Praise for Mo Moulton's
The Mutual Admiration Society

"This is an extraordinary book. Vivid and moving, *The Mutual Admiration Society* makes us think again about how—in private as much in public—modern Britain was made (and remade) through the creative work of women. Beautifully written, animated by a sense of quiet power and amazing ambition, this is essential reading for anyone interested in modern British history."

—Matt Houlbrook, author of *Prince of Tricksters* and *Queer London* and professor of cultural history, University of Birmingham

"Witty and insightful. Tracking lifelong friendships, Moulton reveals how a community of writers and activists transcended the limitations placed upon women in twentieth-century Britain. Their stories are by turns charming and harrowing, revealing how an understanding of women's intimate lives can illuminate the times in which they lived."

—Megan Kate Nelson, author of *The Three-Cornered War: The Union, the Confederacy, and Native Peoples in the Fight for the West*

"Intensely engrossing. Part literary biography, part social history, Mo Moulton's eloquent narrative testifies to the transformative power of creative work."

—Laura Doan, *Disturbing Practices: History, Sexuality, and Women's Experience of Modern War*

"A deeply affecting group portrait of a pathbreaking set of female friends who attended Oxford at the dawn of the twentieth century. If you're a fan of Mary McCarthy's *The Group*, you'll love *The Mutual Admiration Society*."

—Rachel Hope Cleves, professor of history, University of Victoria and author of *Charity and Sylvia*

THE MUTUAL ADMIRATION SOCIETY

HOW DOROTHY L. SAYERS AND HER
OXFORD CIRCLE REMADE THE WORLD FOR WOMEN

MO MOULTON

BASIC BOOKS
New York

Basic Books
Hachette Book Group
1290 Avenue of the Americas, New York, NY 10104
www.basicbooks.com

Printed in the United States of America

First Edition: November 2019

Published by Basic Books, an imprint of Perseus Books, LLC, a
subsidiary of Hachette Book Group, Inc. The Basic Books name
and logo is a trademark of the Hachette Book Group.

The Hachette Speakers Bureau provides a wide range of authors for speaking events.
To find out more, go to www.hachettespeakersbureau.com or call (866) 376-6591.

The publisher is not responsible for websites (or their
content) that are not owned by the publisher.

Print book interior design by Amy Quinn

Library of Congress Cataloging-in-Publication Data has been applied for.

ISBNs: 978-1-5416-4447-2: (hardcover), 978-1-5416-4446-5 (ebook)

LSC-C

10 9 8 7 6 5 4 3 2 1

To chosen family

CONTENTS

Part 4   Visions of a New World, 1939–1945

Part 5   Masterworks and Legacies, 1946–1988

MAIN CHARACTERS

Muriel St. Clare Byrne (1895–1983). Playwright and historian of the Tudor era. Member of the MAS.

Charis Ursula (Barnett) Frankenburg (1892–1985). Midwife, birth control advocate, expert on parenting, and magistrate. Member of the MAS.

Dorothea Ellen Hanbury Rowe (1892–1988). Known as D. Rowe. English teacher and founder of the Bournemouth Little Theatre Club. Member of the MAS.

Dorothy Leigh Sayers (1893–1957). Known as DLS. Detective novelist, advertising copywriter, playwright, essayist, theologian. Member of the MAS.

SUPPORTING CAST

Marjorie Barber (1894–1976). Known as Bar. Muriel St. Clare Byrne's partner. English teacher and author.

Mary Aeldrin Cullis (1883–1968). Known as Susan. Muriel St. Clare Byrne's lover. Secretary, resident tutor at Bedford College.

Atherton Fleming (1881–1950). Known as Mac. Dorothy L. Sayers's husband. Writer and mechanic.

Sydney Frankenburg (1881–1935). Charis Frankenburg's husband. Director of the family firm and philanthropist.

Muriel Jaeger (born Jagger) (1892–1969). Known as Jim. Novelist, essayist, playwright. Member of the MAS.

Catherine (Godfrey) Mansfield (1893–1977?). Known as Tony. Writer. Member of the MAS.

Amphilis Throckmorton Middlemore (1891–1931). Lecturer in English. Member of the MAS.

INTRODUCTION

I T BEGAN IN A QUIET sort of way, over hot cocoa and toasted marshmallows in a student room at Somerville College, Oxford. One evening in November 1912, some new friends, all first-year students, gathered "to read aloud our literary efforts and to receive and deliver criticism." They brought stories, poems, essays, plays, and fables, and they received far more than merely criticism. In the firelight, over economical treats, they created a space in which they could grow beyond the limitations of Edwardian girlhood and become complex, creative adults with a radically capacious notion of what it might mean to be both human and female.[1]

The group was named by its best-known member, Dorothy L. Sayers, who would go on to be a famous detective novelist and popular theologian. Let's call ourselves the Mutual Admiration Society, she suggested, because that's what people will call us anyway. The name both captures the spirit of the group and misrepresents it. They supported each other boldly and emphatically: no false modesty or feminine shame here. They were willing to be relentless and did not insist on being liked, crucial qualities for taking advantage of the real but tenuous space they had to work within. But they were the exact opposite of the simple echo chamber of praise that the name could imply, in its pejorative sense. They were critical, and they were at odds. They fell apart and came together again, over the course of decades and remarkable careers that ranged from birth control advocacy to genre fiction, from classrooms to the stage.

Four members of the Mutual Admiration Society (MAS) are at the heart of this story. Dorothy L. Sayers was known to her friends by her initials, DLS.

Serious and a little weird, DLS was absorbed in her study of French litera-ture and fascinated by the Middle Ages and religion. She would gain fame in adulthood as the creator of Lord Peter Wimsey, the aristocratic detective who starred in her mystery novels. Later, she would be equally well known for the essays and plays she wrote to expound her particular understanding of Christianity and personal ethics.

Muriel St. Clare Byrne, who arrived at Somerville two years later than the others, would become DLS's closest collaborator. Like DLS, she'd loved tales of knights and chivalry and derring-do as a youngster; as an adult, she paid court to the women who became her lovers and partners, immortal-izing the experience in verse and drama. She, too, became a wide-ranging writer, bringing Tudor history and Elizabethan literature to life in popular histories crammed with vivid detail.

Charis Barnett, by contrast, was intensely social, enthusiastic, and em-pathetic, far more interested in people than in ideas. Her career would follow suit, as she raised four children while becoming a nationally known author-ity and advocate on child-rearing, birth control, maternal mortality, and ju-venile delinquency.

Charis's closest friend was Dorothy Rowe, or D. Rowe, the joking trick-ster of the group, who never missed an opportunity for a wisecrack or a limerick that would skewer the foibles and pretensions of those around her. D. Rowe became a beloved English teacher, as well as the founder of a promi-nent and progressive amateur theater club in Bournemouth.

They were joined by a few others at points along the way: the spiky, cyn-ical Muriel "Jim" Jaeger; the otherworldly Amphilis T. Middlemore; and the quiet, serious Catherine "Tony" Godfrey, in particular.

Their words are preserved in libraries scattered across England and the United States, creating a composite archive that is at once deliberate and accidental. Even though they produced copious and vivid letters, stories, poems, and photographs, the members of the MAS resist any attempt by out-siders to know them completely. Jim would stipulate that her personal pa-pers be burned after her death. DLS probably would have destroyed more of her papers if she hadn't died suddenly and relatively young. The members of the MAS kept each other's secrets, too. The question of who knew the truth about DLS's illegitimate son, and when, has always exercised her biographers, but the members of the MAS are like a wall on this subject: the solidarity of their friendship will not be breached. On the other hand, they also preserved

memories and documents. Muriel didn't destroy some fairly frank love letters from another woman, though she had fifty years to do so. D. Rowe wrote
on the backs of all sorts of scraps of paper, creating a double archive of her
own life. She also contributed to the scrapbooks that lovingly document the
Bournemouth Little Theatre Club. Charis preserved her family newsletters
and donated her Somerville diaries to her alma mater, and she told her own
life story in her memoir. Virginia Woolf famously suggested that "Anon, who
wrote so many poems without signing them, was often a woman." Despite
their occasional reticence, the members of the MAS refused to be anonymous. Instead, their abundant archives testify to their insistence that their
work and lives were worth recording.[2]

The women of this generation were well placed to take advantage of the
victories won by the previous era of feminist activists. Whereas the women
of the late nineteenth century had to fight to gain access to higher education,
the members of the MAS enjoyed nearly all that Oxford had to offer, at least
in intellectual terms. In their young adulthood, they saw a raft of legislation
passed that transformed British women into citizens. Women over thirty,
subject to certain property restrictions, would gain the right to vote in 1918;
they were granted the vote on equal terms with men in 1928. Women were
allowed to stand for Parliament, to sit on juries, and to become lawyers and
magistrates. They had increasing access to birth control and well-paid jobs,
as well as scope to smoke cigarettes, wear trousers, and socialize in ways that
would have scandalized their grandparents.

All of this amounted to a revolution in gender relations. But what happens on the day after the revolution? The members of the MAS made the
most of the small but significant opening afforded to them, while continuing to face unequal opportunities, double legal standards, and systematic
discrimination. To be a girl or a woman in early-twentieth-century Britain meant facing pervasive limitations on one's choices, both personal and
professional, despite the recent waves of democratization that had knocked
down barriers based on class and gender. Even as they sat debating poetry
and politics in Somerville College, they were second-class citizens at Oxford
University, where they were permitted to take classes and sit for examinations but could not receive degrees. That would change in 1920, five years after most of the group had finished their studies. That year, Oxford decided to
grant full membership of the university to all the women who had completed
the necessary examinations and coursework, after the passage of the Sex

Disqualification (Removal) Act of 1919 cleared the way of legal objections. The degree ceremony, held one sunny October afternoon in the Sheldonian Theatre, was a brief moment of unalloyed triumph shared by the members of the MAS who received their degrees that day. But they returned home, mostly, to chronic inadequate employment, landlords who didn't want to rent to single women, and relentless pressure to marry and have children.

The Mutual Admiration Society was an incubator. It provided a forum for collaboration, support, and critical feedback, as well as a model for forging other productive partnerships. Although the struggle to build independent lives pulled the members of the MAS apart from each other in the 1920s, the group, remarkably, came back together, in reunions and reconnections around the end of that decade, when its members were in their mid-to late thirties. These reunions led to a series of collaborations that would ultimately transform their careers and reconnect them with work as a life's endeavor, rather than merely the means to financial independence. DLS's much-loved mystery novel *Gaudy Night*, set in a fictionalized Somerville, grew directly out of these collaborations and underscores the importance of balancing the demands of head and heart in this way.

Meaningful, creative work was the birthright of both women and men, they believed. In a pair of essays published in the journal *Christendom* in response to a special issue on "the emancipated woman," DLS and Muriel made that case forcefully. They spent a summer writing back and forth to each other and to the magazine's editor, working out their ideas about why it was so damaging to limit any human being to a narrow set of gendered characteristics. Muriel's partner, Marjorie "Bar" Barber, read their drafts on the beach during their holiday and offered her own opinions. Developed further under the title "Are Women Human?," DLS's response has become an enduring classic. Yes, she argued, women are human, with the same dazzling and bewildering array of talents and foibles as any other subset of humans. In an era when many feminists emphasized the special contributions women could make—to the arts of peace in international relations, say—the members of the MAS were, by contrast, strictly egalitarian. Women, they argued, mostly weren't special: they were just human, and deserved to be allowed to live and work as people first, rather than having all their actions and efforts read through the lens of gender.

For DLS and her friends, the category of "human" was capacious. It could hold all sorts of expression and eccentricity and possibility. "Woman," by contrast, was flattening. It turned half the population into a homogenous lump to be summarized and then controlled. The members of the MAS were profoundly shaped by the fact that they were women, within a changing but still highly restrictive gender order. They thought, consistently and deeply, about that order in all aspects of their work. In their lives, too, they challenged any narrow interpretation of what it meant to be a woman. Their self-expression ranged from the masculine to the feminine, with multiple variations in between, and they experienced romance, sex, marriage, and parenthood in a variety of ways, too. The reluctance around the homogenizing category of "woman," in other words, was grounded in the very real diversity of their own experiences.

Nor were they interested only in expanding access to culture for women *as such*. Their work was usually aimed at "everyone," or at least that subset of everyone who read English and was interested in art and ideas. The MAS intervened, in various ways, in what was arguably the core problem of the first half of the twentieth century: the democratization of culture and politics. This widening of access to cultural and political power brought opportunities and perils. Universal suffrage became the British norm for the first time, and literacy rates improved. Britons became famous for newspaper reading, as well as for being devotees of the new art form of cinema. Giving ordinary people unprecedented access to culture and mass democracy could look promising or dangerous, depending on your perspective. Was the new society a crowd of dupes, easily manipulated by advertisers or, worse, demagogues? Or was it a collective of citizens, able to be educated in improved, scientific ways of living and interacting? Was mass culture, in other words, a liberation or a trap?[3]

Facing these questions, the members of the MAS were simultaneously insiders and outsiders: members of an elite social class, but women. From that very particular position they were able to develop a distinctive set of ideas about the relationships between high art and popular culture, and between elite intellectual ideas and ordinary life. I suspect they would have been somewhat boring men. DLS and Muriel would surely have been full-time academics, DLS a professor of medieval French, Muriel of Tudor history and paleography, perhaps. D. Rowe might have been a headmaster of a small boys' school; Charis, a *pater familias* and competent administrator. (That is, if they hadn't died serving in World War I, as at least some of them would have.) No doubt they would have done good, even excellent, work.

But instead, their marginality within the gender politics of their era served a role like sand in an oyster. They struggled and were pushed out of the main lines of promotion and success, and instead of reproducing the world of their fathers or their mothers, they made something new.

All four worked at the intersections of elite and popular culture. DLS wrote detective novels, that most beloved of middlebrow genres, which merged modernist experimentation with the formulaic delights of thrillers and true-crime stories. Later, she brought religious and ethical ideas to a wide audience, notably through a BBC radio play-cycle on the life of Jesus and a translation of Dante's *Divine Comedy* published by Penguin. Muriel St. Clare Byrne wrote the history of daily Tudor life, for the ordinary reader as well as for the scholar. D. Rowe brought Shakespeare to her students and moderately experimental theater to provincial amateur dramatics. And Charis Frankenburg sought to popularize the latest ideas about parenting, birth control, and healthy motherhood through clinics and advice books. Their diverse efforts were united by a shared conviction in the value of intellectual rigor and artistic integrity.[4]

They were linked, too, by the belief that those values should and could be shared beyond traditional circles and traditional modes. Through theater, novels, plays, clinics, cartoons, and more, they sought to bring the most serious of ideas to the largest number of people. DLS formulated the reason behind this goal most clearly: because serious, creative work is what gives meaning to our lives, and a meaningful life's work is the right of every person. She framed this in religious terms. Creative work is what people share with God, the ultimate creator, and it is our solace in a world defined otherwise by our tendency toward destruction and sin. Charis would have put it differently but meant much the same thing. For her, access to the best science of health and living laid the foundation for a good life in which one could work seriously in respectful cooperation with one's fellows. Underlying all four careers, though, was the core emphasis on the value of rigorous thought for everyone.

They were not naïve optimists. They were well aware, for instance, that mass advertising and pop psychology fooled people into making disastrous decisions, and that mass politics could produce mass destruction. The answer, they argued, was not a return to stifling hierarchies that limited power and learning to a few well-born men. It was rather to educate *better*, to turn the mechanisms of mass culture into conduits for enlightenment and imaginative work, instead of simple tools to generate higher profits or more votes. Their encounter with learning and scholarship had been liberating and joyful and ultimately profoundly humanizing. At Oxford, they were transformed from schoolgirls into creative adults by means of conversation with texts and each other. Their work spanned from midwifery to mystery novels, and from theology to theater, but it was united by the desire to share that transformative education more widely.

On one level, their story reveals the generative power of friendships, which create an intimate local space in which we can become something or someone quite different from our assigned social or familial categories. It also suggests the generative power of marginalization. This is not to argue that exclusion is a good thing, but to recognize that the experience of being marginalized can generate sharp insights, original approaches, and powerful solidarities alongside the toll of damage and loss. The members of the MAS lived at a very particular moment in the histories of both democracy and of women's rights. They experienced radical shifts in inclusion—the ability to attend Oxford and then to receive degrees and the right to vote, most notably. They also experienced the effects of persistent structural exclusions, manifesting most obviously in their struggles to earn adequate salaries independently. As a result, they saw the widening of access to culture as a movement of immense promise and possibility.

They were no revolutionaries. If their position in the gender order rendered them marginal, then class, race, and political affiliation largely placed the members of the MAS in a very central, privileged position. Their party politics varied—DLS once referred to her "vaguely church-&-landed-gentry bias," in contrast to Muriel's "vaguely sympathy-for-labour-&-women bias." But they agreed more than they disagreed. In keeping with the mood of interwar Britain as well as with their politics, they tended to support what has been called "conservative modernity" by historians of this era. The phrase suggests an embrace of new technologies and perspectives—mass communication, political rights for women—alongside a reverence for what was traditional, local, and even insular.[5]

For the members of the MAS, conservative modernity meant recognizing the many benefits to breaking down the walls that kept the ancient traditions of learning and scholarship separate from ordinary people. As DLS recognized early on, even illiterate audiences shaped the development of medieval drama; the grand traditions of European literature grew out of their cheers and boos. She and her friends applied that principle to modern life, believing that vibrant, organic culture only thrived in a society that thoroughly integrated its highest culture with the full range of its population. Through their diverse careers, they worked to make the best ideas, the most creative work, and a joyful encounter with learning accessible to a wide range of people. That, they believed, was one of the greatest achievements to which a democratic society could aspire.

In advance of its sixtieth birthday, Somerville College began, in 1938, to compile information about the careers of its graduates. The *Observer* pointed out the "exceptionally large number of good writers" included in that list, singling out DLS and Muriel St. Clare Byrne among others. But, the paper went on: "not less important are the diligent scholars who live out-of-the-way lives, the scientists, social workers, and school-mistresses who may not be known to the general public, but who continue to raise the level of women's mental responsibility." In their careers, the members of the MAS did more than that. As writers, but also as teachers and public figures, they sought to raise everyone's level of mental responsibility, by insisting that women be heard, finally, as fully human members of society.[6]

Part 1

Oxford, 1912–1918

1

ARRIVING AT OXFORD

O N OCTOBER 11, 1912, CHARIS Barnett and her mother took the train from London to Oxford. Her aunt met them at the station, and together the three women went to Somerville College, where Charis planned to spend the next several years living and studying. They spent the day readying her room, breaking only for lunch at the Cadena Café in Cornmarket, where, as the advertisement said, dinners, luncheons, and afternoon teas were "daintily served with dispatch." Then Charis brought her mother back to the railway station. After tea, they parted: her mother went home, and Charis returned to Somerville to begin her university education.[1]

In its own simple way, the scene, which was repeated dozens of times around the ancient city that week, was remarkable. Charis came from a middle-class family. She was not part of the vast class of young women in Victorian and Edwardian Britain who were expected to work as a servant or in a factory. Had she been born earlier, or into a family that cared less about educating its daughters, she might have assumed she would remain at home until (and unless) she married. Instead, she left home to study, following in the footsteps of centuries of men but only a few short decades of women. Despite the poignancy of leaving her mother at the station, she was already ecstatic the next day, writing home: "I am *very* happy here—I don't know of anything that I would alter if I could."[2]

Somerville College, one of the first women's societies, or colleges, at Oxford, was well designed to foster the transition between a sheltered girlhood and modern adulthood. The culture it created honored both the ideals of middle-class femininity and the traditions of the university. It gave the members of the MAS, as well as their classmates, the necessary support to enable them to master a challenging curriculum and develop their intellectual interests. The MAS took that a step further. Seeing one another without the limiting lens of Edwardian gender roles, they gave each other scope to develop. In their writing, in theatrical productions, in debating societies, and in their relationships, they tried on different styles and personalities and perspectives. They expected, mostly, to use their educations in order to gain paid employment later in life. But for the MAS, work was never only about passing examinations or securing future employment. Writing and thinking instead took on a transcendent importance, not least as the medium through which new friendships and new identities could be consolidated.

Somerville's own position was still tenuous: not everyone at Oxford welcomed the increasing presence of women as nearly equal students at the ancient, masculine university. Even as they studied, the members of the MAS had to negotiate intense anxieties about gender and the place of women within the university.

Although Somerville College was only thirty-three years old, the cohort of 1912 entered "a ready-made inheritance" in an appropriately imposing edifice. Beyond the tiny entrance was a large quadrangle that housed one hundred students, as well as common rooms, dining facilities, and a library. In her first year, Muriel sent postcards home to her mother. One featured the library and another showed the Common Room, where, she explained, "one works after brekker." When it was founded, Somerville had been in a manor house, but over the intervening years it became less and less like a Victorian home and more and more like any other Oxford college. The construction of Maitland Hall and a new entrance in the summer of 1913 would plunge the college into what DLS called "a most grisly turmoil," with "dust & workmen everywhere."[3]

The buildings were tangible evidence of the progress made toward including women in higher education at all levels. This had begun with the establishment of the

Muriel St. Clare Byrne, probably at Somerville (MSBC 9/3)

Ladies' Educational Associations in the mid-nineteenth century, which of-fered instruction for women as well as support in preparing for university examinations. The first university in Britain to offer degrees to women was the University of London, in 1878. By the beginning of the twentieth century, women could study and take degrees at numerous universities in Britain and elsewhere, but not yet at Oxford. Oxford resisted in no small part because its characteristic traditions—boat racing, formal debating societies, and so on—were designed, in the nineteenth century, to promote a professional, imperial, masculine elite. The MAS and their fellow students arrived only a few decades later, and they pushed the university to widen those traditions to include middle-class British women.[4]

Female students living at Oxford were a curiosity, and the spectacle of young women living the kind of studious, single-sex college life that had for so long been exclusively male attracted attention and questions. Writing to her fellow student and future MAS member Tony Godfrey during Easter va-cation in 1913, DLS complained at length about it:

> I'm simply dead sick of telling people about Oxford, & how many there are of us at Somerville & how many dons there are, & why have I got to do an exam in German when my subject's French, & do I see much of the Prince of Wales, & do we have lectures with the men, & is there a tennis-court at Somerville, & what is the name of our Head, & what times are lights put out at night, & how do we get milk when we make our own tea, & may we go to the theatre, & have I made any particular friends, & what sort of people live in my passage, & have I one room or two & will the new buildings be finished when we get back, & do the maids wear caps & aprons, & when was the college founded & are there more women students at Oxford or Cambridge?

But this was at home. Back within the walls of Somerville, students were sheltered from the limelight and assimilated into an ordinary college life.[5]

By 1912, Somerville's leaders had successfully used "modest manners and watchful tact" to win its students most, though not all, of the trappings of university life. Female students attended lectures, took examinations, and had access to libraries and tutors, but they weren't eligible for degrees or to become full members of the university. Somerville, unlike the all-male col-leges, employed female scholars as tutors and in administrative roles. DLS studied French with a scholar named Mildred Pope, whose career highlights the opportunities and limitations experienced by women during this transitional moment. Women's colleges at Oxford had pioneered the teaching of modern languages; a modern languages school was created for the university in general only in 1904. Pope was widely regarded as the leading expert on French philology at Oxford, consulted by students at all levels from across the university. Yet her position was, for many years, tenuous and wholly dependent on her work as a tutor within Somerville. Only later would Pope begin to receive more established university positions: a three-year stint as a Taylorian lecturer beginning in 1920, a term as deputy professor to cover an absence, and finally, in 1928, a readership in French philology.[6]

So the battle for educational equality was far from won. While Somerville students emerged fully Oxford-educated, they were not entitled to receive Oxford degrees. Somerville's principal, Emily Penrose, kept her eye steadily on that ultimate prize. She demanded that Somerville students meet the requirements for an Oxford degree as a powerful demonstration of the fitness of young women for the academic work required by the university. Despite the smaller accommodations, bureaucratic distinctions, and innumerable minor slights, Penrose insisted that her students were as much a part of the university as the young men attending the older, wealthier colleges. And, while she waited for full recognition to come, she diplomatically navigated the social pitfalls of shepherding a hundred young women through their college years in a culture eager to seize upon any misstep as proof that they did not belong at Oxford at all.[7]

THE ROAD TO Somerville College was, for the future members of the MAS, lined with privilege but also strewn with obstacles. Like most university-educated women, especially those who went to Oxford or Cambridge, the members of the MAS were part of the well-off British middle classes. Their families lived comfortably and employed at least a servant or two to deal with the heavier aspects of cooking and cleaning. Their fathers held positions of local influence and respectability: clergymen or headmasters, bureaucrats or businessmen. Jim Jaeger's father was an auctioneer and estate agent who was active with his South Yorkshire town's grammar school and Masonic circles. Amphilis Middlemore was the daughter of a member of Parliament from the Birmingham area. DLS, an only child, was born in Oxford, where her father was headmaster of the Christchurch Cathedral Choir School, but she mostly grew up in the Cambridgeshire fens, where he was a clergyman. Her middle-aged parents doted on her as the center of an otherwise quiet household. Growing up in the seaside resort of Bournemouth, by contrast, D. Rowe was one of four children, and her mother was much younger than her father. Her father, who had been a headmaster of boys' schools before her birth, died in 1905, and her elder brother, too, died, in 1907.[8]

Charis's father was the principal of a teacher training college near London when she was born. He went on to serve in various bureaucratic posts, finally achieving the rank of chief inspector of training colleges. Charis and her family traveled to South Africa briefly when he was seconded to the post of superintendent of education in Natal and Transvaal. Her mother was a writer, the author of a novel and several anthologies of poems for children.[9]

Muriel St. Clare Byrne's parents had married fairly young. Her father, Henry, was just twenty-four when he wed Artemisia Desdemona, a twenty-six-year-old schoolteacher from rural Iowa. Henry assisted his father, a naval architect, in his firm in Liverpool. Like DLS, Muriel was an only child, doted on by parents and grandparents alike. But whereas DLS learned Latin and literature from her bookish parents, Muriel trailed after her dandyish father like a spaniel. She adored every aspect of his hard-drinking masculine world, from the horse races and the jokes to the silk handkerchiefs and the loud suits. His death in 1905, when she was just ten years old, must have been an especially devastating blow. In retrospect, however, she preferred her grandfather's more industrious approach. Whereas her grandfather had designed warships as well as yachts for the Vanderbilts, his sons "were awfully good at doing what they wanted to do," which mainly meant playing golf and bridge. Muriel could not bear either game in adulthood.[10]

Despite the differences in their family lives, D. Rowe, DLS, Muriel, and Charis all remembered benefiting from instruction at home. Charis's parents were

Muriel St. Clare Byrne with her father and grandfather (MSBC 9/1)

strict and committed to education. Muriel's grandfather provided her with tools and careful instruction in their use. D. Rowe's father read John Milton's *Paradise Lost* with her when she was not quite ten, and she savored lines like "Moloch, horrid king, besmeared with blood." DLS's father, likewise, taught her Latin from the age of six.[11]

However, entering Somerville required passing a challenging series of examinations beyond the scope of parental teaching. D. Rowe had started at the Bournemouth Endowed High School for Girls as a young child. She remembered that when her brother left to attend kindergarten there, "I apparently cried out so to follow the boys that follow them I did," and she attended the school from 1896. In fact, as its name suggests, the school was mainly for older girls, the daughters of well-off professional or trading families in the Bournemouth area who came to study English, history, geography, and mathematics and to receive extra lessons in refined accomplishments such as piano, painting, and needlework. After her brother died, D. Rowe left the school but went on to attend Cheltenham Ladies' College in 1911, probably in order to prepare for the entrance exams to Oxford.[12]

Like D. Rowe, Charis attended school from a relatively young age, including the progressive Bedales School and then St. Paul's Girls' School in Hammersmith. DLS, on the other hand, began formal schooling only once her parents realized that they would be unable to tutor her up to examination standard. The transition wasn't seamless. At the Godolphin School in Salisbury, she found sports were a nightmare and French class a rare opportunity to shine, according to her fictionalized memoir. Jim attended a high school for girls in Sheffield. Her letters home to her younger brother are full of action and derring-do: her role as a goblin in the school play and a fistfight with a fellow student that ended in a broken window.[13]

Muriel found salvation at the Belvedere School in Liverpool. As a young child, she had been overwhelmed by stories of her cousin's boarding school, where the girls all wore slippers to avoid sullying the "pure white carpets." In reality, Muriel found that school was not a place of sedate young ladies with "printless feet" but instead a refuge for her restless intellect, which she realized would never allow her to spend her adolescence socializing and waiting for marriage.[14]

In March 1912, Charis, who had graduated the previous year from St. Paul's Girls' School, took the grueling set of Somerville entrance examinations for a second time, hoping to secure a scholarship. Over two days, she spent fourteen hours writing examination answers and was interviewed twice, by English tutor Helen Darbishire and principal Emily Penrose. Two weeks later, she learned that she had been admitted but had just missed out on a scholarship, "as it was an exceptional year." She decided to matriculate anyway, becoming part of that extraordinary cohort. DLS and Jim both won three-year scholarships, and D. Rowe and Tony earned scholarships covering shorter periods. Unsurprisingly, these intelligent young women soon fell in with one another.[15]

ONCE BAGS WERE unpacked and the dining hall had been located, the young women of Somerville embarked on the serious task of finding their place in the social sphere of the college. The older students alternately ignored the first-years and examined them with unsettling thoroughness. But it was among their own number that the class of 1912 found the strongest connections.[16]

New Somerville students often found that they already shared friends or acquaintances, a reflection of the close-knit social world of the Edwardian British middle classes. Muriel would tell her mother happily, "Am discovering so many people with mutual friends." On her first full day at the college, Charis began by dutifully following up on a suggestion made by her parents: that she should go and meet Dorothy Rowe, whose family had a distant social connection with the Barnetts. That day, Charis reported, "I have been to Miss Rowe's rooms several times, but haven't discovered her yet—I left a card there last time." D. Rowe likewise "dutifully deposited" her own card, with all the lack of interest that young people usually show toward potential friends suggested to them by their relations. But then they met while bidding on the same "two-penny pair of tongs" at an auction of "the discards of departed students." The two-penny tongs succeeded where well-meaning parents had failed, and a lifelong friendship was born. The addition of Amphilis Middlemore made a tight trio. Charis soon regarded D. Rowe as "the most amusing person I have ever met!" One night in mid-October, she listened, rapt, to D. Rowe's elaborate stories of her hijinks: the time she stuck her tongue out at a mummy and then apologized, and the time she and her sister "practised the Baton in the British Museum!" Before they knew it, it was quarter past eleven—time to flee back to their own rooms along darkened corridors.[17]

DLS told her family that she befriended D. Rowe when she stage-managed a play in which DLS was involved, though D. Rowe herself remembered meeting DLS before they took their scholarship examinations, bonding over an impromptu recitation of *Cyrano de Bergerac*. In any case, the two became fast friends and soon spent a lot of time together.[18]

Charis was far too practical to rely solely on such happy coincidences, however. She aimed to conquer systematically. On her first full day in Somerville, Charis had "four freshers to tea in my room," and from that moment her diary becomes a dizzying record of more or less daily social engagements with her fellow students. By October 16, less than a week after her arrival, she estimated that she knew sixty people. This impressive feat was the result of a series of coffees that she and a fellow student held for nearly all the Somerville first-years during the first month of classes, a process she described to her parents as "wading through the freshers." Over the course of October and November, D. Rowe, Tony, Jim, Amphilis, and DLS would all come to coffee with Charis.[19]

The friendships that deepened in this atmosphere were a mixture of formality and intense intimacy. As a rule, students at first called each other "Miss Sayers," "Miss Jaeger," and so on, rather than using first names. But as the friendship progressed, "one 'proposed' and Christian names were henceforth used. Etiquette decreed that this advance was made by a senior to a junior." In early December 1912, Charis proposed to Jaeger. And in January 1913, D. Rowe proposed to Charis. Christian names often then gave way to nicknames: Muriel Jaeger became Jim, Amphilis Middlemore became Phil, Catherine Godfrey became Tony, and Margaret Chubb, another Somerville student in this circle of friends, became Cherub. D. Rowe was, briefly, Kiki. DLS began to be known by her initials. When Jim invented a fictional character based on DLS, she explained that she preferred initials to her given name, "which she hated, and would never allow her friends to use."[20]

Cocoa parties and literary meetings unfolded in rooms carefully decorated to reflect the character of their inhabitants and to maximize the opportunities for socializing. Vera Brittain, a classmate who would go on to become a famous author herself, mocked the predominant look as only superficially distinctive: would it be "flowery chintz and pink cushions," or "green chintz and orange cushions"? But Amphilis, D. Rowe, and another student went "into ecstacies" over Charis's room, which featured "an armchair, a corner-cupboard, and a most useful wooden fender which provided extra seating" for parties of up to fourteen fellow students. The college servant who cleaned her room called it "the prettiest room in College," while other people, perhaps less diplomatically, remarked that she must be "an only girl" to have her parents decorate her room so lavishly. Less extravagantly, Muriel had a chair, rug, and screen shipped to her room. DLS, for her part, obtained a large armchair, christened G. K. Chesterton after the popular and rotund author. One Sunday found her writing letters "lying on my back before the fire, my head supported on 3 cushions & my feet" in the chair, "far too hot & comfortable to get up & sit at a table."[21]

Food was a source of enduring concern and interest at student gatherings. When Charis's fire proved inadequate for the task, an entire party relocated to Amphilis's room to roast chestnuts one November afternoon. The students schemed to provide the maximum hospitality on the minimum budget. Charis bought three pounds of apricot jam for a shilling, splurging only occasionally on "bottled raspberries." D. Rowe "introduced toasted marshmallows, which floated deliciously on coffee and were much cheaper than cream." In May 1913, Margaret Chubb and Tony Godfrey set up a tea shop, providing teas from 3:30 to 4:30 daily in return for a modest charge. The following autumn, Charis, D. Rowe, Jim, and some others formed "a sort of cooperative tea association," bringing tea from the common room and contributing jam and other items in turn. In May 1914, it was time for altruism: D. Rowe and Charis issued a standing invitation to students facing the fearsome exams known as "Schools," and served tea to two or three of them each day to ease their "closing efforts." By 1914, in Brittain's memory, DLS was often to be seen "with a kettle in her hand and a little checked apron fastened over her skirt." The students' hospitality did not stop at the college gates—Charis had fifty visits from guests, including her parents, during the 1914 summer term alone, and the amount of washing-up she generated was legendary among the college's servants.[22]

All of this homey coziness bore a serious mission: providing a residential setting that was sufficiently respectable to allay concerns about the propriety of a young lady living without relatives and undertaking serious study. These concerns were physical as well as moral: mental overwork was popularly believed to be a frequent cause of illness for young women. Seeking to calm such fears, Muriel reassured her mother about her physical well-being at college, including the exercise she took, her large appetite, and her increasing weight. In her second term, Charis added her sleeping patterns to the personal details she recorded in her diary. The well-furnished rooms and the tea parties, then, were just two elements in a comprehensive effort to recreate a rather formal version of safe, middle-class family life. Students ate meals together in the college dining rooms, shaking hands with Penrose before breakfast. They were required to dress for dinner, and Penrose liked to have students sit at the high table. Sitting next to the principal was, in Charis's opinion, "rather daunting," not only because Penrose expected intelligent replies but because she ate so quickly. "She was, in fact, known to some of us as 'The Pen that fills in a flash'—a reference to a much advertised fountain-pen." Students were to be in their own rooms by 11 p.m., and the lights in the passages were out at 10, though the judicious use of flashlights enabled after-hours expeditions.[23]

But, ultimately, the young women of Somerville were not living as daughters in a family setting. They were students, in a context that naturally encouraged both intellectual and personal independence. They held college meetings, where they democratically set rules about such things as work hours and noise levels. Members of the MAS served in various roles in college governance, frequently sitting on the library committee, for instance. DLS was the senior bicycle secretary, and at a meeting in October 1914 she "reminded people that bicycles must be marked with the owner's name and kept in bicycle sheds," not left around the college, where they would be impounded and held until a fine was paid.[24]

Even parties in students' rooms could be seen in a different light. Take Brittain's sensationalized description of the atmosphere of an evening Somerville "cocoa-party." The air, she wrote, "was heavy with the fumes of cocoa and cigarette smoke; crumbs of 'College Creams' and the remains of some over-boiled milk clung to the sticky hearth." While sticky spilled milk conjures up spoiled children, the presence of cigarette smoke reveals that these girls were modern women, embracing freedoms, such as smoking, that were traditionally denied to middle-class women and even prohibited at other women's colleges. The fact that smoking was permitted for Somerville students was a source of immediate joy to DLS, who became known, in Jim's semi-fictionalized account, for her "exquisite smoke rings." Somerville's leaders were well aware that smoking was associated with looseness and modernity, but they declined to regulate their students. Their decision was not welcomed by everyone. When Charis ordered a cigarette box carved with the Somerville arms, she encountered "a disapproving shopman," who said, "'I'll carve you a *sweet-box* with the Somerville arms.' I replied that he could call it that if he liked, but that it would hold cigarettes."[25]

Skeptical sales clerks were the least of the MAS's barriers at Oxford. Once Somerville students left the college gates, they found themselves under the scrutinizing gaze of the wider university. Even before she spoke, a Somerville student was often judged on what she wore. Fashion trends became fodder for debate. In the autumn of 1912, for instance, there was a "craze for untidiness" among Somerville students and their contemporaries at other women's colleges. DLS scathingly described a friend who was unbearably "self-conscious in her ungainliness." But by the following spring, the pendulum had swung in the other direction, and everyone seemed to be wearing "fearfully smart" new clothes. DLS and a friend attended church one Sunday in skirts "so tight it took us about 10 minutes to kneel down." Such experiments in fashion brought down official wrath. In 1914, the principal of the Oxford Home Students received "a very tiresome complaint that the men examinees are disturbed by the way our students sit in their tight skirts and show their legs." Even within Somerville, DLS was gently encouraged to dress a bit more quietly when she arrived at breakfast one morning "wearing a three-inch wide scarlet riband round her head and in her ears a really remarkable pair of ear-rings; a scarlet and green parrot in a gilt cage pendant almost to each shoulder and visible right across the hall."[26]

When Charis wore a particularly pretty shot-silk dress, a porter guarding a lecture hall briefly mistook her for an American tourist and nearly barred her from entering. Then a male undergraduate remarked appreciatively, "I suppose there are two kinds of girl at Somerville—freaks and girls like you!" Freak, here, meant someone eccentric in her devotion to learning or other esoteric pursuits and echoed the popular slogan "Somerville for freaks." The incident suggests the pressures on Somerville students to be, simultaneously, sufficiently somber in their clothes to look like worthy students and yet fashionable enough to be seen as attractive rather than freakish by potential male partners.[27]

The members of the MAS were sensitive to the nuances of these stereotypes. D. Rowe proposed a party that would feature a prize for the most "woman-studentish" guest. The plan was ultimately abandoned as too dangerous. These women were students, but they were afraid that, inadvertently, they would appear too woman-studentish and join the ranks of women mocked for their intellectual pretensions. Charis even reassured her parents that she'd heard Somerville had a comparatively high marriage rate for a women's college. In fact, the postwar generations of university women would marry more frequently than the first female university graduates, though educated women were still less likely to marry overall.[28]

Such skirmishes over appearances reveal a deeper truth: Somerville College stood at the margins of Oxford, its students not yet fully accepted as equal. At a dance, one man made himself obnoxious by comparing Somerville with "Oxford colleges," highlighting the fact that it was still, technically, only an affiliated women's society. In one logic course, men and women usually sat on opposite sides of the room, with the men sometimes spilling over into the front row on the women's side. One day, Charis and D. Rowe were seated in the second row on the women's side. When they collapsed with laughter before lecture started as the result of an in-joke about the porter, first one man and then two more transferred to the row in front of them. Charis didn't explain exactly why, but evidently everyone found the whole thing hilarious, especially as the men began a bout of ridiculous fake coughing to spur their giggling on. Integration in the classroom was still novel enough to sustain this rather silly physical comedy.[29]

In her German classes, DLS was frequently the only woman in the room. Even in the literature class where she had a female companion, that student "never says a word & never lifts her eyes from her book." When DLS was the only female student to take a language exam, she found herself seated "severely isolated like a leper" in one corner of the room. When she'd first arrived, "I wandered into the men's part of the room," and the doorkeeper "rushed at me with wildly-waving arms & a terrified expression, & shooed me away to my seclusion like an intrusive hen." Yet even that could not suppress DLS's intellectual self-confidence. It must have been disconcerting watching men of mediocre intelligence and attainments earn Oxford degrees while all women were still denied them, though DLS did not comment directly on the point. Instead, she emphasized her feminine advantages. During an oral examination, one examiner raised a potentially thorny point, saying that he was "very much surprised" to see that DLS "considered Schiller's 'Robbers' a pleasing play." DLS admitted that "my heart sank into my boots," but she decided to try "an individual touch." "Relying on the fact that I had put on my best coat & skirt & a becoming hat, I assumed my most womanly smile & said: 'Oh! don't you think it is?'—He smiled—I was encouraged to give my reasons—he smiled & agreed. At any rate he passed me." The "intrusive hen" would find ways to fight back.[30]

At Somerville, students had to navigate a classic double bind. On the one hand, they didn't want to seem too woman-studentish or too freakishly absorbed in learning. On the other hand, expressions of femininity brought a different sort of criticism and scrutiny down upon them, as porters, lecturers, sales clerks, male undergraduates, and others resisted the integration of women into Oxford. Somerville College tried to balance these imperatives, offering a combination of Oxford student life and the trappings of middle-class domesticity. Such efforts could only do so much. In the end, no one could remain both a sheltered daughter and a university-educated intellectual. DLS, D. Rowe, Charis, Muriel, and their compatriots would, inevitably, be transformed by their education. The MAS would help them make the transformation.

2

MUTUAL ADMIRATION SOCIETY ON STAGE AND PAGE

THE MAS PROVIDED ITS MEMBERS with the space to do serious work and have fun without the highly gendered scrutiny that was so prevalent at Oxford. As a group, it was marked by exuberance and experimentation. No character was too outlandish, no form too ornate, no reference too arcane: it was all grist for the mill, even if meetings were just as likely to end in raucous laughter as in artistic epiphany. On one level, the meetings of the MAS were a variation on the theme of typical Somerville student parties. But the group had something more: a sense of purpose, leavened with a riotous sense of humor. While its members worked out their ideas about gender, religion, and politics through debating societies and theater and in their formal coursework, the MAS was always their intellectual home.

The first recorded meeting of the Mutual Admiration Society took place on November 6, 1912, and is noted laconically in Charis's diary: "M.A.S. with Miss Middlemore at 8.0." Amphilis provided the refreshments and DLS read two of her works, whose titles reveal her ongoing infatuation with medieval themes: "Earl Ulfric" and "Peredur." On November 24, another meeting took place, this one over tea in Charis's room, and she and Jim read their work. Charis's selections were a poem, a fable, and a short story about women's suffrage. DLS also baptized the club, saying that "if we didn't give ourselves that title, the rest of College would." She wasn't wrong. The MAS earned "some little digs" in that year's going-down play, a light-hearted, self-referential production put on by each year's graduating class. Vera Brittain, who never joined the group's ranks, remarked twenty years later that they "took themselves very seriously, and apparently still do." DLS, Charis, and D. Rowe were joined by Jim Jaeger, Amphilis Middlemore, Margaret Petty, and Dimaris Barton to round out the membership of the first term's iteration of the MAS.[1]

The MAS had serious literary range and ambition, but the account of the next term's first meeting is a reminder that the group could be uproarious, too. Everyone had promised to write something during the Christmas vacation, but only Dimaris Barton and DLS actually followed through. Before the holiday, DLS had told the group that she was planning to write a piece from the perspective of the men inside the wooden horse at Troy. Instead, she wrote a miracle play about the three Magi. At the meeting, she launched into her "prose description of the three men—one watching a huge cauldron boil, one studying a horoscope, & the other sitting at a large table." D. Rowe, affecting ignorance about the change of topic, inquired, "But was this happening *inside* the wooden horse?" Charis collapsed into laughter while DLS "explained solemnly that it wasn't." She tried to continue with her reading, but the mood was lost, and Charis was soon giggling at her pronunciation of "pipkin." As Charis told her parents: "O I *was* ill! And so was Dorothy. Why, oh why, was I cursed with a sense of humour?" DLS might have been wondering something similar.[2]

They also enjoyed the macabre, the gruesome, and the eerie. One dull evening in mid-January, D. Rowe and Charis found themselves with time on their hands as they waited for Amphilis to return from London. They crept into her room and assembled a spooky figure on her bed: a "little round mottled work box on the pillow" for a head, with lids for eyes and "hairpins for nose & mouth & a stocking & a hearthbrush for hair." Enhancing the realistic effect, D. Rowe "put cushions for its body, & stuck a pair of shoes straight up at the end of the bed." The crowning touch was "a pair of leather gloves hanging out over the sheet, & holding a bottle with a label 'Suicide by Poison.'" Luckily, Amphilis walked in during the preparations and was delighted.[3]

Perhaps inspired by the success of this practical joke, Jim staged an elaborate ghost party two days later. Somerville College, she had learned, had allegedly been built on the site of an old convent and was supposed to be haunted by the ghost of a nun—a legend that says much about the fear that too much education rendered a woman unmarriageable. Having sworn that she had seen this apparition herself one night on the stroke of eleven, Jim invited eight other first-year students to meet the ghost. She enlisted Amphilis, D. Rowe, and Charis in her aid, and told Margaret Chubb about the plans. Other guests, including DLS and Tony, came to the party in all innocence. DLS contributed her own esoteric elements, drawing a pentagram on the threshold and preparing Latin charms to use in case an exorcism was necessary.

Together, they sat and told tales of ghosts, working themselves into "a most frightfully creepy state with all sorts of grisly stories." As the clock struck eleven, someone said, "I believe Jim has arranged a ghost for us," but D. Rowe quickly began a new story to create a distraction until the cry went around: "there's something white!" DLS saw outside the window "a shadowy figure in the black and white garb of a nun!!" Others noticed that the figure carried a baby in her arms. It was, in fact, Amphilis, dressed up in a white nightgown with a black lace dress as a hood and daubed with luminous paint. She let out an eerie howl. When she reached the window of the room where the party stood gathered, Jim asked her in to coffee, and the game was up. No one had been truly frightened. In Charis's opinion, the "only person who was in the least annoyed, & she may not really have been, was Dorothy Sayers." Amphilis was left to spend hours scrubbing off the paint.[4]

Amid the pranks and the jokes, the MAS continued its work in earnest. In early February 1913, new member F. S. Thomson "read a paper on Shakespeare's fairies," and Charis read two sonnets, one original and the other translated from French. As a forum for literary experiment, the MAS was unparalleled, pushing members to express their ideas through a dazzling variety of forms and styles. DLS captured this range in a suite of poems, "The Last Castle," which she circulated to the MAS and later published in her first book of poetry. Dedicated to "all us vain, sentimental, honest fools of M.A.S., & for any other such that have loved Oxford," the collection is a romp through different styles, each tagged with a name such as "Oxford-cult," "Religious Ornament," and "Metrical Experiment."[5]

Outside of the formal meetings, members of the MAS continued their discussions of literature and ideas. These conversations deepened ties of affection and esteem. As Charis put it to her parents, "Dorothy Rowe is *very* clever: we discussed serious literature the other night—she knows a lot, & talks very well." They began collaborating on articles for the journal for Oxford women students, the *Fritillary*, and, with Amphilis, started reading their favorite poems out loud to each other. But there was always an undercurrent of mirth. In a particularly funny moment, Charis discovered that her last wisdom tooth had come through after an evening of "deep ethical discussion" with D. Rowe.[6]

These meetings and conversations served more than an intellectual purpose. They created a space in which the members of the MAS could try on different selves and different ways of being in the world. They had all been putting on plays and wearing costumes since they were children. The young D. Rowe had been "very good at inventing delightful games" as well as "dressing up and acting." Muriel's youthful library featured classic adventure stories: *The Scarlet Pimpernel*, *The Count of Monte Cristo*, *The Last of the Mohicans*. She wrote stories and created handwritten and illustrated magazines with her friends. She adored acting, too, spending a stretch of time inhabiting the character of the Scarlet Pimpernel himself after seeing Fred Terry portray him. DLS, similarly, was wholly absorbed in the character of Athos from *The Three Musketeers* for a time, and she continued to sign letters using character names into adulthood. In her fictionalized memoir, she remembered the gravity of these games. "If a grown-up said, as most of them tactlessly did, 'Are you going to dress up?,' [she] would reply in a tone of rebuke, 'I'm going to *dress*.'"[7]

Significantly, these costumes and alter egos were often masculine. Muriel, especially, had preferred the "entrancing society of men" as a child and prized the real tools and miniature sailing yachts given to her by her grandfather, who called her Toby. In one of the magazines she created with a childhood friend, there's a story featuring a girl named Tommy who wishes she were a boy. Muriel studied the photographs of her father and his friends, memorizing their flashy clothing: "very high stiff collars, four-in-hand ties or natty bows, and what my mother called 'loud' check waistcoats—lovely waistcoats of pale canary yellow with red lines and flat gold buttons. Their tightly cut trousers are checks, even when their jackets are plain; and they have enormous coloured-silk handkerchiefs, with plain red or blue or green borders." Frustrated with acting in plays at school, she felt "I would be all right if they would only give me a proper man's part." Instead, thwarted, she "took to specializing in drunks—the Porter in *Macbeth*, and Hercules in the *Alcestis*," prompting one scandalized parent to comment that "I had no business, at my age, to know so much about it."[8]

Outside of the rarified discourses of sexology, where cross-gender identification was discussed, named, and sometimes pathologized, there wasn't much language available for the young Muriel to describe her complex experience of gender. Discussing the issue later in life, she would distance herself from "Tommy's" direct wish to be a boy. The social world of Somerville and the MAS, however, provided abundant opportunities to explore and express masculine as well as feminine dimensions, particularly through theater and costume. At a costume party for D. Rowe in June 1913 (held directly after a meeting of the MAS), the guests "had to attend dressed as a character in a melodrama: Dorothy [Rowe] was an adventuress, Dorothy Sayers a racing-man, Miss Kirk the malapropos stage child, Tony the heroine, Jim the detective, Cherub a cow-boy, Phil an innocent country-lad, F.S. 'Madame' from Monte Carlo." Charis, who came as an "innocent flower-girl," was "dragged in shrieking" by Jim the detective, probably the high point in what she described as "the best party we have been to here."[9]

In October 1913, DLS attended a costume dance in old-fashioned masculine attire, playing the violin, dancing until half-past eleven, and impressing everyone with her impersonation. "The Pen was completely puzzled. She stared at me for about five minutes and then had to be told who I was. It surprises everyone that I make up so well as a man. It surprises me rather." Sometimes described by colleagues as masculine in her fearless leadership, Penrose herself also played "trousers roles" in amateur theatricals, appearing in one, for instance, "wearing whiskers and her nephew's coat and trousers." Somerville was an all-women space, but parties like this highlight the ways that it was nonetheless a place where gender diversity and gendered roles could be explored. In their games and their critical engagement, the members of the MAS practiced a wide range of self-expression, laying the groundwork for their understanding of themselves as humans first, women second.[10]

Members of the MAS were also involved in full-dress theatrical productions. In their first year, they put on a mock *Hamlet* that mixed bits of Shakespeare with modern language and turned the whole thing into a cheerful, rather heartwarming comedy. Charis played Horatio and served as stage manager, while Amphilis was Polonius. The star of the show, however, was D. Rowe, in the role of "Hamlet, the Pragger Dagger." Pragger Dagger was Charis's riff on the slangy nickname given to their fellow Oxford student, the Prince of Wales, or the Pragger-Wagger. In their version, Hamlet has been pawning Ophelia's gifts, and the stress of the debt is making him delusional. Those around him try to interrupt his gloomy soliloquies. When Hamlet, pondering suicide, invokes the "dread of something *after* death," the king in-terjects: "that's true—post mortem & the coroner . . . and then the forfeited life policy—Exceedingly unpleasant!" They conspire to cure his troubles with an elaborate ruse involving a false dagger and ghost costumes. At the play's end, the queen is happily looking forward to the wedding of Hamlet and Ophelia and their departure for a honeymoon. The audience, knowing the play well, enjoyed all the jokes and laughed in "one roar from beginning to end." It was a potent demonstration of the MAS's fearlessness in reappro-priating revered high culture for their own purposes.[11]

The next year, members of the MAS were involved in mounting a double-bill production of *Prunella: Or, Love in a Dutch Garden* and *Admiral Guinea*. Amphilis was the driving spirit of *Prunella*: she painted the drop scene, served as stage manager, and starred as Pierrot, the leader of the players. Charis was the producer, and D. Rowe played Scaramel, Pierrot's servant, while Jim Jae-ger was the Boy. A large, enthusiastic audience filled Maitland Hall to see the production, and the *Fritillary* praised Amphilis, who "struck just the right note, and brought out the half poetic, half fantastic spirit of the play."[12]

Student debating societies offered another public venue in which to ex-plore ideas and perform. The Somerville Parliament was a debating society that followed the procedures of the House of Commons. There, the women of Somerville, including Charis and D. Rowe, rehearsed for a citizenship they were not yet entitled to hold. Strikingly, they used not only male titles but masculine pronouns. Charis made her maiden speech in dramatic fashion. In the midst of it, the chairman interrupted, "Order, order, I must ask the hon. gentleman, if his point has direct bearing on this clause." Although oth-ers had meekly backed down when faced with this challenge, Charis refused, to laughter and cheers from her party: "I said 'I *think* so, Sir!' & went on to the end of my speech," earning congratulations afterward.[13]

Somerville students also debated in the all-women Oxford Students Debating Society. In October 1912, they debated the merits of coeducation, and Tony was among those to speak in favor of the motion for it, which was carried 105 to 40. When DLS took part in a debate on impartiality, the *Frit-illary* reported that she had "an arresting manner of speaking, and was ev-idently fully convinced of the rightness of her cause." Somerville students also debated men, although women were not admitted to the main Oxford Union debating society. In 1914, DLS asked her parents to send her black evening frock for one such debate, so that she would "look respectable" when speaking at the debate with Balliol College on the motion that the "educated classes of the present day show a sad lack of enthusiasm." DLS's request was a version of the classic Somerville tactic: look respectable, while strategically pushing the boundaries of acceptable behavior.[14]

THESE FORAYS INTO university politics took place in a charged national context. The campaign for women's suffrage was then at its height, with both militant and moderate groups grabbing headlines in their efforts to win women the right to vote at the national level. Somerville students had formed their own suffrage society and carried their banner in a procession to Albert Hall in 1908. Members of the MAS, too, generally believed that women should gain the right to vote. Charis was the most devoted to the cause; she had heard the famous suffragist leaders, the Pankhursts, speak in Hyde Park. She also wrote a short story, which she shared with the MAS, about a woman who is granted three wishes by a fairy and uses one of them to get her fiancé to support the vote for women. She entered the story twice into competitions run by the *Westminster Gazette*, only to be rejected both times, not on the grounds of quality but because, as she remembered, they would not publish suffrage propaganda. At Somerville, too, she attended suffrage meetings, hearing English tutor Helen Darbishire speak at one in October 1912, and she joined the suffrage society, which was affiliated with the moderate National Union of Women's Suffrage Societies.[15]

On January 29, 1914, Charis took part in a debate in the Oxford Students Debating Society on the motion "that the reluctance of the modern woman to marry is of benefit to society." She argued in favor of the motion, pointing out that reluctance did not mean refusal, and that the profusion of options for women was good for everyone. Indeed, she said, the competition from other professions would even improve marriage. The honorary visitor, Cicely Hamilton, a writer and suffragist, likewise argued that marriage could never be ideal "so long as it is compulsory." Nevertheless, the motion lost by thirty-three votes. Despite this outcome, the event had its benefits. Their honorary visitor socialized afterward with Charis, D. Rowe, Margaret Chubb, DLS, and others, including Diana Whitwill, who opposed women's suffrage. Hamilton drank coffee, ate biscuits, smoked, and "amused us very much, & Diana in particular, by always fixing her when she was going to tell a suffrage story. Di is our only Anti."[16]

Women opposed women's suffrage in surprisingly large numbers and for a variety of reasons, often to do with concerns that votes for women would lead to votes for everyone. In other words, it was better to go without a vote than to open the doors to mass democracy and an end to the dominance of a white, landed elite. Diana Whitwill might have believed that, or she might have opposed suffrage for another reason. More striking was the capacity of the MAS to include a diversity of views on this point—testimony to its plurality, but also to a certain lack of interest in formal politics. As Charis later recalled, the feminist movement was not a major focus at Somerville. It wasn't that the women's movement didn't exist, she explained, "because we made funny speeches about it, and we had our Parliament," but it was "very inactive, I should say. Passive. Sympathetic, but not doing anything about it." In certain respects, she underestimates the work that members of the MAS put into carving out space for women as intellectuals at Oxford. Then and later, though, their focus was cultural and specific to their own areas of expertise, and they didn't, broadly speaking, concentrate their energies on mainstream feminist campaigns or organizations.[17]

If the members of the MAS were largely in agreement on the question of votes for women, they were far more diverse when it came to issues of religion. DLS, in particular, was under considerable family pressure to participate in the religious societies on campus. In her first term, she was cornered by an aunt at a family friend's house in Oxford and told to join the Oxford Christian Union. DLS "behaved as coldly as I could," but still got a "tract" of a letter for her pains later. Unsurprisingly, she reacted strongly against the Christian Union, which she found to be obsessed with "misty theological discussion" and "unprofitable argument." Nor did her aunts let up the pressure as time passed. In March 1914, DLS got a lecture from another aunt, who walked her back to college from tea and enquired "after my soul's welfare." In her preemptive letter to her parents, DLS insisted on her own right to religious exploration and, especially, intellectual development. "What you have been taught counts for nothing," she argued, while "the only things worth having are the things you find out for yourself." Citing G. K. Chesterton, she explained that many "theories of life" were being offered to her, many more than had probably been offered to her aunts:

It isn't a case of "Here is the Christian religion, the one authoritative and respectable rule of life. Take it or leave it." It's "Here's a muddling

kind of affair called Life, and here are nineteen or twenty different ex-
planations of it, all supported by people whose opinions are not to be
sneezed at. Among them is the Christian religion in which you happen
to have been brought up. Your friend so-and-so has been brought up
in quite a different way of thinking; is a perfectly splendid person and
thoroughly happy. What are you going to do about it?"

As she explained, "I'm worrying it out quietly, and whatever I get hold of will
be valuable, because I've got it for myself."[18]

Some of this worrying out happened through reading and writing. DLS
was heavily influenced by Chesterton, a popular defender of Christianity. In
one essay on Blaise Pascal, she made the great seventeenth-century French
philosopher sound like an exceptionally breezy Chesterton. In another, she
rejected the Enlightenment philosopher Jean-Jacques Rousseau's account of
a naturally good man who is corrupted by society. His ideas, she concluded,
do not ultimately accord with the facts. Paraphrasing Chesterton, she described Rousseau as a man "whose philosophy is quite clear, quite coherent &
quite wrong." When she became a popular theologian in her own right, DLS
would return to these ideas, insisting always that religion must stand up to
the most thorough intellectual scrutiny.[19]

But what about that "friend so-and-so" who had been brought up differently? DLS's "worrying it out" also happened in community. On one
occasion, she brought an unlikely companion, Charis, to Sunday services.
Charis was a bit taken aback by the High Church trappings: "my word! We
had, among other things, the bell at the Elevation of the Host! But the music is glorious—Gregorian chants." Her bemused surprise reflects her very
different background. Charis's father was an affectionate, obsessive, vege-
tarian Deist of Jewish descent. Her parents concealed his Jewish heritage
from their two children until Charis was about fifteen and their openly
Jewish uncle came to visit from Australia. She and her brother found
the revelation "immensely funny," she said later, though it's clear that
the question of being Jewish worried not only her parents but, at times,
Charis as well. For his part, her father sincerely "believed that there were
many roads, all leading to the same place." Many roads, many theories of
life: perhaps the elder Barnett's beliefs found their way into the MAS and
helped to create the space for members like DLS to grapple with their religious ideas more freely.[20]

IN BETWEEN DEBATES and meetings and rehearsals and costume parties, the members of the MAS also had their academic work: lectures to hear, "coachings" to attend, essays to write, and ultimately examinations to pass. D. Rowe arrived at Somerville intending to study Classics. But although she was "often ingenious & clever" in her first term, she was also out of her depth. She was, in this regard, like many women who arrived at university with significantly weaker backgrounds in Latin and Greek than their male counterparts. In the words of the tutor who taught her Thucydides, "She has no standard of work at present & no conception of what lies before her, though, on remonstrance, she has made a real effort to pull herself together." Once she switched to English literature, however, the tide began to turn. English tutor Helen Darbishire found that she had "a power of thinking out a question systematically & thoroughly which is unusual in a student of her age."[21]

Tony Godfrey's reports suggest a stronger student, one who was capable of writing first-class essays, though she could be diffident. Jim Jaeger was, perhaps, Tony's opposite. She was confident and independent, but her tutors worried about the lack of time she seemed to spend on her work. Charis was probably the MAS's weakest student. In her diary, Charis recorded her hours of work carefully, perhaps proving to herself (and to her parents) that any academic failings were not due to lack of effort and focus. But she always balanced the social with the cerebral. As she explained in an early letter home, "Somebody says they are going to put in eight hours regularly. Isn't that rather excessive?" After all, she'd been told that it "isn't done" to work in the afternoon! She tended to react to people rather than subjects. In her first term she found her Tacitus coaching "rather trying," because her coach "sniffs violently all the time, & sucks lozenges."[22]

DLS was, without question, the most serious and successful student in her group of friends. At first, some of her tutors worried that she tended to opt for being superficially funny and clever—"smart" was their word—rather than serious. She always found it difficult to restrain her fascination with language. As one tutor noted, "At her worst she runs off with rhetoric or journalistic slang or a pulpit manner & spoils her style." But in general her dedication and quality of thought produced original and well-received essays. Her main French tutor, Mildred Pope, expressed a growing appreciation for DLS. She praised her ability to make "deductions with acuteness & real insight." By her second year, DLS had "laid the foundations of a scholarly knowledge" of Old French, having "shirked no difficulties" on the linguistic side.[23]

DLS's work reveals a mind attuned to the nuances of language and already sensitive to questions of theology and gender. Under Pope's guidance, DLS studied French literature and history from the Middle Ages through the nineteenth century, the English Romantic movement, and literary form. Her essays were written both in English and in French, often quite stylishly. In her fictional memoir, DLS evokes the sensation of falling in love with literature: realizing, for example, that Molière's line "La pâle est aux jasmins en blancheur comparable" is a "symphony on the vowel 'a.'" She loved the "slow mill of textual criticism" and was always a wordsmith and a puzzler. A notebook from her undergraduate days contains a doodle working out the variations to be derived from the word *manes*: *manse, maens, maesn*, and so on.[24]

Training in translation sharpened her skills. In another notebook, she filled eight pages recording the variations of the strophes employed by poet François de Malherbe, counting the appearance of each type with meticulous attention. She scrutinized the changes in language over time. Her translation notes include discussions about the nature, origin, and development of specific words and verb forms. Yet she was apparently reluctant to embrace too fully the identity of translator, at least to her family. When her father asked her to translate a poem for him in June 1914, she put him off, describing it as "practically untranslatable" but offering to pass the task on to a "girl who is very good at translations"—a description that Reverend Sayers no doubt would have thought applied to his own daughter.[25]

Although the MAS was, broadly speaking, a serious-minded group, DLS risked standing out in her innocent, intense investment in her objects of study. In February 1913, she hosted a special supper in recognition of the anniversary of Molière's death. Charis and Jim were there, as well as other students and Mildred Pope, who proposed a toast to Molière's memory. DLS offered the formal reply, and then the second-year students, dressed in deep mourning, recited an original poem honoring the seventeenth-century French poet. It must have been a triumph for DLS, but it also marked her out from her contemporaries—according to Charis, at least, "Nobody took it seriously but Miss Sayers."[26]

Perhaps in reaction, DLS cultivated a studied disdain for academic work. Leave counting hours of work to Charis: DLS claimed to be inveterately lazy. During the Easter vacation in 1913, she wrote an essay about characterization in the "Chanson de Roland," but claimed, in a letter to Tony: "working? No, not half as hard as I should be." And that summer, again, she indulged in "a perfect orgie [sic] of laziness—simply lounging through the day—doing no work, taking no exercise, writing no letters, & spending my whole time puffing cigarette smoke into library novels." The result was that, in late July, she realized an overdue assignment "was still not done." Did such protestations fool anyone? Perhaps, at least, they gave DLS a sense that she could cultivate an identity based on something beyond being a dutiful student.[27]

As their first year wound to a close, the members of the MAS faced their first sets of examinations. Amphilis had found the work taxing and was allowed to drop one examination in Classics in February. She was "fearfully pleased" about it, which led to some teasing. D. Rowe and Charis would ask her how she was getting on in her preparations for the exam, "and she begins again every time to explain to us perfectly solemnly that she isn't taking it."[28]

But Charis's course through examinations would not be smooth either. Her work in the spring had not been strong—"far below what she can do if she tries," in the words of a tutor. On March 3, she stayed in bed, achieving an impressive seven hours of work while suffering from what seemed to be mumps or flu. The doctor ordered rest and then, as the illness persisted, forbade Charis to take the looming Classics examination. Instead, her mother and her aunt brought her home to convalesce. Ultimately, she had to take two sets of exams, on Classics and on theology, at the same time in June, earning the remark from her examiners, "Well, Miss Barnett, it wasn't very good, but we think you've just done it." She immediately sent a telegram to her parents with the joyful news that she'd passed.[29]

DESPITE THE EXAMS, the end of their first year at Somerville was ringed in glory for the inaugural members of the MAS. They were proud of what they'd achieved as a group, planning a "Golden Book" to commemorate five of their literary productions. But they were also ready to enjoy the easier pace of summer. The weather in June 1913 was warm and unusually dry. Jim, Tony, and Charis slept outdoors, in the garden, dragging chairs and mattresses out to arrange a makeshift camp under the stars. Charis wrote home ecstatically, "It is perfectly glorious, & I slept quite well."[30]

DLS took advantage of the start of her first summer holidays by staying in Oxford with local family friends, the Dixeys, for a while after the official end of the term. The visit was a delight. For one thing, the Dixeys slept in and didn't worry about the housekeeping, and DLS relished the contrast with her own orderly background. She stayed in the room usually occupied by the elder brother, Giles, who was around her age, and "desecrated his masculine furniture with face-powder & glycerine & cucumber & hairpins." The family patriarch was Dr. Frederick Augustus Dixey, an entomologist who was then a fellow and bursar of Wadham College. He was an ideal surrogate father figure for DLS. Then in his late fifties, Dr. Dixey had spent most of his adult life in Oxford, and he was a keen amateur musician who sang in his church choir and delighted DLS with his "killing manner" of recounting humorous college stories.[31]

The highlight of the stay with the Dixeys was attending the Oxford Encaenia, the ceremony at which honorary degrees were conferred and other prizes awarded. At first DLS had accepted an invitation to attend with an aunt and cousin, but she abandoned her boring relations when Dr. Dixey gave her two tickets of her own. She immediately went to Somerville to ask Charis to come with her, whereupon Charis "(quite literally) fell upon my neck & said she would love it." The next day, DLS was late getting her hat on. She "tore over to the college as if the fiend was after me, only to find Charis cheerfully guzzling lemonade with Jim & Dorothy Rowe"! Nevertheless the two friends got themselves to the theater only fifteen minutes late, walking through straw-covered Broad Street amid crowds of people.

DLS's account of the event brims over with her enthusiasm for Oxford life. She and Charis contrived to escape a plainly dressed acquaintance who tried to join them in the queue, dubbing her "the enemy in cotton gloves." And they "fell head over ears in love" with the winner of the Newdigate poetry prize, a handsome blond young man from Balliol named Maurice Roy Ridley—"isn't it a killing name, like the hero of a sixpenny novelette?" The Oxford Professor of Poetry gave a speech that, in Charis's estimation, "simply *bristled* with the Prince of Wales," then studying at Oxford. DLS was captivated, too, by the Oxford pageantry on display. Although she couldn't follow all of the Latin speeches, she understood enough to be highly amused at the very imperfect efforts of the dons to use the new Latin pronunciation when addressing the one foreigner present. She recorded that the vicechancellor "addressed all the assembled doctors in a sing-song little speech, beginning something about 'Does it please you doctors of the University that so-&-so should be admitted to such & such a degree—Placetne?' &

then he took off his cap; then said 'Placet' without leaving time for anyone
to make an objection if he wanted to, & put it on again." *Placetne* (does
it please you?), *placet* (it pleases me): the call-and-response would remain
with DLS, reappearing in a pivotal scene in one of her most famous novels,
Gaudy Night.[32]

Back with her own family in Bluntisham in July 1913, DLS was immediately "home-sick for Oxford—not for college—but for that curve in the High
& Radcliffe Square by moonlight, & for the people in the street & the stories about Varsity life." In letters, DLS recreated the atmosphere of the MAS
meetings, giddy with the play of ideas and language. "I *cannot* get any ideas
for prose. Prose is a thing (now is it? is it a thing? it's not a person at any rate.
Well, thing will have to do)—a thing I only write upon compulsion, & then
badly," she wrote gaily to Jim, going on to mock herself for her own mixed
metaphors as well as the bad habits that poetry-writing enabled. In another
letter, she discussed the importance of plot and offered a critical assessment
of a draft of one of her poems: "I am not pleased with all of it, but I thought
the twisty trees & Satan & the Head of the Crucified came out better than I
expected."[33]

Such correspondence was a lifeline. At home at the rural rectory, DLS's
only near contemporary merely giggled when DLS agreed to show her the
same draft poem, to her great irritation: "I'm glad the M.A.S. never got the
giggles." This conveniently omitted the memory of Charis and D. Rowe dis-
solving into laughter at DLS's miracle play in January, but it accurately reflected the value that DLS placed on taking things seriously, which the MAS
supported in spite of its bursts of hilarity.[34]

DLS's exasperation reached even greater heights with another visiting
friend, the "vacuous" Violet. When Violet resisted DLS's efforts to insist
upon a "sensible argument" over dinner, DLS "laid down my ideas in an
offensively dogmatic manner, purposely exaggerated, in order to promote
contradiction. You know that offensive manner of mine?" But Violet parried
with exaggerated modesty and bowed to DLS's "superior knowledge!" Could
anything, DLS asked Jim, make "a fellow feel a sillier ass"? Within the MAS,
this false modesty and circumlocution could never happen. "Oh! Jimmy—I
miss our loud-voiced arguments, everybody certain of being quite right.
Hang it all! What were tongues made for unless to argue with?" Somerville
was a place not just of cocoa parties and cigarettes, but of vigorous debate,
where DLS's "offensively dogmatic manner" and "loud-voiced arguments"

were seen as merely part of playing the game. Undoubtedly tactless and even sophomoric, such arguments nonetheless provided intellectually curious students with a proving ground for their minds.[35]

THE MAS SOON had to consider the serious issue of admitting prospective members. After just one term, it was already the object of desire: "all the first year & some of the seniors are busting themselves with wanting to join the M.A.S. but we are very select." Naturally, members came and went. Margaret Petty resigned from the group because she lost interest, for instance, and DLS urged Tony Godfrey to join by writing "something that I or Jim can produce at the next meeting." In 1913, however, the MAS decided to try a formal procedure of inviting samples of work submitted under pseudonyms, which would then be judged impersonally and used to decide whether to admit the author. It was a plan destined to lead to trouble.[36]

The second year of MAS's existence began in October 1913 with a meeting held in DLS's room. Charis read a chapter from a novel called *Patricia*, and Jim "read an awfully good verse 'soliloquy of Nero.'" The group considered applications from new members, including Agnes Murray, the daughter of Professor Gilbert Murray, a longtime supporter of Somerville College and of women's education. Agnes was admitted, but the process of accepting new members soon led to minor mayhem. An anonymous application, submitted under the pseudonym Scribbler, included three samples of work, one from her school magazine, under the cover of a "very cheeky note." The samples were very bad: Charis cited, as an example, the reference to "The strong right arm / To shield from harm / The sweetness of a feigned alarm!" D. Rowe stuffed a cushion into her mouth, apparently overcome by how terrible the verses were. The group composed a note of rejection, based both on the standard of the work and the anonymity of the submission. Charis hoped the response "will do her good—it was her own opportunity of hearing unbiased & frank criticism! She heard it!" But the plot soon thinned: the MAS was again summoned, and D. Rowe admitted that she and another student, Diana Whitwill, were in fact Scribbler. Charis wrote home: "D. R. has naturally been having the time of her life!!!"[37]

The MAS soon returned to its core strengths: wildly ambitious writing and cozy socializing. Charis hosted Agnes Murray's first meeting, at which DLS read a fragment of her writing, Jim read "a psychic story," and Charis

read "two French translations that I did ages ago . . . & have since repol-
ished." In February 1914, DLS and Dimaris Barton read; Dimaris told Charis
that her "M.A.S. style was 'Gravely amorous!'" Muriel St. Clare Byrne began
at Somerville in January 1914 and soon joined the MAS: "an awfully nice
child who writes quite good stuff." The members also turned their attentions
more emphatically outward in their second year at Oxford, becoming leaders
in the other literary groups. D. Rowe, for instance, was the Somerville representative to the Oxford women's magazine, the *Fritillary*.[38]

The MAS attracted the interest of outsiders and the devotion of its members because it offered a uniquely free space. Its members could try on a vast
array of perspectives and ways of being, unfettered by the social shame that
was otherwise so pervasive. Such experimentation was enormously helpful when it came to working out ideas on the broader stages that Oxford
offered—whether in theatrical productions and student debates or on the
subjects of religion or gender politics. It would prove helpful, too, in navigating the more treacherous shoals of personal relationships and youthful
romance.

3

UNIVERSITY PASSIONS

S TRICT RULES GOVERNED INTERACTIONS BETWEEN young men and women at Oxford, in deference to the particularly sheltered status of middle-class British women in this period. In theory, by creating a series of symbolic and real barriers between men and women, these rules were meant to preserve the ability of Somerville students both to be educated and to remain respectable. In some ways, the immediate prewar years were the strictest on this point: social customs had become rules that were not yet tempered by the social cataclysm of World War I and its aftermath. The members of the MAS accepted the situation, understanding that utter probity was strategically important in their quest for full Oxford membership: "it was up to us to provide no ammunition for the die-hards." Reality, though, also tempered and complicated the apparently ironclad system. Chaperones could be co-conspirators as well as wise counselors. Romantic interests could cross age boundaries, or flourish within the walls of Somerville itself. Unofficially, crushes or "passions," usually shortened to "pashes," provided informal but broadly culturally sanctioned ways to explore romance and desire.[1]

Pashes were considered de rigueur for girls and young women, and those on teachers in particular were a rite of passage. In her fictional memoir, the DLS stand-in chooses, rather instrumentally, to develop a pash for a teacher, whereupon it "ran its course with no more deviation from traditional lines" than a tram in London. But when she writes a letter to her pash "in a rather exalted vein of seventeenth-century *galanterie*, and concluding: 'I kiss your hands and your feet,'" she is told she has gone too far. Her teachers are more concerned with propriety than with her ability to ventriloquize romantic styles of past centuries. This fictional episode echoes a real-life pash DLS had for a teacher, expressed in a poem that began, "Grey eyes / where wisdom lies / Too still for ocean & too deep for skies."[2]

The great pash of DLS's college years was the conductor of the Bach Choir, Dr. Hugh Percy Allen (later Sir Hugh), with whom she pursued a fairly stylized flirtation. DLS was a dedicated member of the Bach Choir, where her feelings were public knowledge and expressed with a mixture of sincerity and self-deprecation. In a letter to her parents, DLS offered several pages of detailed descriptions of various musical events, all focused on Allen, before stating, "I will now stop Allenising if possible." She was fascinated by his emotional style of conducting, which generated an intense group intimacy. At one rehearsal, DLS thought Allen might "burst into tears from sheer misery, & the whole choir follow suit from mere fright." But as the concert drew closer, he was "at his most fascinating," "nice & woolly & kind & making jokes." Another time, she invited Tony Godfrey and Diana Whitwill to choir practice because they were curious to see what all the fuss was about. Allen demanded to know who had brought them, dismissing their vague assertions that they were "from Somerville." Rejecting their offers to leave, he began an interrogation:

> H.P.A.   (in a voice that Stentor might envy): *Who is responsible for these young women?*
> D.L.S.   (in a loud bleat) *I am, Doctor!*
> H.P.A.   (advancing, terrible, mouth open, hair erect) Who?
> D.L.S.   I am!
> H.P.A.   Now I know. (He continues to advance)
> D.L.S.   (aside) Lord deliver us!
> H.P.A.   (sitting down quietly at the piano) I like to make people uncomfortable.
> D.L.S.   I warned them of that.
> H.P.A.   Oh! you did, did you?—Very well. We will sing the "Agnus Dei."

The scene is remarkable for its eroticized power dynamic as well as its humor. DLS concluded: "of course, the two came home, & drivelled over him—said he was so boyish & charming." If DLS thrilled to Allen's displays of faux anger and dominance—she "exulted when he threw up his baton at the tenors"—she also appreciated the more vulnerable aspects of his sensual style, such as his "well-known strip-tease act, beginning with his hat and scarf and ending, with miraculous timing, with the end of the movement, just when there seemed to be nothing but his trousers that he *could* take off."[3]

Not all of DLS's admiration was so sexually charged. She recognized Allen's skill as an effective conductor, drawing on his lessons when she tried conducting her own choir at home in the spring of 1915. But she was drawn in by the personal attention he paid to her, especially through intimate conversations in the organ loft. Allen, it seems, liked to have adoring young women around him. And DLS was certainly adoring, writing multiple poems to and about her idol.[4]

DLS's main confidant on Allen-related topics was fellow Bach Choir member Mrs. Molyneux, who was a friend of Mrs. Dixey. Mrs. Molyneux sympathized with DLS's infatuation. But she also sounded some warning notes. She was evidently less than enthusiastic about a poem dedicated to Allen and decorated "with a really charmingly illuminated cover," that DLS gave her for Christmas in 1914. A couple of months later, as they chose music together for the ladies' choral, Mrs. Molyneux took the opportunity to tell DLS "what a problem marriage was & how unkind Hugh Percy [Allen] is to his wife." DLS bridled a bit—"I really didn't see there was any call for me to know about" that—and blamed the wife for her misfortunes. "If a woman started off by running a man's errands & bowing down before him, she shouldn't be surprised if he made a door-mat of her publicly."[5]

Of course, running errands and bowing down was exactly what DLS was doing. She began, belatedly, to revise her opinion of the revered Dr. Allen. That same month, she admitted to her parents that he was really an "old ass" who wanted to add her to "a long procession of little tame cats who have adorned his organ-loft in succession." But she would not be "anybody's tame cat." If she flattered him, she now asserted, it was only to meet her own ends of getting him to speak at Somerville. It was a bold revision of her previous adoration, but perhaps it was necessary to save her dignity.[6]

DLS had been deeply earnest in her feelings for Allen. A lengthy poem addressed directly to him imagines him as a "master builder" who can only dimly grasp the religious significance of his achievements. Its final stanzas offer a blessing and a farewell: "God keep you. I have set you in your place / Among the holy streets of this grey town." The theme of an arrogant but skillful artist would recur in DLS's writing, as she began formulating the idea that creative work put ordinary, even sordid people in direct touch with the transcendent, holy power of creation. This idea would animate the series of religious plays and essays she would write in the 1940s and would come to occupy a central place in her vision for a better society. Back at Somerville, it served, perhaps, to distance her from Allen, who could be seen as a flawed human being rather than an idol. Although she shared her crush on Allen openly with her parents, Mrs. Molyneux, and her classmates, it is impossible to know what deeper feelings she might have kept concealed in her heart, or whether what was said and done in the organ loft ever crossed the bounds of what DLS considered appropriate. The pattern of abject, ashamed love for a charismatic, unattainable man would recur in DLS's life.[7]

Pashes also developed between Somerville students. Charis had a pash for a fellow female student who ran the Christian Union, which prompted her to attend a Christian conference with her. "And for one blissful moment I was converted and went and told her, and she said, 'Wait a bit,' and of course, it went off the next day." Her diary and letters home also recount an intense crush, perhaps the same one, during her first term at Somerville. Charis was embarrassed to have been a spectacle in the eyes of her fellow students, but at least it ended amicably: "we have had no bust-up, & just smile sweetly & pass each other by." For the future, Charis swore off such entanglements. She reassured her family: "I am just good friends with several people, & friends with many more."[8]

In the spring of 1914, DLS developed a pash for D. Rowe, at least according to Charis, who reported merrily to her family that this development "fills us all with joy." When D. Rowe needed to change her room for health reasons, DLS lobbied the college administration for D. Rowe to remain in her building, "so that they could arrange M.A.S. meetings more easily." DLS and D. Rowe sided together against Charis in an argument about poetry, too. Yet, at the same time, Charis and DLS attended a mixed-sex dance, and Charis reported happily on their interactions with men, suggesting that pashes for women were not incompatible with the rites of heterosexual courtship.[9]

Muriel St. Clare Byrne had been enmeshed in complicated romantic relationships with girls since her adolescence, according to her autobiographical writings. As an early teenager, Muriel developed a crush on Helen, whose effortless, triumphant femininity elicited a potent mixture of misogyny and desire from Muriel. Playing tennis, "I am contemptuous of Helen's underhand service—a girl's service. I mean to serve overhand, whatever anybody says—a great slashing sliding drive of a service, like a man's." But despite Muriel's strength, "Helen always wins," with her reliable style and her "knack of putting a twist on her ball that baffles me nearly every time."

But while her friendship with Helen was meaningful, it was soon over-shadowed by more intense crushes. First, Muriel fell in love with the actress Ellen Terry, to the amusement of her family. Next, she developed a crush on an older girl at school, Frieda. Together with another infatuated student, she walked Frieda back to the station after the morning's school session, discussing *Macbeth* and women's suffrage and proportional representation.

Then came a crisis. Muriel was invited to join Helen every day for lunch for a week while her mother was away. Although Muriel happily accepted the invitation, she was gobsmacked to realize that it implied giving up her walk with Frieda. So Muriel walked Frieda to the station and only then joined Helen for a belated lunch. Her callow behavior was revealed to her when she secretly read a letter Helen's mother had sent her daughter. "The plan to bring us back, easily and naturally, into our old relationship, had failed: I could not free myself of this new infatuation. . . . And her mother wrote counselling patience, forbearance, hope." Paralyzed by shame and overwhelmed by Helen's mother's wisdom and love, Muriel did nothing.[10]

While at Somerville, Muriel wrote poetry that described, in various indirect ways, the experience of same-sex romance there. One poem describes a series of ecstatic encounters taking place in what sounds more or less like a student's room. The narrator hears, for instance, the sounds of "quick feet that passed along the corridor," as well as "traffic noises" outside. Another poem laments the necessity of staying in and doing work alongside "blear, be-spectacled fools." "You are probably out on the river now; I shouldn't find you if I did go round," but still, the narrator can't stop thinking "that you'd be pleased to see me, are wanting me." In "Denial," Muriel suggests a sublimated version of sex. The narrator tries to reach the soul of a desired woman: "but it was bright / And glassy, hard, impregnable, / A barrier / Between me and herself." At last, desperate, the narrator makes a final attempt: "and wild / With misery I hardly knew / The thing I did, / But pushing madly through / At last came where she hid . . . I found her crying like a child."[11]

"Favete Linguis" (or "Hold your Tongue"), by contrast, describes a relationship based on peace and serenity rather than fraught emotions and hectic conversation. While most relationships were defined by "their restless brains, or mine," with this person Muriel found peacefulness: "the gift of

quiet on your brow / Like some long benediction now / Closes upon me."
It is tempting to imagine that this last poem heralds the arrival of Marjorie
"Bar" Barber in Muriel's life. The two attended Somerville at the same time,
and photographs show them socializing there. They would move in together
later. For them, same-sex pashes were a rehearsal, not for heterosexual marriage, but for adult same-sex partnership. [12]

Muriel's poetry exists in a very particular historical moment. Victorian
women used passionate, overheated language in their same-sex friendships
as well as in their romances. The distinction between friendship and romantic partnership was not so much about passion as about sex and long-term
marital commitment. All of the Somerville pashes should be read partly in
this light. They were a fun pleasure that, to their Victorian-bred parents at
least, wouldn't raise automatic anxieties about lesbianism. But Muriel wasn't
a Victorian. She lived in an era when an emerging science of sex was beginning to categorize homosexuality in new ways. It was possible, by this time,
to see intense relationships between young women as potentially unhealthy
or linked to a deviant sexuality. Because of this, all-female institutions attracted particular anxieties.[13]

What risks, then, were those with same-sex pashes (or fully fledged
relationships) at Somerville running? Muriel seemed to wink at the issue.
One short poem, entitled "Sublime Mediocrity," reads in its entirety: "A life
without desire / Is a hearth without fire, / But who desires too well / Fries
in the fires of hell." DLS was skeptical but not condemnatory, asserting,
"Few friendships among women will stand the strain of being romantically
considered—all those I've ever watched have ended in dead-sea apples (the
romantic ones I mean), & I avoid them like the plague." Nevertheless, by
request, she contributed two poems to a short-lived publication called *The
Quorum: A Magazine of Friendship*, a very early magazine focused on homosexuality. One of these poems, "Veronica," shows an understanding of the
complex possible meanings of "friend": "I am not sadder that we have been
friends, / Nor lonelier, loving you." Yet the narrator promises not to add to
her friend's burdens by revealing the depth of the pain she's caused: "not
God Himself, Who knows all things, shall know / That you have made me
weep." Is there a commentary, here, on the love that dares not speak its name
and seems to be capable of being hidden even from God? Although the poem
is written in the first person, of course, the narrator need not be DLS herself.
Perhaps she cribbed notes from Muriel.[14]

ACCORDING TO THE official rules, Somerville students were not supposed to socialize with men except in the presence of an approved chaperone. These were often local relatives or friends of the family, who hosted mixed but eminently respectable parties. Visits from family members could also provide a context for mixed social events. When Charis's mother came to visit, Charis arranged a full round of social visits, including a tea party in her room. DLS held a mixed-gender tennis party in honor of her own mother's visit in June 1913.[15]

Within these rules and customs, there was room for maneuver and compromise. Charis flirted mildly with a man who took the rules rather less seriously than she did. He had asked her to punt with him, "but as he apparently intended the punt-pole to chaperon me, it hadn't come off!" D. Rowe received a marriage proposal from an acquaintance during a cinema performance—but given the hilarity of the retelling, she, at least, does not seem to have taken it seriously. Another time, she agreed to pretend to be engaged to a male undergraduate so that the train guard would let them have a carriage to themselves. At a production of *Iolanthe*, DLS found herself in an apparently compromising situation when she ended up seated alone with Giles Dixey; his mother hadn't turned up, and they had been separated in the queue from Tony and Jim. "Appalling situation for a Somerville student!— Alone with A Man in the gallery!!" Of course, it really wasn't such a crisis as all that. Although DLS tried to assure Giles that "I shouldn't be fried in boiling oil on his account," he was still anxious, so she clambered past other audience members to explain the situation to a Somerville student with more seniority and authority. This woman "roared with laughter and said it didn't matter in the least," adding that Giles must be an "unusually nice young man" even to have worried about the situation, and in the end everyone was able to enjoy the show.[16]

Marriage was still a highly coveted goal for most Somerville students. Through the Dixeys and Mrs. Molyneux, DLS was introduced to potential appropriate suitors. She met Frank Brabant at the Dixeys' home in February 1913, but, although she became friends with the Brabant family, she described Frank only as a "not bad, but, I fear, rather an earnest young man," who "wants shaking up a bit I fancy." A more promising connection developed between DLS and Giles Dixey. The two were exactly the same age, and they formed a friendship mainly through their shared literary endeavors, swapping poetry and offering advice. Yet after rapidly achieving "a sort of mountain-top of intimacy," the friendship soon found itself, to follow DLS's own metaphor, "clambering awkwardly down in the plain of ordinary life, and endeavouring not to miss its footing by the way." At least one of DLS's friends thought the quarrel suggested that the relationship would soon become romantic, but this DLS stoutly denied, insisting that it was a misunderstanding between writers who were merely seeking "a free & friendly exchange of criticism." In any case, Giles had his own adventures to seek as he departed Oxford for a stint as a sailor.[17]

Although she valued her literary friendship with Giles, DLS was unlikely to fall in love with a moody young man afflicted with wanderlust. DLS's interests were firmly rooted in England; while Oxford attracted students and visitors from around the world, her own gaze was not particularly global or cosmopolitan. In November 1913 she went, with Tony, to meet "some copper-coloured potentate—the King of the Fee-jees, I think." Having met him, she improved the accuracy of her reference but maintained her flippant tone in a letter to her parents: "the king of the Fi-ji Islands was really a charming potentate, but I don't think you need be afraid of my becoming queen of anything." Although she related Giles's overseas adventures happily enough in letters home, the lot of an English wife overseas did not appeal to DLS in the slightest. She wrote with horror of the niece of a friend who, freshly married, "went out with her husband to his new station in some beastly part of Africa, & when they arrived they found there had been a rising or something, & the government had issued new orders, forbidding any white woman to go there."[18]

DLS and Tony both grew close to Arthur Forrest, a fellow student of French and a serious musician. In June 1913, DLS and Arthur had talked about music at Balliol, and he followed up with an invitation to tea, "so my 'womanly expression of intelligent ignorance' was after all not wasted." It is hard to imagine that "womanly ignorance" was a particularly winning strategy for someone as keenly intelligent and argumentative as DLS, but the friendship continued. In February 1914, she and Tony had Arthur to tea, an event DLS recorded with the somewhat reserved remark, "He talked a great deal & enjoyed himself very much, I think." The three again met over tea with Mrs. Molyneux in May, enjoying music and tales of Arthur's recent vacation in the Pyrenees. One month later, DLS spent her twenty-first birthday again dining with Tony, Arthur, and Mrs. Molyneux. After the dinner, she wondered, to her parents, about the possibility of romance with Arthur: "he seems to have taken rather a fancy to yours truly; shall I make a bid for him? He has plenty of money and plenty of brains, and I rather think plenty of sense, and is not more excitable than most musicians!" But the relationship stumbled. Was he, perhaps, more interested in Tony than in DLS, or did she lose interest? DLS's later references to him are slightly dismissive, and give the impression that he was seeing more of Tony than of DLS.[19]

As THEIR SECOND year at Somerville progressed, the MAS faced other challenges and distractions, too. Jim had to stay away from Oxford for a while that winter, to avoid the risk of spreading measles after her sister fell ill. More distressingly, in January 1914, Amphilis left Somerville abruptly. She told Emily Penrose that she needed to leave for "family reasons," but her father wrote and said that she was beginning a new venture, though he doubted its success. She collected her things one Friday and left Charis a note, merely asking her to return some library books. Her departure caused considerable speculation. The "favourite theory" was that she had left to become a hospital nurse. More likely, however, was that she was struggling with illness of some kind, possibly the mental challenges that would trouble her later life. Penrose was surprisingly sympathetic and perceptive about the effect of Amphilis's departure on her friends. She told D. Rowe, "One of the three gone, Miss Rowe; we *are* sorry." In June, Amphilis visited Oxford to make arrangements for returning to her studies as a "home student." She would live with the family of Greek scholar and Oxford don Arthur Sidgwick, who was a champion of women's education at Oxford. According to Charis, Amphilis was "exactly the same as ever," a remark that sounds like an unconvincing effort to paper over the major disruption her sudden departure had caused.[20]

Charis and D. Rowe both gave into the temptation to coast a bit, academically, after Amphilis left. Charis confessed with disarming honesty to her parents that one tutor "says that I am no linguist but that I work hard. (I'm afraid that she is not telling the strict truth, but I'm glad she thinks she is.)" The dawn of her second year had found D. Rowe sitting on Jim's floor, while Jim translated to her "the *whole* of the Anglo Saxon she ought to have done" during the vacation. In a Chaucer seminar, D. Rowe wrote a paper that was "superficially clever, but lacking reality, & scholarship." Finally, in June 1914, the Somerville bursar lectured her: she was not "sufficiently serious-minded." D. Rowe responded, initially, with a theatrical overcommitment to reform: she would join the Fabian Society and give a talk on the history of trade unions, and attend morning prayers, and sit at the high table for meals.[21]

Even the first MAS meeting of 1914 was dubbed "frivolous," though the next meeting was somewhat more focused. Agnes Murray sent a poem and Charis read something called "Pink-nose," which she hoped to publish. But D. Rowe, perhaps unintentionally this time, again lightened the mood. She read a ballad that her fellow members were unable to take seriously, "because the refrain 'With a Derry Down Dee' struck us as more humorous each time she came to it." In May 1914, a "first rate M.A.S. meeting" celebrated the fact that nearly all of the leaders of the college literary societies for the coming year were drawn from their ranks. "Everybody except Jim read something. . . . Sayers & Rowe—lyrics, Barnett—Shaw paper, Godfrey—part of a novel, Byrne—poem, & Barton sort of dramatic dialogue." The membership of the MAS evolved again, and Jim Jaeger and Diana Whitwill became "honorary members."[22]

In late June 1914, the MAS (honorary members included) celebrated another successful year by having lunch on the river. The group sat in a hayfield next to wild roses and read their work in turn, nearly everyone making a contribution in the idyllic setting—while the ever-practical Charis warded off her perennial hay fever by sniffing "good old 'No-Germo'!" Only a few months before the outbreak of war, there seemed to be not a cloud in the sky, and nothing more serious to worry about than pollen and the complexities of shifting from girlhood crushes to adult romances. Such challenges were real and important, but they were about to be overwhelmed by a global cataclysm.[23]

4

BATTLEFRONTS

ORLD WAR I LASTED FROM the late summer of 1914 until the autumn of 1918. It crashed into the lives of the members of the Mutual Admiration Society at a moment that would have been fraught no matter what, as most of them began to look ahead to their final year of undergraduate studies. The transition from the supportive environment of Somerville to independent adult life would always have presented challenges, particularly for ambitious young women who wanted to earn their own livings. Instead, members of the MAS found themselves facing the completion of their education in the context of a total war that would kill many of their contemporaries and inflict traumas that would shape a generation. If they remained at Oxford, they experienced an intensified form of female intellectual community, as male students and lecturers left for war service. The war was also a democratizing force: they encountered a wider range of people, in a wider range of contexts, than they would have otherwise, with important consequences for their future work.

Vera Brittain's *Testament of Youth* has provided an enduring archetype for understanding the experiences of well-off young British women during this conflict. Brittain lost both her brother and her sweetheart at the front, and the image of her in her nurse's uniform, somehow both innocent and utterly transformed by war, has come to stand in for a whole category of women's experiences. Charis loathed *Testament of Youth*. Her brother died at the front, too; she also lost friends, some of them, maybe, boyfriends. She, too, worked as a nurse in France. But she understood her experience differently. Together, Charis and D. Rowe read Brittain's memoir with distaste when it came out in 1933; later, Charis kept the book in what she called her "chamber of horrors," recoiling at its insistence that the war had somehow meant more to Brittain than to other people. For Brittain, as for some other writers, the war opened up a chasm between those who had truly suffered and those who sat complacently at home. Charis would have none of this, perhaps because, in her instinctive empathy, she was well aware of the various—sometimes mysterious, but always profound—ways that the war had shaped the lives of each of her friends.[1]

THE SUMMER OF 1914, and the whole period leading up to the war, is sometimes imagined as a kind of long garden party. Indeed, the members of the MAS enjoyed a summer of traveling and socializing. The war found DLS in France. Having been invited to join a friend, she gamely bought some new thin frocks and a hat and tried to ignore the local chemist who commented, gloomily, about how dire the European situation looked. She found much to thrill to in Tours that summer: the cathedral and the old houses, and the novel experience of being in a Catholic country. She even claimed to have enjoyed "splendid 15th century & Renascence smells," though she did complain about the lack of modern plumbing and hot water: "Old England for me!" When war broke out, she and her companions struggled to get back to England amid scenes of mass mobilization.[2]

Charis had also had a cheerful summer, including a visit to a "very lively houseparty" with her father's cousin's family in Cheshire. Among that family was Sydney Frankenburg, a young man who would play an increasingly significant role in Charis's life. Such visits were a regular highlight for Charis. Sydney's father, Isidor, would buy her a first-class return ticket toward the end of her stay, so that she would have to visit again before the return portion expired in six months. Years later, she learned that he used to remark that he "wouldn't mind if Sydney married that Barnett girl."[3]

Charis was back with her family when war was declared. She canceled all her tennis dates and went immediately to London with her beloved younger brother Denis, who was called Dobbin, after his initials. Over six feet tall, Dobbin was a vision of young English manhood, excelling in Classics and sports and looking forward to a scholarship at Balliol College, Oxford. Graceful, clever and masculine, he had been openly favored by their Aunt Louie, who lived with the family. In later life, Charis could still recall her slights with vivid, burning detail. But the sibling bond was stronger than all that. In Charis's memory, the most important fact was the way that Dobbin stood up for her, time and again.[4]

DOBBIN HAD BEEN due to join Charis at Oxford that autumn. Instead, like thousands of other young men, he put all his plans on hold in order to enlist. Britain had an all-volunteer army for the first two years of the war, relying on patriotism and peer pressure to generate the numbers needed to sustain the conflict. In London, Charis and Dobbin hastily reopened their family's house, which became a meeting point for their friends as young men converged to join the war effort. There were no servants, so Charis played at housekeeping. "I bought food and fed him and his friends, and some it went bad and I didn't know why, and it was a most exciting time." The streets were full of enlisted men, and Dobbin himself enlisted with the Artists' Rifles. By September 1914, DLS had heard that over half of Oxford's men had enlisted. Arthur Forrest, the musician who had socialized with DLS and Tony in the spring of 1914, joined up, too, and DLS was sorry to miss seeing him since she'd heard "he looked very nice in uniform." Giles Dixey returned from sea several months later in order to join the navy, but he ended up instead with a commission in the artillery.[5]

Faced with the prospect of returning to Oxford without her brother, Charis immediately applied for leave from Somerville to undertake war work. "The men did, and why shouldn't I? And the principal said, right you are, bless you and go." Charis's situation was unusual; the university generally encouraged its female students to remain at their studies. This would keep the university going and assist in helping women students qualify for teaching as a form of national service, to make up the shortfall in male teachers. Two-thirds of Oxford students had left by 1915, most of them men. Somerville student Vera Farnell found the predominance of women in lectures and classrooms uninspiring. "Many of them felt restless and useless and were anxious to serve their country in some more direct and strenuous manner than seemed open to them as University students."[6]

Even the music had turned patriotic in the autumn of 1914. D. Rowe and DLS attended a concert conducted by Hugh Percy Allen, and "we sang 'God Save the King' all through—twice!" DLS wrote a letter home in the style of war-time reportage, parodying the excesses of censorship. Under the heading "Heroic Exploit of a Student," for instance, her parents read: "on __ Miss D. Sayers of Somerville __ __ __ __ __ and __ __ __ __ __ (censored)."[7]

Refugees arrived from Belgium, fleeing the German advance. Agatha Christie would find the inspiration for her famous sleuth Hercule Poirot in this unfortunate community. Providing aid and welcome to these refugees was a major form of war work available to young women during that first year of the war. In November, Somerville hosted a party for the Belgians, with tea, Morris dancing, and renditions of both the Belgian national anthem and "God Save the King." Charis dressed as a "Belgian Father Christmas" in 1914 and distributed toys to refugees at a party at her family's home. Undertaking her own volunteer work, DLS was assigned a "Belgian lady," whom she helped to find lodgings. She had a hectic, hilarious time assisting another refugee into her new home: "you should have seen Lady Mary Murray's cook explaining the kitchen range to us in English, Miss Jones and myself explaining to Madame Rüdder in French, and Madame Rüdder passing the explanation on in Flemish to the cook and housemaid!"[8]

Few English men and women actually thought the war would be over by Christmas, despite the persistent legend to the contrary. But there was still a perceptible shift as the year ended and the patriotic music and light-hearted parties for Belgians began to be replaced with a more thorough transformation. In a humorous song, DLS satirized the wartime constraints of Oxford life, emphasizing the tedium:

> Skimming lists of German crimes
> In the "Standard" & the "Times"
> Reading unconfirmed reports of victories & slaughter,
> Sick of arm-chair strategy—
> Knitting socks for men at sea—
> Here's a song for you & me,
> Alma Mater's daughter—[9]

The War Office took over the Somerville buildings for use as a military hospital in 1915, and Somerville decamped for rooms in Oriel College and elsewhere. Students were informed about the new living arrangements over Easter vacation in a letter, which DLS referred to, rather tactlessly, as "Emily's bomb." The change of venue provoked a variety of reactions. DLS mourned the fact that her beloved overstuffed chair, good old G. K. Chesterton, would not fit in the more cramped quarters, telling Jim: "it is quite melancholy to think he will never preside over our revels again." Tony and Muriel recalled that narrow cliques thrived in the new fragmented living arrangements, but also felt that the situation shed "new light on old relationships." Men were made anxious by the increased integration of women into the heart of the university. According to one oft-circulated story, an Oriel alumnus, spotting a Somerville student leaving his alma mater one day, muttered, "O, *hateful* sight! *hateful* sight!"[10]

Amid the changes, academic work and writing continued. D. Rowe seems to have found a new focus. By the start of 1915, her tutors remarked that she had "advanced in wisdom & insight" and was finally "substituting honest and even penetrating study of her authors" for "specious theories." DLS claimed to feel out of step with classmates who were looking ahead to their careers. Nevertheless, she and other MAS members were beginning to enjoy external recognition and publication. Reviewing *Oxford Poetry 1915*, the *Aberdeen Daily Journal* made special mention of DLS's "Lay," a "really fine piece of work that lets a flood of passionate enthusiasm into the Oxford life," and of D. Rowe's "An Old Rhyme Resung," which is "full of colour and of good-humoured banter."[11]

Muriel served as the editor of the *Fritillary* in 1914–1915. She seems to have been a tough critic. In March 1915, an editorial took Oxford women to task for the "careless attitude" they adopted toward the magazine, which ought to have been "symbolic and affirmative of the union existing between all women students at Oxford." Muriel demanded commitment but also quality, and she did not hesitate to publish scathing criticism of the submissions for prizes in the spring of 1915. D. Rowe won a guinea for her poem "The Dream Merchant." But DLS's submission, "Mirth," was published alongside the editorial comment that it "has some very good lines in it, but has also too many serious lapses to justify the award of a prize." It was a bracing beginning for what would become a fruitful collaboration.[12]

In the summer of 1915, DLS earned first-class honors in French, while Amphilis and D. Rowe earned second-class honors in English. At the end of each school year, the members of the final year put on what was known as a going-down play, "going down" being the phrase for leaving Oxford. This play usually featured self-referential humor set to popular tunes. In 1915, D. Rowe and Amphilis produced the play, and DLS was the musical director. Their characters were based on real faculty members: DLS, triumphantly, got

to be Dr. H. P. Rallentando, the absurd version of her erstwhile crush, Dr. Hugh Percy Allen. Another song teased DLS for her vigorous execution of her duties as bicycle secretary. Behind the laughter, though, was the bittersweet sense of the looming end of college's happiness. To the tune of "Tipperary," then a standard song associated with service in World War I, they sang, "Goodbye to the Bodley / Farewell Radcliffe Square / It's a long long way to Never Country / But we're going right there."[13]

DLS as Sir Hugh Percy Allen in the going-down play, 1915 (Somerville)

Leaving Somerville was painful. On June 23, 1915, DLS wrote a short, elegiac poem entitled "Last Morning in Oxford," conveying an unwillingness to let go. Yet she was wary of nostalgia, too. In another poem, she promised, "I would not hold too closely to the past." Instead, she advised, "Sweet friends, go hence and seek your own renown, / Now that we have gone down—have all gone down."[14]

Not all the members of the MAS went down from Oxford with DLS in 1915. Having missed considerable time due to illness, Jim, for one, would be a student until 1916. DLS was invited to help for a few days with the Somerville library in October 1915 and looked forward to seeing Jim, "who will be feeling a bit stranded, I expect, poor darling." Muriel remained, too, having begun her studies later, and made plans to put together a book of MAS writing called *Blue Moon* (in reference, presumably, to how often it would appear).[15]

War, and the competing demands of adult life, made holding MAS meetings difficult. In September 1915, when DLS was at loose ends, she planned a trip to Bournemouth to see D. Rowe, only to have war work take precedence when D. Rowe's hospital put her on night duty. But she made it to London to see Charis, and planned another London trip over Christmas break that would feature "a M.A.S. dinner" with Tony, D. Rowe, and Jim present.[16]

The regular cocoa parties, then, were a thing of the past. The MAS could have been a nostalgic relic, as DLS hinted when she wrote breezily to Jim,

"Good old M.A.S. We got some good fun out of it, didn't we?" Nostalgia was in the air: both Jim and Tony considered publishing novels about Oxford. Jim's draft reimagined the bittersweet excitement of leaving Somerville, and claimed that the fictionalized MAS had been "disbanded, because its first members arrogantly refused to face the prospect of the certain decline" of the club once they'd left it. At the last meeting, one of the members proclaims, we've "drunk the toast: Let us break the glass." In fact, though the real MAS did not continue as a student society at Somerville, the most important aspect of the club endured, because its members kept sharing their work and offering criticism to one another. Jim sent a sonnet to DLS that has not survived but evidently included a "charming and undeserved compliment" to its pleased recipient. D. Rowe and DLS spent the winter of 1915–1916 "corresponding in parodies" of one another's poetry. Night duty might prevent socializing, but it couldn't prevent literary banter. DLS also sent carefully assembled copies of her poetry cycle, "The Last Castle," to members of the MAS, including Jim, Charis, and Tony.[17]

From a group of college friends, the MAS was becoming a community of writers. In April 1916, DLS asked Jim, Tony, and D. Rowe to be her literary executors if she died in an air raid. Would they accept "full powers as to publishing or destroying, but not letting anything be published at the expense of pious relations? . . . nobody cd. do it as well as the M.A.S." DLS's first published book, entitled *Op. I.*, was a volume of poetry in Basil Blackwell's series for new poets. It, too, is a testament to the significance of the MAS as a writing community. The book's epigraph is individualistic and bold: "I will build up my house from the stark foundations, / If God give me time enough." This individualism is at odds with the book's contents. Throughout, DLS is thinking about Oxford and the community she had gained there. Poignantly, she conjures up Somerville and the world of the MAS as "that last faery castle, where we met, / And dwelt three years together, you and I!" The dedication is even more explicit: to "the Stage-Manager of 'Admiral Guinea' [D. Rowe], the Conductor of the Bach Choir [Hugh Percy Allen], and the Members of the Mutual Admiration Society."[18]

AS THE POMP of 1914 gave way to prolonged battles with enormous tolls, the traumatic consequences of the war became ever clearer. All the members of the MAS would have known someone who died or was permanently changed by war service. DLS had an uncle and a cousin serving in the war; by the summer of 1915, both have "got nervous breakdown, one has neuritis and the other has damaged his eye gazing at aeroplanes." Her friend Giles Dixey hated his war service, becoming too despairing even to enjoy poetry. He was in "the big push" in the summer of 1917, and DLS feared for him, but he was one of the lucky ones, surviving the war and earning a Victory Medal.[19]

Arthur Forrest wrote to DLS in November 1914 from a camp near Woolwich, offering her an "airy apology" for his recent silence. Toward September 1915 Arthur was sent to the Dardanelles. In DLS's account, he "hates the whole thing, I think, but takes it very high-spiritedly"; he was focused on the idea of getting back to music and Oxford. That was not to be. Arthur Forrest died on December 9, 1915, in Malta from septicemia that developed after frostbite. In her poem "Epitaph for a Young Musician," DLS reflected on the transcendent quality of death, which took her friend from the ordinary chances of life into a realm of perfect, eternal sacrifice. Death "robbed him of occasion to transgress, / He lost the chance of failure; perfectness / Was his alone."[20]

Death robbed others as well. Amphilis fell in love with a former Oxford man, Hugh Sidgwick, one of the sons of the family with whom she'd lived while finishing her studies. After she left Oxford, Amphilis had returned to Birmingham and undertaken a mix of low-key voluntary war work and domestic caring (for instance helping her friend, former Somerville librarian Margery Fry, to care for her ailing father). It is easy to see why Amphilis would have liked Hugh, then a civil servant in his early thirties. He loved walks in the countryside in southern England and was a writer and a fan of literature, including Jane Austen's novels. He joined up in 1915, but was eloquent about his disgust at war, calling it "horrible and indecent," as well as "a triumph of machines over men." Amphilis, who railed against the treatment of conscientious objectors, would have found his qualms sympathetic, too. Their romance developed slowly; he was the sort of person to value friendship before committing to marriage.[21]

When Hugh returned to London in February 1917 on temporary leave to resume work at the board of education, though, things moved more quickly. In March, Hugh visited his sister Rose, a university teacher, in Birmingham, and the three walked together in the Clent Hills. By April, Amphilis realized that the relationship had altered in intensity and meaning. She "knew suddenly that when we met again we should have to talk things over; & that seemed easy & natural." To Fry, whom she regarded as a "kind of a mother or aunt," she explained in late May that she and Hugh were thinking about marriage, though nothing was definite yet. "It's all very easy & comfortable & feels like being real good pals whatever else we may or may not be."[22]

Hugh, too, was cautious in his letters home. He was concerned that his family might disapprove of him marrying someone who had become a kind of daughter to his parents. To a good friend, however, he wrote "so much of the (nameless) girl he loved." For her part, Amphilis seems to have been worried particularly about what she'd bring to the marriage. She talked the matter over with her sisters and concluded that "if he realised really what he was in for (because I know I am rather an unaccountable person) that I was game." Here, again, seems to be a veiled reference to something like mental illness.[23]

But before Amphilis could tell Hugh that she was willing to move forward, he died from internal bleeding after a bomb fell on the car he was traveling in. Amphilis was staggered by the news. From the General Hospital in Birmingham, where she was training in nursing, she sent her effusive sympathies to his sister Ethel but asked for nothing in return: "answer unnecessary—this is my affair." Yet she soon found solace through grieving with the Sidgwicks, who accepted her as Hugh's "wife-elect" and then as "Aunt Amphilis" to his brother's children. She received the letter he'd left behind for her and hoped that he'd known, in the end, that she loved him. "From his last written letter to me I am inclined to believe it; but I should be very glad of more certainty." When his mother received his personal effects, she gave Hugh's wristwatch to Amphilis, who buckled it on, noted when it had stopped, and then wound it and held it up, so that his mother could hear it.[24]

Charis and her parents received brave, cheerful letters home from her brother, Dobbin. November 1914 found him sheltering in a greenhouse in France, which was "rather cold," though bright. He was still enthusiastic enough to be excited to meet the Prince of Wales—or the P-Wagger, as he put it—coming off parade, and to pity the working-class regular soldiers who "can't see the eternal fun of the thing." He got his first taste of shell fire at the end of the month, though he reassured his parents, "I found it did not worry me." But things changed fast at the front, and boys grew up quickly. Dobbin became adept at firing on German soldiers building trenches on their side. It was as exciting, he said, as shooting his first rabbit, though he hesitated to describe what he'd seen: "well, he was done in, but I won't tell you." The killing took its toll despite the homely metaphors. "I *am* having a glorious time, but you can't imagine how old I am now." Dobbin met his cousin Sydney Frankenburg while in France and enjoyed a lighter moment. "Dear old Sydney" took him to what both were surprised to discover was not a lace-making establishment, as advertised, but apparently a brothel. "But we emerged with our good Semitic morals unsullied," Dobbin assured his sister, enclosing a piece of lace that she kept for the rest of her life.[25]

Dobbin returned home on leave in early 1915. Charis wanted him to stay in London, rather than go to the family's rural home, but she was overruled. He was wounded in May 1915, but only slightly. Far more painful was the mounting tide of death around him. He saw the men he commanded killed, injured, or driven mad. Then came news that a good friend from childhood had been killed. Dobbin's letter home underscored the widening gap he felt between his experiences and his family's: "you at home have not taken the progressive course in the death of friends, and I am very sorry for you."[26]

By June, Dobbin was working in a dangerous "gas area," confiding this only to a friend who could share the details with his family if he were killed. The glamour of war had all but faded. He was recommended for an award but explained bleakly, "It was for carrying some wounded machine-gunners out of a farm that was being shelled. I think they all died, so it was a wash-out." Dobbin had been in the army less than a year but he was already a jaded survivor. In July 1915, he returned home on leave for the last time, confiding to Charis that "he sensed an enemy behind every tree, and was on the alert at every rustling leaf or cracking twig." The next month, he was back in Flanders, where he served as a highly successful bomb officer. On the night of August 15, he led a working party in a trench closely adjacent to the German trench. Despite the proximity, he directed the soldiers from a parapet. He was lit up by a flare and in an instant was hit by a German bullet. Dutiful to the end, he attempted to give further instructions about finishing the work as he was carried from the trenches, but his mind began to wander, and he died in the small hours of the morning of August 16 at Poperinghe.[27]

The news made its agonizing way home. On August 19, his family received a War Office telegram saying that he had been wounded; that evening, they received letters from the front informing them of his death. The next day, Charis's father wrote to the War Office asking for confirmation: "I do

not doubt that he has died," he wrote, "but I cannot publish the announce-
ment before I hear from you." The attention to detail is characteristic of the
man, as is his brave disavowal of hopeful doubt. A month later, Percy Barnett again wrote to the War Office, on black-edged paper, to complain that
Dobbin's glasses, regulation revolver, and automatic pistol had been left out
of the effects forwarded to his family. The grieving father explained that the
items were wanted for a cousin headed for the front—but it is hard not to
hear, also, the final outrage at the idea that Dobbin was being robbed even as
he lay dying far from home.[28]

Charis's world was torn apart by Dobbin's death. What consolation
could the members of the MAS offer? Their efforts were awkward but sincere. DLS wrote a letter of condolence immediately, but wondered about its
efficacy: "I'm sure if I was in trouble I should hate all the letters saying the
same things—but perhaps I shouldn't when it came to the point." Probably
Charis did appreciate it, since she wrote a "perfectly ripping letter" in reply.
DLS also expressed her empathy through poetry:

> I found him in the church-yard,
>   My brother who had died,
> With white lilies above him,
>   And a hemlock by his side.

The poem offers a brief, vivid glimpse into the complex terrain of grief. Of
course, for DLS, such a glimpse could only be secondhand. But when Charis
read D. Rowe's copy of the poem, she said "that it rang perfectly true."[29]

A short time later, DLS, Tony, and Charis planned a shopping trip in
London together. DLS was anxious about the trip. Would Charis be "in a depressed state"? In fact, the visit was a delight. Charis, Tony, DLS, and another
young woman (probably Hilda Rowe, D. Rowe's sister) "lay on the floor,
round a gas-stove with no gas in it for fear of zepps., and the eider-downs
and pillows all over us, and talked late, and pretended we were at college."
The shopping expeditions were a success, and Charis helped DLS to navigate
her very first experience of riding an escalator, taking hold of her friend's
arm "lest I should get giddy or anything." Late-night laughter and rides on
department store escalators might have been exactly what Charis needed.
She kept a stiff upper lip, but DLS admitted, "of course, one can't help feeling
Dobbin in every corner of the house."[30]

CHARIS'S GRIEF PUSHED her to find a way to do war work in France. As she put it later, "I just wanted to get away and do something . . . really in the war." There was a great deal of work available to those who wanted to support the war effort but were unable to fight. In a poem published in *Oxford Poetry 1918*, Muriel seems to allude to that sort of work: "the steady, silent effort, / Only the toilsome moulding, the shaping the weapon, / None of the keen sword-glory." In their answers to a survey circulated in 1917, current and former Somervillians reported being engaged in hospital work, ambulance driving, relief work, work on the land, administrative work, and many other war-related efforts.[31]

As a group, the members of the MAS undertook work in several of these categories. D. Rowe volunteered in a military hospital in 1916. Faced with the task of boiling thirty-eight eggs simultaneously for the patients in one ward, she admitted in verse: "it was the sort of, kind of egg / No decent hen would lay." Jim left Somerville in 1916 with second-class honors, much to the disgust of Emily Penrose, who regarded her work as first class. Jim found employment in a series of positions in various ministries, spending much of the war's final year at the foreign intelligence section of the statistical department in the Ministry of Food and learning in detail about the horrors of starvation in Germany and Austria, where the governments increasingly struggled to feed their populations. Amphilis also earned second-class honors in 1916 and received Penrose's condolences; she went on to voluntary war work and then nursing. Tony worked with the Ministry of National Service and enjoyed it very much.[32]

Charis had been doing all sorts of work with the Women's Emergency Corps and the Women's League of Service since 1914, including interpreting and working at an infants' clinic. After Dobbin's death, she visited the Friends War Victims Relief Committee because she had heard that they were sending volunteers to the continent. She told them that she spoke good French and hoped to work with young babies, and received the unexpected advice to train as a midwife. She tells the story with typical humor in her memoir: "my mother, at Burnt Hill, next day received a telegram, 'Unless you object am entering maternity hospital immediately.' She returned post-haste to London to amaze me with her misinterpretation of my plans. (It is relevant to explain that nobody in the family had ever shown interest in a medical profession.)" Charis was not pregnant, but she was on the cusp of a life-altering adventure. Midwife, she remembered, "wasn't really a respectable word" at the time, but she was determined.[33]

Charis went to Dr. Annie McCall's Clapham Maternity Hospital to be trained, in accordance with the legislation that had, since 1902, regulated the necessary education for registered midwives. Dr. McCall was a pioneer in the field, emphasizing ante-natal diet and care. Trainees worked thirteen-hour days in full uniform and attended evening lectures: "through a haze . . . comes Matron's voice, 'Nurse Barnett will answer that if she's awake.'" In the wards, they changed diapers, oversaw feeding, and made sure the supplies were in good order. On top of this, they could be called to assist at late-night deliveries. On her first day, Charis observed three births. To get over the shock, "I had to steel myself by imagining that I was acting in a play." It was a long way, perhaps, from Somerville, but her education made the memorization of Greek and Latin medical terms far easier. Charis was a survivor, and she soon thrived in the hospital context, befriending both matron and cook, keeping exhaustive lists, and even sewing a special pocket in the seam of her dress to keep from losing her cuffs, which were obligatory at meals or in a doctor's presence but removed for actual work.[34]

She presided over a birth solo for the first time on an unusually busy day. A new nurse was sent to assist, and Charis noticed that she was black only after the baby arrived. In her memoir she writes, "Coloured people were almost unknown to us then so it was an additional jolt. All went well, but my first solo midwifery case is unforgettable." Charis would certainly have seen nonwhite people as a child in South Africa. But although the moment is meant to be comic, it highlights the way that Charis's war work continued the process, begun at Somerville, of widening her world and moving her beyond the somewhat narrow expectations of her parents.[35]

Charis traveled to France as a certified midwife at the beginning of October 1916. It was a rough crossing over the English Channel, made worse by a two-hour delay because of an enemy submarine nearby. Things were better in Paris, where Charis enjoyed "chocolate with whipped cream and glorious cakes." She spent most of October working at a convalescent hospital in Samoëns in the Haute-Savoie, helping to care for forty women and forty-six children in austere, difficult conditions. She was one of the few trained members of staff, apart from Dr. Katherine MacPhail, who was posted there while recuperating from illness after working in Serbia. An American nurse made matters even more difficult: she "despised female doctors, and, to show her disdain, used to dive under the bed with a duster, and answer Dr MacPhail's questions over her shoulder."[36]

Once her war zone permit came through, Charis continued onward to the maternity hospital at Châlons-sur-Marne, where the Friends were caring for Belgian refugees. This was one of a set of institutions founded through the efforts of one British woman, Dr. Hilda Clark, who wanted to address the needs of the refugee mothers and children behind the front lines in a moment when most resources were being sent to support the military. The new maternity hospital, presided over by Clark's partner, Edith Pye, was set up in the former workhouse, which was ugly but well lit.[37]

When Charis arrived, she struggled with the antique plumbing that had amazed DLS in Tours, but on a whole different scale. Water had to be heated on coal-fired stoves ventilated by long iron pipes; drains were clogged, frozen, or both; there were no bathrooms; and the food "was sent from the workhouse in pails." The work was relentless. She got a septic thumb, but was "merely told to keep my hand in a sling and do as much as possible." The hospital, nicknamed the Maternité Anglais, was run according to English notions of scientific baby rearing: "feed them only at the proper times, and not to cuddle them every time they cried!" The women found it strange, but, in Pye's recollection, they soon enjoyed the leisure time and good sleep the system allowed both mothers and babies. Charis, for her part, would always remember the bitterly cold Christmas she spent there, singing carols over the noise of fussy babies.[38]

Charis had approached the Society of Friends because they would send her to France, but she came to resent their pacifism. She was sickened, at one prayer meeting, by the "smug self-righteousness" of the conscientious objectors present, who presumed that they were purer than men like Dobbin who had lost their lives fighting. Inside her coat, as a silent protest, Charis wore a Military Cross given by one of her friends. Yet she found joy in her work as well, reflected in a parody of *The Gondoliers* she wrote to describe night duty at the hospital. "We proceed to *cherche* a light / For the duties of the night. When at last we've found the matches / Then we polish off the batches / of the cases they've collected in the day; / And if business isn't heavy / We may hold a sort of levée / And hot cocoa and *bouillottes* we give away." Hot cocoa and a party to put things right: Charis remembered more than just Greek and Latin from her Somerville years.[39]

War work was frequently, for young women, interrupted by family duties. Charis left Châlons at the end of March 1917 and worked for a short while at a maternity home for officers' wives. But then she suspended her war work and returned home to help her mother care for Aunt Louie, who died in October 1917. D. Rowe likewise put her hospital work on hold for home nursing duty after her mother needed a minor operation. Such interruptions are a reminder that war work, however dramatic and far from home, did not fundamentally undo the social expectation that dutiful daughters would put their families first. A Somerville education disrupted that narrative more, by placing young women in a context in which the development of their minds was meant to be the primary aim.[40]

Decades after the war ended, a historian asked Charis how her generation felt about those who had died. The loss didn't overshadow her, she said, but it was always present: "I think you always feel you owe a lot to them." In the last years of the war, the members of the Mutual Admiration Society began to embark on the process of forging adult lives and careers. Those lives would always be, as Charis admitted, informed by the cataclysmic conflict of World War I. But they were also shaped by the ongoing limitations on women's public work and independent lives, and by the communities, including the MAS and Somerville, that sought to transcend those limitations.[41]

Part 2

Slough of Despond, 1918–1929

5

TEACH OR MARRY?

IRGINIA WOOLF FAMOUSLY DEMANDED ON behalf of female authors, "Give her a room of her own and five hundred a year." At Somerville, the members of the MAS had rooms of their own. Between parents and scholarships, all the necessities of life were provided. The Somerville students were the direct beneficiaries of the feminist struggle that had gone before them. In the decade after their graduation, they were, by contrast, on the front lines of the struggle for independence. No one would give them a room of their own—outside the family home and family duties, of course—and earning an adequate salary was no simple task. Jim's second novel featured a character who, after university, gets a job as a secretary to a woman in politics and takes a small flat in Bloomsbury where, "in modern fashion," she lives alone. This was a highly idealized vision. In fact, getting started was a great deal more difficult for the members of the MAS.[1]

The decade after 1918 was hard on the MAS. They faced a job market that actively favored men returning from the war, in addition to the universal struggles faced by young people trying to get a career going. They were provisional citizens, in a kind of limbo professionally, socially, and politically. They couldn't even vote until they turned thirty under the terms of the 1918 legislation that gave women parliamentary suffrage. They also faced the complexities of adult sexual and romantic lives. Dealing with these challenges pulled the members of the MAS in different directions, but, out of the messy fog of trying to make ends meet, a life's work began to crystallize. Among DLS's papers is a pamphlet, dated December 1920, from the British Federation of University Women. It argues, "Women have claimed and won the right to responsibilities of citizenship, but their public work will be judged by no lenient standard." In different ways, all the members of the MAS would find a way of intervening in public life. But in these early years, claiming even the most minimal footing of authority for public intervention was crushingly hard. Balancing that work with the demands of the heart was even more difficult.[2]

According to a survey of Somerville alumnae of their generation, they were as likely to become teachers as they were to marry—mutually exclusive options, generally, in an era when teachers were usually barred from marriage. Both options could offer long-term stability and fulfillment. For most of the MAS, though, neither option was ideal. In the last years of the war and the first years of the postwar period, these two poles—teaching and marrying—would exert a kind of gravitational pull, shaping the choices made even by those who wanted to do neither, at least not right away or exclusively. When, if ever, would they become wives? How could they be good daughters, if they cost their families money and offered nothing in the way of filial duty? The members of the MAS were at a transitional historical moment in this regard. Muriel's own teaching notes demonstrate her awareness that Victorian middle-class women had a far more circumscribed array of choices than her own. Discussing Charlotte Brontë's novels, she argued that the Victorian world "simply didn't give a chance to & had no room for a woman with either a brain or a soul of her own." If a Victorian woman didn't want to be dependent on her family, her only real options were marriage or working as a governess for a pittance. The members of the MAS had more choices than that, and teaching in a secondary school, though still not well paid, was far more secure and remunerative than being a nineteenth-century private governess. For those who did not make a career of it, teaching could also fill the gaps as they waged prolonged, multifaceted campaigns to make a life beyond teaching, marriage, or dependence on family.[3]

Nearly every MAS member taught secondary school at some point, a job into which many university women "drifted . . . on the principle of least resistance." Even Charis, one of the exceptions, had to argue with her father to avoid teaching. He was, himself, prominent in education, and he wanted her to follow in his footsteps. Indeed, he said that he would never have allowed her to go to Oxford if he had realized she didn't want to teach, and "he took no further interest in me, and to subsequent enquiries whether I was at college or on vacation, he replied that he hadn't the slightest idea."

Only the war, and perhaps her mother's steadfast support, eased this painful breach.[4]

D. Rowe took up what was supposed to be a temporary teaching job in 1916 at her old high school in Bournemouth, and made a life's work out of it. In some respects, she was returning to familiar ground; her mother was still on the school's board of governors. She was carrying on a family tradition in another sense, too. Her father had worked in education and had been the headmaster of Tonbridge School, leaving a few years before D. Rowe's birth. In other respects, though, she joined a growing, changing institution. Bournemouth High School had its origins in the drive to provide more formal education to women in the late nineteenth century. By 1919, it had twenty-one regular members of staff and 349 pupils, a substantial increase over prewar numbers. Its buildings were increasingly inadequate as the school continued to expand, and in 1935 it opened at a new site with brand-new buildings, becoming the Talbot Heath School in honor of its new location.[5]

D. Rowe was a demanding teacher whose department earned special praise from the government inspectors who visited in 1928. She had no patience for typical student excuses. One pupil told her, "I know what it means but I can't explain it," and was met with the unanswerable reply: "if you really understand what it means, you will be able to explain it." But she also pushed her students to become thoughtful, responsible adults. To a grumbling sixth form class, she said, "No one, you know, can *make* you do what *you* decide not to do." The students were startled: who could disobey Miss Rowe? "Perhaps, for the first time, we realised that our obedience had been based on trust and that, as we were grown up, we must accept responsibility for our actions."[6]

Her success as a teacher was fueled by her ever-present sense of humor. Students remembered her mordant comments on their essays' missteps. She sent her favorite student mistakes on to members of the MAS. For instance, she sent Charis a student's explanation that quarreling nobles disturbed the army by causing "dysentery among the junior officers." She could be humorous in the classroom, too. Mentioning the fact that husbands and wives could not be forced to testify against one another, she "added with her familiar mischievous look, 'So, if you meet a young man who knows evidence which could put the rope around your neck, marry him.'"[7]

D. Rowe cultivated a reputation for eccentricity at Bournemouth High School. She grew flowers and strawberries in the school garden and was an amateur beekeeper. One student remembered "the sight of her on her bicycle in the rain sitting bolt upright holding her umbrella in one hand and steering with the other!" She would solve her colleagues' problems by opening the collected works of Shakespeare at random and pointing to a passage. She was famous for listing points—A, B, C, and so on—and one pupil dreamed that her list had stretched to K—a glimpse, maybe, of one of the traits that bound her tightly to Charis, another inveterate list maker. A colleague once asked in the staff room if anyone knew where to find a costume of a Turkish lady. D. Rowe immediately came to her aid, explaining, "Oh! I always keep the costume of a Turkish lady on my shelf, just in case."[8]

These stories suggest the importance of theater to D. Rowe. Many former students credited her with their subsequent enjoyment of Shakespeare, whose works she brought to life in the classroom. While her most storied performance was her one-woman *Macbeth*, her students averred that she "could play Juliet or the nurse, Macbeth and the witches." She held the attention of the class for an entire hour merely by lecturing on the meaning of the first two words of *Hamlet*: "who's there?" Many former students found that her voice still echoed in their minds whenever they read, quoted, or saw Shakespeare. As one student told her later, "You lit up our minds and the light has never gone out. I have never been to a performance of Shakespeare without you."[9]

D. Rowe would become head of the English department, equipping generations of students to cope with the particular burdens of being intelligent, witty women. When someone said, dismissively, "Oh, well, you're so clever!" D. Rowe advised one student, the future translator Anthea Bell, "You must smile sweetly and say, 'No, dear, not clever, only amusing.'" Despite her success in the classroom, this telling quip hints at the limits of teaching for her. Bournemouth High School was not a sufficient outlet for her extravagant, over-the-top theatricality, which would find expression in what was essentially a second full-time, unpaid job running an amateur theater.[10]

For many others, teaching secondary school was merely a painful station on the journey to other endeavors. Tony Godfrey tried it but found it too draining. By the end of her first term at Blackheath High School, she was ill from overwork and being looked after by Jim Jaeger. Muriel St. Clare Byrne spent the first two years of the war finishing her studies at Somerville in English language and literature, earning second-class honors. As the end of her university career approached, teaching beckoned. Her first teaching job was at the Liverpool College junior school, teaching young boys. The principal of the college described her as "willing and punctual, bright in her lessons, and effective in discipline," a young teacher who had learned "where the real difficulties lie" and made a good beginning. Given her background, she was well placed to sympathize with her students. She compared notes with the black sheep of her class on matters such as making paper airplanes and eating an orange in class without being caught, and concluded that he and his fellow twelve-year-olds "know as much of the means of alleviating the dulness of being educated as we did."[11]

But teaching children in her hometown was, perhaps, too tame. In the autumn and winter of 1918–1919, Muriel moved on to a post with the YMCA in France teaching English literature to active servicemen. Her supervisor there described her as "thorough and interesting," and said that she had helped the men to develop "discriminating judgments on books." Her own retrospective assessment was more cynical: the "men didn't want education," but she, at least, made some "friends of a lifetime." Possibly one of them was Mary Aeldrin Cullis, a Somerville graduate a dozen years older who was in France running concert parties, driving ambulances, and organizing a bookshop, and who would later become a significant figure in Muriel's life.[12]

Immediately after leaving Somerville, DLS had bounced about for lack of things to do, despite having achieved first-class honors. One aunt discouraged her from nursing, given her lack of "patience & sympathy." She applied to work for the Board of Trade, but nothing came of it. She also considered accepting an unpaid clerical position back in Oxford with Emily Penrose. Meanwhile, a male friend from Oxford, Frank Brabant, who had only gotten second-class honors, "is going to be a lecturer in philosophy somewhere in place of a man gone to the Front," she wrote to Tony. "No time for more. I'm cross."[13]

What was left? Teaching. DLS, "sick of hanging about" her parents' home, wrote to an agency and immediately got two interviews, one with a school in Harrow and one with a school in Hull. Despite the distance from London, the Hull job appealed to DLS immediately. The headmistress was new in her post and was undertaking a thorough reorganization. "At the word 're-organise' the Bicycle Secretary lifted her head & sniffed the air like an old war-horse." She was offered the job on the spot and accepted it after talking it over with her family.[14]

DLS arrived in Hull in early 1916. She was pleased with her fellow staff and befriended the energetic, red-haired headmistress, but she struggled with the students, who were passive, ignorant of major French authors, and accustomed to learning by rote. Already by February she knew she would leave before she could truly bring things right, "because my brain will be growing rusty, and I can't afford that." She found Hull a bit stifling too—the Hull Vocal Society was no Bach Choir, though the town "simply bristles with excellent cinemas." Air raids were another source of stress. DLS had to crawl home in the dark when the alarm went during a Vocal Society rehearsal. After witnessing her landlady's attack of shudders during one air raid in November 1916, DLS wrote to Jim: "I had never seen fear before—believe me it is brutal, bestial and utterly degrading. I should say it was the one experience which is neither good for man nor beast." Luckily, she had some spirits handy to share with the suffering woman. By summertime, DLS had developed a bald patch on her head, which her doctor attributed to the shock of the aerial attacks. This, from DLS's perspective, was far preferable to the alternative diagnosis: mental strain from the work of translating medieval French to keep her mind sharp while maintaining a teaching job.[15]

In the early spring of 1917, DLS made the momentous decision to leave Hull and take up a position as a sort of publisher's apprentice to Basil Blackwell in Oxford. To Jim, she wrote first with the news; to Tony, she "sent a minute dissection of my emotional condition"; and to D. Rowe, the "business details." It brought her back to her beloved Oxford and into a world of literature far more suited to her temperament than the reluctant French pupils in Hull. As she told her father, who fronted the money for the change, there was "*no future* in teaching" for her.[16]

For DLS, the link between meaningful work and a good life was becoming apparent. The work at Blackwell, which involved learning the business of bookselling and publishing inside out, would be strenuous and require long hours, but DLS relished the challenge. "It's immoral to take up a job solely for the amount of time one can spend away from it, which is what most of us do with teaching." Emily Penrose saw it differently, reacting with what DLS perceived as disapproval because "publishing isn't work of national importance." DLS not only disagreed but found that working at Blackwell suited her immensely, because it combined a commitment to serious literature with a fundamentally popular, and indeed commercial, endeavor. As a writer, DLS was keen to explore this intersection of high and low brow, to understand why aspects of her own writing appealed to some people and not others, and to experiment with writing that offered simple, direct joys: "the clank and gurgle of alliteration, and the gorgeousness of proper names," as she put it to D. Rowe. Literature was serious business, but it was also sheer pleasure. At Blackwell, DLS served as an assistant publisher and junior bookseller. She edited volumes of *Oxford Poetry*, contributing a translation of a twelfth-century French poem to the 1917 edition. In February 1918, she agreed to stay on at her current rate, with the promise that, eventually, she'd get higher pay and a management role.[17]

DLS also continued to write. She published another book of poetry, this one on religious themes, entitled *Catholic Tales and Christian Songs*. Having apparently learned a good deal about bookselling at Blackwell, she turned her attention immediately to the problem of marketing the volume. She and Jim cooked up a plot to generate a minor controversy, in the guise of angry letters to publications that reviewed the book. "Anything said is better than nothing said," she wrote, every inch the future proponent of the idea that advertising pays. They considered involving D. Rowe in the scheme, but DLS hesitated because of her "strange way of arguing." The ultimate result was a series of letters battling over the nature of Christ and religious symbolism. These hinged deliberately on arcane terms and interpretations, underscoring the power of language both to enlighten and to mislead. As she told Jim, "'Jargon' is responsible for nearly all the snarls people get themselves into." The manufactured controversy bore fruit, though unfortunately not in the form of robust sales. Instead, it brought her engagement with other religious thinkers, including her future friend, the novelist and theologian Charles Williams. The experience didn't turn her into an established poet or authority on religion (at least not yet), but it did sharpen her sense of the power of language and publicity.[18]

WITH DLS BACK in Oxford, MAS reunions were somewhat easier. One "gorgeous Whit-week-end" at the end of May 1917 saw a glorious reunion that recalled the joys of Somerville life. "Tony, Cherub, Jim, & Amphy Middlemore were all here, & we went on the river all day, & were very noisy & jolly." DLS and Muriel also enjoyed a deepening friendship. By the end of 1918, DLS described Muriel to Jim as an "amazing woman." But there were outside forces that kept the MAS from seeing as much of each other as they might like. Some of this was related to work. Their schedules had become too hectic: on one occasion, DLS canceled a proposed reunion in order to entertain some visitors who were writing a book for Blackwell on psychic communications from excavations at Glastonbury. So, "alas! the Tribal Meeting, quâ Tribal Meeting, has collapsed."[19]

New relationships also demanded time. Always highly sociable, Charis maintained friendships with men serving in the military, including two who arrived to visit her together in a taxi after a maddening journey through London—they could recall that she worked at a maternity hospital, but not which one. Her bedroom was filled with pictures of young men in uniform for whom she wore hobble skirts and high heels on numerous dates. As she put it, "There was a stream of men on leave from the front anxious for companions for dinners and theatres, and *Gather ye rosebuds while ye may* was much in our minds."[20]

Sydney Frankenburg, Charis's Manchester cousin, was one of this stream. Initially rejected for the army because of bad vision, he had gone to France anyway, converting his car into an ambulance. After conspicuous bravery at the battle of Neuve Chapelle in March 1915, he won a commission and also did chaplaincy work for Jewish soldiers. Home on leave, he took Charis to tea and proposed marriage, but she refused. She arrived back late for her shift, escaping a scolding because the matron had seen her and Sydney getting out of a taxi and said to her colleague, "Something's happened to those two; tell them to leave the girl alone." He returned to war, serving in Egypt from July 1916 to February 1917 and then in France.[21]

After Charis turned Sydney down, he ordered roses and violets to be sent to her weekly at the hospital where she was training. This persistence seemed charming to Charis in retrospect, but DLS had a similar, less-welcome experience that highlights the vulnerability of young women navigating the field of marriage proposals. In the summer of 1917, she began a friendship with Reverend Leonard Hodgson, who bought *Op. I.* and told her he liked it. After just a few meetings, though, Hodgson proposed marriage, much to DLS's surprise and alarm. He stopped by the Blackwells' house unexpectedly and cornered her in the drawing room while Basil and his wife made coffee, informing DLS that "he loved me with his whole heart." "Oh Lord!" she replied, before remembering to say that, although he had done her a great honor, she had never thought of him in that way. At this critical juncture Basil returned, with cigarettes in hand, to interrupt the awkward conservation. On her way home, later that evening, Hodgson overtook her on his bicycle and apologized. "He then said all the same things over again, and I said all the same things over again." She had to write to him again the next week to refuse the proposal for good.[22]

Even after she reiterated her refusal, he kept turning up at her office, "looking like a Good Friday cod." He pressed his case into the autumn, even joining the Bach Choir. With a striking frankness that perhaps reveals the depth of her frustration, she wrote to her family: "*but* could I bring myself to do it with L.H.?—Perhaps if I shut my eyes—But no!—he has the wrong sort of hands, & one can't shut one's sense of feeling, more's the pity." No wonder that by November 1917 she exclaimed, "Oh my dears! I will never get married!" Finally, in December 1919, Hodgson got engaged to another woman, writing DLS an odd, formal letter acknowledging "that you were right and I was wrong," and thanking her "for the firmness with which you prevented me wrecking both our lives." DLS called the letter a "perfectly graduated series of insults."[23]

Charis and Sydney's story took a much different turn. In November 1917, she saw him again while he was on leave from France and realized that she had changed her mind about marrying him. Perhaps his brush with injury changed the dynamic—he had been hurt by shrapnel from a faulty grenade during live bombing practice in July that year. Or perhaps Charis's months in France had given her new perspective and time to heal from the loss of her brother. They went to a play the next day, and during the intermission she took out a "rather faded chrysanthemum" and asked if he wanted it. Yes, he replied, bewildered. "Then why didn't you ask for it?" said Charis. Sydney realized, then, what Charis was driving at. "With an exultant smile he exclaimed, 'Does that mean you've come to your senses?'" It was an unconventional proposal but one that suited its protagonists well.[24]

Sydney told everyone that Charis had refused him at first, in order to protect her from the accusation of marrying for money, but in truth their engagement completely altered Charis's relationship to work and finances, at first in quite conventional ways. She had been studying public health, with the idea of doing district work with babies as a social worker, continuing what she'd done as a high school student. But after she and Sydney agreed to marry, she gave this up and bought silk stockings for herself and a fur coat for her mother—perhaps the most classic sartorial expressions of feminine success in this era.[25]

Charis and Sydney were married on February 18, 1918, just a week after her twenty-sixth birthday, at St. Matthew's Church in Hammersmith. Her uncle H. C. Beeching, the dean of Norwich, presided, and her father and Sydney's mother served as the official witnesses. None of the day's challenges could disturb Charis. She slept soundly when a Zeppelin flew over early that morning, and when Sydney, being Jewish, balked at having to kneel in the ceremony, "I mumbled something to my uncle about a war disability, and he carried on undisturbed." Charis Barnett became Mrs. Sydney Frankenburg, but she changed his name, too, and began calling him Bill rather than Sydney. They spent their early married days in Whitby, where Sydney had been posted to join a cyclists' battalion with other "tired officers" who had done several years of active service. Rather insensitively, Charis's parents also sent along two young cousins for the couple to care for. In October, Sydney rejoined his regiment in France, leaving a pregnant Charis in London.[26]

WORLD WAR I ended on the morning of November 11, 1918. Scattered across England, in the midst of taking their first steps into independent adulthood, the members of the MAS were nonetheless united by this moment. D. Rowe was spotted "sitting on the open hood of a taxi ringing a large handbell" in Bournemouth's main square. In Oxford, DLS was "original, as usual—I heard the news while seated in the dentist's chair!" Muriel had just collected her papers authorizing her departure to Rouen to do educational work with the YMCA, "and I was in Trafalgar Square when the whole world went mad. You wouldn't have known there were so many people in London, cheering, shouting, singing." Charis, seven months pregnant, was also in London, walking in Oxford Circus with her friend and midwife. As the cheering crowds took over public transport, the two walked back to Kensington. Charis could not rejoice fully. She had learned only the day before that her husband had been badly wounded in his shoulder. It would be twelve more days before she was able to see him in the hospital.[27]

A month after the armistice, Tony Godfrey, embroiled in her own romance, told DLS that London had become "quite sex-ridden," and DLS wondered "how much of all this marrying & giving in marriage is pure infection." Her comment on Tony was affectionate but acerbic: "methinks she is ear-marked for Matrimony!" Indeed she was, marrying Francis Turquand Mansfield in the spring of 1920. Margaret Chubb got married shortly after the war, too, to Geoffrey Pyke. DLS joked to Jim that, in a moment of feeling poor, she considered joining the trend, but then her finances improved and she changed her mind.[28]

What about romance that didn't lead rapidly to marriage? In an essay published in 1919, DLS lamented the lack of practical experience in love and sex allowed to educated women of her generation. They grew up sheltered, then entered an education that supposed that such matters could be discussed but not experienced. Women "cannot grow wise in an atmosphere in which going to tea with a youth ranks as a thrilling dissipation, and inviting the same man twice in a term is considered too desperately exciting for all concerned." Going straight from that to teach in "the cloister of a girls' school," these women were soon well past the age when youthful scrapes might have provided the requisite learning. A friend told DLS that, at the age of twenty-six, "I see now that I do not want an independent career; but I am unfit for marriage because I have been taught to demand too much, and I do not know how to give men what they want." DLS disagreed. She wanted women to demand more—of sex and everything else. She concluded that women ought to be able to enjoy love and life. "The right to work is not enough for the woman of to-day; she demands the right to understand."[29]

In real life, DLS enjoyed an easy, open social life while living in Oxford and working at Blackwell: staying up late, trying to establish Thursday salons in her Oxford rooms, and describing love as a "foolish thing" to Jim. She became a recognized chaperone for Somerville students, so that she could invite them to her salons. More personally, she continued to flirt with and admire relatively unavailable men. When she had her appendix out, she embarked on a flirtation with her married surgeon, but found, after a couple of months, that she had to put a stop to it. She even called on his wife, remarking to Jim, "How complicated our latter-day civilisation is!" She doted on Basil Blackwell, too, casting him, despite his relative youth and vigor, in the role of "a helpless male thing" who needed to be provided with proper tea in the office by his more practical assistant.[30]

All of this looks carefree, but it wasn't really. DLS found that a single woman who was neither a student nor an academic had no obvious place in Oxford society. Her landladies were dubious about her. One told her plainly that she'd prefer a transient undergraduate to a "permanent woman" as a lodger, and she grumbled over DLS's social habits, such as what DLS described as a very respectable tea for wounded soldiers. Single women were poorer, too. DLS philosophized that at least one advantage of being a woman was that people "simply dare not overcharge me as much as they would if one were a man." But even that was a mixed blessing at best: "that's why they don't like women." In April 1919, she switched to working freelance for Blackwell, supplemented with casual tutoring and journalism. Bills mounted up, and opportunities did not. DLS soon found the constant money pressure "a kind of nightmare," compounded by the "damnable feeling of being no earthly use to anyone."[31]

During the winter of 1918–1919, DLS advised Doreen Wallace, then a student at Somerville, on her unrequited crush on their mutual friend, Captain Eric Whelpton, who had been invalided out of the army in 1916 and returned to finish his undergraduate degree in 1918. In his memoir, Whelpton recalls DLS as striking in her role as salon hostess. Her "grey eyes radiated intelligence, her mobile features vividly expressed her thoughts and emotions, and her voice, though rather high pitched, was a pleasant one." She dressed in black, paired with "large pendulous earrings and exotic strings of beads." He teased DLS about her propensity for listening to all her friends' love troubles, and she joked about graduating in the subject of love "and giving coachings at 8/4 an hour." She was aware, though, that deeper feelings often went unsaid. In a poem from this era, she notices "the things you did not say / And thought I did not know," which, together, make up "the web that we call truth."[32]

In May 1919, Whelpton took a teaching job in south Normandy at a boarding school called L'École des Roches. The school had been founded in order to bring the best of English public-school education to France, along progressive lines rather than traditional ones. His headmaster suggested organizing an educational exchange bureau that would offer French students and teachers a chance to go to England and vice versa. This provided DLS with the opportunity to escape Oxford, where her options were increasingly limited and where she was about to be turned out again from her lodgings. By September, she was in France, working as Whelpton's secretary in the educational exchange bureau.[33]

While in France, DLS nursed an unrequited love for Whelpton. He complimented her appearance, including her "beautiful shoulders." She found him "handsomer than ever," she told Jim in September 1919, though "that does not interest you." Perhaps Jim was only uninterested in Whelpton, though it's more likely that DLS was acknowledging that Jim didn't care about men's beauty in general. DLS was far more susceptible to masculine charisma. She went beyond ordinary office duties in France and "nurse-maided" Whelpton, ensuring that he was provided each day not only with office supplies but with a range of other comforts, including pipe cleaners, chocolate, flowers, and smelling salts to aid his nervous disposition and delicate health. She refused to cut his hair, but told Jim, "I shall be surprised if I don't have to darn socks before I've finished!" He recalled later that "she did a great deal to complete my literary education," discussing topics ranging from seventeenth-century poetry to French literature.[34]

Whelpton treated DLS as a somewhat dim confidant rather than a potential love interest. He moaned about his health and his thwarted ambitions, professional and romantic, resting his head on her knees and telling her she was "the only person who ever understood." DLS saw herself, rather than Whelpton, as the problem here, promising her parents "that if I find I'm hurting him, I'll leave him like a shot." In February 1920, she offered to do exactly that. Whelpton refused, blaming himself for the awkwardness that had developed between them, and the two agreed to carry on and continue cooperating. But by April, he was looking for a new job, and DLS sounded heartily sick of him: "he would get on so much better if he didn't think himself a much bigger person than he is." Whelpton, meanwhile, had fallen in love with another woman and arranged a secret engagement while on a visit to London in the spring of 1920.[35]

Less than a year after she'd arrived, DLS was once more in a stressful dead-end situation. Her hair was falling out again, though she reassured her mother that even her "black times" didn't last too long. Both marriage and permanent teaching jobs offered ways forward for the members of the MAS, with milestones to achieve on the road to full adulthood and a respectable place in society. Refusing those options could easily mean getting trapped in a kind of antechamber, circling endlessly around the same problems: low pay, few opportunities, unsatisfactory relationships. Finding a way out of that cycle would occupy the next half decade of DLS's life.[36]

6

DETECTION AND DESPAIR

I N THE SPRING OF 1920, it was clear that DLS needed to leave France and impose some sort of direction on her life and career. By moving to London, she took the first steps that set her on the course to become both a successful advertising copywriter and a famous mystery novelist, author of the beloved Lord Peter Wimsey stories. Her continued involvements with unavailable men would nearly wreck her chances of independence. But she would emerge from the resulting crisis with a clearer sense of her professional and personal priorities.

DLS's friends helped her to build the path out of France and toward a writer's life in London. Formal MAS meetings were scarce in these years, but the friendships remained strong. In September 1919, DLS told Jim that D. Rowe "is with Charis at the moment, & seems full of beans." DLS's bank account book from 1919 reflects small sums paid to friends, including Jim and D. Rowe—reimbursement for books sent, perhaps, or other favors or errands undertaken. They reflect the ongoing connection between them. The job at L'École des Roches brought DLS back to London with some regularity, where she took advantage of the opportunity to catch up with MAS members. She and D. Rowe corresponded about a play that DLS planned to put on at the French school in the spring of 1920. Jim visited DLS regularly: in Oxford in the spring of 1919, and in France in the summer of 1920.[1]

Together, DLS and Jim developed an expertise on Sexton Blake, a fictional detective who starred in a vast array of comics and pulp fiction popular in this era. In early 1920, DLS, stricken with mumps, was reduced to begging her friend to send more Sexton Blake books, in "discreet packages of about two at a time" to avoid customs fees. She proposed writing an article comparing the series with "the old romance cycles" and figures such as Robin Hood. "Now is the moment to study the growth of a popular hero-cycle on the spot." The two energetically undertook the project. Adopting the pseudonym of Alexander Mitchingham—a "nice, scratchy sort of name for a professor of comparative religion"—DLS connected Sexton Blake with phenomena ranging from "the Osiris mysteries" to "the Oriental Jesus-cults." Jim spotted a "John-James-Peter trio" in the stories, which, DLS enthused, "places my original Sexton Blake = Christus identification beyond all question."[2]

On one level, this is just a charming game. But it points to deeper thoughts afoot for both DLS and Jim. It broke down the division between art with a capital A and popular, trashy literature. If the Sexton Blake stories could be analyzed as a popular hero cycle, that meant that they were, in essence, the authentic folk art of the moment. Expending intellectual and creative energy on popular genres could be a continuation, in another register, of the critical training they had received at Somerville. DLS began to wonder, too, about the link between mass democracy and education. As things stood, she reflected, a working man would not have the time or energy to study sociology or economics and so fit himself to govern. And yet, "obviously, by divine law & human social tendencies, he ought to govern—so where are you?" DLS's ultimate answer, in part, would be to make sociology and economics, as well as ethics, accessible to the ordinary person through clear writing and popular culture. But first, she needed to get published and find a way to make a living.[3]

DLS began to plan actively for a full-time writer's life, using her London stints to make useful contacts, though she increasingly understood the "paramount necessity of being always on the spot." She befriended publisher and author Michael Sadleir and urged Jim to meet him, too. While traveling from France to London in the summer of 1920, she met Cecil Mannering, the Scottish film actor and director. He offered her advice about writing film scenarios for money, suggesting that she try writing up a scenario for a particular book and send it to him when she'd finished. DLS immediately turned to the MAS, and used her short leave time to travel to Bournemouth and meet with D. Rowe for a few days to put something together. As she told her mother, "Now I couldn't do it alone, but D. Rowe and I could make something of it together." Although Mannering did help her to develop and try to place a film scenario, ultimately nothing came of it.[4]

DLS arrived back in England in time to take part in a moment of triumph for everyone involved with women's education at Oxford. DLS confessed to her mother, "I want so much to be in the first batch" of women who would claim Oxford degrees.[5] On October 14, 1920, a placid, dreaming day, when red flowers bloomed on the heavy vines that draped the ancient stone and newer brick, Oxford University granted degrees to women for the first time. The grand auditorium in the Sheldonian Theatre was crammed with graduates, supporters of women's education, friends, family, and perhaps a few who came simply to see the remarkable sight. DLS, Muriel, and Jim retroactively received their bachelors and masters of arts degrees that day.

The great ceremony began when the south doors of the theater were thrown open and the principals of the five women's societies walked in. They had received their Oxford masters of arts degrees in a private, earlier ceremony. These women were veterans of the long fight for women's education. One of them had been the first woman ever to complete the honor examinations in modern history, while another was the third woman to do the same in the Classics course. They had had to earn their official degrees elsewhere, at more progressive universities: one in Dublin, another in Paris. The leader of the small procession, Mrs. B. C. Johnson, had presided over the home students, or women attending Oxford while living in private homes, for forty-one years. She walked using an ebony cane for support, but her back was straight and her demeanor proud. There was a hush, and then an explosion, as the audience unanimously rose to its feet and burst into cheers. Together, the principals made their way slowly and with dignity to the front of the theater, where they bowed to the vice-chancellor and then took their seats.[6]

The men, with looks of studied casualness, took their degrees first. Cheers erupted once more, amplified and redoubled under the vaults of the auditorium's roof, as the women were presented by their deans to the vice-chancellor and proctors, who doffed their caps to the candidates. Then, the women left the theater to change out of their ordinary academic garb and into bachelor of arts gowns hooded with white fur. Thus attired, they returned and knelt before the vice-chancellor. He touched each woman on the head with the Holy Gospels—revealing his nerves only once, when he accidentally tapped one woman with his own mortarboard instead of the scriptures. At last the deed was done, with the Latin words pronounced in the ceremony for the first time in the feminine gender: *domina, magistra.*[7]

Some fifty women received degrees that day. Many more of the four hundred or so eligible for them would take part in other degree ceremonies over the next year. Charis took her degree in the summer of 1921. Sydney brought their eldest son, then aged two and a half, to the ceremony, and she ruefully recalled that he nearly overshadowed the whole thing. "He announced in such a loud voice that he had a nicer dressing-gown than the Vice-Chancellor's, *and* green pyjamas, that the Vice-Chancellor had him removed." Charis loved that story, which captures the arrival of women into Oxford in all their dimensions—they were mothers and scholars, and it was no contradiction, just a bit of colorful variation.[8]

After the heady experience of receiving their degrees, the MAS turned back to more prosaic concerns. In moving to London, DLS joined Jim and Muriel in what Vera Brittain memorably described as "that slough of despond which lies just inside the gateway of every path to the literary life." DLS and Jim discussed sharing a flat, but neither of them was making enough reliable money. After working as a secretary, Jim tried her hand at journalism, earning a diploma in the subject from the University of London in 1920. She worked briefly that year for the feminist newspaper *Time and Tide* and then as a headline writer for *Vogue*. DLS despaired at Jim's tendency to quarrel with her employers and to disdain "what she's doing at the moment because she thinks she ought to be doing something grander." To make ends meet, Jim spent stretches of time at home when unwell and also relied on financial support from her family "or somebody," in DLS's cynical phrase.[9]

Still, the two friends lived close to one another and socialized frequently. It's easy to imagine them laughing together over Jim's tongue-in-cheek essay about archaic Oxford regulations that now governed female, as well as male, students: "alas! for the good old times before we were admitted to the University, when I fought my cocks in Christchurch quad, and drove my four-in-hand along the High!" One hectic day in the month after the degree ceremony, DLS and Jim rushed after lunch to Golders Green to see Jim's sister and brother-in-law, who wanted to photograph them in their academic gowns. Then they hurried on to a meeting of some sort of spiritualist sect, where the minister, controlled by the spirit, "hurls fearful inspired speeches at

DLS and Jim in their academic gowns (Collett)

one in the dark." Another time, they went to the theater together, gleefully anticipating a new series of plays that "surpasses everything else in grisliness."[10]

DLS supported herself in various ways in the autumn of 1920. She taught for about six weeks in total, at Clapham High School (where she lectured on English verse) and at South Hampstead High School. She did translations from French to English for the Comité National Polonais en Amérique. In her application to use the British Library reading room, she put her new academic status to immediate use: she was, she explained, "a Master of Arts at Oxford," and what's more, she was hoping to begin a postgraduate bachelor of letters degree. Her proposed thesis attempted to translate her merry course of Sexton Blake studies into something more serious: "the Permanent Elements in Popular Heroic Fiction, with a special study of Modern Criminological Romance."[11]

DLS wrote with dedication, branching out from the poetry that had defined her so far. Even before arriving in London, she was thinking about detective fiction. While in France, she had requested Jim's local information about exactly when and how Big Ben was adjusted for the switch from summer time to winter time, a crucial detail in a story she was writing. Early in 1921, she was inspired to begin another detective story that opened with someone found dead in a bathtub wearing nothing but a pince-nez. Why a pince-nez in the bath? "If you can guess, you will be in a position to lay hands upon the murderer, but he's a very cool and cunning fellow," she told her mother.[12]

This was the birth of DLS's most famous creation, the aristocratic sleuth Lord Peter Wimsey. The body-in-the-bath story would become *Whose Body?*, and it would be followed by a series of novels and short stories that were wildly popular at the time and have proved enduring classics of the so-called Golden Age of detective fiction. With his monocle, his diffidence, and his habit of quoting literature, Lord Peter Wimsey stands alongside sleuths such as Hercule Poirot, Miss Marple, and even Sherlock Holmes. But DLS could hardly imagine such an outcome as she began writing in a somewhat grim state of mind in 1921, giving Wimsey all the luxuries and comforts that she could not afford.

MONEY WAS NOT her only problem. DLS was in a paradoxical position, living an apparently liberated flapper lifestyle but without a particularly feminist framework through which to understand it. Throughout her young adulthood, for example, she consistently expressed the idea that male babies were superior. Indeed, she even endorsed adoption, somewhat facetiously, on the grounds that you could choose a boy. Writing about "a woman doctor," DLS admitted, "I instinctively doubt her word." Visiting the National Portrait Gallery, she found the famous women all ugly. The ones who might have been a personal inspiration to her—writers such as Elizabeth Barrett Browning, Charlotte Brontë, and George Eliot—were only "a depressing sight." She had little sympathy for a friend who had the misfortune of being called for jury service on the same day as her bachelor of letters viva voce examination at Oxford: hadn't women brought it upon themselves? "I can't help chuckling at the way people resent these patriotic responsibilities which have devolved upon them with votes & things." And she was happy enough to be still too young, at twenty-nine, to vote in the October 1922 election, since she didn't "care much which set of idiots is in!"[13]

In her efforts to relate romantically to men, too, DLS was both invested in very traditional gender roles and irrepressibly strong-minded—not an easy combination. Her friend and fellow writer Norman Davey showed up one afternoon "*dreadfully* cross" because his lunch companion had "thoughtlessly endeavoured to tell him his own views about something." DLS was, he said, to serve as the antidote to this demoralizing experience, since, as he put it, "you let *me* talk to *you*." It was all acting, she told Jim, and a total concealment of her "natural disposition."[14]

Such concealment, in the pursuit of male companionship, came at a cost. DLS would soon be involved with a man whose ideas about female submission and free love would push her into a profound personal crisis. She moved in December 1920 to a building in Mecklenburgh Square. Her new landlady was "a curious, eccentric-looking person with short hair" who "thoroughly understands that one wants to be quite independent." There, DLS entered the orbit of a rather glamorous, somewhat older crowd of writers and friends whose emotional entanglements were operatic.[15]

One of this crowd was John Cournos, a Jewish Russian American novelist who had moved to London in 1912. In between journalism and creative writing, he had a complex, intimate relationship with the modernist poets Richard Aldington and Hilda "HD" Doolittle—who were married at that time—while continuing his on-again, off-again love affair with Dorothy "Arabella" Yorke. Aldington, in turn, began an affair with Yorke, who, like HD, lived at Mecklenburgh Square. These overlapping romantic attachments were all very Bloomsbury. Cournos's apparent commitment to free love, though, should not obscure the significant currents of misogyny among his friends. John Gould Fletcher, a fellow American, wrote to Cournos that the "shameless luxury flaunted" by women in New York made him pray for "a few Bolsheviks" looking "for blood and rape." Later that year, around the time DLS met Cournos, Gould urged his friend not to pursue this "new woman affair." He remonstrated, "You admit that you are no longer interested in the thought of adding to your harem; so why do so?"[16]

Cournos seems to have made DLS wait, in any case. She enjoyed an expanding social life, "lots of parties—theatre and a night-club (!!) last week, teas and things this week, lunch at the Ritz next week." But in the hot summer of 1921, as the translation work dried up and connections in the cinema and publishing world all seemed to lead only to more meetings and introductions rather than paying work, DLS found herself frustrated, unable even to get a reply from D. Rowe about whether she could come visit Bournemouth. She exploded: "I can't get the work I want, nor the money I want, nor (consequently) the clothes I want, nor the holiday I want, nor the man I want!!"[17]

DLS and Cournos grew steadily closer, but in a way DLS never did get the man she wanted. She invited him, it seems, to visit her at her parents' home in the late summer of 1921. That didn't work out, nor did her vague plan of bringing him to Christmas that year, though, she assured her mother, he "really wants to know you." He didn't approve of her detective stories—he spelled "Art with a capital A," after all. Nor did he enjoy taking her out to light entertainment, preferring more serious fare. On the rare occasions he consented to go to the cinema, "it was a fearful job" to find a film he'd agree to see. One time, DLS "tramped half London with a bad blister on my heel" before he would "settle down."[18]

Over the next two years, DLS's life would pull in two opposite directions. On the one hand, she found increasing stability in her living situation and her working life. On the other, she became increasingly embroiled in destructive romantic relationships. At the very end of 1921, she left Mecklenburgh Square and took an initial three-year lease on a three-room flat on Great James Street, which Jim helped her to find. She got a cat, a "vulgar little tabby Tom" named Agag, to keep down the mice in her kitchen. He was soon growing to a "monstrous size." By the summer, she was well settled in. D. Rowe paid her a visit for a few days and was "delighted to be able to picture you, when I can't see you, lying in your flat with your head pillowed on works of criminology and your feet on the onion saucepan with a cigarette in your mouth, the word on your lips and Agag on your tummy. (N.B. this is a composite picture—I'm not referring to the size of the kitchen.)"[19]

DLS's relationship with Cournos, conveyed through two novels and a searing stack of letters, is so appalling that it attracts a kind of fascination. The question of whether, and how, to have sex is at the heart of it, surrounded by dense layers of misogyny, mistrust, and misunderstanding. DLS wanted a complete relationship with him, one that could culminate in marriage and children. She objected to using birth control, which is not so strange. Many people in the 1920s saw mechanical methods of birth control as unnatural and unsavory, even if they were willing to use more traditional methods of family limitation, such as withdrawal. And many women associated condoms, in particular, with prostitution. DLS wanted to be a partner, not a mistress; using a condom would have been at cross-purposes with that. She also saw Cournos's preferred methods as unnatural: "for all your talk about being free to live & love naturally, the first thing you insist on is, the use of every dirty trick invented by civilisation to avoid the natural result." For his part, Cournos probably saw birth control as a responsible measure, given his lack of interest in commitment to DLS; in his autobiography, he would criticize his stepfather's prolific, irresponsible approach to procreation.[20]

They reached an initial crisis point in January 1922 when, as DLS put it, she and Cournos had a difference "on a point of practical Christianity (to which he strongly objects!)." This was a veiled reference to the use of contraception. Despite the disagreement, DLS had Cournos to dinner in February 1922. He was short of money and upset about the poor sales of his latest autobiographical novel. DLS was somewhat skeptical when he blamed the publisher, but she also seemed ready enough to believe that he was a suffering hero who "deserves something better of life." She let Cournos stay in her new flat when she was away in March, though her mother was dubious about the arrangement. On her return, Cournos left his free lodging and relocated for a few months to Oxford. She saw more of him that summer, cooking him another elaborate meal in July 1922. D. Rowe underscored the centrality of food in their relationship, but also, perhaps, the worrying sense that DLS was in over her head when she advised her, "Don't let John worry you: he's probably hungry and what you think is an aggressive yell is a squawk for food."[21]

Cournos fictionalized these dinners in his 1932 novel, *The Devil Is An English Gentleman*. At her flat in London, "Stella" prepares a steak dinner for "Richard," with wine and soup and cheese and Bénédictine—a fair recounting of the actual dinners served by DLS to Cournos. After dinner, on the couch, Richard undresses Stella. They agree that he should undress, too. "She did not resist him, and he might have taken her; but he did not take her," instead waiting for "a token of abandonment on her part; it did not come." Finally, she pulls away and bursts into tears. They repeat this pattern several times; in between, he takes her to the cinema and the theater, and they start quarreling. He suggests that she could be his mistress, and then "if we pull along alright for a space we can discuss marriage!" Stella refuses, and the affair is broken off. Too late, she understands that total submission "would have bound them forever."[22]

Both the pattern of foreplay without intercourse and the obsession with submission are themes in Cournos's life and writing, and his books idealize women who offer sex freely to their adored male partners. DLS put Cournos's emotional manipulation at the heart of her own novelistic retelling of the relationship. Published in 1930, *Strong Poison* introduces Harriet Vane, who is on trial for the alleged murder of her ex-lover, the rather loathsome poet Philip Boyes. Boyes had convinced Vane to live with him outside of marriage, allegedly because he was opposed to the institution. Once she moved in, he revealed that cohabitation had actually been a test; having passed it, she could now marry him. Instead, Vane leaves. But when Boyes dies suspiciously, she is, of course, the prime suspect.[23]

DLS has a great deal of fun, in the novel, pointing out exactly what a dreadful, pretentious writer Boyes is. One jury member, for example, mentions that he "had had the misfortune to read some of his books, and considered the man an excrescence and a public nuisance." Boyes's loyal friend Vaughan, meanwhile, blames Vane unreservedly and says her motive was jealousy: "you'd think it would have been enough for her to help and look after a genius like Phil, wouldn't you?" But Vane is clear that what really haunts her is the deception—the fact that Boyes convinced her to do something she thought was wrong on the basis of a lie about his own beliefs and in order to test her willingness to obey him. In real life, DLS was infuriated by Cournos's claim that he'd set her a test and, by refusing to offer unconditional sex, she'd failed.[24]

Cournos left London in October 1922. DLS complained in late November that he hadn't "so much as sent me a post-card," though she heard from someone else that he was fine. He would soon marry Helen Kestner Satterthwaite—oddly enough, she was also a mystery novelist. DLS heard the news in the summer of 1924. By then, she pointed out, they had both done what they'd sworn they wouldn't: she'd had sex using birth control, and he'd gotten married.[25]

IN THE MIDST of this year of emotional turmoil, DLS made slow, painful progress toward having her own career. Her parents helped to pay the typist's bill for her first novel, but she was increasingly uneasy about relying on them as she approached thirty. She apologized to her mother for being "such a hopelessly shaky investment." She would have saved money by living with Jim if she could, "but it's too risky when we're *both* dependent on charity." At her parents' behest, she agreed to consider temporary teaching assignments, promising to take a job as a teacher by summer 1922 if nothing else turned up. She kept writing her second Wimsey novel, because the work "prevents me from wanting too badly the kind of life I *do* want, and see no chance of getting." She was reduced to trying to sell her fiddle for cash but found even that hard to do.[26]

She did find inspiration and emotional sustenance in Bournemouth. While visiting D. Rowe, she met Sir Arthur Marshall, a barrister and Liberal politician who gave her legal details for her new novel, which involved a peer being tried for murder before the House of Lords and would later be published as *Clouds of Witness*. Otherwise, her visit was lighthearted and fun. She went "to a few cinemas & theatres," and carried on "a few little flirtations of no importance, but it was all very care-free & pleasant." She returned in mid-March, "chasing after a will o' the wisp of a job."[27]

In the late spring of 1922, things finally began to happen—DLS got a proper job and Lord Peter Wimsey gained traction. In April, a literary agent who knew Cournos agreed to represent DLS and her detective fiction. In July, he sold her first novel, *Whose Body?*, to Boni & Liveright in New York. D. Rowe was staying with DLS that weekend, going to the theater and having a good time. On the night that DLS got the news from New York, they went together to another friend's flat, and as DLS entered, she exclaimed, "I am rich! I am famous!" Then, appropriately enough, they all began to discuss the murder trial of Edith Thompson and Frederick Bywaters, which was then in the news. D. Rowe went home with the draft of "Lord Peter" in tow, promising to "guard it with care" and return it when she'd finished.[28]

Slowly but surely, DLS began to earn larger sums of money for her writing. She exulted in "a dictum of Philip Guedalla's in the *Daily News*: 'The detective story is the normal recreation of noble minds.' It makes me feel ever so noble!" *Whose Body?* introduces Lord Peter Wimsey and marks the start of an extraordinary series of novels that lived up to that dictum, making witty and serious points in the guise of the unashamed fun of the detective novel.[29]

A classic flawed hero, Wimsey is both a brilliant amateur detective and a man scarred by his experiences fighting in World War I. He solves baffling murder mysteries in an eccentric, whimsical style, dropping literary quotations and peering through his trademark monocle. DLS's biographers have often sought to find a real-life model for Lord Peter Wimsey. This is misguided. The early Wimsey is, above all, an idealized version of DLS herself, with bits and pieces of her experiences and her fantasies woven in to make a genuinely fictional character. From Eric Whelpton, for instance, she probably got the details about the apartments in Paris where gentlemen met and housed their mistresses, which she used to give Wimsey his slightly risqué sexual history. As part of his translation work in the early 1920s, Cournos received letters in Russian written in a strikingly beautiful hand; these, perhaps, became the beautifully written Slavic letters received by the unfortunate victim in the later novel *Have His Carcase*. In any case, regardless of his parentage, Wimsey would make DLS's name.[30]

Written in an admittedly escapist frame of mind, *Whose Body?* dwells lovingly on the imagined luxuries of Wimsey's aristocratic lifestyle: the posh flat, the hobby of collecting antique books, the devoted butler, the excellent food and drink. Even here, however, Wimsey has surprising emotional depth. What seems to be a lighthearted thriller that opens with a body in a bathtub becomes a haunting meditation on shell shock, trauma, and loss. The body turns out to belong to a respected Jewish banker who had been happily married to a Christian woman. Wimsey experiences a mental breakdown when he realizes what happened to the banker, and why, and he relies on his faithful butler, Bunter, and his friend on the police force, Charles Parker, to assist him in completing the case.

Sometimes criticized as anti-Semitic, *Whose Body?* relies on stereotyped language but also treats the victim as an admirable person who falls prey to someone else's grotesque prejudice and jealousy. The plot reflects a personal knowledge of circumcision, probably gained from DLS's relationship with Cournos. In its sympathetic treatment of a mixed marriage, the novel also seems to echo Charis Frankenburg's experiences, as the daughter of a marriage between a Christian woman and a nonpracticing Jewish man, and the wife of practicing Jewish man. She defended DLS from charges of anti-Semitism: "being half Jewish, I should certainly have noticed that!" Charis's own feelings about Jewishness were complex and sometimes contradictory. In an era when anti-Semitism was increasing, none of the members of the MAS fully embraced it, but they also engaged in discourse that contributed to the sense of Jews as fundamentally different, sometimes in ways that perpetuated discrimination and negative stereotyping. *Whose Body?* is the most nuanced of DLS's novels in this respect; in other novels, both Jewish and Scottish people are simply used as shorthand for greedy moneylenders and play walk-on parts.[31]

WHEN A RETURN to teaching loomed, since writing wouldn't pay all the bills, DLS got a job as a copywriter at the advertising agency of S. H. Benson. London was, in this era, a global center for the advertising industry. Interwar advertising was a relatively hospitable place for a woman to work. There were women in high-ranking positions in London firms, which recognized the significance of the female consumer and sought to market directly to her. Still, it was a male-dominated industry. Once, traveling with a colleague to

Kendal to inspect a boot factory, DLS discovered that the hotel had booked them both into the same room "under the impression that we were both gentlemen."[32]

The job suited her; she loved the days filled with "energy and rush," even when she was "exhausted with trying to find arguments for using tea and margarine." Her first published advertisement was for Sailor Savouries. "All lies from beginning to end—at least, a tissue of exaggeration," she said. Her employers were delighted. They agreed to keep her on permanently and they gave her a pay raise to boot, removing at last her dependence on her parents.[33]

DLS would spend nearly a decade working in advertising. At S. H. Benson, she was at the center of some of the most famous campaigns of the era, including the Guinness toucan who championed "Guinness is good for you!" and Colman's Mustard Club. These ads helped to define the visual reality of interwar Britain, especially London. The 1933 Wimsey novel *Murder Must Advertise* conjures DLS's office life with vivid reality. In order to test the spatial elements of the plot, DLS brought Muriel to the office. Years later, Muriel remembered "with pleasure going up and down the iron staircase in Bensons," which served as the model for the all-important staircase in the novel. Work-related incidents were also fictionalized. One of her real-life colleagues had fallen between the platform and the train at the Baker Street tube stop, incredibly surviving with only minor injuries. His lucky escape would form the basis of a villainous bit of derring-do in the novel. In later life, DLS rebuked interviewers who assumed that she resented the work because it distracted from her more serious calling as a writer. Work was work, and writing for the public could take many forms.[34]

ONCE COURNOS WAS gone, DLS began a new relationship almost immediately with Bill White, who had been staying with her upstairs neighbors. White was married, though it's not clear at what stage DLS realized this. He had worked as a bank clerk before the war, but his real passion was anything with a motor in it. After war service, he and his wife struggled to settle down. By 1922, she and their daughter were staying in Southbourne while he looked for employment in London. DLS brought him to her family's home that Christmas, arriving on the back of his motorcycle. He was, she said, "an absolutely rock-bottom, first-class driver." Although he lacked "literary intellect," he knew "all about cars, and how to sail a boat and so on—and in fact he's the last person you'd ever expect me to bring home, but he's really quite amiable." He was, in that respect, a good antidote to Cournos.[35]

Their relationship involved socializing, sex—this time with birth control—and a certain degree of domesticity. He stained her sitting room floor for her, and she made him food. They went together to her office dance in January, and they socialized with Norman Davey and a few other friends, or tried to. In February 1923, these friends reneged on a plan to go dancing because of the foggy weather—this, after a day in which DLS had worked at the office and White at manual labor at his shop, while the others merely lounged about. DLS told them they were "damned unsporting," and she and White went to the Hammersmith Palais de Danse on their own.[36]

DLS evidently felt that the relationship was not one she could share with most of her friends. As she told Cournos, "It's such a lonely, dreary job having a lover," because of the need for secrecy. She couldn't force introductions, and "besides, it's so dirty to be always telling lies, one just drops seeing them." Soon, even more lies were necessary. The birth control she used with White hadn't worked, and she was pregnant. The whole hard-won structure—flat, job, cat, writing career—was in dire jeopardy.[37]

CHARIS AND DLS both had children in the 1920s. Their experiences could not have been more different. And yet, in some respects, the central problem of balancing motherhood with the demands of work and personal life linked them. For DLS, having a child was a transformative and profoundly dangerous event. Maternal mortality was a stubborn issue in England in the 1920s. But far greater, for an unmarried woman bearing a married man's child, was the risk of social disgrace. DLS's ability to earn a living, to build her career as a writer, and to live independently as a respectable middle-class woman—all of it was thoroughly endangered by her situation.

In the immediate aftermath of her pregnancy, DLS saw the failure of the birth control device as evidence that "nature refuses to be driven out, even with pitchforks—or other implements." In fact, as Charis would have told her then and probably did tell her later, commercially available devices were often unreliable, but medically supervised and fitted devices were far less likely to fail. Not that it would have mattered; doctors rarely offered birth control to unmarried women. In any case, by the summer of 1923, DLS was thirty years old, pregnant, single, and facing a very limited array of choices.[38]

Abortion was illegal and extremely dangerous. DLS also opposed it. While at L'École des Roches, she had convinced an unmarried mother working there to keep her baby, providing practical assistance of various kinds. The woman's family wouldn't help her, but DLS and Whelpton found her a place to stay; she would go on to work at the Berlitz school for languages while her son stayed in the countryside, presumably being fostered. In a way, this provided DLS with a model for her own trajectory. She rejected the idea of turning to her parents. Instead, she embarked on a lonely, daring plan based on a set of resolutions: first, that she, not her parents or child, should suffer most from her lapse in judgment and, second, that she must preserve her employment and her independence above all. She actively deceived her parents about the situation. In a letter sent as if from London but actually from the nursing home where she gave birth, DLS chatted lightly to her mother about various relatives and attributed the delay in finishing the next Lord Peter Wimsey story to problems with the plot, rather than personal complications. "I had to re-write a couple of chapters owing to a change of plan, which has thrown him back a good bit."[39]

Keeping the secret at S. H. Benson was not, perhaps, the greatest of her obstacles. She took eight weeks leave in total, claiming illness, and when she returned, she was "congratulated on looking so much fatter than when I left." But this was probably some combination of obliviousness and discretion on the part of her coworkers, in addition to being a testament to DLS's ability to maintain her privacy and her poker face. Benson was not a place with overly exacting moral standards. Earlier in 1923, DLS and a colleague had traveled to a perfume factory, and to her amusement he brought his mistress along. If she was willing to tolerate a mistress on a business trip, it's not hard to imagine that her closest colleagues were willing to ignore signs of her pregnancy, nor would they have been outside the norms of the time in doing so.[40]

Bill White told his wife, who was then living with their daughter in a flat belonging to his brother in Southbourne, that DLS was pregnant with his child. His wife not only agreed to help but went to remarkable lengths to provide DLS with care. She brought DLS down to Southbourne for the birth, arranging for her to stay at a nursing home called Tuckton Lodge under the care of her brother—who, apparently, merely thought DLS was a friend in trouble. White's wife and daughter stayed in DLS's London flat while she was away, watching her cat and forwarding her mail in order to maintain the fiction that she was still at home.[41]

Tuckton Lodge was close to where D. Rowe lived, which raises the question of when, if ever, she told members of the MAS about her child. Decades later, a researcher pressed D. Rowe about details connected to DLS's personal life. She offered this magnificent reply: "perhaps I should say that if I had ever promised her not to reveal any secrets of her private life I should still not consider myself free from such a promise, but I never did." On the face of it, this declaration suggests that DLS simply did not confide in D. Rowe, which is of course plausible. At a deeper level, though, D. Rowe's answer suggests an impenetrable wall of friendship. In 1938, dealing with a deceased relative's affairs, D. Rowe joked to DLS that she had learned all she wanted to know about "the penalties for giving false information when registering the birth of an illegitimate baby, (not from any personal or family experience)." Perhaps D. Rowe kept DLS's secret to the grave, and the joke about registering the birth of an illegitimate baby is an in-joke. More likely, perhaps, in her answer to the nosy biographer, D. Rowe is sending a message across time to DLS that she would have kept that secret, had she been asked.[42]

John Anthony was born on January 3. DLS was not going to keep him. Her doctors recommended that she start by breastfeeding anyway, to give him "a good start in the natural way," even though he'd have to "struggle with the change of food" in a few weeks. Notes in DLS's papers prescribe the typical feeding regime—every three hours—with the poignant remark: "suggested food: Manna in bottle if constipated or Demerara sugar."[43]

If sex had been fraught, giving birth was, for DLS, a rare moment of feeling proud of her physical body—her "truly magnificent body," as she described it to Cournos. In a draft written about a decade later, DLS imagined the feelings of a new mother, "unaccustomed to success in any physical sensation," who experiences a sense of relief at being able to be utterly normal in this respect. Her body "might not be able to play hockey or tennis, but in this important particular it had not let her down." In a letter to Cournos, DLS even suggested that having children was, for women, what having sex was for men. Both he and White "behave pretty callously as regards the crying need *of* a woman for children, which is physical completion for a woman as 'tother side of the business is for a man."[44]

Two days before her son was born, DLS had written to her cousin Ivy Shrimpton, asking her whether she would take charge of an infant. As biographer Barbara Reynolds has pointed out, this seems a bit late to be making this sort of inquiry. Reynolds suggests that DLS might have agreed to an adoption and then changed her mind, preferring to reach out to someone she knew well. But there's no way to know for certain. Adoption would not become legal in England and Wales until 1926, though informal adoptions were commonly pressed on unwed middle-class young mothers—perhaps another reason why DLS hesitated to lose control over the situation by confiding in her parents.[45]

DLS had been close with Ivy Shrimpton as a child. She visited the family from time to time when she lived in Oxford, though it's clear that they weren't at the top of her social priorities. Ivy's father died in the spring of 1921 after a long illness, leaving her to care for her mother. Ivy also fostered babies and children in their home, and DLS had done her various small kindnesses—sending her an old winter coat, for example, in the winter of 1921. After a visit in the early summer of 1922, DLS's mother praised Ivy's management of her foster children to DLS.[46]

Reaching out to Ivy, then, was logical if belated. DLS wrote as if for a friend, explaining that the baby "won't have any legal father, poor little soul," and that "everything depends on the girl's not losing her job." The child would be, she promised, "extremely healthy" and in her charge "for some years—till circumstances enable the mother to take it herself." Ivy agreed, and a few days later DLS wrote to announce the birth of a "sturdy little boy" who would arrive in Oxford "with all paraphernalia and particulars on or about Jan 30th."[47]

Three days before the transfer, DLS came clean to Ivy: John Anthony was her son. "I won't go into the whole story—think the best you can of me—I know it won't make you love the boy any the less." She'd held back, she said, to hear Ivy's honest response about the terms for raising the child, and in order to give her the chance not to tell her mother, DLS's Aunt Amy, if she didn't want to. DLS asked, too, that she refrain from telling DLS's own parents. "It would grieve them quite unnecessarily." If at some point her son spilled the beans, "it can't be helped—I've done what I could to spare people's feelings, but it can't be carried to the point of letting the kid lose anything he might be having." She conceded, too, that if she died before DLS's own parents, they should be told.[48]

And so DLS delivered her son to Ivy. On the last day of January 1924, she returned to London alone. Her keys were locked inside her flat, and she had to wait to get the charlady's spare set, sitting by herself at the cinema until the charlady returned. The next day, she got a letter from Ivy: John was eating and sleeping, and another child in the house was already very fond of him. It was a "great relief" for DLS to read all this. Within days, she returned to work, where her office mates were "all charmed to see me, and very sympathetic about my 'illness.'" DLS's letters to Ivy in the months to come were full of details about food and digestion and the general minutiae of small babies—including a warning not to make him wear round caps that would give him "elephant-flaps" for ears, after she had put so much effort into giving him "nice, flat ears." DLS took up photography as a hobby. It was a respite from the blizzard of words that surrounded her professionally—by day in the copywriting office, by night as a novelist. Photography, too, is a favorite hobby of new parents, and photographs of John Anthony are mixed in with letters to Ivy about prints and negatives, evidence of DLS's visits.[49]

By April, DLS was having a harder time with it all. She sent a "little woolly jacket" for John Anthony as well as a copy of *Whose Body?* for Ivy, but her sleep was troubled and her mood anxious. She dreamed that her son had "grown elvish & wizened & was decaying away!" Of course it wasn't true, but in the next line she pressed Ivy not to forget to finish up his vaccinations. A few weeks later, her feelings were even more conflicted. "Poor little J. A.—I hardly know whether I love him or hate him—but he's happy enough so far, anyhow." She had seen her family at Easter and nearly told her mother what had happened. But in the end, she told Ivy, she decided to wait. She didn't want to cause her family "worry and embarrassment," nor did she want to answer their questions, and "being sympathised with and bothered" would only make her angry with the child. "As it is I can't see that anyone suffers but myself so far, and therefore, so far so good."[50]

HER TWO DISASTROUS relationships—with John Cournos and with Bill White—continued to haunt her. DLS hoped that White might want some involvement in his son's life and tried to foster a sense of connection early on, but to no avail. By the start of May, she'd told him to "go to hell." But their social circles, at least, continued to overlap for a while longer. She encountered his new girlfriend in a restaurant that autumn, which was uncomfortable for everyone. Still, DLS hoped that her son would be "mechanically-minded" rather than "musical or artistic." "I'm so bored with writers and people like that." Even so, she wasn't quite done with Cournos either. She wrote to him in the summer of 1924, having heard that he was going to marry. Their correspondence soon became lengthy and rancorous. Cournos suggested that they meet. They did meet one Saturday early in 1925, and she felt so sick and miserable the next day that she stayed in bed. In February she told Cournos, "It frightens me to be so unhappy—I thought it would get better, but I think every day is worse than the last, & I'm always afraid they'll chuck me out of the office because I'm working so badly."[51]

Then, in April 1925, Ivy's mother died, causing a new potential crisis over where she would live and whether she'd be able to keep the foster children. In a letter to her own mother, DLS affected an air of detachment. Ivy "would be sorry to give up the children," of course, but the baby, she gathered, "can, if necessary, be disposed of, if time is given to make arrangements." What was DLS envisioning? At first she imagined her son going to her mother, with whatever explanation was necessary. Ivy could "shove J.A. off onto Mother and tell her, and I'll weigh in and explain." Within a few days, though, she had thought better of this plan. She would find an alternative fostering arrangement. She had written to "an old college friend who is a sort of trained authority on babies, and who might very probably know of some person who would take charge of him." Though DLS doesn't name the friend, she must mean Charis, who did in fact help many single mothers out of difficult predicaments over the course of her career. Probably DLS again wrote as if for a friend, explaining the situation without admitting that John Anthony was hers. Luckily, by the end of the summer, the crisis was averted, and John Anthony stayed with Ivy, where DLS continued to visit him.[52]

As she planned for every contingency to protect her son, DLS's instinct for self-preservation also returned that summer of 1925. Cournos sent a letter in late June, but she postponed reading it until the middle of August—when, as she was already miserable for a different reason, she decided to read it, since "one may as well be hanged for a sheep as a lamb." In her relationship with Cournos, DLS had experienced sexual intimacy for the first time, and she had appreciated being treated as something other than "a kind of literary freak." She had been ready to agree to a lot—to accept that he might have other lovers, to be "moulded into any set of interests," to be "overborne, like any Victorian fool." But she was not prepared to accept his casual, self-centered proposal for sex and occasional companionship. By 1925, she was finally able to say so. DLS had survived Cournos and all his mayhem, and then a secret pregnancy; she was preserving her independence while supporting her son alone. She was no Victorian fool.[53]

She still wanted to find a partner. Bizarrely, Cournos seems to have offered to find her a new lover as early as January 1925. Although she was understandably skeptical, DLS played along, describing to him the qualities she now sought. She wanted someone jolly, who wouldn't judge her for liking crosswords and photography. Ideally he would be less intellectual than she was. "Marrying a highbrow (or living with one) would be like marrying one's own shop." It was a marriage she was after, not another secret lover, and she wanted someone who could meet her interests and desires. "I have a careless rage for life, & secrecy tends to make me bad-tempered," she wrote. "Give me a man that's human & careless & loves life, & one who can enjoy the rough-&-tumble of passion."[54]

A man who enjoyed motorcycles would be good, too. With the money from the American serial rights to her second novel, *Clouds of Witness*, DLS had bought herself a motorcycle. It was an unusual choice for a woman in 1925, though to Cournos she claimed that it was motivated by practical and maternal considerations—it would save her the train fares to visit her son. Driving in those days, particularly on a motorcycle, was an adventure beset with breakdowns and bad weather. But she loved "to feel the engine purring along in the lovely, velvety way that means that everything is exquisitely adjusted & happy together." In December 1925, she got a sidecar and considered spending Christmas on the road, and she joked with her father that she should "come & set up a motor-cycle repair & first-aid establishment" in her parents' town. This seems to be a new, freer DLS, one willing to dabble openly in hobbies and interests, beyond scholarship, that were usually associated with men.[55]

She soon found a motor-enthusiast partner in Atherton "Mac" Fleming, a divorced man in his mid-forties who earned his living as a journalist and photographer and had also worked for an engineering firm. A veteran of the Boer War, he had married in 1911 and had two daughters. In World War I, he served with the Royal Army Service Corps after spending two months with his own car assisting the French Red Cross in Arras. During the war, however, he began to suffer ill health, affected by experiences at the front. In August 1918, a doctor found him unfit for duty as a result of gastritis and mucous colitis.[56]

After the war, Mac returned to journalism, publishing a book on battlefield tourism. He also became involved with a London crowd that seemed to marry and divorce with dizzying speed in the early 1920s. Men who sued for divorce on the grounds of adultery had to name the other man as co-respondent to the suit. Mac was duly co-respondent in the divorce suit of the already twice-married wife of a motor agent, with whom he'd been involved since 1922, despite still being married to Winifred Fleming. In 1924, Winifred, in her turn, sued Mac for divorce, alleging that from October 1923 he had lived in South Kensington and committed adultery with another woman. She was part of the first wave of women able to sue for divorce on the grounds of adultery alone, rather than having to cite an additional factor such as cruelty, after the divorce laws were made more egalitarian in 1923. Their marriage was dissolved, and Fleming was ordered, in January 1926, to pay yearly sums toward the support of his children, who remained with their mother. He was not involved in their upbringing—meeting them only briefly for a lunch in 1928—a decision for which one of his daughters would blame DLS.[57]

It is not known how DLS and Mac met, though their shared interests in motors and writing meant that they probably moved in similar circles in London. They married, at a registry office rather than a church because of his divorced status, in April 1926. DLS was, by then, a very different person from the one who had fantasized about being overborne by John Cournos four years earlier.[58]

DLS was not born a feminist; she became one, through bitter suffering and the stark realization of the precariousness of her position in a world that denied female sexuality in all sorts of ways. Despite her glib remarks about the superiority of baby boys to baby girls, giving birth to her son began a process that would change how DLS thought about gender and equality. Having experienced her body in new ways through sex and childbirth, DLS would be increasingly concerned with her right to be treated, not as a woman or a literary freak, but as a human being in control of her body and her destiny.

DLS ALSO TRANSFORMED from someone who wrote detective stories to generate cash into someone at the forefront of the reinvention of the genre. She was a pillar of the Detection Club. This storied club, whose members included DLS's childhood hero G. K. Chesterton as well as Agatha Christie and Margery Allingham, defined the Golden Age of detective fiction and forged a stable, enduringly popular literary form. Fascinated with what made detective fiction work, DLS read widely, reviewing dozens of other murder mysteries and even working on a biography of Wilkie Collins, whose novel *The Moonstone* is said to have been the first real detective story in English.[59]

DLS credited authors including Collins, Sir Arthur Conan Doyle, and Edgar Allan Poe with originating the key elements of the detective genre. These men wrote in the late nineteenth century, when the development of professionalized police forces attracted considerable public interest in the subject. They integrated the thrills of sensational crime stories with the intellectual satisfaction of trying to solve a logical puzzle. And they established certain stock elements: the unconventional amateur contrasted with the conventional policeman, the "surprise" solution, and the significance of psychological clues. But it was DLS and her fellow Detection Club writers who turned those elements into a compelling cultural phenomenon, the murder mystery, which remains one of the best-selling categories of books for its combination of predictability and surprise. Within a reassuringly familiar framework, the detective novel offers an engaging puzzle. It touches on issues of violence, greed, and deception, but promises resolution and a return to stability as the detective reveals the truth in the final pages.[60]

The Detection Club codified the conventions and ethics of the murder mystery. Their oath expresses the main idea, asking prospective members, "Do you promise that your Detectives shall well and truly detect the Crimes presented to them, using those wits which it may please you to bestow upon them and not placing reliance on nor making use of Divine Revelation, Feminine Intuition, Mumbo Jumbo, Jiggery-Pokery, Coincidence or Act of God?" Elsewhere, DLS expanded on the list of silly, unsporting devices. "Avoid use of homicidal lunatics, drugs unknown to Science, impenetrable disguises, pan-European crime conspiracies with unlimited powers, electrified houses full of concealed trap-doors, hypnotism, supernatural interference and other things which the reader can't be expected to guess."[61]

No evidence was kept from the reader. Clues were hidden in plain sight so that in theory any reader could solve the mystery. But they were introduced so skillfully that few readers would actually guess the solution before the final pages. This was a subtle game of revelation and concealment. As the club's jointly authored publications make clear, a set of rules did not make for a mechanistic genre. But there were tricks of the trade. DLS told fellow novelist George Orwell to keep an eye out for horrifying details. It didn't mean the author was morbid, only that the gruesome particulars were being carefully placed to distract from the clue "which it is his business honourably to present you with and at the same time prevent you, if possible, from noticing."[62]

Over the course of the 1920s, DLS became a master of this genre. She would publish eleven novels featuring Lord Peter Wimsey between 1923 and 1937, most of them enduring classics, as well as several coauthored novels and numerous short stories. She could be very playful, even answering fan mail on Lord Peter Wimsey's behalf and passing along "his" greetings and reminiscences as appropriate. In time, however, her interests grew more serious. As the decade wore on, she began to ask harder questions about the limits and possibilities of detective fiction.

For one thing, she wondered about the ultimate aim of writing to manipulate, whether through advertising slogans or well-placed red herrings. Her novel *Murder Must Advertise* deals with this issue explicitly. Its bifurcated plot shows that the advertising industry and the drug trade are two sides of the same coin, both of them fooling people into spending their money on things they emphatically do not need. Speaking at the Oxford Union in 1935, DLS suggested that detective fiction was guilty, too. It "drugged and doped people," giving them a "passionless technical view" of murder.[63]

The Oxford Union speech was lighthearted, but the deeper question remained: what could detective fiction, with all its sleight-of-hand, contribute? At the start of her writing career, DLS had rejoiced in the idea that detective fiction was recreation for noble minds, asserting, "I can't write for low-brows. It's the merry high-brows who like my books." As she wrote, she became more ambitious. Even as she participated in a movement that brought increasing technical sophistication to detective fiction, she believed that it was limited by being "over-intellectualized" and refusing to consider great emotions and passions. It was time, she argued in the mid-1930s, to find a way to combine that technical expertise "with a serious artistic treatment of the psychological elements, so that the intellectual and the common man can find common ground for enjoyment in the mystery novel as once they did in Greek or Elizabethan tragedy." She now criticized writers who wrote things that could only be understood by their own small groups. It would not do, she believed, to leave ordinary people to read only the work of inferior writers. Detective fiction could do more.[64]

7

PROFESSIONAL MOTHERHOOD

LOOKING BACK OVER HER CAREER, Charis Frankenburg said, "I do rather bull-doze into things, but you get them done that way." And so she did, be-coming a force to be reckoned with in national and local politics around issues of maternal and child welfare. Well-off and married, she had four children between 1918 and 1928, all of them desired and planned. Instead of ending her public work, she made maternal welfare her focus as an expert on child-rearing, a tireless advocate for midwives and for access to birth control, and later as a magistrate. She became a public authority on motherhood, em-phasizing the need for mothers to be able to maintain their own health and outside interests. For middle-class parents, she wrote and lectured on par-enting, promulgating a modified, humanized form of the rigid routines then being popularized by baby expert Dr. Frederic Truby King. For working-class mothers, she promoted affordable birth control through clinics and advocated for increased state provision of services.[1]

After the war, Charis and Sydney moved to the Manchester area, where they lived in a series of substantial houses. The Frankenburgs were a promi-nent family, part of a close-knit local Jewish community that had expanded as a result of immigration from eastern Europe during the nineteenth cen-tury. Sydney's father Isidor had immigrated from Russian Poland to the northern industrial city of Manchester and set up a business manufacturing leather bags and then waterproof clothing at a factory in Greengate, Salford, that employed over one thousand people by 1893. The business was one of several owned by Jewish entrepreneurs in the region that ingeniously used the by-products of coal to make waterproof clothing. Isidor Frankenburg was very successful, serving as Lord Mayor of Salford three times. Sydney, in his turn, was a director of the family firm.[2]

All of the Frankenburgs, Sydney and Charis especially, were also involved in philanthropy and social work. The couple once had a session with a psychiatrist "for a joke," and "she said, 'Are you both the sort of people that get onto a committee and then you're made chairman of it?' And we both giggled and said yes." Sydney particularly worked to improve the lives of British Jews, because they "weren't getting a fair deal, he always said." He founded a special branch of the British Legion dedicated to Jewish ex-servicemen, which bore his name. He was a magistrate in the adult and juvenile courts in Salford, as well as holding positions on the boards and committees of organizations dedicated to youth, health, and Jewish life: the Jewish Lads' Brigade, the Salford Juvenile Employment Committee, the Salford Royal Hospital, and the Greengate Hospital and Open-Air School, to name a few.[3]

Sydney and Charis lost no time in starting their own family. Peter was born in 1918, followed by John, then Miles, and finally Ursula in 1928. Sydney and Charis were generous and systematic in their approach to family life. They arranged their household according to a rule that gave her the final word on household management and the children, and him the final word on finance and "other less personal matters." She took a while to adjust to having a great deal more money: the discovery, for example, that her husband considered buying chocolates a reasonable housekeeping expense was a startling delight. Occasionally he asked her to economize. In her memoir, she recounts the story of discovering that during such a period of austerity he had hired out-of-work ex-servicemen to dig a swimming pool for the children. "'Good idea,' said I, 'and now can I stop economising?'"[4]

Religion was somewhat more complicated. Charis and Sydney raised their children as nominally Anglican, though rooted in the Frankenburgs' Jewish context. Sydney spent Passover with his family, while Charis sometimes went to church and occasionally brought the children. She joked that Sydney was Jewish "when it was inconvenient," clarifying, generously, "to himself, I mean." But, she insisted, neither of them "really were labelled," and the children ended up like them, holding a general faith "in a good God." To the outside world, she would claim her Jewishness when it was relevant. She sometimes described herself as "half Jewish." And she reflected, later, that her own Jewish antecedents might have helped her in public life, because "it's helped me to understand a lot of people." But within the world of the Frankenburgs, she wasn't half Jewish; she wasn't Jewish at all. Her mother-in-law chided Sydney for calling Charis a shiksa, which Charis translated as a non-Jewish woman who could do the work forbidden to observant Jews on the Sabbath. Perhaps they didn't avoid labels so much as hold them lightly, accepting the religious diversity that informed their family life without making too much of it.[5]

Like others of her class, Charis had a good deal of help in managing her brood—notably servants and access to a range of schools, including boarding schools. This was crucial to her ability to do so much outside of the home. However, she was closely involved in raising her children, making decisions based on her understanding of scientific theories rather than on custom or prejudice. In this, she took after her parents. Her father had had an impressive career in educational bureaucracy and teacher training. One of his most widely known books, *Common Sense in Education and Teaching*, argued that children "must be treated as persons in the process of development," and that teaching could form habits, for good or for ill.[6]

As educators, the elder Barnetts emphasized child development and behavior modification. And they practiced what they preached: Charis's upbringing was characterized by intense control. Visiting cousins from South Africa were "horrified at the way I was under my parents' thumb." Some of this was salutary. Charis remembered that her mother brought her and Dobbin up "to be so very, very conscious of other people's feelings," yet without being a doormat. Her father was more rigid, as can be seen in his *Little Book of Health and Courtesy*. This volume, which Charis described as "an entertaining handbook on manners," provided a cornucopia of maxims and rules to live by, from the sensible to the idiosyncratic. Percy Barnett advised keeping windows open day and night and drinking at least half a pint of water thirty to sixty minutes before breakfast. Codes of masculine chivalry are in evidence: men should take the "less pleasant side" of a narrow path and step into the road, for example, to let a woman pass.[7]

In her father's warnings to "*be* cheerful and *look* cheerful," we can glimpse some of the physical and emotional regulation that characterized Charis's upbringing. Her memoir records her father's habit of leaving notes around the house, as well as his efforts to improve her hay fever through regimented diets and his insistence on sensible clothing and shoes. As for cheerfulness, Charis absorbed this to the extent of retelling Goldilocks as a child with the following dialogue: "Baby Bear said (whining) 'Someone's eaten my porridge,' and Mummy Bear said, '*Cheerfully*, Baby Bear.'" This training stayed with her. Initially, she quoted the story approvingly, but she came to feel that it had "made more harmful the stresses and strains that came later," by preventing her from speaking up about her own needs. When she had her tonsils out as an adult, for instance, she lost weight rather than complain about the painful hospital food, until her husband intervened.[8]

Charis took these lessons to heart. Unusually for an upper- or middle-class woman in this era, she breastfed her children and believed strongly in the value of doing so, though some of her friends said she was "like a charwoman." Charis's only conventional nanny lasted a mere five months on the job, while she was pregnant with her second child. The nanny complained when Charis got her son's hair cut—because the nanny felt it "was her business, not mine"—and finally got the sack when she dosed the child with castor oil, which Charis had forbidden. Henceforth she would instead train housemaids in childcare herself. When her youngest child was ill, she curtailed her public activities in order to attend to her more closely.[9]

Based on her wide reading and personal experiences, Charis decided to write her own manual of advice on raising young children. First published in 1922, *Common Sense in the Nursery* would establish her as an authority on child-rearing and would go through multiple revised editions and printings over the subsequent decades. The first edition of the book was dedicated to her parents and her children. Like her parents, Charis believed strongly in the importance of early training: "the inclination of the branch really does depend on the bending of the twig." Yet the overwhelming impression in her writings and papers about parenting is not one of rigid control, but of a careful structure designed to foster happy, caring children. Her advice strikes the modern reader as occasionally quaint, but never heartless.[10]

Charis Frankenburg (*Not Old, Madam*, Vintage)

Perhaps some of Charis's greater openness, and her comparative emphasis on serenity and joy, was informed by her friendship with D. Rowe, whose own parents had been far more indulgent than the Barnetts. D. Rowe was a consistent presence in the Frankenburg household, enlivening holidays with her unique blend of whimsy and fun. She thrilled the children by dressing for dinner in the most extravagant costumes: "once it was as a Persian nobleman and once as a Chinaman," and on another occasion "a delighted parlourmaid was called upon to provide coffee-spoons for earrings." At Christmas, as the children opened presents, Charis kept a list of who got what from whom, while D. Rowe folded wrapping paper and sorted ribbons and string. She also regaled the children with a series of stories about Felix the Cat. "Once, as the bedtime-to-be-continued point was reached, a sixteen-year-old, who had pretended to be reading, wailed, 'Oh, you can't leave him like that!'" If the Barnetts provided a rubric of correct behavior, the Rowes contributed a playful joy.[11]

THE SCIENCE OF motherhood received increasing expert and official attention in the early part of the twentieth century. If the population was to be improved, mothers needed to be educated in a range of skills that would ensure not only their children's survival but also their participation as ideal citizens, according to the proponents of the new ideologies of motherhood. Child-rearing advice, of course, fell on often-skeptical ears. When DLS read a doctor's recommendation that babies over six months should do a half hour of exercises daily, she was scathing: "people really don't seem to know how to be silly enough." Charis was far more open to applying science to parenting. Ever the maker of lists, Charis advised parents to keep careful records of their children. Information about vital statistics and milestones would aid the doctor, as well as flag possible issues early on and provide data for analyzing differences between siblings. A diary noting important events plus an ordinary day, recorded every six months or so, was another invaluable aid. A doctor at one school remarked, "Methodical Parents," when he saw the notes Charis had made.[12]

Common Sense in the Nursery was an interpretation of a particular school of thought within the new science of parenting, recently imported to Britain from New Zealand by Dr. Frederic Truby King, who emphasized breastfeeding and the need for a strict routine governing sleeping, feeding, and even bowel movements. Truby King encouraged fresh air and discouraged interaction, including cuddling, which could lead to overstimulation. Contemporaries, as well as later researchers, disputed this rigid approach.[13]

Truby King's ideas are evident throughout *Common Sense in the Nursery*, particularly its first edition. Charis advocates a firm feeding schedule—every three hours for tiny babies, and every four for older ones—and describes overstimulation as second only to "deliberate and persistent cruelty" in the harm it can cause a baby, warning parents even against pointing things out to their child. There was likewise to be no "patting, rocking, perambulator-pushing, or singing" to coax the baby to sleep.[14]

Yet Frankenburg did not slavishly copy Truby King's approach. Instead, she humanized his mechanical system, paying attention to the needs of both mother and child. She defended him against what she saw as the "silly slander that he advocated leaving a baby to cry for hours until the feed was due," a defense that was equally a reinterpretation. Her instructions encourage a parent to return frequently to a crying baby, and she offers tips on distinguishing the meaning behind different cries. She pushed back, though, against the "bad old superstition that it is dangerous to allow a boy baby to cry," which had made boys less self-controlled. In the 1934 edition, she added: "feminists can, and no doubt will, carry this theory into later life!" She also reinterpreted Truby King in light of her recognition of a mother's needs as an individual. Her suggested measures aimed to increase the child's self-sufficiency and the parent's efficiency, with the result that mothers would have some free time from very early in their children's lives.[15]

The book's core theme was this: "children should be, of all the people in the house, the most important and the most seriously considered, but they should think that less attention is paid to them and to their likes and dislikes than to any other member of the household." Beyond a regular schedule and no overstimulation, *Common Sense in the Nursery* consistently emphasized the importance of fresh air and long hours outdoors, which made children stronger and healthier. Years later, her daughter recalled that Charis kept them outside even in wintertime, though protected from the cold by "felt overboots and mittens" as well as "a small electric fire when there was frost." Charis advocated for children to spend a small part of each day alone. In letters from boarding school, her son refers to his "private box" at home, generally granting one or the other of his parents permission to look in it for specific things, evidence of Charis's belief in a child's right to private space and time of their own.[16]

Her opposition to corporal punishment was implacable. Instead, parents should firmly but gently teach "obedience and self-control," as well as initiative and decision-making. Challenged about how she would deal with a child who insisted on pressing lift buttons and inconveniencing other people, she explained that she would tell the child to leave the elevator, and remove him if necessary, "on the principle that he is not the only person in the universe." She would tell him why his behavior was unacceptable, but postpone the talk until he was receptive, and she would not allow him to use lifts "until he could be counted on to behave like a grown-up person." In real life, her emphasis on self-sufficiency could have hilarious results. Charis wondered aloud one day, "Do I need an umbrella?" and heard her children reply, "Now, Mummy, you can decide that just as well yourself."[17]

In the 1934 edition, *Common Sense in the Nursery* shows the influence of new ideas that went beyond Truby King's simplistic behaviorism and includes attention to child psychology, particularly in the thorough revision of the chapter on bad habits. Charis had long insisted that parents should be honest and straightforward about all things, including the basic facts of sex. In 1922, she had argued that bad habits were a sign of neglectful parents who had failed to nip them in the bud. Although emphasizing the need to address underlying causes, such as boredom, she had focused on methods for preventing particular habits or retraining behavior if necessary. Masturbation, which she called "undesirable handling," was described as a moral and physical danger that could easily lead to dire consequences. In the 1934 edition, by contrast, bad habits are a sign of "something wrong in the child's emotional life." She reassures parents on masturbation, which is now mentioned without euphemism, because scientific study has proved it will not cause physical or moral harm. While it should still be discouraged as "not a socially desirable habit," Charis impresses upon parents the need to avoid causing any feelings of guilt to develop around the subject.[18]

Even in 1922, Charis had urged that boys and girls be dressed together, to make nudity and physical differences natural and unremarkable. From 1934, her advice incorporates a nod to the Freudian notion that girls might envy their brothers' genitalia and develop "an inferiority complex"—but she adds her own feminist twist. She simply explained to her own daughter that "she was really the luckier of the two, as she had in her a little house where she would be able to make a baby when she was grown up, and her brother would not be able to do this."[19]

By 1946, Charis increasingly saw "the importance of personal relationships," which allowed parents and children to "tackle difficulties *together*, in fact, make friends." She admitted that her method was not perfect. When her daughter had to take a despised medicine, she "sometimes said, 'You go away Mummy, and when you come back it will be gone'; so, practising my psychology, I left the room, and returning rejoiced that, sure enough it had gone. Under the rug, but that I did not know till years later."[20]

COMMON SENSE IN the Nursery enjoyed decades of popularity and established Charis Frankenburg as an authority on children. She lectured widely on the subject of raising children and wrote newspaper advice columns for parents. She reviewed other child-advice manuals, too, praising especially those authors who wrote from personal experience. She tried to aim her advice at a broad audience, arguing that her recommendations generally "are within reach of a small income," and that much of the advice would actually save parents money. Some of her public advice, though, must have sounded like it was directed to a much narrower band. In the *Manchester Guardian*, she advised mothers to take their children Christmas shopping themselves, rather than entrusting the task to an ill-prepared chauffeur, for example. And she lamented the decline in the presence of a dedicated nursery in the home, where a child could play freely without being constantly surrounded by "adult tools, such as matches, scissors, and saucepans, which necessitate a thwarting stream of prohibitions."[21]

For Charis, motherhood and career were not in conflict. In a newspaper debate on the tension between work and family demands for women with university degrees, Charis insisted that the separation was spurious. Her university degree enabled her to communicate her knowledge about parenting clearly and effectively. It also gave her the Classics training that inspired her next project, a collaboration with D. Rowe: the strikingly popular *Latin with Laughter* books, which used simple storytelling and illustrations to introduce the basis of Latin grammar to small children. Here, again, Charis followed in the footsteps of her father, who had translated *Robinson Crusoe* into Latin to help schoolchildren learn the language. Charis wrote the text for *Latin with Laughter*, and D. Rowe provided the illustrations that brought the hilarious little stories and vignettes to life.[22]

The first book was dedicated to Charis's children: to her three sons, "who have used it as a stepping-stone," and to "the baby-she-bear who likes it." The books encouraged children to use Latin to tell stories and express their

ideas from the start. Its themes go well beyond the realm of classical literature. A typical, if particularly feminist, example begins: "a woman-doctor is
preparing medicine, but the women avoid the medicine. The woman-doctor
tastes tears. She prepares a feast in-front-of a woman." After the story, a glos-
sary offers translations (*medica* for woman-doctor, for example) and notes
about grammar.[23]

The title page proclaims Charis's educational qualifications—"M.A.
(Oxon.)"—but in the text she candidly admits that she did not have a first-
class honors degree in Classics. But what matter? It "is by no means always
the expert who most clearly sees the beginner's difficulties." Indeed, the book
was aimed at "the mothers who, having learnt no Latin, or having forgotten
what they learnt, wish to give their small sons and daughters a foretaste of
the subject before school life begins." *Latin with Laughter* brought the ability
not only to learn but to teach Latin into the realm of possibility for ordinary
mothers—an example of the MAS's growing commitment to bringing their
own elite educations to a widening, if still somewhat rarefied, audience.[24]

IN HER WIDE-RANGING career in public health, as a voluntary organizer,
committee woman, board member, and advocate, Charis broadened her
scope well beyond the concerns of middle- and upper-class parents. She built
on Victorian and Edwardian traditions of women's public engagement. Like
previous generations of well-off British women, she helped the poor through
instruction and charity, the mainstays of traditional middle-class philanthropy. Although she never ran for office, politics was a crucial arena for her
work. Like elite nineteenth-century women, she wielded influence instead on
committees and deputations at the local and national levels.[25]

At the same time, her work was forward-looking. It was founded on a
belief in the importance of women's full citizenship. She was active in the
women's sections set up by the Conservative Party to court this new group of
voters. More profoundly, she was motivated by the conviction that women,
especially working-class mothers, were getting a raw deal and deserved better. Unlike earlier philanthropists, she didn't assume that the middle-class
example was always the right one. Instead, she turned to scientific expertise,
in the form of the "mothercraft" movement and the emerging consensus
that mothers—their physical presence and their emotional attachment—
were crucial to child development. In a final departure from her Victorian

forebears, Charis also believed in the importance of working with the expanding, although still tiny, welfare state in Britain. While she saw important roles for charity, she believed that the state had a crucial, central role to play in the provision of health care for its citizens. Even her philanthropy was undertaken partly in order to shift state policy in the direction she believed would be most beneficial for women and their children.[26]

Charis's initial foray into a public role was in setting up a baby clinic in her home. This seems to have been a private, charitable version of the antenatal clinics that were being established locally across the country after the 1918 Maternal and Child Welfare Act required them. Her family doctor ran the sessions, with Charis serving as nurse and Sydney helping with organization and business practices. The local council took the flourishing clinic over when the Frankenburgs moved in 1923.[27]

In 1925, Charis contacted the famous birth control advocate Dr. Marie Stopes and asked for advice about setting up a birth control clinic in the Manchester area. In her own family, birth control had always been normalized. She wanted to have her first child quickly, since Sydney was returning to the front, but they used birth control thereafter to regulate the timing of her pregnancies. She was aware of her privileges: her early knowledge of birth control, the wealth and education that made it easy to secure it, and "then I was a midwife and I know how to insert into a vagina and all the rest of it."[28]

Like other interwar campaigners, Charis saw the birth control movement as part of the broader women's movement, "because if a woman was having a baby every year she couldn't do much else." The birth control movement sought to ensure, in the longer term, that poor women would have reliable access to information about birth control through local authorities and mainstream medical providers. As Charis told the conference of the National Council of Women in Manchester in 1926, she and other advocates "do not regard the provision of specialised birth control clinics as the ideal means of achieving their end," but hoped that soon the Ministry of Health would allow birth control advice to be given in the state-funded maternity and infant welfare centers. In the meantime, however, advocates began setting up private, low-cost clinics where women of limited means could access information about how to use safe, effective methods of birth control.[29]

Stopes put Charis Frankenburg in touch with Mary Stocks. Charis and Mary had been acquainted at high school and at Oxford. Reintroduced, they immediately got to work. The first planning meeting for the clinic was in October 1925; by November there was a committee and an advisory council, which included the actress Sybil Thorndike. To raise money for the clinic, Charis remembered afterward, "we just went around among our friends and begged." The Manchester, Salford, and District Mothers' Clinic opened its doors on March 1, 1926. The clinic was staffed by a doctor and a nurse-midwife, and ran twice weekly for between ninety minutes and two hours above a baker's shop in Greengate, Salford. In addition to making it an innocuous building to enter, the bakery gave the whole place "a lovely smell of bread." Once again, Sydney pitched in, helping to decorate the premises and secure medical case sheets for record keeping.[30]

Charis worked in the front room, welcoming and interviewing the women. Mary Stocks was the chairman and Charis the honorary organizing secretary; Flora Blumberg served as the honorary secretary. Dr. Olive Gimson provided medical services, assisted by the midwife Nurse Pulford. They generally advised the use of a type of cap or diaphragm (the Dutch cap, the Prentif cap, or Stopes's Prorace cap) along with a spermicidal ointment or pessary. Each patient, often with her children in tow, met first with Charis Frankenburg, Mary Stocks, or another helper, "always a married woman and an experienced social worker," who interviewed her about the details of her case. "Great care is taken that nobody shall feel hurried." After washing her hands, the patient was then examined by the doctor, who offered personalized advice. Finally, the patient met with the nurse, "who instructs her until she thoroughly understands and has practised the doctor's orders." All this was checked again through follow-up appointments. There was only a fee for the first appointment and appliances were supplied at cost, though donations were also accepted.[31]

Conducting her initial interviews, Charis was "very kind and confidential and helpful." She would ask the woman, What can we do for you? And then the woman would "generally burst into a flood of tears" and tell her painful story, and Charis would say, "Well, you know, that's what we want to help you about." She would, reassuringly, describe how the doctor would help, explaining that "it wasn't an operation, it wouldn't hurt you," but that the "nice lady doctor" and the nurse would "be able to tell you exactly the best way to help you."[32]

Such work was very controversial. Charis had, at Sydney's request, consulted with her mother-in-law before proceeding. Surprisingly, this formidable woman replied that Charis's record of charitable work in Salford gave her the right to do what she wanted. She was, perhaps, personally "doubtful about it," but Charis believed "she was converted in the end." This is not to say that Charis caught no flak from Sydney's wider community. One member of his family wished that she hadn't opened the clinic quite so close to the family's business in Salford. Nathan Laski, a pillar of the Manchester Jewish community, infuriated both Sydney and Charis at a British Legion branch event by making, in Charis's words, "an extremely vulgar speech about my beautiful figure," and how surprised he was that, as a birth control advocate, she had four children. Sydney was "boiling over and I had great difficulty in keeping him quiet, but I assured him that when my turn came to speak, I could flatten him out all right—which I did." Even when Laski died in a road accident years later, Charis refused to mourn him.[33]

The medical profession, in general, was indifferent or hostile to birth control. Some women arrived at the clinic from hospitals where they were told to avoid further pregnancies for their own health but then were offered no further advice. Such reticence was partly the result of official limits on providing birth control information in state-funded institutions, but it also reflected a lack of knowledge among doctors. Some doctors who wanted to know more "used to come after dark" to learn from Dr. Olive Gimson.[34]

ON ITS OPENING, the clinic attracted a storm of public controversy, fed by the active opposition of the local Catholic bishop, Dr. Thomas Henshaw. He linked the clinic to eugenics, the pseudoscience based on the idea of controlling reproduction to improve the human race, usually in explicitly racist or ableist ways. Connecting this to birth control, Henshaw sarcastically described eugenics as a science "which aims at the improvement of the race by securing its extinction." He conjured a wicked coalition of women, bent on promoting evil by instructing "their sisters in the art of thwarting natural laws, defeating God's plans, indulging in sin, and avoiding some of the physical penalties attached." Why, he wondered, could the police not shut the clinic down? Failing that, he said, local fathers and mothers should "rise up in arms against those who dare to defile the minds of the people and hound them out of the district," putting an end to "the evil in their midst." The *Catholic Herald* emphasized Henshaw's warning not to be fooled by the clinic's apparent respectability: sin was sin, even if it was promoted by a clinic staffed by nurses and "under the patronage of a 'lady.'" The Salford *Catholic*

Federationist printed a call for birth control to be "thrust back to the sewer to which it belongs and from whence it came."[35]

On April 13, there was a protest meeting at Salford Town Hall. One speaker, an "eminent physician" who worked in gynecology, warned that birth control would produce "various stages of mental derangement, leading up to insanity," and would promote sex outside of marriage with a consequent rise in venereal disease. The canon of St. Philip's Church, which was Anglican, argued that the lack of self-control engendered by birth control would damage the nation's manhood. Unlike the Catholic bishop, he made his case on the basis of racial eugenics: birth control should not be promoted, because the Dominions, such as Australia and South Africa, required high birth rates among whites in order to counter Asian and black populations. This was a bit much for the audience; a voice of protest was raised. The canon replied, "I believe as much as anybody that the black man is a brother. But I would ask, do you desire him as a brother-in-law?"[36]

Some of the rhetoric against the clinic was misogynist and anti-Semitic. Charis kept notes on the worst of it: a reference to her allegedly "German-Jewish name," for example, or to "those over-dressed, well-fed, & badly bred women who throng the matinées every day, & publicly flaunt cigarettes between their painted lips." There was a brick thrown through the clinic's window, but the intervention of the chief constable persuaded the bishop to soften his rhetoric. There were no personal physical attacks. Charis weathered it all and reflected later, "I must have been pretty brazen I think."[37]

Charis was skeptical about the church's objections. If birth control was wrong because it prevented reproduction, how did the church justify celibacy, to which the same objection surely applied? She was outraged, too, by Dr. Edward Lyttelton's 1929 pamphlet, *The Christian and Birth Control*, which included a parable about a man, who couldn't be celibate for health reasons, and his wife, for whom pregnancy posed a grave risk. She ultimately died in childbirth, her husband's health being judged more important that her own. Adding insult to injury, Lyttelton praised not her sacrifice, but her husband's Christian approach to his loss. In a letter on the book to *Time and Tide*, Charis was incandescent: "*her* health had suffered unto death; *her* work had suffered; who cared for the two motherless children? But *his* health and work were unhampered, and presumably he married again, as continence would have been injurious, and he had emptied and thrown away his bottle of medicine."[38]

Nevertheless, Charis, like DLS, was well aware that all publicity was good publicity. At the intake interviews, patients were asked how they'd heard of the clinic. They frequently answered, "At the protest meeting" or "We were told in church not to come." Yet the religious opposition meant that patients needed more reassurance that what they were doing was good and not evil. As Charis remembered, "You had to, you know, rub in the fact that you'd got your children and you loved your children and you were wanting to help children and that's what it was for."[39]

The clinic also organized its own positive publicity by holding public meetings. The first was in May 1926 and featured future member of Parliament Eleanor Rathbone and prominent birth controller Dr. Norman Haire. Charis Frankenburg and Mary Stocks addressed many smaller meetings across the region, at cooperatives, Women's Institutes, the National Council of Women, and "all political parties." Charis would bring her baby with her, so as not to miss the evening feeding: "this was a graphic illustration that we were not *anti-births*." She emphasized that her qualifications were not political or economic. Instead, she acted out of sympathy with mothers, and sought, not an end to births, but the spacing of children in a way that would maximize health for all. Her father came to hear her address two meetings, for the National Council of Women and the National Union of Societies for Equal Citizenship, and she valued his "generous comments" on her performance for the rest of her life. Already by the second year of the clinic's operation, she and Stocks found "considerably less opposition to the movement than was at first felt."[40]

But Charis was tireless. She even worked the topic into her speech at the National Conference on Maternity and Infant Welfare in 1928, despite the fact that references to birth control had been officially banned at the meeting. In May 1931, she spoke at the Annual Conference of Conservative Women in support of granting welfare centers the right to offer birth control advice. At the International Midwives' Union Congress in May 1934, she argued for the inclusion of contraceptive methods in midwifery training. In all of this, Sydney was a staunch supporter. He drove Charis wherever she needed to go—in 1931, this amounted to seventy-four meetings.[41]

The clinic was careful to steer clear of any association with prostitution. Charis compared this to the extraordinary pressure on her generation of Oxford women to "be purer than the pure," in order to avoid criticism. Officially the clinic only treated married women who had been pregnant at least once, though the doctor had some discretion on this point. Openly treating unmarried women would mean that clinic would "be called a whorehouse and then that would be the end of it." Personally, though, it's clear that Charis believed that supplying birth control information to all women was appropriate. It was wrong, she felt, to punish the illegitimate child in order to punish the mother, who had ended up pregnant because she had been denied "the proper information" about birth control in the first place.[42]

The clinic did not provide abortions, which were illegal. Moreover, they cautiously declined to register pregnant women as clients in their records, "lest our Caesar's wife reputation should suffer from a subsequent self-induced abortion." Pregnant women who arrived at the clinic were encouraged to attend an ante-natal clinic instead, where they would find support for a healthy pregnancy. But "we had awful scenes with them." They wanted help ending a pregnancy, not sustaining it, and a visit to an ante-natal clinic might expose their attempts. "Those who were frantically experimenting with abortifacient drugs and more violent methods were not likely to submit themselves to medical scrutiny."[43]

As THE SCENES with pregnant women suggest, women already sought to limit their reproduction in various ways. Besides abortion, the clinic found that women relied on what they called "being very careful"—or in the clinic's language, "incomplete intercourse"—or on commercial appliances that were expensive and, if used by someone with an undiagnosed medical issue, potentially dangerous. Women learned about birth control, the clinic argued, mainly from commercial advertisements run in many cases by companies supplying drugs for abortion.[44]

Birth control was crucial in an immediate sense on grounds of preventing illness and death for mothers and babies. The clinic calculated that the first 108 women they treated had collectively experienced 509 pregnancies. One woman had, at the age of forty-one, been pregnant eighteen times, suffering three miscarriages and the deaths of four infants. Infant mortality was officially calculated per live birth, but the clinic argued that abortions, miscarriages, and stillbirths should also be included. In meetings, Charis also cited the case of the wife of a man with tuberculosis. Her husband had been in and out of a sanatorium for years, unable to provide for the family, but there was "a baby every time he came out."[45]

However, Charis and her fellow advocates refused to limit the need for birth control to narrow medical necessity. She was unflinching in her insistence that economic and personal concerns were also valid, and indeed that they were all part and parcel of the same thing: healthy, happy families. Charis spoke vividly about the need for birth control, citing "that awful story of the woman who said, when they told her the baby was stillborn, she said: thank god." Most of the clinic's patients wanted to limit their families because of "inadequate housing and wages," a sign of their "profound sense of parental responsibility." Women working full-time in factories needed to be able to control their reproduction, and would turn to drugs and desperate measures if alternatives were not available, Charis told a National Council of Women conference in Manchester. "You cannot expect working women to manage their babies unless they have two or three years rest in between." Charis argued, too, that birth control was important for a sense of security and a happy sex life. Constant pregnancies weighed on fathers. It was the "man's job to earn," but weekends were easily taken up with looking after children if pregnancies were too frequent. Well-spaced families, by contrast, meant a comfortable home. Husbands and wives could enjoy sex, rather than women fearing it and men turning to paying for it elsewhere.[46]

As Charis knew, arguments for and against birth control in this era often referenced eugenics. The clinic was affiliated with the National Society for the Provision of Birth Control Clinics, and it cooperated with the Eugenics Education Society, the Malthusian League, and the Society for Constructive Birth Control. This list underscores that the idea of improving human beings through deliberate choices about reproduction was mainstream in this era. The language of eugenics was sprinkled throughout casual conversation, too, bringing with it notions of health versus degeneracy, the inheritability of traits and disease, the possibility of breeding better people, and, always, a strong flavor of racism and white supremacy.[47]

All the members of the MAS were white. Their direct references to non-white people were rare, but they made use of casually racist phrases with an unreflective ease. Some of this echoed popular eugenicist ideas. In 1918, DLS rejoiced at the immediate social consequences of demobilization, remarking with considerable tactlessness, "It is really splendid to be seeing men about again who are not black or diseased or degenerates." Jim's 1927 novel, *The Man with Six Senses*, touches on eugenicist themes in its story of a man who has an unusual ability to sense mineral deposits in the earth. His gifts are unrecognized in his lifetime, but the novel's heroine deliberately bears his child in order to preserve his special ability in the human race. The novel ends ambiguously, leaving the reader unclear about whether this attempt at positive eugenicist breeding has worked and whether it will be worth the sacrifice of the heroine's career. However, Charis's clinic avoided most direct eugenicist arguments. They did suggest that birth control would increase the percentage of healthy, "fit" children, but the implication was usually more about environment than heredity. Fewer babies would be injured by botched abortions, for instance, and more children would grow up with the benefit of adequate resources and healthy, engaged parents.[48]

In its first year of operation, the clinic saw 423 patients. By September 1931, it had advised 2,025 women. At this stage, the clinic undertook an effort to prove, contrary to the claims of naysayers, that birth control was effective at its basic goal: preventing unwanted conceptions. As early as 1928, Dr. Olive Gimson had argued that the rare failures of the method seemed to be down to patients not carrying out instructions. In 1931, Flora Blumberg visited current and former patients of the clinic and interviewed them about their experiences. The results were published in a pamphlet, *Only Eight Failures*, that pushed back against the reports of other clinics—which admitted high rates of failure—as well as official skepticism by distinguishing between failure of the method itself and failure of women to follow instructions consistently and accurately.[49]

Yet the report's conclusions were rather more nuanced, suggesting the need for better instruction and simpler methods of contraception. The clinic's original aim had been to advise women on contraception, with the idea that they would "go away and practise it, and in this respect live happily ever after." This had been, to a large extent, successful. The "eight failures" of the pamphlet's title refer to cases in which women swore that they had followed all instructions consistently yet had become pregnant—an extraordinarily low rate of failure. More positively, it found twenty-eight women who had successfully stopped using contraception in order to become pregnant, "a complete answer to the silly assertion that contraception induces sterility." Whether pregnancy was intended or not, women who had become pregnant after successfully using birth control for a while felt "they had had a rest, and felt much stronger and better."

Far more numerous were lapses: cases in which women had failed to follow instructions, or had alternated an approved method with something less reliable. The indifference and ignorance of many medical practitioners contributed to the problem, as did dodgy advice from "the lady next door, the chemist's assistant, and the rubber shop." The clinic had to reckon, too, with the complexity of the recommended method itself. Some women did not have sufficient privacy to make use of the method, for instance. Elsewhere in the report, the authors echo generations of social workers who emphasized the individual's responsibility for overcoming poor conditions and who claimed to be able to read a great deal into superficial details of housekeeping. "The success or failure of present methods depends almost entirely on the efficiency of the woman concerned," so that a "spotless doorstep" heralded successful use of birth control, while the homes of those who had lapsed were messier: "a half-tin of Nestlé's milk on the table, together with a half-loaf, and butter or margarine in its original paper, and several layers of dirty dishes" foretold a woman who struggled to comply, in their view. A birth control clinic, then, must also be an "educational agency," offering the encouragement and training necessary to comply with the approved method of birth control.[50]

Over time, the birth control advocates won an ever wider section of the public to their cause. It is telling, though, that even the other organizations that Charis worked with were often divided or hesitant. In 1933, the Manchester, Salford, and District Mothers' Clinic asked to rent some space at the Greengate Hospital and Open-Air School for its expanding practice. Greengate was one of the Frankenburgs' main charities, and Sydney was chairman of the committee. The clinic's request caused debate, with some committee members wondering whether the opposition to birth control would make the arrangement detrimental to the hospital. Ultimately, after two meetings, the clinic was granted a space to rent.[51]

Charis was a member of some of the more moderate women's organizations that pursued equal citizenship in the post-suffrage era. Here, too, birth control was controversial. The Women Citizens' Association was one such organization. Formed in January 1914, this organization pressed both for greater attention to issues affecting women and children at the local level and for more female representatives on public committees and boards. In 1927, Mary Stocks defended the clinic against "innuendo" published in the organization's magazine. Giving birth was dangerous work, and should be "accorded greater consideration and more adequate safeguards." In reply, the author of the original article defended herself, arguing that the clinic was not interested in "maternity welfare" but in "how to prevent conception," two very different things. Nevertheless, the Women Citizens'

Association came to support birth control provision, overcoming the challenges launched by its Catholic members.[52]

The National Council of Women was similar. At the group's 1929 conference in Manchester, "there was a visible quickening of interest" when Mary Stocks put forward a resolution calling for maternity and child welfare clinics receiving government grants to be empowered to provide information about birth control. Opponents of the resolution cited its potential to drive doctors and nurses away from clinic work if they opposed birth control on ethical grounds. They argued, too, that self-control was part of morality. In the words of one speaker, "Suffering borne in the right spirit was not the greatest evil in the world." Ultimately the resolution passed, again over the opposition of conservative and Catholic groups within the organization.[53]

Birth control advocates also made progress in their original goal of securing greater official provision of birth control advice. In 1927, a Salford councillor raised concerns about the welfare clinics sending clients to the birth control clinic for information, "contrary to the Ministry of Health's instructions." Charis visited the Ministry of Health and spoke with Dame Janet Campbell, the senior medical officer on the subject of maternal and infant welfare. Campbell assured her that it was quite alright for a doctor at a grant-aided welfare center to refer a patient on medical grounds to a birth control clinic.[54]

Soon they were able to cut out the middle step, when the Labour minister for health released a memorandum in 1930 allowing local authorities to provide birth control information to married women in their welfare clinics. That year, Salford did so, and Manchester and other British cities soon followed suit. As a result, the clinic took on the task of training the nurses who worked in the local welfare clinics and providing advice to visiting medical officers from the region.[55]

By 1934, then, the clinic was well established, and an enormous change in attitude had come about. The Lambeth conference in 1930, at which the bishops of the Church of England relaxed their opposition to birth control, had contributed to this, as had the global economic depression, which fueled the need to limit family size while times were hard. The clinic was now working with several different municipalities and holding a busy weekly session at its new home in the Greengate Hospital. Flora Blumberg became chairman of the clinic in 1936, as Charis's attention turned to other things. In 1939, it expanded further and moved into new premises in Chorlton-on-Medlock.

By 1954, it was linked with the Family Planning Association and holding sessions four days a week, teaching contraception as well as offering sex education and fertility advice. Dr. Gimson remained a medical officer.[56]

IN ADDITION TO her work with the clinic, Charis advocated for the health of mothers and children in other ways. She and Sydney hosted parties in Salford for expectant mothers, sending them home with parcels to assist in preparing for the new arrival. Sydney included cigarettes for the fathers in the parcels, telling the mothers, "And don't forget that if it hadn't been for them you wouldn't be here!" More seriously, Charis, like many others, was deeply concerned with the issue of maternal mortality, which had not declined like other causes of death. The search for an explanation to this conundrum pitted general practitioners against specialists and advocates of home births against advocates of increased hospitalization.[57]

Charis was one of the opponents of hospitalization for childbirth. Only 23 percent of births took place in a hospital in 1923. Charis always emphasized that maternal deaths were as common or more common among wealthy women, linking this to their high rates of medical intervention. With the assistance of a friend from her maternity hospital days, Charis gave birth to each of her four children at home without a doctor or the use of anesthetics or painkillers. Had she and DLS been able to discuss the issue, they might have found much to agree on. Charis believed "that childbirth is a natural process, not an illness," designed "to function smoothly and to induce a feeling of satisfaction." More graphically, she told a later interviewer, "I always said it's like passing a very hard bowel movement." In other words, it "is a normal pain," and not something to be afraid of. It was best undertaken at home, where the laboring mother can be "the centre of interest."[58]

Controversially, Charis opposed efforts to ensure the universal availability of anesthesia in childbirth, arguing that it would actually increase the danger of the process. In 1931, she clashed with some anonymous medical professionals over the issue in the pages of *The Manchester and Salford Woman Citizen*. There, she asserted that a midwife should be in charge of normal labor, and she implicated the use of chloroform and instruments in the persistently high levels of maternal mortality. She criticized the "idiotic" campaign of the National Birthday Trust Foundation to provide anesthetics more widely, when "a hot cup of tea and a baby and a nice midwife and a fire" would be far more beneficial. Instead, she supported Grantly Dick-Read's Natural Childbirth Association. Decades later, she still believed that doctors and midwives remained "a bit too sold on anaesthetics," and she was critical of medical interventions made for doctors' convenience rather than maternal health. In 1964, she decried as "misguided" the campaign to normalize hospital births in all cases. By then, however, maternal mortality had declined as a result of sulfonamide drugs, introduced in the mid-1930s, and later other antibiotics that greatly reduced the incidence of infection after childbirth.[59]

Charis was personally galvanized in the fight for the rights of pregnant women by the death of Molly Taylor in 1934. Taylor died after being transported from one hospital to another immediately after giving birth, and Charis served as an expert witness in an inquiry into the case. That November, the national Maternal Mortality Committee hosted a meeting bringing together about 1,300 delegates. Charis, as representative of the National Union of Women's Conservative and Unionist Associations, seconded the main resolution in support of full implementation and expansion of measures to improve childbirth facilities. She was part of a deputation that met with the minister of health, Sir Kingsley Wood, in December 1934. There, she spoke about maternity hospitals, arguing that they "should co-operate with other organisations as part of the social services." The minister, in reply to the deputation, agreed on the need to expand services, including antenatal care, midwives, and hospitalization where necessary.[60]

At the heart of Charis's effort was advocacy for the role of the midwife. Midwives were, and are still, a central part of childbirth policy and practice in Britain. They attended some three-quarters of births in this era. As with birth control, midwives were easily available to those who could pay, so Charis's efforts focused on getting local authorities to provide similar access to poorer women. She gathered statistics and medical opinions, and, through her work with the Salford Maternity and Child Welfare Committee, got the city to agree to pay for midwives for "necessitous cases," before such payment was mandated at a national level. She was a tireless advocate for the Midwives Act of 1936, which would improve pay for midwives. Charis attended Parliament to see the bill progress. "The man who got me the seat, a member of Parliament, kept coming in and saying would you like to come out," but she stayed until the small hours of the morning, "so excited and pleased." The Midwives Act transformed the profession, requiring local councils to retain and pay a salaried staff of midwives.[61]

Even after 1936, Charis continued to advocate for midwives, arguing that married midwives should be treated equally, for instance. She served, too, as the Salford representative on the North Western Federation for Maternity and Child Welfare and on the Council of the Midwives' Institute. She continued to emphasize the importance of midwives in facilitating home births, which would allow mothers to "avoid an atmosphere of apprehension and disease." And she defended an increase in midwives' salaries in 1943, pointing out that they were on call at all hours and often working alone, in contrast to district nurses and health visitors.[62]

IN MANY OF her views, and in much of what she advocated, Charis was progressive, pushing up against and often right past the assumptions and conventions of her world. Like the rest of the Barnetts and the Frankenburgs, she was also a member of the Conservative Party. Much of her work was in line with the party's own efforts to adapt to the new, mass-democracy world. Conservative Party leaders made a concerted effort to attract women to the party after 1918 and developed large women's organizations, though they were less successful at bringing women into leadership. In addition to specific policy positions designed to appeal to women, particularly housewives, the Conservatives developed a rhetoric of being the party of common sense and middlebrow pragmatism, which resonated with their female membership. Charis served in a variety of Conservative women's organizations, and probably could have held elected office; she declined an invitation to run for Parliament against Labourite Ben Tillett.[63]

Like others in the party, she pushed more old-fashioned Conservatives to modernize and engage with social problems. She wanted her fellow Conservatives to move past the "old feudal idea that they were the lords of the manor," required to do nothing more than distribute coal and blankets to the needy. She asserted her right to be respected as a woman within the party, too. In the women's Moss Side Conservative association in the early 1930s, she earned the nickname of the Moss Side Tigress. When the other members complained that the Co-operative Society supported the Labour Party, she asked who shopped at the Co-op. A "forest of arms" was raised. "Now, hands up all who go to the meetings and vote on policy," she said—and got no response but a rapid agreement that members should attend Co-op meetings "or forever hold their peace." She clashed with the chairman of the men's association over her advocacy for birth control. He called a meeting to censure her, without even inviting her to attend and offer a defense, which she called "the dirtiest trick" ever played on her in public life. She ignored the meeting, and his resolution of censure failed. "And a few days later he had a heart attack and died. And my women said it was a judgment."[64]

Although Charis's modernizing outlook chimed with party policy, she was still a maverick. As a Conservative, she was in the political minority in many of the movements in which she worked, particularly birth control. Her efforts earned her respect from members of other parties. Her Labour Party friend Eleanor Cuddeford, a Salford councillor, "said I was too nice to be a Conservative"—just as one of her maids had said "I wasn't a real lady, I wasn't afraid of work." As she remembered, "I've had some funny compliments in my days." Others on the left were more skeptical. In 1933, Charis clashed with author Walter Greenwood over his portrayal of Salford in his classic book on Depression-era Britain, *Love on the Dole*. She called it a "caricature of my city," but he skewered her pretensions as "the calm effrontery of self-appointed, economically-secure apologists of degraded humanity." For Greenwood, Charis was no better than the condescending, well-off philanthropists of the nineteenth century, and certainly not too nice to be a Conservative.[65]

Charis Frankenburg took her training as a scholar and as a midwife, and her personal experience as a mother, and used them to establish herself as an influential authority on motherhood. In her advice books, complicated issues of language, human development, and morality are conveyed to audiences that stretch far beyond Oxford scholars. Although Charis made use of science and what she regarded as the most convincing, up-to-date theories, she never suspended her own judgment. She was both mother and expert, seeing no contradiction between the two roles—indeed, she saw them as necessarily complementary. Experts on parenting ought to be parents, and parents ought to rely on expert advice, in her view. And mothers of all classes ought to benefit from the ability of science to allow them both enjoyable sex lives and well-planned, healthy families.

8

SLEEPLESS NIGHTS

MURIEL ST. CLARE BYRNE WAS beset by insomnia in the early 1920s, and for good reason. She wanted to be an academic and researcher, but she struggled to break into that world, hampered both by her gender and her need to support herself and her ailing mother. At the same time, she and her former Somerville classmate Marjorie "Bar" Barber formed an enduring partnership and household, which provided crucial stability as she dealt with family obligations and financial strain. She would never be a full-time academic, but, with Bar's support, Muriel instead wrote popular history emphasizing women and everyday life in Tudor England.

After teaching in Liverpool, Muriel had spent a term back in Oxford doing postgraduate research on Anthony Munday, an English playwright and predecessor of Shakespeare. She registered in October 1917 for an MA in English at the University of London. The research on Munday would culminate in an edition of his manuscripts published through Oxford University Press in 1923. An erudite, detailed introduction, unsigned but almost certainly by Muriel, discusses the original manuscript in detail, explaining, for example, how she interpreted ambiguous handwriting using references to other texts from the period. She spent the winter of 1918–1919 teaching for the YMCA in France, before returning to London for good.[1]

In London, Muriel began living with Bar. Photographs suggest that they had been friends, or perhaps already lovers, at Somerville, though no letters between them survive from that era. Like D. Rowe, Bar was a born teacher with a flair for theater. She had taught English at Edgbaston High School in Birmingham in 1917 and 1918, and from spring 1920 began what would be a

long and illustrious career at South Hampstead High School for Girls in London. She
made a deep impression on her students.
On the first day of class, one remembered,
Bar said, "Good morning, class," to which
the students mumbled a reply. She wrote
her name on the board and then said, "I am
going to forget this happened. I am leaving.
I will come back, at which time you will
all stand together, and when I say Good
Morning to you, you will respond by saying, 'Good morning, Miss Barber.'" And, of
course, they did. Bar was this student's favorite teacher: "I think everyone absolutely

Marjorie Barber (MSBC 9/5)

adored Miss Barber. She knew how to move and how to dress." Another student remembered Bar as "an inspiration," speculating that she was "probably
a frustrated actress." Her rendering of Portia's speech from *The Merchant
of Venice* remained vivid years later. She also produced plays for the school,
especially the annual Christmas play, which she imbued with a literary sen-
sibility and a visual style inspired by Italian Old Masters. Theatrical, self-
assured, and literary, Bar was a memorable teacher—and a perfect match for
Muriel.[2]

Beyond the classroom, Bar produced edited collections and other texts
relating to the teaching of English, including a series of Chaucer's *Canterbury Tales* in the late 1920s. In 1928, she published a book aimed at assisting
secondary-school students preparing for examinations. It's easy to imagine
Bar discussing some of the sample questions with Muriel: "what was the
Elizabethan ideal of a gentleman?" for example. Her question about how
Jane Austen or Charlotte Brontë might have written about "the feminist
movement of this century" echoes the concerns Muriel addressed in her own
lectures. Bar knew that teaching was no picnic. In her fiction, she wrote with
clear eyes about its challenges. One story features a teacher who finds that,
after twenty-five years in the profession, all sentimentality is gone. Teaching
is a kind of "virgin motherhood," she feels, conducted at an extraordinary
scale: "after all, it's not natural to have four hundred children." Nevertheless,
Bar found scope for professional satisfaction and intellectual engagement
teaching English at a secondary school.[3]

Muriel did not. Although she, too, taught at South Hampstead to pay the bills, she kept looking for ways to make the leap to teaching and research in higher education. Her headmistress allowed her to take on additional work in the pursuit of this aim. She was an assistant English tutor at Somerville for one term in 1919, and coached undergraduates at Oxford on weekends from 1920 to 1925. She also took on a class for the Workers' Educational Association (WEA), teaching mostly women and a few men about nineteenth-century novelists. Meanwhile, she applied to more permanent and research-oriented university positions, usually at women's colleges: a research fellowship at Girton, Cambridge; the role of tutor in English at St. Hilda's Hall, Oxford. In a letter of reference, her old Somerville tutor Helen Darbishire wrote that Muriel had carried out the research on Munday "in the teeth of considerable difficulties," showing "the true scholar's passion for the pursuit of knowledge."[4]

But it was to no avail. Muriel remained at the margins of elite academic life. Darbishire was on her side, but she struggled to attract other necessary patrons. The literary scholar Percy Simpson, for example, thanked her for her work tutoring his students, but he hesitated at writing her a reference, since he said he knew only a few aspects of her research. The legacy of that struggle can be glimpsed in her decision, decades later, to leave money in her will for a scholarship for Somerville students, like herself, who had not received a first-class honors degree but were nonetheless cut out for academic research.[5]

By 1920, Muriel found herself restless. Bar reached out to their mentor Darbishire, explaining that Muriel was "bothered with sleeplessness again, brought on by worry." Darbishire, on holiday in Rome, wrote immediately and at length to Muriel. "I don't want to speak as a preacher or teacher (that you know) but only as a friend, man to man," she wrote. "You are chafing in some way or other against life. If you could accept it with your spirit, the restlessness would cease." Darbishire reminded Muriel of the importance of the good salary she was earning as a teacher, which "relieves your financial anxiety in regard to your mother," who seems to have been living with Muriel at this stage. It also "means immense spiritual gain for yourself & also for Marjorie," opening the way for both of them to enjoy things like "music, drama, going abroad, getting good holidays." Research and writing alone would never pay the bills. If she truly could not accept her situation cheerfully, and was still troubled with sleeplessness, she ought to consult a doctor.[6]

Muriel's reply doesn't survive, but she made it clear that she could no longer tolerate schoolteaching. Darbishire thanked her for explaining "exactly how things stand," and agreed that she ought to quit her teaching job at the end of the school year. Indeed, Darbishire now advised that she adopt the philosophy, "My life is in my own hands. No one & no thing can make me do what my mind & spirit tell me not to do." If Muriel kept at the research and worked toward the DPhil degree, Darbishire hoped she'd get a university lecturing post eventually, though she warned this was far from certain. She advised, once more, that Muriel see a doctor about the insomnia, since mental and physical troubles "are absolutely interpenetrated & interpenetrating." Muriel's task, from the summer of 1921, was to salvage her mental state while continuing to meet the demands of family responsibility—and to find a way to turn her abilities to something other than teaching adolescents.[7]

Muriel was with her mother when she died at the Florence Nightingale Hospital on Lisson Grove on February 21, 1923, aged fifty-five. She buried her in St. Marylebone Cemetery, under a granite Celtic cross. The following month, Muriel arranged to be buried in the same plot herself, when the time came. As her family duties eased, her professional options became clearer. That same year, she began lecturing at the Royal Academy of Dramatic Art (RADA) in London on English poetics and the history of drama and Shakespeare. This affiliation would continue until 1955. She supplemented this with occasional substitute lecturing at Bedford College, a women's college in London. As a lecturer, she was remembered "for her stylish delivery (and appearance) as well as her power of making the past live; and her generous, spontaneous interest in the work of beginners in the field," which "soon tempered the sense of awe at her expert knowledge." Muriel would never be a university don. Instead, she fashioned a career that stitched together temporary or casual teaching with historical research and writing that, although it was grounded in serious study, was aimed at a far wider audience.[8]

BAR AND MURIEL shared their lives on every level. Muriel's appointment diaries trace the outlines of Bar's life, too. They had joint finances, reflected in their complex system of loans and repayments of fairly small amounts to settle their accounts. They celebrated their birthdays and took holidays together: Bruges, Dijon, Provence. If they visited the interwar lesbian nightlife in Paris, or the clubs in Soho that welcomed queer patrons, however, their diaries remain silent on the subject.[9]

They created a shared home in their rented London flats. In one of her short stories, Bar offers a glimpse of this environment, as seen through the eyes of a high school girl. Dulcie adores her English teacher, Miss Dryden, who opens to Dulcie an intellectual world that "stretched as far as Greece and Rome" and has its capital in Stratford-upon-Avon. Its emotional center, though, is the flat that Miss Dryden shares with the history mistress, where "the casual arrangement of dark wood, polished floors and cream walls, the tawny curtains and blue chair covers, the tulips in pottery jars, the Medici prints, above all the shelves of books had in themselves provided a new horizon." This, surely, is Bar's world as she would like it to be seen. The home she shared with Muriel is conjured as a bastion of welcome and erudition, its style reflecting an educated, modern alternative to traditional Victorian clutter while also evoking a distinctly queer domesticity.[10]

They shared this home with pets, doting on them and commemorating them with photographs and poems. Bar wrote a poem dedicated to "the luckiest cat alive." It lists various reasons why the cat is so fortunate in his life of ease and comfort, culminating with, "You're lucky, cat, in that you own / Two such charming mothers." Their papers include a 1925 book of advice for cat lovers with handwritten notes about veterinary care and local chemists who supplied feline medicines. One can only hope that the handwritten recipe for "stomach trouble" involving egg white, brandy, sugar, and water, to be administered every three hours, was calming to the owners as well as to the cat.[11]

NEITHER MURIEL NOR Bar, nor DLS, D. Rowe, or Charis, ever labeled her own sexual identity, at least not in the documents that have survived, using a modern label for gender or sexuality—straight, lesbian, heterosexual, transgender—or older sexological or cultural labels such as invert, sapphist, or New Woman. None of them directly described their sexual practices or desires, either. Their lives, however, tell eloquent stories about the diversity of the choices they made. Charis and DLS both married men and had children, though Charis followed a far more traditional trajectory. D. Rowe never married and seems to have remained single throughout her life. She was also a free spirit, moving frequently within Bournemouth, flirting casually and cultivating a reputation for eccentricity. Members of the MAS transgressed expectations, too, in terms of gender expression, adopting masculine nicknames and male prerogatives in various ways at different times. In some respects, it would be possible to argue that they each lived a queer life, in that they refused neat categories and pushed beyond the boundaries of feminine womanhood in twentieth-century Britain.[12]

Muriel, however, is distinct. Her life offers a glimpse into the domestic and personal realities of a household headed by two women living in a marriage-like commitment to one another, at a very particular moment of transition. Such households were accepted in Victorian Britain, provided certain norms of discretion and decorum were maintained. By the mid-twentieth century, a distinct lesbian identity would emerge. In the years of Muriel's early adulthood, then, such same-sex relationships were in a state of flux and subject to new scrutiny.

Relationships between older women and younger women, especially between students and teachers, were particularly pathologized. Relationships between two equal women operated in a different cultural zone: accepted in some respects, even as references to sex between women were subject to profound anxiety and silencing. Sex between women was not specifically prohibited by law, though it had attracted legal punishment in various ways. In 1921, an amendment that would have outlawed sex between women was introduced in Parliament—though its proponents never intended it to be passed. Its purpose was to kill the bill to which it was attached, and it was successful in that. Outlawing lesbian sex would have broken the enforced official silence around it, and some in Parliament even argued that passing such a prohibition would introduce the concept of lesbian sex to English women. They were, of course, much too late. Lesbian sex was at the center of several different scandals in the 1920s, most famously the obscenity trial over the 1928 novel *The Well of Loneliness*, by Radclyffe Hall, which narrates the unhappy life and loves of a masculine "invert" who was roughly Muriel's contemporary.[13]

Despite its cultural salience, *The Well of Loneliness* was not the only British novel in this era to address lesbianism. In the 1927 Lord Peter Wimsey novel *Unnatural Death*, DLS distinguishes between different sorts of same-sex relationships. The murder plot hinges on the character of seductive, manipulative Mary Whittaker, who corrupts a much younger woman. Yet

the novel also depicts the domestic contentment of a long-term female couple, one more masculine and one more feminine, who are a part of the fab-
ric of their rural English community. This couple is much more typical of
the women in same-sex relationships in the Wimsey novels. In 1928, DLS
claimed to her collaborator Dr. Eustace Barton that "inverts make me creep,"
using the contemporary sexological language for someone who is both homosexual and expresses gender in a way that does not match their socially
assigned category. Perhaps there is a vestigial measure of defensiveness about
her own unfeminine aspects here, or perhaps she did not want to reveal her
friends' personal lives to her collaborator. In any case, her overall body of
work and her friendships suggest that such an opinion about "inverts," if
it was genuinely held, did not survive the late 1920s intact. Beginning in
Strong Poison (1930), DLS created the recurring characters Eiluned and Sylvia, friends of Harriet Vane, who seem more or less a couple along the lines
of Muriel and Bar. In *The Five Red Herrings* (1931), set in a fictionalized version of Kirkcudbright, the Scottish village where DLS and Mac spent their
holidays, Miss Selby and Miss Cochrane are Wimsey's neighbors. In real life,
the artist Dorothy Johnstone lived with her then-partner Vera "Jack" Holme
in Kirkcudbright in 1919 and was part of a network of female artists there.
Though there is no firm evidence that DLS knew them, they, or couples like
them, might have inspired these characters.[14]

Jim Jaeger wrote sympathetically about homosexuality and gender
transgression. In a 1936 play, a character is shocked when she realizes that
one of her colleagues, "the sanest, most generous person I ever worked with,"
has a same-sex lover. She'd thought "that sort of thing" was "wrong and
unhealthy," and "associated with rackety studio parties and cocktails and
women masquerading as men—and all the rest of it." But she comes to realize that this woman actually is much happier and more balanced than most
other people, and as a result a better person. In another book, Jim praised
the French novelist George Sand, urging the reader to accept Sand's own explanation for her decision to dress as a man—that it was more comfortable
and convenient.[15]

Muriel would explore the issue of her own cross-gender identification
later, in her 1942 memoir. She and Bar touched only lightly on the subject
of homosexuality in their writing. In her teaching notes, Muriel argued that
Charlotte Brontë wrote to her friend Ellen Nussey with "the very ardour of
a lover," though she concluded that this did not necessarily suggest a sexual

connection. In a draft play, Muriel mentioned homosexuality in order to criticize excessive parental dominance. Isn't it "inconsistent," one character suggests, to praise possessive parents but "ostracize the love-perversions dealt with in Leviticus"? She consistently used the second person in her poetry in order to express her romantic impulses: not he or she, but you. She wrote of "your hand, slender and strong," for example, and "your hair, just stirring in the cool night breeze." Another poem hinted at the burden of silence around desire. "If I owned the earth . . . I could then say the thing / Of my heart's unburdening,—/ Have words of joy and might / To sing of you aright." Bar was more direct in her poetry. Held in thrall by a violinist, "I only know I loved her while she played." Another poem imagined an encounter between the narrator and a maiden, which could be an encounter with a lover or with the self: "half of me she was, / I half of her—so we were mingled." Muriel's poems tended to proceed in the chivalrous mode—the knight and the lady, the lover and the beloved. Bar's vision was more expansive. She wrote, in 1924, about her pleasure walking with two others. "A golden spell held the hearts of us / And bound them with tender witchery." In real life, Muriel's attachment to more than one woman would challenge Bar's sense of herself and her relationship. But that was in the future.[16]

GROUNDED IN HER life with Bar, Muriel began, in the mid 1920s, to find her voice as a historian. Muriel had written since childhood, entranced from the start by the extravagant language of sprawling heroic epics. "I had the gadzookery of it at my finger-tips." Beginning in 1925, she put that gadzookery to the serious task of conveying the texture of the past to a modern audience. That year saw the publication of her first major book, *Elizabethan Life in Town and Country*. Bar compiled the index, read the proofs, and provided, in Muriel's words, the "continuous help which made it possible to carry through the work on top of ordinary duties." Her mentor, the scholar Alfred Pollard, helped too, reading the book in manuscript.[17]

Elizabethan Life situates Muriel squarely in two of the major currents of popular history writing in the interwar decades. First, there was a widespread revival of interest in the Tudor era. Films such as *The Private Life of Henry VIII*, directed by Alexander Korda, are an example of this, turning the famous king into a modern celebrity to be consumed and enjoyed by a mass audience. Like many of her contemporaries, Muriel was fascinated by both Elizabeth I and her father Henry VIII. In *Elizabethan Life*, she described the queen as "a naturally gifted and extremely well-educated young woman, with all her father's charm of personality, who had been schooled and disciplined for over ten years" by "bitter experience." Though she would never have made the comparison in print, these words could apply equally well to Muriel at this stage of her life.[18]

Second, *Elizabethan Life* was concerned with "the daily life of ordinary people." Some of the best-selling history books in the interwar years were volumes from *A History of Everyday Things in England*, a series published between 1918 and 1934 by husband-and-wife team Charles and Marjorie Quennell. These books came from a liberal, middle-class outlook, and they were founded on the idea that readers should be able to encounter the past directly through ordinary objects. Muriel's book, too, covered a dazzling area of topics, from mousetraps to labor legislation that recognized the need for a midday nap. She drew on both historical documents and literature, placing a special emphasis on the personal writing and diaries of women, which had not been fully valued by scholars.[19]

That same year, she also published a reprint of educational writings by two French Huguenot teachers who worked in Elizabethan London. Here, again, Muriel's interest was in the vivid, humorous, everyday details of Elizabethan life: the "thick-headed" young man who keeps passing the bread by hand even though it isn't polite, for example, or the acerbic comment of the Frenchman: "they say commonly in England that God sendeth us meat and the Devil cooks!" There was evidently a market for this sort of thing. The first limited edition of these educational dialogues soon sold out, and a subsequent expanded edition was brought out in 1930. In 1926, Muriel edited a limited edition of reprinted extracts from an Elizabethan naturalist's works, under the title *The Elizabethan Zoo*. The extracts represent both real and mythical animals. Only in this way, Muriel argues, can the reader get an authentic sample of Elizabethan zoology, in which "superstition and fact, myth and observation are all inextricably mingled," and unicorns are real "while the cat and its habits are described with real accuracy."[20]

These books, with their plethora of detail, delight the reader with the contrast between the familiar and the strange as everyday people of the past describe their daily lives. Such details, Muriel argued, were crucial in allowing ordinary people of the present to understand their own history. "An Elizabethan portrait often holds us at a distance," but the records of daily life

reveal "people who lose brooches and wear their shoes out. These are people we know." In reviewing other works of popular history, Muriel argued
that this was the goal of the genre. In addition to vivid writing and rigorous
accuracy, it was, above all, necessary to bring historical figures to life for
the modern reader. As Muriel put it, "The historian to whom the ordinary
reader's heart warms is the one who assumes that behind and beyond the
documents and dates are real people, with temperaments, nerves, and bents
of mind, who make mistakes, and generally function like human beings."[21]

Writing about domestic lives for a popular audience was a way for women
to write saleable history in this era. But Muriel went beyond the limits of the
genre, arguing that everyday life ultimately revealed the most fundamental cultural and political transformations. To do this, she delved ever more
deeply into personal correspondence and diaries. Often, this meant looking
at the words of overlooked women. Anne Bacon, the mother of philosopher
Sir Francis Bacon, for example, "left us a bundle of explosive correspondence
which gives an extraordinarily vivid idea of her personality." Elizabethan
women, Muriel argued, were "vigorous, masterful women; strange, assertive,
dominating women," even as they lurk, "secret and smug as cats . . . half-
hidden behind their silent and purposeful impenetrability."[22]

In 1932, Muriel made a discovery that would alter the course of her career. She had been making her way through the letters of King Henry VIII
for an edited collection of his correspondence—when she came across something else. "We invite our fate. Mine was waiting for me," she wrote later.
In the stacks of Tudor letters held by the Public Record Office, she found
the collection belonging to Arthur Plantagenet, Lord Lisle. Far more than a
political correspondence, here, at last, was the perfect expression of "the lost
moment that was Tudor England." Interviewed decades later, she explained,
"I must say I wasn't looking for a life's work. . . . But I was caught . . ." She
would spend the next four decades, on and off, working her way through
these letters, producing an edited collection that remains a standard reference work in early modern English history. Although she relied on the professional context and mentorship of male scholars, especially Alfred Pollard
and W. P. Kerr, she also credited the Victorian ladies who produced collections of letters from old records with inspiring the project.[23]

Popular histories that reintroduced English people to their Tudor forebears, while also emphasizing daily life and ordinary objects, reflect the
sometimes opposing interwar impulses toward modern democracy and

national nostalgia. As Bar's story suggested, Stratford-upon-Avon was the capital of the MAS's cultural universe, signifying the golden age of English achievement. But Muriel was never interested only in celebrating past great-ness. Unable to secure a career as an academic, she instead wrote history that was both rigorous and popular. She wanted to make an era defined by the towering figures of English history—Elizabeth I, Shakespeare—accessible to ordinary people by illuminating its everyday life, from the minor hilarities of foreign-language teaching to the quotidian letters out of which Elizabethan literature would blossom. In doing so, she crafted an argument that ordi-nary lives and mundane words are, in fact, the very stuff of history, which, taken together, produce the grand movements worthy of admiration and nostalgia.[24]

Part 3

Head and Heart, 1929–1939

9

DEPARTURES AND REUNIONS

N THE DECADE AFTER WORLD War I, the members of the Mutual Admiration Society had embarked on individual struggles to establish independent, self-sustaining lives. The pressures of work and family duties preoccupied them; the burdens of shame, too, created barriers where easy intimacy had once flourished. DLS, caught up in a series of unfortunate love affairs and then a pregnancy, felt burdened by the secrets she had to keep from her friends. Muriel struggled under the weight of financial responsibilities and the need to make a life while not compromising too much on the kind of work she wanted to do. D. Rowe was absorbed back into her Bournemouth life and her work as a teacher. And Charis gave birth to four children while launching a career as a public authority on motherhood. Then, something remarkable happened: they came back together. For varied reasons and in varied ways, Charis, D. Rowe, DLS, and Muriel renewed their connections with one another in the years right around 1930. By then, of course, they'd made other friends and alliances as well. But the reunited MAS produced extraordinary results. As a group, they provided one another with the stability and space that allowed for more honest and vulnerable work—or, to put it another way, that allowed them to take the risk of putting head and heart together, instead of separating them in the service of mere survival.

The reunited MAS was a smaller group than the original. Tony Godfrey, Amphilis Middlemore, and Jim Jaeger had been central to the MAS at Oxford but would fall out of its orbit more or less permanently. Others, such as Margaret (Chubb) Pyke or Diana Whitwill, who had been brief or peripheral parts of the MAS, also remained in only occasional contact. Charis and

Margaret Pyke were distant colleagues in the larger birth control and family planning movement, for instance, and Diana Whitwill came to Charis's house during World War II and heard a play by DLS on the radio. But these ties were looser and more haphazard.

Tony Godfrey and Muriel St. Clare Byrne collaborated on a published history of Somerville, but after her husband Francis Turquand Mansfield's death in January 1922, Tony seems to have lost touch with the members of the MAS. Although she appears briefly in various records—she might have had a daughter with Francis, she was briefly engaged to someone else, and she seems to have traveled with her father and lived to an old age—she disappears, too, from our story.[1]

Amphilis Middlemore briefly had the most conventional academic career of the group. She taught English at Worcester High School from 1918 to 1920, but then moved to the United States to teach English at Bryn Mawr College from 1920 to 1922 and then at Swarthmore College. While teaching at Swarthmore, Amphilis began graduate work in English at the University of Pennsylvania. She had never taken her degree from Oxford, having never completed one of the required examinations, but with the assistance of Swarthmore's president, she convinced the authorities at the University of Pennsylvania that this was more a formality than anything reflecting the seriousness of what she'd accomplished. The plea worked, but you can almost see Emily Penrose shaking her head: this was precisely what her policy of requiring Somerville students to complete all examinations had been designed to prevent. But Amphilis had left partway through her time at Somerville and returned as a home student, so she eluded Penrose's supervision.[2]

In the United States, Amphilis was a voice of England for her students. She taught English literature, including specialized courses on poetry and nineteenth-century prose. Returning home frequently in the summers, she brought back firsthand information about politics and society. In March 1922, she directed and acted in two plays put on by the Bryn Mawr faculty to raise money for victims of the famine in Russia. In one, set in England, she played a "kitchen maid of unbeautiful aspect and romantic leanings," complete with cockney accent. She insisted on the importance of intellectual people, telling one YWCA group that "they are giving something to the world that no one else can." She was also, it seems, a somewhat absent-minded professor. Jokingly, the Swarthmore student yearbook suggested that her New Year's Resolution should be "to comb her hair at least once a day."[3]

In the spring of 1926, Amphilis fell ill with what the doctor at first thought was typhoid fever, though apparently it was measles. She was initially confined for two weeks. But in early May a temporary replacement was appointed to cover her classes for the rest of the year. Later that spring, Amphilis returned to England, sailing from New York to Southampton and arriving on June 11, 1926. By the end of summer, she was still too ill to return to the United States for start of the 1926–1927 school year. Was it the aftereffects of the measles, or something more? In a personal letter to the Swarthmore president, Amphilis wrote, "I am so very sorry to fail you in this way. I have asked my doctor to write & explain the situation to you & all I can do now is to apologise very sincerely," adding that she was sure he did not "want an inefficient teacher around." It seems possible, again, that mental illness can be read between these lines. She did return in the summer of 1927. But in April 1928, after just one academic year back, she tendered her resignation as instructor of English at Swarthmore, offering her "affectionate thanks for the pleasant years that I have spent here." She remained until the end of term and arrived back in England in mid-July 1928.[4]

Amphilis Middlemore died on July 18, 1931. She fell from a window at St. John and St. Elizabeth Hospital in London, and the inquest held two days later found that she died by suicide while of unsound mind. She was forty years old. Following the will she'd made in 1929, most of her estate went to various relatives, with a walnut cabinet left to a friend in London and an emerald and diamond ring left to a friend at Swarthmore. In an interview in 1977, Charis recalled Amphilis as "a delightful person who died before she finished at college, she went down and she died soon afterwards." Time is foreshortened in Charis's memory, collapsing Amphilis's sudden departure from Somerville in 1914 and her tragic death seventeen years later. It underscores the sense of rupture Charis felt when Amphilis left Somerville, as well as the way that Amphilis's subsequent career and final illness brought her firmly outside of her old friend network.[5]

Jim Jaeger, by contrast, stayed in the same geographical and professional realms as the other members of the MAS, and their paths crossed or neared at several points over the subsequent decades. Like the others, Jim wrote novels, essays, and plays that tried to make sense of issues relating to mass democracy and the place of ideas and culture in the modern world. But she was not a part of the core group of the MAS after the early 1920s.

Jim seems to have returned to Yorkshire for a long stretch of time beginning around October 1922, unable, due to lack of money and ill health, perhaps, to keep making a go of it in London. The rural life might have suited her better—D. Rowe noted that Jim "does like pigs and ducks and weekends in the country better than me." DLS's first novel, *Whose Body?*, is dedicated to Jim: "if it had not been for your brutal insistence, Lord Peter would never have staggered through to the end of this enquiry." DLS visited North Yorkshire with Jim in the summer of 1924. There, DLS enjoyed good food and long walks while scouting locations for the next Wimsey novel, *Clouds of Witness*, which is partly set at Wimsey's brother's hunting lodge in the area. But after this, their friendship seems to have lapsed.[6]

This holiday happened only a few months after the birth of DLS's son. Did she confide in Jim and receive an unwelcome, perhaps unforgiveable, reaction? One of DLS's biographers has suggested that Jim might have expressed romantic feelings for DLS. By 1924, though, they'd been good friends for a dozen years—rather late in the day for such a revelation. They stayed in some kind of contact after the holiday, though no further letters survive between them. In December 1925, DLS mentioned in a letter to her mother that "Jim Jaeger is having a book published in January—all the best people seem to publish them!" Jim herself had received the offer from the publisher only in late September, so DLS was still relatively up-to-date with Jim's news, whether at first- or secondhand. Discussing homosexuality and "introverts," DLS later told a collaborator that she'd had a friend "who was rather that way—a very fine person of powerful intellect" who now refused to see her "because marriage revolts her." If this is indeed a reference to Jim, it could be, then, that DLS's conduct with men in general, or perhaps her marriage to Mac Fleming specifically, was the source of the rupture. Or, perhaps, the friendship simply faded.[7]

As a writer, Jim Jaeger produced a diverse body of work—novels, history, essays, and plays. Her early novels were published by the Hogarth Press, run by Virginia and Leonard Woolf, and were experiments in the relatively new genre of science fiction. Her 1926 novel *The Question Mark*, which may have influenced Aldous Huxley's *Brave New World*, grappled with the problem of the socialist utopia. Ultimately it is a commentary on the dangers of any attempt to isolate the intellectual from the ordinary and a plea for friendship rather than adherence to doctrine. It imagines a future in which the ever-widening gap between the "intellectuals" and the "normals" is a source of agonizing personal pain. This would be a theme throughout Jaeger's career: how to build a better world without replicating, or even worsening, the problems of intellectual and social hierarchy that blighted the present.[8]

Although she would work as a journalist, reviewer, and publisher's reader, in addition to publishing novels, plays, and some enduring works of history, Jim never achieved the renown accorded to DLS or Muriel St. Clare Byrne. Although she worked with the same literary agency that they did, her publishers struggled to make her books commercially viable. Even more galling, they suggested that she ought to draw on her old connection to DLS—by asking her for a blurb, for instance, or even by writing her own "analytical Detective Story" in the style of her erstwhile friend. Still, Jim's preoccupations and interests often echoed those of DLS. Her 1933 quasi-mystery novel *Hermes Speaks*, for example, is concerned with the power of unscrupulous schemers to manipulate the masses. The novel is no match for the Wimsey stories in complexity and execution—indeed, the reader probably guesses the solution well before the slightly hapless protagonist does. But its preoccupation with modern methods of duping the public can be read alongside DLS's own *Murder Must Advertise*, published two years later. A draft novel, "Murder at Hangerden," was, perhaps, Jim's attempt to write that analytical detective story; it skewers the pretensions of overactive local bureaucracies in a small town, but was never published.[9]

Jim's subsequent life drew her near to other MAS members occasionally, suggesting that the rupture with DLS did not wholly isolate her from the rest of the group. She and D. Rowe worked together on theater in the 1930s. In January 1933, the Bournemouth Little Theatre's repertory company produced a play by Jim—titled for production *The Sanderson Syndicate*, though published as *The Sanderson Soviet*. The play focuses on the four Sanderson children, who are engaged in a constant competition to curry favor with their father and assure their inheritance. At one point, one of the siblings advises another not to count on her friends: "one's friends are quick enough to chuck one back at one's family as soon as one shows signs of becoming a nuisance." Is there a hint, here, of Jim's own experience? Did she feel chucked back onto her family by unsympathetic friends during her run of illness, injury, and patchy employment in the early 1920s? Maybe. But D. Rowe was a stalwart friend and critic after the *Sanderson* production, reading drafts of plays and other work by Jim and by her brother Bernard, and providing lengthy commentary on them. Although D. Rowe brought other work by Jim before her theater's selection committee, no more productions seem to have transpired, and their correspondence trails off in the mid-1930s.[10]

Jim dedicated her most enduring book, a study of changing social mores entitled *Before Victoria*, and published in 1956, to Somerville classmate and onetime MAS member Margaret Pyke, calling her its "first reader and friendly critic." Beyond that, no further traces of connections between Jim and the MAS survive. Jim Jaeger died on November 21, 1969, in Royal Tunbridge Wells, leaving most of her estate to her siblings, apart from small bequests to two friends, and requesting that her personal papers be burned.[11]

IN 1929, THE members of the MAS were in their mid-thirties. Their lives and work had pulled them in different directions. Around this time, though, D. Rowe, Charis, DLS, and Muriel all reconnected with one another. In their reunions, their shared holidays, and their resurrection of their writers' community, they consolidated friendships that would last for the rest of their lives.

DLS's personal life underwent a series of shifts in the late 1920s. Her parents died—her father in 1928, and her mother in 1929. She and Mac moved into the house she'd bought for her mother, in the small town of Witham in Essex, though she also retained the lease on her London flat. Amid all this upheaval, reviving her connections with her friends was an important first step toward writing more dimensional, convincing literature. Back in 1925, DLS had wondered if the trouble with her writing was that it wasn't "very close to her heart." Four years on, she would find the ability to put her heart back into her work.[12]

Sometime in 1928 or very early in 1929, DLS reached out to Charis. She no longer needed help finding a place to foster John Anthony, who would grow up in Ivy Shrimpton's home, though he was informally adopted by Mac Fleming in 1933. She did, however, want advice on getting reliable birth control. Charis put her in touch with Dr. Helena Wright, a prominent doctor and friend of Dr. Marie Stopes, as well as the author of a sex advice manual. As DLS rather laconically put it: "by the way, many thanks for your suggestion with regard to the woman doctor etc. Dr Wright was very nice, and fixed me up quite satisfactorily. So that's that."[13]

Charis, in return, pressed DLS to attend that year's Somerville Gaudy. Oxford colleges hold feasts at the end of the academic year for their alumni; these celebrations have the nickname "Gaudy." DLS was tempted, telling Mac, "I think I must go to the Gaudy this year." "Certainly," he replied "why not." But, nine years after she had earned her degree, returning to Oxford had become a fraught ordeal for DLS. She confessed to Charis that she had delayed actually writing to make the arrangements. "It's one of those deep inner repugnances that the psycho-analysts are always talking about. I don't *really* want to go." Returning to past locations, rekindling old connections—these things threatened to stir up emotion on a subconscious level. DLS told Charis that she hated looking back, nostalgia, the whole business. She didn't want to think about her past self, or to be encouraged to feel sentimental in the company of her former companions. "I like for instance, to see you and D. Rowe, because you are both people whose company is in itself delightful—but, my God! a collegeful of people with whom I have no other bond than that we once were all there together!" Even if she went, "everybody will say that I am just as intolerable as I was fifteen years ago—and with every justification! I *am*!!" At the end of the letter, DLS told Charis that she had finally written to Somerville to request a room for the reunion. "I will sing the song. I will even sit on the floor and talk jolly. But I will not drink cocoa. There are limits."[14]

DLS would dramatize her feelings in her most beloved novel, *Gaudy Night*. In that novel, Harriet Vane, also a detective novelist, is oppressed by the idea of her former classmates and tutors seeing her through the lens of the scandal that had threatened to engulf her life. She feels a rising sense of dread as she drives toward Oxford from her London flat. The increasingly familiar countryside and roads spark not nostalgia or joy, but anxiety and shame. If DLS followed her promise to Charis and attended the 1929 Gaudy, she might have felt the same churning stomach, reminding her of the gap between the promise of her degree and the complex realities of her life.

At the 1929 Gaudy, held on the first weekend of July, merrymakers dined well on salmon mayonnaise, roast duck, lamb, peas, and new potatoes. The dessert, strawberry ice pudding, echoed both the season and the sweet joys of childhood and adolescence. They heard toasts by principal Margery Fry, Professor Gilbert Murray, and the vice-chancellor. Muriel's commemorative program for the evening is signed by Bar, D. Rowe, and Margaret Pyke, among others—but not, it seems, by DLS, who, if she did attend, perhaps thought signing souvenir programs was as bad as cocoa.[15]

DLS had dreaded rejection and mockery at the Somerville gaudy. Instead, in returning to her alma mater, whether that summer or a bit later, she rediscovered the importance of the MAS. *Gaudy Night* celebrates that rediscovery. Surrounded once more by her old friends, Vane begins, at last, to thaw and to trust in other people. The novel's true hero is the community of women who make the college what it is. In the book's denouement, Lord Peter Wimsey pays tribute to "the remarkable solidarity and public spirit displayed by your college as a body." He links that solidarity to intellectual integrity. Early on in the case, he established that "there was not a woman in this Common Room, married or single, who would be ready to place personal loyalties above professional honour." Thanks to that solidarity and integrity, Vane's alma mater weathers serious peril, while Vane, and perhaps DLS as well, is restored to her community and able to balance head and heart at last.[16]

BEYOND GAUDIES, THE members of the MAS began spending more time together. Muriel's diary records regular visits with both D. Rowe and DLS, sometimes around the time of the January meetings of the Somerville Association of Senior Members (the alumnae association) in London, but also weekends and dinners and teas and Shakespeare plays at other times. In January 1931, DLS, D. Rowe, and Muriel all had tea together, nearly a Mutual Admiration Society reunion.[17]

Muriel St. Clare Byrne dressed as a sailor (MSBC)

Muriel, Bar, D. Rowe, and, often, D. Rowe's sister Bena began spending August holidays together on the south coast, often in Stoke Fleming, Devon. On one level, these were classic beach holidays. There was the search for a good bungalow to rent, with "the right kind of oil-stove, flat beds, real armchairs, good thick carpets." There was leisurely tourism as well as lazy days on the beach. In Cornwall in 1931, Muriel and Bar were joined by D. Rowe and Bena, and Muriel's diary records visits to Tintagel and nearby villages. It also contains the delicious entry, for August 5, "All day on beach. Sun bathe."[18]

In between the sunbathing and the touring, these holidays were a time of creative renewal. Decades later, D. Rowe would write to Muriel, "Never do I forget our lovely times at Stoke Fleming and our excursions, bathes, backchat, front-chat on Shakespeare and all the other joys we had with you and Bar. . . . Such things are imperishable." Neither D. Rowe, nor Muriel, nor Bar became a poet, beyond the occasional poem published in a magazine or newspaper and Muriel's early volume with Blackwell, but they wrote a great deal of poetry and shared it with each other. These holidays by the sea recreated the combination of intimacy and creativity that they had enjoyed at Somerville. In August 1929, at Stoke Fleming, D. Rowe wrote a poem entitled "Record E.489 (Chorale from Cantata No. 147, Bach)." It imagines a prince coming forth to "speak consolation and the intents of love." Beyond the obvious religious analogy, the poem conjures the Stoke Fleming scene: the sense of being in nature but also surrounded by culture, music, and conversation that provided a context of friendship, love, and perhaps a consolation for the realities of working life.[19]

Muriel helped D. Rowe to collect her poems, seemingly with an eye to eventual publication, though there's no evidence this ever happened. At one point, D. Rowe sent Muriel a list of poems that she'd written, including ones that had appeared in Oxford magazines, suggesting that the project as a whole was imagined as a kind of lifetime retrospective. It is clear, though, that many of the poems had been written more recently, perhaps in the enthusiastic glow of the Stoke Fleming holidays.[20]

In a sense, these poems represent D. Rowe's reckoning with her own artistic presence. They exude an enthusiasm for life: for the sounds, sights, and textures of the world, particularly the natural world, and for the power of ideas. They are also grounded in the daily life of a provincial teacher. One poem is written on the back of an examination paper for trade scholarships in September 1930. Another poem, "In the National Gallery," is more a fantasy about that place of high culture than a real encounter with it. She sent a draft of this poem to Muriel and admitted some uneasiness about the line that refers to the National Gallery being "twelve steps above Trafalgar Square." Of the twelve steps, she confessed, "I haven't counted them, but no more could Wordsworth have seen that there were exactly 10,000 daffodils at a glance."

And then, even more uncertainly, "I hope it *is* in Trafalgar Square!" In "For a Diary," D. Rowe was frank about the challenges of working long days to earn a living. The all-consuming work provided little scope for poetic inspiration.

> How many days go by
> That I behold
> No dawn-star in the sky
> Nor eve of gold,
> But from my bed
> To toil go, heavy-hearted,
> And raise my head
> To find the light departed.[21]

Muriel, too, thought about the relationship between work and inspiration in the poetry she wrote around this time. How to balance intense emotions with daily duties? In August 1930, she published a poem that wryly summons the imagery of the historical researcher, only to suggest that even in the dullest work, true inspiration is possible. She's comfortable enough, her mind in its "book-lined groove," where it enjoyed "adequate lighting, silence, and ink." There, she produced "many quarto pages, evenly written / All the footnotes included, references verified." This is drudgery, until "suddenly, a word flowers, and the senses, smitten, / Rise from their death, insurgent," pushing the poem and the historian at last toward intellectual and romantic consummation. Another poem from the same year uses shipbuilding as a metaphor for gallantry in love. That choice was personally resonant for Muriel, whose grandfather designed ships. In the poem, she equates her grandfather's work with wood and her own work with words. "I would build you my song as men build a ship, / Had I the skill; / A gracious, swift, high-hearted, gallant thing / To match your will."[22]

If trying to write meaningful poetry while earning a living was difficult, what was the alternative? DLS and Muriel both wrote for wider audiences, one way to square that circle. Bar contributed to this conversation with a poem humorously evoking the dangers of leaving one's lonely garret in order to write more popular work. In "Lucifer: a Moral Tale," Bar imagines a starving poet who decides to advertise his services as a poet for hire. He hangs a brass plate on his door and places advertisements in newspapers: "saying 'Follow the fashion! / Be patrons of passion! / Just write for free sample! No subject I bar!'" Soon, business is thriving, and, rather like Lord Peter Wimsey, he's enjoying "a flat with a butler, a cat, and a parrot." But all is not as it seems. He's haunted by dreams that suggest he has betrayed his calling. The poem has a cheerful, if heavy-handed, ending. He dies suddenly, but in heaven his fate is simply "to sing for his Muse in an Attic once more." Be careful what you wish for, Bar warns: the work itself is what matters, and the trappings of success a mere distraction.[23]

DLS WOULD JOIN these summer gatherings later in the 1930s. First, however, she had to reestablish friendships that had atrophied. Muriel recalled that she had only learned of DLS's marriage to Mac Fleming in a roundabout way when she invited DLS to the production of a play she'd written and got no reply. "Some time later I received a letter from her to say she had only just got mine, they had got married and were spending their honeymoon driving all over Kirkcudbrightshire while she was busy collecting local colour and accurate location information for the Five Red Herrings." DLS invited her to dinner, promising Mac's excellent cooking, though in fact, Muriel recalled, DLS made the meal. "But I found Mac very debonair and charming, and they seemed happy together."[24]

There is much about this account that is questionable: for one thing, Muriel remembers it all happening in September 1928, though DLS and Mac actually married in 1926. Moreover, the letter that Muriel mentions was written later. In October 1930, DLS wrote apologetically to Muriel from Kirkcudbright, explaining that she'd misplaced Muriel's address and proposing that they get together when she returned to London. She and Mac had spent most of the summer in Scotland, while she finished *The Five Red Herrings*, "full of Scotch scenery and real railway time-tables." Muriel's memory telescopes these events, but she accurately recalls the relative distance between them at this stage. They were in touch, having the occasional dinner or tea, but they were not particularly close.[25]

Over the course of the early 1930s, this began to change, as DLS and Muriel forged new bonds of intellectual and personal connection that would become a fruitful long-term collaboration. DLS brought Muriel into her professional network, where an interest in the Tudors frequently provided the initial link. Most importantly, perhaps, DLS introduced Muriel to her close friend Helen Simpson, who had just published a biography of Henry VIII. In her review of Simpson's book, Muriel wrote admiringly of Simpson's ability to write intellectually demanding history for a wide public. "Her book may be meant for a popular audience, but she demands in her reader the adult mind." The three would remain friends and embark on a joint project together at the start of World War II. DLS also introduced Muriel to her literary agent, Nancy Pearn, who invited both Muriel and Helen Simpson to a Queen Elizabeth–themed party she held in 1934. Occasional dinners became regular ones, which sometimes stretched into weekends. On her fortieth birthday—June 13, 1933—DLS dined with Muriel. In a letter from April 1934, Bar was still "Miss Barber" to DLS. Yet the same spring, one of Muriel's friends ended a letter to her with "Love to you both & always to DLS if she's within hail," suggesting that Muriel and Bar, too, were incorporating DLS thoroughly into their world.[26]

DLS and Muriel discussed their current projects: DLS's never-finished biography of Wilkie Collins, Muriel's arguments with her publishers. They respected each other's expertise, while serving as the ideal educated audience for each other's work. DLS brought Muriel to Detection Club annual dinners, even asking her to speak, in 1934, from the point of view of an ordinary reader who could describe what she liked in detective stories and what she loathed. Beginning in the mid-1930s, Muriel would read and comment on drafts of nearly everything DLS wrote, up until her death decades later.

Likewise, DLS enjoyed and supported Muriel's historical work. DLS bought Muriel a book in the Farringdon Street bookstalls in 1933 that she thought might be useful "if you are still engaged in considering the equipment of Tudor households." In return, Muriel gave DLS a copy of *The Elizabethan Home* for Christmas 1933. DLS, Mac, and her Aunt Maud spent Boxing Day reading passages to one another, sympathizing with the "various culinary & domestic difficulties," such as "the pie that is too much baakt" and "the tartes that bee cold." Another time, DLS sent Muriel a long letter about her success in deciphering an Elizabethan cookery book, though she added somewhat bashfully, "no need to hasten to read it, until (if ever) you feel inclined for such talk." Soon enough, they were entertaining each other with long letters written in faux-Elizabethan style and sometimes even handwriting—DLS, for example, informing "Mistresse Byrne" that "it wille greatlie rejoice ye to learne that y golde ffishe bee yet in sounde healthe." The linguistic larks of the MAS were fully resurrected.[27]

AS THEY APPROACHED middle age, the members of the MAS had every reason to look forward rather than back. As DLS put it, "paradoxical as it may seem, to believe in youth is to look backward; to look forward, we must believe in age." Of course, aging had its drawbacks. D. Rowe remembered that "when we were all round about middle age and all except me had put on weight pretty heavily I suggested that, to preserve the initials M.A.S. we should accept that these now stood for 'Middle-Aged Spread.'" But growing older could also bring the stability and self-assurance necessary for undertaking important work. Years later, DLS would tell an audience of schoolgirls that things got better with age. While "youth was a worrying, rather embarrassing time of life," at forty "life will really begin to be interesting." D. Rowe made similar points in a pair of poems about growing older. In "Forgiveness," she was glad to move beyond her youthful faults, "my follies, my ungenerous mind," and to embrace her new traits, which she compared with the "autumnal royalty" of the changing leaves. More humorous was "Youth Gone." In this poem, D. Rowe exclaims: "youth gone? / I never said goodbye!" But now, here was "Middle-Age," with "graver smile and more forgiving eyes." Accepting the inevitable, D. Rowe asks Middle-Age to

> walk with me a stage.
> The sun rides high; up, heart! up, load!
> This is the next adventure of the road.[28]

10

SUBVERSIVE SPINSTER

S EEN FROM ONE VANTAGE POINT, D. Rowe was a classic spinster aunt, close
to her sisters and nieces and serving as a caretaker for family and
close friends. But such an interpretation misses much of what D. Rowe
achieved. Formidable, flirtatious, and funny, she was an innovative producer
who brought cutting-edge ideas to the theater she helped to found, while
working full-time as an English teacher. Rather than a spinster, she is better
understood as a single woman who built enduring community and bonds
of kinship around herself outside of the norms of the family. Moreover, she
insisted that amateur theater in a seaside resort could be serious, modern,
and exciting. As she put it in a review, "One need not necessarily be bored,
half-witted, broken-hearted, drunk, dissolute or late for rehearsals simply
because one happens to live by the seaside." There was no reason, she suggested, why Bournemouth could not sustain theater that challenged conventions, valued language, and took its audience seriously.[1]

The figure of the spinster haunted the imaginations of the members of
the MAS in various ways. DLS, for instance, contrasted the opportunities
available to her generation with the fate of her paternal aunts, "brought up
without education or training," who found themselves thrown, after their
father's death, "into a world that had no use for them." One trained to be a
nurse, "by my father's charity," while another joined an "ill-run" religious
community. The third "lived peripatetically as a 'companion' to various
old cats, saving halfpence and cadging trifles, aimlessly doing what when
done was of little value to God or man." DLS was appalled: "from all such

frustrate unhappiness, God keep us." Although she created a sympathetic, fictional version of this kind of woman in the form of the recurring character Miss Climpson, who runs an information-gathering bureau called the Cattery funded by Lord Peter Wimsey, DLS was clear about the horrors of such an existence in real life.[2]

D. Rowe never married, and she was both a dutiful daughter and a devoted aunt. She helped to care for her mother, who died of cancer early in 1923. She also maintained a close relationship with her family friends, the Liberal politician Sir Arthur Marshall and his wife, Louise, shepherding them through their old ages as a surrogate daughter. They spent holidays together—at Christmas 1937, for instance, D. Rowe and Arthur both enjoyed the pamphlet about Wimsey family history that DLS sent. D. Rowe was, too, a dedicated aunt to her sister Hilda's daughters and also to Charis's brood. Meanwhile, she had no fixed household of her own, but moved from place to place in the Bournemouth area, as a lodger or tenant.[3]

At times, D. Rowe merrily embraced the role of aunt, telling one student, for instance, that an aunt "is qualified to put her elbows on the table during meals—though no one else may." She was well aware that being a dutiful daughter did not have to end as miserably as it did for DLS's aunts. Just before Christmas 1938, D. Rowe's own eighty-four-year-old aunt died suddenly. This woman had made a living selling paintings of flowers while caring for her aging parents. After their deaths, she moved to an isolated cottage in the hills beside the river Wye, refusing letters, solicitors, and bank accounts alike.

Her aunt was not cast off by a world that had no use for her. Instead, she cast off the world, having no more use for it. When she died, D. Rowe traveled out to deal with her affairs. To DLS, she wrote, "You would have approved of the scene on the night before Christmas Eve, when Police Constable Nicholas and I tramped miles of hill road above the Wye Valley, where all bus-service was suspended owing to roads like frozen glass, with a mist rolling up from below, by the light of a bulls' eye and bearing a rat-eaten will in a biscuit tin." The life and death of a self-denying spinster is

D. Rowe (BLTC)

reimagined here; instead of the usual tropes of pathetic cadging and triviality, D. Rowe offers us a dramatic, eccentric climax worthy of a film.[4]

D. Rowe, though eccentric, was no hermit. Indeed, she made use of every minute in her busy, social Bournemouth life. Her great creative endeavor was born one summer evening in 1919, as she and a friend, George Stone, were walking home after taking part in what he called "a particularly crude alfresco cabaret." Stone was a businessman as well as a semiprofessional theater director. Together, they decided to create a new theatrical venture, one that would make proper use of local talents to do something a bit more interesting. This was the start of what would become the Bournemouth Little Theatre Club.[5]

This was not as quixotic an undertaking as it might sound. True, after the war, the commercial theater had begun to suffer from the competition of the cinema. At the same time, however, local and amateur theater groups were rapidly expanding, and more people were involved in making theater for themselves. D. Rowe and Stone had meant to start small, with simple performances staged in members' homes, but the club outgrew that idea almost immediately. Just two months after they'd dreamed the club up, on a night pouring with rain, came the first production: two one-act plays, one of them written by a club member. Between November 1919 and May 1920, there were no fewer than seven productions, and membership was already over two hundred, growing to nearly five hundred by 1925 and over seven hundred by 1928. DLS visited D. Rowe in October 1920 and found her house was "full of lovely early Victorian frocks" to be turned into costumes.[6]

D. ROWE ACTED in club plays from time to time. Far more significant, though, was her work as a producer (as directors were generally called) and as a leading member of the selection committee that decided both what plays to put on and which actors to cast in them. D. Rowe was a sociable, efficient presiding figure. Charis remembered following her around the club on one visit, meeting various people as they went. After one such conversation she asked D. Rowe, "What's he done?"

"Nothing," came the surprised reply.

"But why are you angry with him?" Charis persisted. "That's the first man we've met this evening whom you haven't addressed as 'King of my Heart.'"

"Well, I can't remember their names, and I have to call them something!"[7]

Some of D. Rowe's work with the club required diplomacy. The selection committee was a frequent target of members' ire, especially when they found themselves not getting the roles they wanted. The club was a collective endeavor: there were no individual curtain calls, and flowers were sent to dressing rooms after performances, rather than handed to individuals over the footlights. As an amateur club, it existed, on one level, to provide acting opportunities for its members, who paid a fee in order to be part of it. In 1926, over 80 percent of acting members had been offered parts in that season's productions. Two years later, however, the club's annual general meeting clarified that admission as an acting member did not mean that someone would necessarily be cast in one of the main productions. Members should take advantage of the lower-stakes opportunities in the club first, such as play readings or informal productions staged just for members. The issue was debated again in 1936, when the meeting resolved that the quality of club productions must ultimately take precedence over the goal of giving everyone a chance to act—though D. Rowe suggested that women's parts might be offered first to members who hadn't acted yet that season. But when it came to casting, someone had to make the difficult decisions. Pressed by one woman who had acted in the private productions but hadn't been offered a big role yet, D. Rowe apparently replied frankly, "Well, perhaps they do not consider you good enough."[8]

Over time, the Bournemouth Little Theatre Club expanded and evolved. In its early years, it had raised significant sums for charities, particularly those that were connected with World War I veterans. That charitable emphasis took a back seat to an increasing focus on growth and commercial experiments. By 1929, the club was producing its own monthly magazine and had, according to local press coverage, a larger membership "than that of any similar club in England." At the same time, it began the process of procuring a site in order to build a physical theater that could serve as "a central home for the continuation and enlargement of its activities and for the development of Amateur Art."[9]

The decision grew out of the broader "Little Theatre" movement, which saw local theaters springing up across the country in these years, providing high-quality and often political or experimental theater to watch and take part in, well beyond the commercial theaters of London. The Bournemouth

Little Theatre, Limited, was formed on October 24, 1929; D. Rowe took ten preference shares in the new company. The timing couldn't have been worse, coinciding almost exactly with the Wall Street stock market crash that would trigger a global economic depression. But the Bournemouth Little Theatre persevered, inaugurating a series of garden parties to raise funds. In December 1930, D. Rowe attended the formal ceremony in which the foundation stone was laid. Six months later, on June 15, 1931, the new theater opened. At the Bournemouth High School, D. Rowe received a telegram of congratulations from Charis, who was in Macclesfield: "LUCK TO THE THEATRE AND LOVE FROM BARNETTS AND FRANKENBURG."[10]

Boasting over five hundred seats and a Green Room Club where food was served and smaller productions could be staged, the new theater was praised in the *Everyman*: "without being luxurious, the building will add to the pleasure of theatre-going." There were two plays to celebrate the theater's first week, one of them produced by D. Rowe. The audience cried "producer" at the end, but D. Rowe declined to step onstage to receive the applause.[11]

Leading figures in British theater praised D. Rowe's club for its courage. At the theater's opening, the playwright St. John Ervine, who was also the drama critic for the London *Observer*, said, "They were building their own theatre and producing plays that would make West End managers faint, and not only producing plays but writing them as well." Sybil Thorndike, a famous actress (and also a member of the board of Charis's birth control clinic), praised the club for the leading role it had taken in the revival of amateur theater in England. Amateurs, she argued, could experiment and develop methods of performance that professionals could not. They gained something, too: taking part in amateur theater provided "the value of personal expression which could not be obtained by sitting with one's feet on the mantelpiece and listening to a gramophone." C. B. Purdom, likewise, argued in a review of the new theater that the "mass production methods of the cinema have made people perceive the need for local and individual dramatic expression."[12]

The theater as a whole was profitable almost immediately, apart from the brief, loss-making experiment in running a repertory company that performed, among other things, Jim Jaeger's play *The Sanderson Syndicate*. Signs of prosperity included the wide range of benefits enjoyed by members in the mid-1930s: special performances of club productions, three annual programs of short plays in the clubroom, a musical or opera presented by the operatic section, and social sections dedicated to outside pursuits such as motoring, cinema, debating, and poetry. In 1935, the club changed the theater's name to the Palace Court Theatre, after an adjacent building. Advocates of the change were keen to stop being seen as "little," and with some good reasons. By the end of the 1930s, the theater club was one of the leading amateur societies in the country. It had an income of £2,000 a year and a membership of over 1,400, producing eleven shows each year and hiring out the theater for further commercial productions and concerts.[13]

THE BOURNEMOUTH LITTLE Theatre Club's success and prominence was due at least in part to the innovative direction that D. Rowe brought to her work there. Women generally had limited opportunities to work as professional producers in this era. In the Bournemouth club, however, D. Rowe and other women frequently directed productions. On one level, this could be seen as a natural outgrowth of women's participation in home theatricals and amateur drama in the nineteenth century. However, it also provided women, including D. Rowe, with the opportunity to shape the direction of British theater, at a moment when amateur companies were in many respects taking the lead.[14]

As a leader on the dramatic selection committee, D. Rowe was committed to high artistic standards and interested in pushing the club beyond the usual limits of amateur theater. The club had to please many constituencies in its choice of plays; they had to attract audiences, provide juicy roles for acting members, and offer a wide range of material. In 1930, defending their choices, the selection committee pointed out that the past season "offered realistic tragedy, romantic comedy, farce, a murder play, drama, Grand Guignol, and an operetta." But it was not easy to find exciting, worthwhile new material that had been passed by the censor and yet not taken up by a major commercial producer. No one wanted reheated London leftovers, either—that is, provincial amateur revivals of productions that had recently been successful in the West End. As one club member put it, "Let us, in the name of moderate highbrowism, have a taste of caviare from time to time."[15]

D. Rowe developed a keen instinct for what would work, and what wouldn't, on the Bournemouth stage. In letters to Jim Jaeger on the subject of writing for an amateur club, she advised introducing one new character per act and changing the setting or the time of day at least once to maintain the audience's interest. An episode like a visit from a newspaper reporter, inserted in the middle of a play, means that "the audience can take its attention off the story for a breather." And she warned: "the damnable thing about the drama is that the audience is more interested in the individuals in a story than in the implications of the story itself," and were quite happy to cheer on a likeable immoral character if the playwright gave them the opportunity.[16]

But if D. Rowe considered the audience's needs and weaknesses, she also, as a producer, demanded their attention and intellectual engagement, providing that "taste of caviare" in Bournemouth. Some of this work had a decidedly feminist bent. The club's first public production was *Diana of Dobson's*, a feminist play by Cicely Hamilton that followed the adventures of a shopgirl who inherits £300. D. Rowe was stage manager. After a special matinee performance in February 1920, "loud and continuous cries were made for 'stage manager,' and these did not cease until Miss Dorothy Rowe came forward and gracefully acknowledged the tribute." Five years later, she produced Clemence Dane's play *A Bill of Divorcement*, which asked the audience to envision a world with modernized divorce laws.[17]

D. Rowe's productions earned critical praise and the recognition that she was working far above the usual amateur standard. The judge in a British Drama League competition called her 1926 production of *Barbara's Wedding* "all very slick and professional," for example. In the early 1930s, she experimented with different genres: a one-act farce described in the club's journal as "a wonderful feat of pantomime foolery," and two years later a melodrama selected by the club's acting members. Here, again, the local reviewer praised the production: though "the majority of amateur societies" might have struggled with the play, here, "the carefully chosen cast" was up to the challenge. After these dalliances in farce and melodrama, D. Rowe returned to form, focusing on serious plays of literary merit. She produced *St. Joan* by George Bernard Shaw in 1936. The production was dogged by issues and postponed due to a cast member's illness. But it received a rapturous notice in the club magazine. D. Rowe had produced "one of the outstanding successes of our Club since its inception," and had done so through commitment to the drama itself rather than trendy tricks. The reviewer praised, particularly, "a long scene played by only three characters without a single change of position," which proved "that the continual restless movement, now so fashionable, is unnecessary if the players are sincerely interested in their own theme." D. Rowe was a producer with faith in the power of language well delivered by skillful actors.[18]

She was also increasingly interested in using costumes and settings to challenge received wisdom in the theater. Grounded in amateur theater, she was well aware that elaborate costumes placed a heavy demand on everyone involved. In one review of a big costume play, she thanked "our properties and wardrobe manager and her ever-efficient helpers" for their tireless work in "measuring all the characters from top to toe" as well as "ordering, unpacking, sorting, distributing, mending, remaking, collecting, checking and returning." She understood, too, that choices about clothing, props, and scenery had an immediate and profound effect, signaling to the audience from the start whether they would be watching a comfortable rehash or a bold new interpretation of a familiar work.[19]

As early as 1924, D. Rowe created a sensation when she coproduced a play that had been inspired by a local antiques dealer who agreed to provide some of his treasures as props for the production. The result was a hit: for the evening performance, "there were no fewer than three lines of cars drawn up in Hinton Road quite half an hour before the commencement of the performance, and at the time of the rising of the curtain there was offered the unusual spectacle of a number of smartly dressed people vainly looking for seats."[20]

In the 1930s, D. Rowe began to experiment with historical settings in more audacious ways. She was certainly capable of producing straight historical drama—her adaptation of Jane Austen's *Emma* was praised for the "amazing skill" with which the production had rendered the "spirit and atmosphere" of its era. But she was also interested in productions that confounded audiences' expectations about time and place. She was delighted, for instance, with the club's production of Oscar Wilde's *The Importance of Being Earnest*, in which the decision to keep both costumes and set strictly black and white gave "a fresh and entirely delightful impression" to a play that could no longer hope to surprise audiences. "In times past the Selection Committee has been frightened off new ground by the Club's expressed distaste for plays of an 'experimental' type," she wrote, but hopefully the success of this play would keep the door open for future experiments.[21]

Should plays written long ago be produced with modern costumes? This was a question that exercised interwar theater lovers, including the MAS. In her book of examination questions for English students, Bar asked: "Do you think the method of playing Shakespeare in modern dress is more suitable to the comedies or to the tragedies?" A milestone in this debate was Barry Jackson's 1925 modern-dress production of *Hamlet* at the Kingsway. DLS evidently saw this, telling her mother that October that she'd seen "the modern clothes Hamlet & found it very impressive." Muriel argued later that it had made people realize that they'd only ever seen *Hamlet* produced as a vehicle for a star actor, rather than "*as a play*—a closely-knit, clear and exciting drama, full of vigorously conceived and varied individuals." As this might suggest, Muriel was no fan of unthinking orthodoxy when it came to Shakespeare and costume. Apart from a few exceptions, she argued that the evidence suggested that Shakespeare's plays had always been played in whatever people were wearing at the time. Shakespeare in modern dress, in other words, was a venerable tradition.[22]

D. Rowe made her own contribution to this debate in 1933, when she produced Richard Brinsley Sheridan's 1777 play *The School for Scandal* in modern dress. She went far beyond costume choices in modernizing the play. A soliloquy was delivered into a telephone, people played bridge rather than piquet, and syncopated jazz complemented the "almost ultra-modern settings." The club's magazine explained the decision in an article that was unsigned but probably written by D. Rowe. Echoing Muriel's perspective, it argued that "period" dress is itself a convention. For the Victorians, for instance, nearly all Shakespearean heroes wore "coloured tights," while their fairies "always wore butter muslin and tinsel crowns." Shakespeare, for his part, "always dressed his cast in the latest Elizabethan fashions." Modern ideas and norms shape every aspect of production. Shylock, the Jewish character in *The Merchant of Venice*, is "played today as a semi-tragic figure," for example, but Shakespeare wrote the character mockingly, intending his audience to laugh at his final exit. All this, the article argued, proved that modern dress was a reasonable choice for Shakespeare. If that was true, then "how much more so for Sheridan, who was so much nearer the modern outlook?" Staging plays in modern dress made them accessible to audiences in a new way, breaking down the barriers of strange clothing or manners in order to reveal the universal human realities at stake. There could be no better symbol of the MAS's ability to blend an informed appreciation of cultural classics with an enthusiasm for modern invention.[23]

D. Rowe had to fit her theatrical productions in between teaching full-time and caring for relatives and friends. As the founder of an amateur theater, she also had to cope with a variety of local issues and emergencies—the lack of understudies, for example, or the pique of members who didn't get the parts they wanted. None of it stopped her from creating an institution that took its place in the front ranks of the revival of amateur theater in interwar Britain. She did so above all as a producer who insisted that the brain didn't go on holiday just because the body was in a seaside resort town. She produced a wide variety of plays, all of them linked by a sense of professional production values and intelligent interpretation. Most strikingly, she used the theater to reinterpret traditional culture for a truly modern audience. If women could get Oxford degrees, she seems to say, then why can't an eighteenth-century soliloquy be delivered into a telephone, and so made real and comprehensible to a twentieth-century audience? In asking that sort of question, and producing these sorts of plays, she changed what amateur theater could mean.

11

THE PROBLEM OF MARRIAGE

WHILE D. ROWE BUILT HER life as a single woman, Charis, DLS, and Muriel all had romantic and marital partnerships of different sorts. The nineteenth-century middle-class ideal of marriage between men and women had emphasized a thoroughly dependent, domestic wife—the "angel in the house," maintained in sheltered splendor. Such a model was rarely fully achieved in practice, but it was underwritten by a set of laws that subordinated a woman to her husband in legal and financial terms. Late Victorian feminists had challenged this situation— D. Rowe's mother, for example, had insisted on the right to continue selling her paintings after marriage. She'd believed, too, that women should keep their surnames and give them to their daughters; failing that, she inserted her maiden name into her daughters' names, so that D. Rowe's full name was Dorothea Ellen Hanbury Rowe. By the 1920s, though, the ideal marriage was changing form, with a new emphasis on companionship and sexual compatibility.[1]

Charis's marriage was unusually egalitarian and companionable, in an era that increasingly valued those qualities but struggled to achieve them. Muriel and DLS experienced rocky times in their respective relationships. DLS wondered whether to leave Mac Fleming, and Muriel embarked on a new love affair that turned her partnership with Bar into an uncertain threesome. These experiences raised fundamental questions about the nature of romantic partnership between equal adults.

SYDNEY FRANKENBURG HAD sustained a serious wound to the shoulder in the last days of World War I. He convalesced in an officers' hospital. Once he was released, Charis dressed the wound faithfully for months. By 1919, the wound was still discharging, and Sydney suffered from limited movement at the elbow as well as stiffness in the wrist and fingers. He was declared permanently unfit for general service and granted the rank of captain. In September 1922, the shoulder wound reopened, but then it re-healed and seemed unlikely to cause further trouble. In Charis's words: "he was able to play tennis and squash; in fact the only sphere in which he was incapacitated was in carving for the family!"[2]

But in February 1935, the wound again became infected. Charis insisted that he receive a second opinion from Dr. Langley at the Salford Royal Hospital, who reacted quickly, admitting him to the hospital for surgery the next day. Charis's focus turned to nursing her husband, and they both dropped their usual public responsibilities. She stayed with him in Salford Royal on his two subsequent admissions and cared for him at home in between with the help of a night nurse and regular visits from Dr. Langley. She relied, too, on the assistance of Edith "Bonn" Bonnell, Ursula's governess, and Ted Briggs, her husband's agent. Sydney was "desperately ill" all summer, though he greeted the guests from his wheelchair at their annual garden party for ex-servicemen and their families.[3]

By October, Sydney seemed much better, and he and Charis traveled together to Bournemouth for a holiday. It was a natural choice: a seaside resort, but also, of course, the home of D. Rowe. Their eldest son, Peter, wrote to his parents in early October, sending his love to D. Rowe and asking his parents when they'd be able to visit him at boarding school. In fact, only a short time after their arrival, Sydney collapsed, and the local doctor told Charis that there was little hope of a recovery. She cared for him in Bournemouth for a couple of weeks. D. Rowe came every day to be with them; Dr. Langley also traveled down, and Charis's father visited once as well.[4]

They evidently broke the news only slowly and gently to the children. Bonn had taken Ursula, the youngest, to Blackpool, and Peter wrote from school with thoughts about his university aspirations and hopeful remarks about his father's health. Finally, Sydney said that he wanted to be at home, and Charis rapidly made arrangements to ensure an adequate staff there. They traveled back to Manchester on October 23 in a railway ambulance coach. Ursula and Bonn came home, and other friends and relatives began to gather. Peter joined them briefly to have a bad tooth taken care of. He returned to school on November 4 and wrote again the next day, claiming that the unusual frequency was merely part of an effort to "improve my handwriting." But the gravity of the situation could not have been lost on anyone. On November 7, 1935, Sydney Frankenburg died. The children all returned home, and D. Rowe came to join Charis as well.[5]

Sydney had died a few days before Armistice Day; decades later, Charis remembered the ex-servicemen on her household staff standing to attention while listening to the Armistice Day service, broadcast from the Cenotaph on the radio. The Sydney Frankenburg branch of the British Legion honored Sydney with a memorial service at the Park Place Synagogue in Manchester. The Greengate Hospital and Open-Air School sent their sympathy to Sydney's family and used money sent as donations in lieu of flowers to build an extension that would provide them with ten more beds.[6]

In her memoir, Charis's fluent flow of words stumbles when it comes to Sydney's death. It was, she wrote, "difficult to write about our marriage. There is nothing in it that I would have changed—except its duration which was less than eighteen years." And, finally, she adapted the words of Izaak Walton: "doubtless God could have made a better marriage, but doubtless God never did." Charis donned mourning attire, though it was unusual by 1935, because she felt it was a "useful caution to friends encountered unexpectedly, who have not heard of your loss." She had to cope with a range of new responsibilities and struggled both to maintain her own work and to fill some of the roles left empty by Sydney. She now had to deal with financial matters, including the large estate Sydney had left to her and the children; neither her solicitor, whose health was failing, nor the guardian Sydney had nominated to assist with raising the children provided adequate assistance. The headmaster of the boys' boarding school, however, was "always a source of strength." With Dr. Langley's assistance, the British Legion branch, too, advocated for her to receive his army pension, though the pension authorities at first did not admit that his war wound had been the cause of his death.[7]

At first, Charis tried to return to a semblance of ordinary life. She resumed her work in Salford a month after Sydney's death, and the children returned to school. She also took on some of Sydney's former roles, becoming vice president (later honorary life president) of the British Legion branch and chairman of the Greengate Hospital committee. But it was difficult. At the beginning of August, Charis suffered a breakdown and spent two months in bed. At the garden party for ex-servicemen, her eldest son Peter hosted and she merely made a "short speech from the balcony outside my bedroom window." Her doctor insisted on a real period of rest, telling her, "I want you to think it *right* to read a novel in the morning!" She was prescribed pills that she later described as "especially adapted to pale languid females who feel exhausted upon slight exertion."[8]

D. Rowe seems to have stepped back, briefly, from a few of her roles at the theater in 1936, perhaps freeing up time that year to support Charis and her family. She had always been a kind of aunt to Charis's children; now she became a surrogate extra parent, too, as Charis navigated grief and single parenthood. Her steady presence was one reason why Charis was able, mostly, to remain in her public roles despite the immense loss. She and Dr. Langley both provided help with the emergencies of parenting during this time. In May 1937, Charis's middle son, John, was ill with appendicitis. Dr. Langley visited his school, and Charis canceled her committee meetings to attend to her son. After surgery, she took him to Bournemouth, where they both stayed with D. Rowe while he recovered. It's a testimony to the strength of their bond: what could have been a place tinged with the memories of Sydney's final illness instead remained a refuge, because D. Rowe was there.[9]

In October 1938, Charis's family and household moved to a new home, Oughtrington Hall, in Cheshire. Dr. Langley insisted that she not be present for the move itself, so Charis went to Bournemouth to stay with D. Rowe again and only arrived in Cheshire at the start of November. Even so, the transition wasn't easy. By the middle of the month, Peter was urging his mother to visit Oxford, where he was now a student at Balliol College, so that she could see her friends from her own university days. "Do, Mum, I think it would do you good." Meanwhile, she also had to cope with another son's accident at school, again relying on Dr. Langley's help. But by February 1939, Peter was able to remark lightly, "You seem to be having fun with all your callers and all."[10]

CHARIS AND SYDNEY had adopted traditional gendered roles in their marriage to some extent—he had handled the finances, for instance, while she became Mrs. Sydney Frankenburg. But, although rooted in a kind of separate-spheres outlook, their decision-making was explicitly egalitarian, and they supported each other's work in tangible and intimate ways. Years later, DLS would argue to Mary Stocks (Charis's old partner in the birth control clinic) that gendered patterns of behavior in marriage were more a matter of circumstance than innate nature. When the wife was the breadwinner and the husband lived on her earnings, "you often find the man developing a whole series of 'feminine' weaknesses, such as nagging, niggling," and jealousy of the partner's work. The wife in such a setup, for her part, "develops a number of the alleged 'masculine' qualities, such as a free and open way of handling money, indifference to domestic trifles, the subordination of the subjective to the objective, etc." Indeed, she went on, the pattern extended beyond male-female relationships. When two women live together, and "one does all the housekeeping while the other just does 'a job,'" the one who does the job will behave to the one who keeps house "exactly as a man does to his wife," "taking the housekeeping part for granted and never saying 'thank-you' for it, being inconsiderate about the servants (if any), developing a curious 'masculine' incapacity for understanding how rations work, demanding in one breath that the house should be spotless and grumbling in the next because the other party insists on spring-cleaning, etc., etc."[11]

Stocks disagreed with this analysis, at least as far as the two-woman household went: "I believe that when women live together, they have an incurable tendency to nurse one another." Yet in both cases, DLS was writing from experience. She was describing, in the first case, her own marriage to Mac, which was shaped by her increasing fame and success and his bouts of illness, bad temper, and begrudgery, and in the second case, the relationship between Muriel and Bar. Rather than divide these relationships into separate heterosexual and homosexual categories, she grouped them both as forms of marital or quasi-marital partnership, and argued that the inequalities that bedevil them are the consequence of gendered hierarchies in society, not the sex of any particular partner.[12]

The differences between Muriel and Bar's relationship and DLS and Mac's marriage are obvious. DLS and Mac were legally married, though they couldn't get married in the church in 1926 because of Mac's divorce. Muriel and Bar made a shared household in a moment when relationships between women were under new scrutiny. Although they functioned as a married couple socially, as had Victorian women before them, they were not legally bound. References to sex between a married woman and her husband were increasingly acceptable—witness the raft of advice manuals for married

couples wanting to improve their sex lives—but open allusions to sex between women immediately conjured scandal. For DLS, Muriel, Bar, and perhaps Mac, though, the similarities between their relationships were far more
compelling. Over the course of the 1930s and 1940s, and through the twists
and turns of evolving relationships, the friends embarked on a joint project
of making sense of their partnerships, putting what we might now categorize as "gay" and "straight" marriages into the same frame of analysis. They
make clear, too, that Muriel and Bar's relationship, far from being essentially
secret or illegitimate, was constructed in community and using the limited
legal structures at their disposal.

DLS and Mac had a challenging marriage. Biographers have speculated
that they were sexually compatible, though only on the strength of reading
between the lines of DLS's writing. D. Rowe never met Mac, though DLS
talked to her about him. Muriel and Bar, by contrast, knew Mac well, and
Muriel considered him easy to get along with, jovial, and full of funny stories
about his life and past work. But funny stories over dinner are one thing;
the daily intimacy of pulling together in marriage is something else. DLS
retained her professional identity as something strictly independent, continuing to use Sayers as her surname in most circumstances, with the explanation that it saved her from the mistakes she would inevitably make if she
tried to use Sayers in professional life and Fleming elsewhere. In the early
years of her marriage, DLS expressed the opinion that all women, "married
or not, should be able to make money for themselves," believing that it would
soon be regarded as equally degrading for a wife or a husband to be merely
"kept." In fact, DLS's earnings would largely support Mac, especially as he
was increasingly unwell, bothered by various stomach complaints, rheuma-
tism, and, perhaps, the mental aftereffects of war service.[13]

The unhappy marriage of the Fentimans in the 1928 Wimsey novel *The
Unpleasantness at the Bellona Club* offers a flavor of the difficulties of DLS's
own married life. In that novel, the shell-shocked George Fentiman is relent-
lessly critical of his wife, Sheila, on whom he must rely financially. Fentiman
remarks bitterly, "No wonder a man can't get a decent job these days, with
these hard-mouthed, cigarette-smoking females all over the place, pretend-
ing they're geniuses and business women and all the rest of it," though he
apologizes to Lord Peter Wimsey later for his outburst. Increasingly unwell,
forgetful, and prone to fits of rage, Mac, too, was no longer able to work in
any steady way.[14]

Mac published a book of recipes with commentary in 1933, dedicated to "my wife, who can make an omelette." *Gourmet's Book of Food and Drink* suggests a man who enjoyed not only food and drink, but old books, historical detail, and tall tales. There's a certain Fentiman-like preoccupation with the difficult position of the modern British man. The reader learns, for instance, that whereas in most places women value being able to cook, in Britain it is out of fashion. An entire chapter, meanwhile, is devoted to remedies for hangovers.[15]

In the late autumn of 1933, DLS and Muriel went on a road trip, stopping at bookshops along the way to place orders and drum up sales for Mac. Even while she made this generous gesture, though, DLS was considering whether to divorce him. It was, as Muriel put it, "the tour that we took for her to make up her mind." Muriel and DLS went to Oxford. There, DLS took Muriel to Ivy Shrimpton's house and they both saw DLS's son, John Anthony. Muriel told Bar she'd met the boy, who was "about ten," though it's not clear exactly what she thought his relationship was to DLS. From Oxford they went on to Bath and then around Somerset tourist spots, visiting Wells Cathedral, Cheddar, and Glastonbury before Muriel returned to London on December 11. Somewhere along the way, DLS decided to stay in her marriage, and, in Muriel's recollection, "the subject was never mentioned again, at any rate not by me."[16]

In a draft story written in these years, DLS imagined the feelings of a mother of two whose husband asks for a divorce. He accuses her of wanting to "turn into a sort of Bloomsbury frump with all your Museum friends." Apart from being a "frump," this is fairly accurate, the wife in the story admits: "I might go back to some of my historical work, if I haven't lost touch too much. Professor King could probably give me some work on her Elizabethan Lives." With a few twists, it's not far from what DLS might have imagined her life would be like if she divorced Mac and was more fully absorbed into Muriel and Bar's London world.[17]

Instead, she stayed. Mac, who almost certainly knew that DLS was John Anthony's mother, informally adopted the child and gave him his surname. The fundamental tensions in the marriage—around Mac's temper and illness and DLS's absorption in her work—remained. They slept in separate rooms, perhaps because of Mac's poor health. Nevertheless, they found ways to make it work. Much later, DLS would rebuke John Anthony for blaming a quarrel with his wife on his "impossible temperament." This, she said, was just another way of describing bad behavior, "and the mere fact that we use that word implies that we intend to take no serious trouble to control ourselves." This would not do. In marriage, she went on, "one can do without love, one can do without common interest, one can even, at a pinch, do without fidelity; but one cannot do without courtesy and consideration." In spite of it all, DLS would find enough of these qualities to make her own marriage last. But that didn't make it easy. Years later, Muriel remembered Mac asking, emotionally, "What can I do to please her? She doesn't think I love her, but I do. Nothing I can do seems to make any difference."[18]

MURIEL AND BAR faced challenges as a couple, too. Muriel's writing around this time hints at difficulties. In "Two Silences," a poem from February 1931, she describes two very different sorts of silence that might exist between partners. One silence is "the unquestioning peace" that lies beneath the surface level of passing words. The other silence is the one between two lovers who are afraid to admit that something has come between them, a silence of secrecy and distance. "There hangs a shadow on your brow. / I almost fear to search your eyes, / Lest in my own you should surprise / The answering shadow's faint surmise."[19]

What was the source of the trouble? An unpublished play by Muriel suggests one possible answer. The play mainly concerns Margaret and John, a married couple in middle age. Sweetly, their daughter is a kind of miniature Charis, an Oxford graduate who dreams of running for Parliament and meanwhile makes "enormous charts and statistics which are going to prove something or other about birth-control." Most of the play, though, is taken up with horrible marital arguments. Margaret says to John, for example, "You're cleverer than me, and you hammer away at me till you've beaten me to a pulp. . . . You make me feel like a trapped animal." Over time, Margaret comes to understand that the fundamental rot at the core of her marriage is the desire for absolute possession. This must be overcome, she realizes, so that rather than possessing people, she can learn to be "free with them, enjoying them, loving them, in that same sort of free way."[20]

Free, non-possessive love was at the heart of what came next for Muriel and Bar. It's hard to say how many lovers Muriel had: at least two, counting Bar, but possibly more. There are hints in her diaries of other intense attachments. In the late 1920s and very early 1930s, her diary records many meetings, sometimes almost daily, with "G." This could be Gladys Wheeler or Gladys Scott Thomson; she collaborated with both around this time. What is certain, however, is that, from the early 1930s, Muriel embarked on a serious and lasting relationship with another woman.[21]

In the acknowledgments to her 1936 collection of Henry VIII's letters, Muriel gave pride of place to "Miss M. M. Barber," who had endured "Henry's giant bulk and overwhelming personality in the house for over two years." She thanked many others, too, including DLS and, for the loan of some books, "Miss M. A. Cullis." Miss M. A. Cullis had in fact become an important part of Muriel's life: a long-term lover and partner, as well as a frequent presence in her and Bar's household.[22]

In Muriel and Bar's extended network of friends and professional acquaintances, long-term romantic partnerships between women were commonplace. Many of these involved multiple, simultaneous long-term partnerships, or what in today's terms might be called polyamory. At Bedford College, the women's college where Muriel taught on temporary contracts, she would have come into contact with Professor Caroline Spurgeon, who was involved with two women at the time: her longtime companion Lilian Clapham and Barnard College dean Virginia Gildersleeve. All three spent considerable time at a cottage in the South Downs, nicknamed the Old Postman's Cottage, which Gildersleeve bought in 1925 and gave to Spurgeon in 1931. Nearby, theater producer Edy Craig, dramatist Tony Atwood, and painter Christopher St. John had their famous queer household at Smallhythe Place. Radclyffe Hall, the author of *The Well of Loneliness*, and her partner Una Troubridge were frequent guests there. Muriel noted passing Smallhythe on a walking holiday in 1926, when it still belonged to Craig's mother, Ellen Terry. Craig was also friends with Vera "Jack" Holme, who lived with Margaret Ker and Margaret Greenlees from the 1920s until their deaths forty years later. Monogamy, then, was no requirement in their social milieu.[23]

M. A. Cullis was also part of this world—she was a frequent guest at the Old Postman's Cottage, and she traveled to the United States as a personal secretary to Spurgeon. She was a woman of several names. Born Mildred Augusta Cullis, she changed her name after World War I to Mary Aeldrin Cullis. To Muriel, she was at first "MAC," and briefly Aeldrin, but then, for the rest of their relationship, Susan or merely S. Bar and DLS referred to her as Susan as well. Some of these shifting names may have been an effort to protect her identity in the letters she wrote to Muriel, which she usually signed Aeldrin, A., or S.[24]

She, too, had attended Somerville, completing her studies about ten years before Muriel. She taught English at various schools, including a stint at the Bedales School shortly after the time when Charis and her brother were pupils there. She might have met Muriel through their Somerville connections, or possibly through war work, when they both served with the YMCA in France. After the war, Susan spent two years traveling the world as a secretary to a "lady doctor" before returning to London in 1922. If they hadn't met already, Muriel and Susan would certainly have encountered each other at Bedford College, where Susan got work as a resident tutor for temporary stints in the 1920s, and then permanently from 1931. In this role, she looked after the health and welfare of residential students and offered them advice on their postgraduate careers.[25]

In Susan's telling, her love for Muriel had been born, appropriately, in a theater. In February 1933, Muriel produced D. Rowe's play *Very Well Then, Curtain*, as part of a program of entertainment put on by the Bedford College Dramatic Society, of which Susan was vice president. At this performance or another, Muriel walked down the aisle, "head a little humble, but spirit a good deal defiant." Then she turned her head, and "the lights from above scattered the gold of your hair over the dark foldings of your coat," and Susan was smitten. Slowly, Muriel revealed that she, too, valued Susan. When Susan first "realised that you like coming into my room," she told Muriel, she had felt "a little tremor of expectancy" like the earth does "just before dawn." Then, when Muriel had left, Susan called herself "an old fool," and wished she'd "managed life better, because I thought it would be such fun to play in full daylight with you beside me."[26]

From February 1933 onward, Muriel began seeing a lot of Susan, at a cocktail party and then for more intimate lunches and dinners. During the summer of 1933, as their romance gained intensity in the holiday locations of Sussex and Cornwall, Susan sent Muriel a series of extraordinary, passionate letters. She frequently pleaded with Muriel to burn them all: "another Forest Fire for this letter, please." Yet Susan admitted that she had not been able to burn Muriel's own letters, for "one day I shall want to read them all again." Muriel, too, did not burn Susan's letters, and instead they survived in her personal archive, where they form a remarkably frank testament to an intense affair.[27]

Take this letter, in which Susan expresses her belief in the restorative power of their growing intimacy. She hopes that their time together "has really & truly added to your store of resistance & buoyance." For her own part, she is restored: "to be with you is to feel all my own response to sheer living—returning after so long a time away." That morning, Muriel had departed. After a final glimpse of "the back of an entirely uncompromising head," Susan had been left with a "queer ache." Their time together had not been only about rest and relaxation. "And to my shame, you were tired." Susan gestures, here, to a physical as well as an emotional connection, aware, as she writes, of the explosive nature of her candid language.

> My arms are round you now & always—I suppose whether you want them or not, because there things remain—You must burn this— *definitely!* as soon as you get it—& so for once I will write, as generally it is very unwise to write—& whisper that I love you; somehow you have walked straight into my heart & I hold you there with all the pain & the pleasure that that nearness means.—And all the place is beautiful where you have been & all the sunshine is the warm feel of you in my arms—& if I write more, there will be no furnace and no waste pipe bushel big enough to hold the fragment of this paper which has done its work when you have read it & must not exist a minute afterwards.

As she watched the pink evening light, Susan missed their physical intimacy: "part of me is swinging into happiness & the other part is knocked dumb because when I turn there is nothing to touch. Sleep well my darling."[28]

In her letters, Susan praises Muriel with a kind of besotted ecstasy. Muriel had been made by the fairies with "scintillating opal colours." Her life was "radiant with the same thing that brings the look into your eyes that I love, & gives that darling curve to the corners of your mouth & total quietness to your hands—& makes me want to hold you for ever so close that you too shall be aware of nothing but love." Susan was deeply affected by Muriel: "and all of you is very disturbing in a queer beautiful way sweetheart."[29]

Susan reassured Muriel that she was ready to cope with her dark, difficult moods, and would never confuse that surface querulousness with the deeper beauty of Muriel's nature. Muriel did not need "to pretend, or act, or try to cope with me, & if you want to let off steam,—in person or in writing, well, let me have it." Is there a subtle critique of Bar here, or a reflection, at second hand, of what Muriel found frustrating in their relationship? Susan soon claimed a privileged knowledge of Muriel's inner nature, "that other you, which you keep so self protectively locked away that I feel as if I know it better than you do yourself (forgive my arrogance darling!)."[30]

For Susan, the relationship was an unexpected grace in the middle of her life, "a gift from the gods so tremendous and so god-like, that I can only hold out my hand foolishly,—& say nothing." It had given her life "a shake (which it badly needed)." Ruefully, she admitted her own verbosity: "and I could have spared you this long scribble, by writing instead just 'I love you.'" There were domestic touches, too. Muriel had left her gray socks at the cottage where she had stayed with Susan, who washed them and mailed them on to Muriel with a pencil that she might have missed.[31]

After Muriel had returned to London, Susan found Cornwall changed. The beach where she had sunbathed "was the ghost of itself without you." All colors had turned to gray, and hills and cliffs had been leveled to nothing. She continued to write to Muriel while they were apart, though she had sworn not to and knew that Muriel had no time to reply. The start of the new school year was approaching, but "instead of the usual iron ropes of nausea," Susan was elated by the thought that Muriel would be there. She advised Muriel to enjoy the rest of her holiday, "till we meet wearing our London faces and the drive of work thoughts again in our minds—but with a warm & furious pleasure underneath it all." More practically, she urged Muriel to think of a "convincingly good play" that she could put on at Bedford that year. Then, Susan would arrange for her to stay in a guest bedroom at the college next to Susan's own room, "and you shall get some quiet times mixed up with it." Indeed, she looked impatiently forward to spending time with Muriel back at Bedford, promising to "keep my evenings quite free if I possibly can, & my noon free also," to be available whenever Muriel might have a spare moment.[32]

Arriving back at Bedford in late September, Susan found it "like a vault" in the midst of the London fog. She was greeted by a stack of grim letters to work through, but in them, one from Muriel. And then, even better, there was Muriel's voice over the telephone, arranging for lunch on the following Tuesday. Susan lamented only that her hand was injured "just now when I want *all* hands on deck!" Her letters that autumn were full of a sense of the deepening intimacy of the relationship. Susan worried that she was no longer young and vibrant enough for Muriel. "I feel as if I had done such a selfish thing; I did not know all at once you would walk straight into the depths of my being as you have done—I only knew it was so great a happiness to hear you say 'I love you,' because already my arms were round you & already I had waited a long time for you." Nevertheless, she looked forward to seeing Muriel and talking about "the plan 'what next,' &—everything. You'll have to tell me a thousand times more that you like being with me, because I stop short constantly—stand still & think *Can* she?"[33]

In December, Muriel went on her road trip with DLS to help her decide what to do about her marriage with Mac. Did Muriel confide her own romantic complications? Susan wrote to her while she was on this trip, and her letter is focused squarely on their relationship. What was their plan for the future? It's certain that at some point, Bar learned about Muriel's relationship with Susan. Did Muriel talk over the complexities of that situation, too, as she and DLS drove through Oxfordshire and Somerset? And did Muriel, like DLS, opt for stability and decide to stay with Bar—while also bringing Susan more fully into their lives? Susan seems to have spent Christmas with Muriel and Bar later that December, the start of what would become a tradition. By 1935, their connection seems to have been normalized. Susan sent Muriel a cheery postcard from a vacation spot that ended with "Love to Bar & all the family."[34]

For Susan, at least, this might not have been quite what she wanted. She sometimes complained about her talks with Muriel being "so curtailed." She fantasized about traveling, but didn't want to leave the London-bound Muriel, who was "more sunshine than sunshine itself." After the first flush of romance, Muriel and Susan didn't have quite so many lunches and dinners together. Nevertheless, Susan was a significant part of Muriel's life. When Muriel and Bar held a party on January 10, 1936, both Susan and D. Rowe came to stay; the next day was the Somerville Association of Senior Members winter meeting in London, which all four of them probably attended. In February, Muriel produced and designed the sets and lighting for *Tobias and the Angel* for Bedford College. It was truly a

Susan in Madeira (MSBC 1/6)

chosen-family affair. Susan was the vice president of the dramatic society, and DLS provided a prop in the form of a weapon. The play even seems to have featured a walk-on performance by Bunter, the dog that Bar and Muriel had adopted.[35]

In the autumn of 1937, Susan took extended paid sick leave from her job. DLS heard the news almost immediately, and wrote to Muriel, "I am so awfully sorry about her illness, & I do hope it hasn't too much destroyed your chances of getting a bit of rest on holiday." For Susan, it was a long hoped for opportunity to travel again, for a rest cure in the more congenial climate of Madeira, a set of Portuguese islands off the coast of Africa.[36]

Muriel and Susan maintained their connection across the distance. Muriel saw Susan just before her departure, and also sent roses and a card to be brought to her shipboard cabin. Susan found it "almost like being able to kiss you again before we actually started, instead of just remembering the picture of you standing on Euston Station." Muriel had sent, too, more practical gifts: medication, apples, biscuits, and brandy. The roses made it all the way through the rough journey, providing "a sense of companionship that helps me to keep my eyes shut to the rest." On arrival, Susan rode the launch to the quay, "grimly grasping roses," and she made it through customs with the flowers as well as three hundred cigarettes and a bottle of whiskey.[37]

More gifts followed, as Muriel kept Susan plied with small comforts: assistance in developing her photographs, plus a Woolworth cushion, green bath foam, and a brown silk dressing gown on one occasion; medicine, paints, and film on another. Susan reciprocated with poinsettia and bougainvillea—fresh tropical flowers sent by post and arriving in surprisingly good condition. Susan offered, too, to send a set of "really attractive table mats" for Muriel's new home at 28 St. John's Wood Terrace. "Those things here are so lovely it would give me great pleasure to transfer something to 28." The gesture underscores Susan's sense of investment in Muriel's London life, including the home she shared with Bar.[38]

Gifts of money were more fraught: evidently Muriel and Susan quarreled over this issue. When she went on leave, both Muriel and Caroline Spurgeon offered Susan money, but Susan said she only wanted to accept it from Spurgeon. At some point, Muriel had told Susan that she was a "fool" about money, an accusation that Susan considered unfair but unanswerable: "I see that until I have paid back my debt, you have a right to think & say whatever you like."[39]

Despite the tension over money, Susan missed Muriel. She worried over Muriel's health and wished they could be together in the sunshine. "You have I think *all* my love darling—& are more precious to me every time I think of you." Some of this emotion she expressed through concern about the pets, hoping that Muriel's cat "has grown a suitable coat for the outrageous winter & that someone will give poor little Bundog a proper dressing gown in his stocking; I'm sure he must need it." As her return approached, Susan felt "very ambivalent," especially as the political news from Europe grew ever grimmer. "If my friends are to be bombed, I'd rather be on the spot; but I feel too shaken in head & legs to dare think all facing the world again will involve." She made her way home but would struggle again once bombs did begin to fall.[40]

The members of the MAS made marriages and partnerships as diverse as they were. Charis's marriage was a genuinely cooperative enterprise, well organized and purposeful—just as Charis was. It transcended religious differences and found room for Charis's burgeoning public role as well as for four children. Its tragedy was its end. For DLS, marriage was more fraught. She and Mac shared interests and a certain joie de vivre, but these were overshadowed by his illness and behavior, as well as his apparent impatience with her growing success. Muriel and Bar seem to have had a spate of tough times, too, and their dynamic was altered by the arrival of Susan. The MAS's romantic relationships encompassed many of the experiences that made interwar marriage modern: experiments in non-monogamy, the option of divorce, and a commitment to equality, in theory at least. Small wonder, then, that the question of romantic partnership and adult intimacy would be a central concern of the collaborative work of the MAS in the latter half of the 1930s.

12

DOES IT PLEASE YOU?

Bᴏᴛʜ Mᴜʀɪᴇʟ ᴀɴᴅ DLS ꜰᴏᴜɴᴅ themselves at creative impasses in the early 1930s. Muriel wanted to be a playwright but struggled to succeed; DLS wanted to write more emotionally dimensional work but felt stifled by the genre of detective fiction. On road trips and over dinners and weekend visits, they must have discussed their ongoing efforts to resolve the complexities of their personal lives: DLS's marriage, if not her ambivalent motherhood, and Muriel's evolving relationships with Bar and Susan. Seen in this light, it is perhaps not so surprising that the result was the collaboration that produced the Lord Peter Wimsey play *Busman's Honeymoon* and, indirectly, the novel *Gaudy Night*. In these works, DLS and Muriel imagine a solution to the problem of balancing emotional intimacy with the need to maintain intellectual and professional integrity—or, put another way, the problem of balancing the egotism of devotion to work with the ethical requirements of being in relationships with other people.

DLS had dragged her feet at the idea of introducing romance to her detective novels: "women and love stories and psychology" were "generally a nuisance in crime-stories," she said. But in 1930, seven years after the first appearance of her famous hero, DLS told Muriel that she was "getting a bit weary of Lord Peter," who brought in money but was "growing older and more staid." That same year, she published a novel that took the series in a new direction. *Strong Poison*, which fictionalizes DLS's unhappy experiences with Cournos, introduces a proper heroine in Harriet Vane. If Lord Peter Wimsey is the brilliant, clownish, damaged, hero version of DLS, Harriet Vane is the modern woman who has been hurt by love but whose intelligence carries her through. Harriet is more than a love interest. She is not the heart to Peter's head, but instead they are both engaged in a struggle to reconcile the desires of heart and head. What's more, Harriet, as a detective novelist, struggles with exactly DLS's problem: how to make detective novels more emotionally realistic while working within their comfortable narrative conventions.[1]

Have His Carcase develops the Wimsey-Vane relationship. Very like Muriel, Harriet takes off on a solo walking tour of the south coast, but when she discovers a corpse on the beach, she finds that she'd like Peter around after all. The novel is a meditation on courtship and gender. Gingerly approaching one another, Harriet and Peter are surrounded by grotesque exaggerations of masculinity, femininity, and heterosexuality.[2]

Charis was delighted to find herself name-checked in the novel, one of two "female gigolos" named Charis and Doris, though, as DLS told her, "I daresay their godparents in baptism called them Evelyn & Muriel." Charis also spotted the key to the mystery, and DLS praised her. "Nobody else seems to have done so up till now." DLS was, perhaps, less patient with D. Rowe, who saw through another character's disguise. In fact, D. Rowe greatly admired DLS's professional skill. Later, when Muriel loaned her Agatha Christie's *The ABC Murders*, she said that novel "left me with increased respect for D.L.S.'s integrity." Despite being "the world's boob at spotting whodunit," D. Rowe had worked out Christie's central plot device immediately and felt that it wasn't "playing fair."[3]

But if *Have His Carcase* seems to lead Harriet and Peter to a new level of intimacy, the next two novels ignore Harriet almost entirely. Peter continues proposing marriage at suitable intervals, we're left to understand, and Harriet refuses them. Meanwhile he goes on solving thorny mysteries in two of DLS's finest novels, *Murder Must Advertise* and *The Nine Tailors*. Both of these novels move beyond the lighthearted detective-story formula, offering complex commentary and atmospheric settings. Most of all, they provide new psychological complexity. *Whose Body?* had presented Wimsey's shell shock in realistic but raw terms, establishing his tendency to dissociate mentally while solving a case, as well as his penchant for putting himself in danger. In these later novels, by contrast, the complicated tangle of motivations and fears and triggers that define Wimsey's reactions are more fully explained, and the self-sacrificial embrace of danger is more finely rendered. *The Nine Tailors* revisits the world of DLS's childhood in the Cambridgeshire fens, providing a touching cameo for a clergyman modeled on her father. Its closing scenes are set in the eerie environment of the flooding fens. Once again, Wimsey deliberately puts his life at risk at the very moment when he must take responsibility for solving the mystery. In this majestic, otherworldly sequence, his gesture is matched, not by the arrest and explication that usually end a mystery novel, but by the murderer's own silent self-sacrifice. *Murder Must Advertise* recreates the world of S. H. Benson, where DLS had ceased working in 1931. It, too, raises questions about temptation, justice, and the moral complicities of modern life that go far beyond her earlier novels.[4]

Taken together, the Lord Peter Wimsey novels from *Strong Poison* onward establish DLS's growing interest in the problem of living an ethical life and, especially, in how to become a better person by engaging in the push and pull of relationships. But what would become of Harriet and Peter, if anything? DLS passed the dilemma off lightly to D. Rowe. "Lord P. says he is very anxious to get spliced but Harriet is still holding out on him. He is now 42, but still active for his age & hopes to bring it off before he is actually decrepit."[5]

MURIEL, MEANWHILE, HAD begun writing plays as an outlet for her ideas about modern life and relationships, which would not fit neatly into her historical research. She had been writing and teaching on the history of theater, especially costume, since the 1920s. She reviewed books related to theater and historical costume, mainly for the *Times Literary Supplement* but also for the *Sunday Times* and specialist publications such as the *Review of English Studies*. She wanted, though, to put all that expertise to use as a playwright.[6]

Although most of the plays Muriel wrote in these years were never produced, they reveal her evolving ideas about the complexities of modern love. *All at Sea* was a comedy crossed with a parable, with characters bearing fabulous names like Mr. Sinwell and Lady Flinteye. It strikes an arch, knowing tone. One character, for instance, proclaims, "Oh, I'm just crazy about sex. I'm one mass of sex myself, Mr. Sinwell." The excesses of the fast set in the modern era, Muriel suggests here, are no more than ancient vices updated. Another, more sincere drama was *Cash Down*, which presented the working out of tangled romantic feelings among a group of friends.[7]

Set in Provence in the late fifteenth century, *Paul, A Prisoner* was a religious drama with a complex plot. After the woman he loves witnesses what she believes is a miracle and decides to become a nun, Paul turns against religion. He decides to start staging his own miracles, involving public "healing" in the streets. In a twist, it turns out that he apparently really can heal the sick, but he rejects the church and sets out on a pilgrimage. The play ends in an epilogue set seven years later. Paul is dying in a monastery cell, and the moral of the play is made clear at last. The true miracle is his ultimate healing of himself and his ability to find faith before he dies.[8]

Susan regarded *Paul* as especially significant to Muriel. She read a draft of the play in bed in the summer of 1933 and stayed up thinking about it: "what it means to you, & why." It must have meant a good deal, since Muriel persisted through multiple rejections to try to get it produced and sought advice from theatrical friends about how to make it more commercially viable, though to no avail. Perhaps the temperamental, skeptical main character, overly invested in his romantic relationships at the expense of his development, is a reflection of some aspects of Muriel's own self-assessment in these years.[9]

Muriel had more success with two other plays, which were produced by so-called Sunday societies that put on low-budget productions on a subscription basis. One of these was *England's Elizabeth*, produced in September 1928 by the Royal Academy of Dramatic Art Players. The play, written in verse, is an attempt to redress popular misconceptions of Queen Elizabeth I and replace them with a real, human version of her. It has a patriotic vision: Elizabeth realizes, for instance, that she must renounce the happy, normal course of love and marriage and embrace, instead, the fate of being a strong ruler. As produced in 1928, the play received a fairly negative notice in the *Times*. Here again, Muriel persisted, with Susan's assistance. Caroline Spurgeon read the manuscript and called it, Susan reported, "a work of great *national* interest." The Postman's Cottage, she joked, had "harboured a genius unawares!" Spurgeon urged Muriel to put up any amount of money necessary to get it published, which she thought would lead to a full theatrical production. Her partner Lilian Clapham agreed, exclaiming, "*I think Miss Byrne will arrive, with a splash! Very soon!!*" But not much came of it, though RADA produced the play again in 1953 as part of the London County Council open air entertainments.[10]

If *England's Elizabeth* dramatized Muriel's preoccupations as a historian, her next produced play took her into Lord Peter Wimsey's territory: crime and punishment. In 1932, Muriel collaborated with Gladys Wheeler on a play entitled *Well, Gentlemen . . . ?* This play created a dramatic argument against capital punishment by presenting, first, the jury's deliberation over evidence, and then "what no jury can ever see—the events as they actually happened and the circumstances that caused them." In this case, the audience sees that a man had been provoked to murder his girlfriend's cruel employer who had, among other things, drowned kittens. Even if the details are somewhat unconvincing, as reviewers noticed, the point remained: juries are fallible and the death sentence irrevocable. Wimsey's own increasing qualms about sending criminals to the gallows should perhaps be read in light of this play, which was produced in October 1932 by the G Club Players at Cambridge Theatre in Seven Dials.[11]

Detective plays, or dramatized murder mysteries, were popular in this era. Jim Jaeger even satirized this sort of play in one of her novels, describing "a detective thriller, full of sliding panels, masked murderers, stalkings in the dark, weird lights and shadows." DLS had long considered making the leap from novel to stage, since, as she told her parents in 1923, "that's where the money is!" Muriel, too, saw the commercial appeal of the thriller on stage or screen. At one point she dreamed up a skeleton plot for a movie involving an ordinary English office worker in an adventure featuring cars, jewels, and an Argentine lady. In 1933, she asked DLS about the prospects for dramatizing one of Agatha Christie's stories. DLS knew Christie personally, since both were members of the Detection Club. DLS sprang into action. Christie was "in Ur of the Chaldees or some such place, which is rather a good thing, because she isn't very brisk at answering letters," she told Muriel, so she'd rung up her agent directly and told them to expect to hear from Muriel with the request.[12]

Nothing came of Muriel's proposed Christie adaptation. Someone else suggested to Muriel that she should consider writing a play based on DLS's characters. Muriel declined that particular offer, but turned to DLS herself: what about a collaboration? DLS and Muriel had seen each other for lunch, as usual, the day after the Somerville Association of Senior Members meeting in London in January 1935. Then, on February 10, DLS visited Muriel and Bar's flat, and over dinner, they began to sketch the outlines of a play. That night, they stayed up late talking "about this play business till early next morning." The next day, over lunch at Rules, they "mapped out a plan." At Muriel's suggestion, they agreed to use DLS's three "proprietary" characters (Peter, Harriet, and Bunter the butler), complemented by "new versions of her usual types," and write a collaborative play that would adapt her novels' style to the stage. By the time DLS left London, an outline had emerged.[13]

The play would be set during Harriet and Peter's honeymoon, and would provide scope not only for a charming, cozy mystery in an English village, but also for a fuller exploration of their relationship. It was obvious, by the end of *Have His Carcase*, that Harriet and Peter needed to reinvent marriage in order for it to suit them; *Busman's Honeymoon* would show them doing that. As DLS soon realized, this would also mean getting the characters engaged on the page, so that fans could understand why Harriet had decided, at last, to accept one of Peter's many proposals. This she would do in *Gaudy Night*, written after *Busman's Honeymoon* was completed but before it was performed.

READING BOTH *GAUDY Night* and *Busman's Honeymoon* as the product of collaboration between DLS, Bar, and Muriel changes the texts. It's clear, for one thing, that Lord Peter Wimsey and Harriet Vane as characters are not just ego projections on DLS's part. They are also composite portraits, capturing the conversations she had with Muriel and Bar about relationships and love and work. In a sense, Muriel and Bar become alternate models for Harriet and Peter. There's Muriel, with her curly blond hair, her scattershot brilliance, and her moods; there is Bar, with her grounded intelligence, her dark-haired comeliness, and her ruby cabochon ring, exactly like the ring Peter gives Harriet in *Busman's Honeymoon*. Bar's students passed along a rumor that she'd been given the ring by a fiancé who had died in the war, but this is probably mixing two things up. Bar's brother, Graham, was killed leading his company into action in August 1918. It would be reasonable to imagine that the ring, meanwhile, was a gift from Muriel, a "fiancé" who was invisible because of her sex, not her death.[14]

The writing of *Busman's Honeymoon* was a true collaboration: "honest 50-50" in Muriel's words. Back home in Essex, DLS consulted with her solicitor to confirm that the financial arrangements envisioned by the play's plot were realistic. And she was keen to conduct an experiment to ensure that the "murder-machine" was physically realistic, too. By February 16, DLS had written about four thousand words of dialogue for act 1. She sent this to Muriel, who worked on it in turn. The pair spent another weekend together at the end of February. In March, there was a lunch, then Muriel went to stay with DLS for a few days. In between these visits, they spoke on the telephone and sent each other detailed drafts and long letters with questions and ideas—one signed, charmingly, "Your partner in guilt, Dorothy L. Sayers." Drafts of the play show additions, edits, and stage direction amendments in both Muriel's and DLS's handwriting. Their notes reveal that the core issues of motive and method were worked out early in the process, when even characters' names were still uncertain. They are filled, too, with ideas and queries: "what about 4 acts? with the last one snappy?"[15]

In an interview with the press before the play opened, DLS argued that *Busman's Honeymoon* brought two features of her detective novels to the stage. First, it followed the rules of the Detection Club: "every movement is done, every clue is laid, in full sight of the audience, so that the audience has as much chance as the crime investigator of solving the problem." Second, "the 'love interest,' so painfully extraneous in most plays of this type, is here an essential part of the theme." Both accomplishments were hard-won.[16]

Muriel and DLS spent a lot of time on the problem of how to present a mystery plot onstage in a way that both fulfilled the genre's rules and made for good drama. In mid-February, DLS wrote to Muriel suggesting ways to portray the murderer's reactions in a natural way in early scenes without calling the audience's attention to that person. She suggested, too, how to place a red herring that would lead the audience to suspect the wrong person. But if DLS was the master at constructing a satisfying detective story, she deferred to Muriel's expertise about drama. She admitted that, when several people were onstage, "I find it difficult to keep them all talking!" On the question of establishing the possible motives for the murder, she told Muriel, "If you think these points need rubbing in more strongly, then do rub them in." (Muriel's marginal note: "rub in word *motive* here.")[17]

Of course, the two elements, detective and dramatic, were linked. It was crucial to the plot that the honeymoon cottage, where Peter and Harriet find the dead body, should be locked when they arrive. Muriel worried about the locked door: why hadn't the housekeeper alerted someone when she found it locked? DLS admitted this was "undoubtedly awkward," and could be explained only by the housekeeper's general lack of goodwill. Muriel found that satisfactory; as she noted in the margin of DLS's letter, "This won't worry any audience." DLS explained, too, how the discovery of a corpse behind a locked door was not as shocking in this case as it would otherwise be. The audience knows there is another set of keys; and they know, because the doctor tells them that the victim didn't die right away, that he might have locked the door himself before expiring. This is important, because, as DLS put it, "the audience are not then *forced* to look for a murder-machine." Muriel was reassured. "With your help & my own insertions in the dialogue, I've now quieted my uneasiness about the lock, so I hope you'll find it all right."[18]

DLS and Muriel paid close attention, in mid-March, to the timing that needed to underlie the action of act 2. This involved a careful consideration of the constable's and the superintendent's actions after the body is discovered. How, for example, will the constable convey a message to the police station about the situation, and how long will it take? When might the superintendent realistically be expected to arrive on the scene, and what will he do there? At one point, Muriel told DLS that she had "worked over Act II to my uttermost," and could not "do any more until we've gone through it together."[19]

Balancing the requirements of a murder mystery with those of a realistic, sensitive portrayal of a complex relationship was an even greater problem. As DLS and Muriel would later tell producers of the play, the emotional balance rested on Peter and Harriet, "the complete sincerity of whose emotion is the touchstone by which all the rest of the action must be tested." Early in the drafting process, DLS tended to postpone the problem of presenting realistic feelings. "I don't think Peter and Harriet say too much in Act I about the upset to their honeymoon when the corpse is discovered. It looks heartless." But it was soon clear that they needed both a proper quarrel scene and a proper love scene for the play to work on an emotional as well as a technical level. Fretting about it on one train ride, DLS wondered why she'd ever introduced such complexity into her work. Using the slangy abbreviation for "detective," she asked Muriel, "Why can't I just write a nice little 'tec play & be damned to it?"[20]

Character sketches written for the play suggest the emotional landscape that DLS and Muriel sought to evoke. At forty-five, Lord Peter Wimsey is still deceptively youthful looking but "his face, in its rare moments of repose, is beginning to show the marks set there by time & experience." Certain features, "above all a certain nervous tautness of gesture & carriage," suggest a family tradition of aristocratic inbreeding and highlight the biological wisdom of marrying Harriet. On the other hand, the authors are clear that his more exaggerated affectations—the monocle, the "drawl"—are merely "make-up which he can & does put off when he is earnest." None of this prevents the villagers from recognizing him "at once as a hereditary ruler," a phrase that underscores the conservatism that tinges this portrayal of an otherwise modern marriage. Harriet, at thirty, has a less delicate bearing. She is "tall, strongly-made & vigorous in speech, movement & colouring," and her unhappy past experiences have "matured but not tamed her." She has "an immense intellectual sincerity," which Peter loves in her, and she needs her passions and her reason to be in alignment.

Admitting that Peter and Harriet are a "curiously assorted couple," Muriel and DLS argue that their shared educational background allow them a "common understanding." More importantly, perhaps, the adverse circumstances of their pasts—Peter's shell shock, Harriet's traumatic relationship with the poet whose murder formed the basis of *Strong Poison*—have grounded them both. As the mayhem of the murder mystery unfolds around them during what was meant to be their honeymoon, their past suffering makes them philosophical. "This, after all, is life as they have always known it—one damned thing after another—& they are able to preserve a sense of humour & proportion which, all things considered, is highly creditable to both of them." This outcome is not assured. In the play, the characters of Miss Twitterton and Crutchley form a kind of evil version of Peter and Harriet. Miss Twitterton, too, has been shaped by a painful past, which leads her to recreate the violence of her childhood in her adult life. She is the older of the pair, over forty; Crutchley, "about 30," has "sulky good-looks which women find attractive." He casts the "dreadful menace of male violence" over the play, to quote the stage directions, resurrecting the threat of Miss Twitterton's own abusive father and, briefly, raising the question of whether Peter, too, might have a violent temper once he's married. In the case of Crutchley and Miss Twitterton, vanity, greed, and foolishness swamp all possible happiness. Peter and Harriet must marshal their moral resources in order to avoid a similar fate.[21]

On the subject of the relationship between Harriet and Peter, Bar came into her own. She objected, for instance, to the idea of them sharing their wedding night on a dead man's mattress. DLS was apologetic: "tell Bar I'm sorry about the bride-bed!" She'd been thinking pragmatically; they wouldn't choose a secondary bedroom in their own honeymoon cottage, and after all, "the old boy didn't *die* in the bed." DLS was willing to concede the point to Bar: "but if it really disgusts her, cut it out." Instead, they provided for the airing of the mattress. Muriel thought the whole thing was funny: "I feel sure the aired mattress will satisfy Bar!!! I only mentioned it to illustrate the way in which your female fans are all 'mad about the boy,' & because it gave me a good laugh." But if Bar was a stand-in for Wimsey's female fans, she was also correct about the importance of getting the emotional resonance of the play right.[22]

DLS struggled with this. By March 6, she'd written the love scene "except for the infernal quotation, which won't come right. It is too, too shy-making for words, and kept on falling into blank verse in the most unfortunate manner." She briefly considered using a version of the lines of her own invention that would feature in *Gaudy Night*: "we have come / to that still centre where the spinning world / Sleeps on its axis,—to the heart of rest." In the end, she turned to Muriel to verify that the center of the play held. Working out the denouement at the end of March, she wrote to Muriel, "I think that in this scene my mind has been so closely set upon the *construction* of the thing—the making it *water-tight*—that I have probably missed some of the necessary emotion." She was worried, especially, about the balance between comedy and the inevitable tragic note, "which is bound to creep in if a real murderer is going to be really detected and hanged. The least tip the wrong way, and the thing will become either heartless or really grim." She beseeched Muriel, "Please don't mind altering anything at all that seems to you weak or inadequate. I trust your judgement quite implicitly."[23]

Even thornier was the quarrel scene, which was the emotional climax of the play. Here, Peter offers to give up his work of detection, which, he fears, has allowed the specter of violence to disturb the peace of his honeymoon. In mid-April, DLS was agonizing over how to get the tone exactly right. "It will have to be frightfully earnest, I'm afraid—because Harriet will never do the 'you are my lord & master' stunt, & Peter would have fifty fits if she did." She wrote to Muriel, "I have made a valiant attempt to tackle the accursed quarrel scene. It is extremely pompous!" In the final version, Harriet simply insists that Peter must carry on with his work. "What kind of life could we have if I knew that you had become less than yourself by marrying me?" she asks. "If we disagree, we'll fight it out like gentlemen. But we won't stand for matrimonial blackmail." Traditional heterosexual marriage is founded on falsity; in building something new, Peter and Harriet will be two gentlemen, honest with each other and approaching their work with integrity. In the end, DLS felt they had created something good. She told Muriel that she was struck by the "curious and (to me) unconscious symmetry" produced in act 2, when "*all* the masks come off" at last. "I don't want to exaggerate about it all—it is mere comedy—but I have a feeling that, since it worked out naturally so, it is, in its small way, right. Probably you saw this side of it before I did."[24]

IF PETER AND Harriet were to have a honeymoon, they needed to agree to get married. This would be accomplished in *Gaudy Night*, which DLS began to write at the same time as *Busman's Honeymoon*. Muriel was "*dreadfully* contrite" for interrupting the writing of the novel with more queries about the play in March. In fact, play revisions would drag on until the middle of April, long after DLS was ready to be done with it: "curse this ruddy play!" She wanted to work on *Gaudy Night*, since "Peter must be got safely engaged!" But Muriel was not the only distraction. Mac was "gloomy & suspicious" about the play. "Everything is bound to be wrong, in his opinion." DLS found herself in a depression, "rather Peterishly," reacting to the completion of the play by summoning a host of worries about a film being made using her characters, about *Busman's Honeymoon*, and about *Gaudy Night*. She planned a visit to Muriel in London to cheer herself up: "what I should have done without you in all this, I simply do NOT know." The visit might have cheered DLS, but it didn't get the difficult novel written. Again, on April 17, with Mac in bed with a stomachache, she told Muriel, "I must try & pull myself together & get on with *Gaudy Night*, dismissing these other matters from what I call my mind." She later said she'd rewritten the first third of the novel three times, "cursing continually."[25]

Ostensibly another book in the Wimsey series of detective novels, *Gaudy Night* is not only, or even mainly, a novel about the slow romance of Harriet and Peter. Instead, it is a novel about intellectual integrity and the enduring power of a scholarly female community. Harriet's central problem, and the larger theme of the novel, is how to balance head and heart: how to stay true to her work while also allowing herself to engage emotionally and sexually with another adult. The community of women at the heart of *Gaudy Night* provides the missing link, allowing her to be both intellectually honest and emotionally engaged.

In *Gaudy Night*, just as in *Busman's Honeymoon*, the emotional dimensions proved the most difficult to handle. DLS described Peter and Harriet as "the world's most awkward pair of lovers" to Muriel. They were "both

so touchy and afraid to commit themselves to anything but hints and allusions!" On August 19, 1935, DLS sent Muriel six chapters of *Gaudy Night*
with the promise of the rest shortly thereafter. She was jubilant, she said in
her Tudorbethan style: "for whereas our late sovereign lady Queene Elizabeth of glorious memory did advisedly say lett time passe, yet the time that
hath passed in the making up of this marriage is run out of all reason."[26]

Muriel's reception was critical, as DLS had half-suspected it would be.
She felt that the average reader "doesn't want the real Oxford." DLS replied
that she might be right, and that as a result the book might not be popular. But she could not create a "deliberate falsification for personal gain,"
when the book itself was all about how such a lie was an unforgiveable "sin
against intellectual integrity." She admitted that the "first three chapters
move slowly," though she justified it on the grounds of needing the background. And she argued that the book "is personal (not autobiographical) in
the sense that it presents a consistent philosophy of conduct for which I am
prepared to assume personal responsibility." Ultimately, she had written the
book that she wanted to write, the one that was "there to be written."

On one level, DLS's reply reasserts her ultimate control over her characters, despite the *Busman's Honeymoon* collaboration. It also suggests the
depth of the transformation that DLS was undergoing. What bothered her in
Muriel's response "is that you should worry so much about what the average
reader or reviewer may think." DLS was turning away from the practical,
market-driven approach that defined her early writing career and insisting on the overriding importance of professional and creative integrity. She
closed her letter to Muriel, though, with thanks for her frank criticism and
an implicit invitation for more: "it will be splendid when you are back & we
can have a good argufying evening."[27]

WHILE DLS AND Muriel wrote *Busman's Honeymoon*, Phoenix Films was
making a movie about Lord Peter Wimsey, starring Peter Haddon, called
The Silent Passenger. Although it was loosely based on one of her stories, DLS
loathed *The Silent Passenger* and had nothing to do with it. She even offered
to send Muriel the tickets to the trade show, if she were given any, rather
than make an extra trip to London to see it herself: "life isn't long enough."
She wasn't opposed to movies on principle. Reacting to Muriel's film script,
Doubles and Quits, she praised its attention to "the kind of thing that *only* the

camera can tell." But after the *Silent Passenger* debacle, she was hesitant to let Wimsey appear again on-screen. While negotiating contract details over *Busman's Honeymoon*, DLS argued that she and Muriel must retain the right *not* to do a film. Yet she sent Muriel to do the in-person negotiations and told her, "Anything you decide I shall be ready to agree to."[28]

The question of rights and contracts took on new significance in the summer of 1935. Nancy Pearn, DLS's agent, had worked at the Curtis Brown company. But when the founder brought his son, Spencer, in as the head of the company, she decided to leave with some colleagues and set up their own shop. DLS corresponded about all of this with Muriel in her mock-Elizabethan style. She was inclined to be loyal to Pearn, and she was disgusted with Spencer Curtis Brown's condescending efforts to get her to stay with the agency. He had spoken to her "as though I were a littel headstrong Child running sans Councell or Consideration into I know not what." She'd wanted to point out that while he was but twenty-eight years old, she was forty-two, and "I had learned one thing, wch was, never by no means to treat anie man as a Foole to whom I came as a Suitor; but having sett all these Wordes upon paper for the easing of my Stomack, I did tear all upp againe, & so leave him as they say to stewe in his own Juice." Unsurprisingly, she stayed with Pearn.[29]

The question of whether or not the actor Peter Haddon would take the role of Lord Peter Wimsey in the stage production of *Busman's Honeymoon*, as he had in *The Silent Passenger*, became a source of considerable angst for DLS and Muriel over the spring of 1935. DLS saw Haddon's name on a playbill in Oxford in early March and wondered to Muriel if it was a portent—for good or ill, it isn't clear. In the end, Haddon turned the role down, precisely because of its psychological complexity. While he could have been the Wimsey from *Murder Must Advertise*, the *Busman's Honeymoon* Wimsey "rather frightens me, and I cannot see myself getting my teeth into the part." Looking around for alternatives, DLS discovered that the chaplain of Balliol was "the *perfect* Peter Wimsey," and reported to Muriel that her heart "is BROKEN" at the unfairness of the situation. This was actually Maurice Roy Ridley, who had thrilled DLS as the Newdigate Prize–winning poet at Oxford back in 1913. He did accept DLS's invitation to attend the Detection Club dinner in 1935, and DLS implored Muriel to come with a friend, to balance the numbers and "to meet Ridley, who is fun." But, fun or not, the chaplain of Balliol was not going to play Lord Peter Wimsey onstage.[30]

Having finished *Gaudy Night*, DLS turned to the novelization of *Busman's Honeymoon*. Although the play was not yet placed, she warned her publisher that the novel could not come out before the play was produced. By mid-December 1935, she was "struggling with the Dowager," Wimsey's mother, who provides a witty running commentary on the events leading up to the wedding. DLS wrestled, too, with the difficulties of book versus play. How to prove, for instance, that "nobody *could* have entered the house" between the murder and the couple's arrival? Where exactly should the cottage be located?[31]

More significantly, the novelization provided the chance to elaborate on the founding of the Wimsey-Vane partnership. There was much controversy over the introduction, in the widely adopted new Anglican prayer book of 1925, of two options for the marriage service, one in which the wife promises to "obey" her husband and one in which she does not. DLS gave her characters a chance to weigh in on the topic. Harriet and Peter opt for the older version, for idiosyncratic reasons. She'd obey if, for example, he shouted "run!" during a fire. He, of course, would obey her in precisely the same circumstances, but decides not to add the word to his own vows only because it would generate so much gossip in the press.[32]

Muriel gave D. Rowe a draft of the *Busman's Honeymoon* novel to read during Easter 1936, which they spent together. D. Rowe "enjoyed it enormously, all the more so for having had your pointers as to which bits were being transfused into the play," and she felt that there "really are some splendid bits of writing in it, though the theme doesn't allow for anything quite as jolly as the bells of the Nine Tailors." But she warned both Muriel and Bar to make sure they didn't find themselves overworked, between teaching, writing, and trying to get the play produced. She advised, inimitably, "Do, oh do remember that when stern duty, daughter of the voice of God, is at the other end of a telephone the only thing to do is to ring off."[33]

They took her advice, to an extent. In late August 1936, DLS joined Muriel and Bar in Cornwall for a bit of holidaying.

DLS on holiday with Bunter the dog (MSBC 9/5)

Muriel had "secured a bungalow" near Padstow, which, Bar reported, was "in a good position with a little garden sloping to the low cliff edge." DLS wrote cheerfully to Bar, to ask whether she should bring "the thing that makes ice," and hoping "that you and Muriel are feeling more rested. At the moment I feel thoroughly frazzled out, and shall probably come and sleep solidly all day—so please reassure Muriel that I shall not be hankering for metropolitan dissipation!" Finally, while still on holiday, Muriel got a wire: someone wanted the play.[34]

FROM THEN, IT was a mad rush to opening night. *Busman's Honeymoon* was produced by Beatrice Wilson, who was Muriel's colleague at the Royal Academy of Dramatic Art. Muriel remembered "the *fun* we had with rehearsals & the whole business of production." When Dennis Arundell, cast as Wimsey, complained about a line being too short for the amount of stage he was meant to cross during it, they "soothed him" with, "Of course, darling, we will give you all the words you want"—whereupon, Muriel recalled, "he performed the existing line . . . brilliantly." This was "the way to manage your actors!"[35]

Muriel was in Birmingham when the play first opened there at the start of November. It opened in London on December 16. By then, the play's treatment of a marriage between an aristocrat and a commoner with a complex romantic history had become, in DLS's words, "fraught with an appalling topical significance." The relationship between King Edward VIII and the American divorcée Wallis Simpson was public knowledge, and a constitutional crisis loomed over his desire to marry her. In London, when Harriet Vane said, "What kind of life could we have if I knew you had become less than yourself by marrying me?" Muriel overheard a woman hiss: "Mrs. Simpson!"[36]

The critical reviews were mixed, but the public liked it. DLS was heartened by the views of her gardener, who told her, "There was a bit of everything—a bit of a thrill and then a bit of a laugh and then a bit of what I call the sob-stuff. . . . It's natural, ain't it? because life's always a mix-up." To Muriel, DLS commented, "I really do not think, if we had tried with both hands for a fortnight, we could have stated our own theory—or Will Shakespeare's practice—very much more forcibly or concisely." Though their letters are full of jokes and complaints about cooks and cleaners—and DLS's novels tend to rely on unflattering, stereotyped portrayals of lower-class people—DLS and Muriel valued the validation they received from working-class readers and audience members. It demonstrated that they were right to work in popular genres and to look beyond the narrow prejudices of a particular educated class. If Shakespeare's dramatic logic could be found in a gardener's words, it was only sensible to write plays that spoke to gardeners and secretaries, as well as to novelists and lecturers.[37]

In *Gaudy Night*, Harriet relies on her college community to provide the support and context she needs to find her way to a workable relationship with Peter. In much the same way, writing *Busman's Honeymoon* in collaboration with Muriel and Bar allowed DLS to break through the emotional barriers that had increasingly seemed to stultify her work. Doing so allowed DLS and Muriel to connect with far wider audiences in direct and meaningful ways. The play's commercial success, too, would equip them with expanded financial and social capital. DLS would use that capital to work in new realms, exploring the moral questions introduced in her later Wimsey novels more and more explicitly.

13

WHAT THE BUSMAN WROUGHT

USMAN'S HONEYMOON BROUGHT SUCCESS AND opportunity to its authors. In addition to their work on the production itself, Muriel and DLS gave talks on the play, always "as an unrehearsed double turn, which went over very well." Victor Gollancz published the text of the play in 1937, with Muriel serving as consultant. More than a strict acting version, it was designed to appeal to general readers, too. Nonetheless, it would be used by repertory and amateur companies to stage many productions over the next decades. All of this provided both Muriel and DLS with a much-needed infusion of cash, allowing them to live more securely and spend time and energy on projects of their own choosing. Muriel improved her material circumstances and focused more deeply on her historical research. DLS moved away from detective novels and toward writing plays and essays dealing with ethics, morality, and religion. The turn toward theater, in particular, gave her a new sense of common ground and collaboration with D. Rowe. DLS also took a leading role among Somerville alumnae, having overcome the deep ambivalence and shame that had kept her away in the 1920s.[1]

Muriel and Bar adopted a dog, Bunter, a Cairn terrier, in 1935. He was named after the character in the Wimsey novels and "was graciously patronised" by DLS herself. Muriel and Bar had visited "one of the lost dogs' homes," where Bunter won their hearts. "We've got a cat, and we live in a flat," they had protested, but of course he had joined them and the cat, Timothy White, anyway. Muriel joked that he immediately ruled the roost. "The cat never once ungloved his disciplinary paw; and within eighteen months we had given up the flat and taken a house with a garden." Indeed, in 1937,

Bar and Muriel moved into a house at 28 St. John's Wood Terrace that would be their home for the rest of their lives—the receipts from *Busman's Honeymoon* providing the means for an upgrade worthy of Bunter's needs. They showed it to D. Rowe in January and moved in April, hosting a party the day before the furniture arrived. Here, again, their legal arrangements, including a joint insurance policy on the house, suggest the ways that they built a shared household without a legal marriage.[2]

In another sign of *Busman*'s benefits, DLS and Bar traveled to Europe together, visiting Venice in 1937. Bar made their travel arrangements, booking their cabins and their hotel rooms "at demi-pension so that we can lunch at restaurants if we like." In Venice, DLS let Bar, the more experienced traveler, take the lead. DLS "asks humbly intelligent questions about the history of Venice," Bar told Muriel, signing off with the cheery promise: "I shall spend lashings of money! I love you." DLS used the trip as inspiration for a new play, *Love All*, which features a woman who becomes a successful playwright rather than pining after her caddish husband—a fairly pointed theme, especially given Mac's doubts about *Busman*.[3]

BACK IN LONDON that September, DLS assisted in the process of moving the production of *Busman's Honeymoon* to a new theater. DLS kept Muriel and Bar, who were now traveling together, abreast of the developments by letter, hoping that this business was "not poisoning your holiday & turning it into the Busman's variety." DLS visited the theater with various souvenirs from Venice for the cast, who enjoyed the "presents of little glass fish & things." The original actors playing Peter and Harriet had decided not to carry on with the relocated production, so DLS assisted, too, with the process of finding their replacements. The new Peter was Basil Foster, and, after some reversals of fortune, DLS was able to secure the role of Harriet for her original top choice, Ethel Glendinning. As DLS put it to Muriel, "It is true that her ankles are more meaty, but so is her personality." And that, of course, was what counted, when it came to playing Harriet Vane.[4]

DLS relied on Muriel's absence to discourage Foster's more harebrained ideas. When she and the director were sure something was a bad idea but couldn't think of a suitable objection quickly, they simply said, "Well, let's try it your way, and when Miss Byrne and/or the producer are here, we'll ask them." On the other hand, DLS used flattery to get Foster to reverse changes that the previous Wimsey had made, which she and Muriel hadn't liked. It was hard work, no doubt, but satisfying to DLS, as her dream of writing for the theater was finally a reality. Even Mac was convinced, and now believed "that *Busman* is (for some reason or other) the goods!" Muriel and DLS, the proud collaborators, marked the one-year anniversary of *Busman*'s opening on November 9, 1937, and DLS suggested that they celebrate by going to see some other plays together in London.[5]

Muriel used the proceeds of *Busman* to finance a partial "sabbatical year" which she later described as "necessary mainly on grounds of health." This gave her the time and mental energy to delve into the Lisle letters in the Public Record Office. She seems also to have begun working on the book that would become her memoir. D. Rowe read a draft of this, as well as a manuscript of one of Muriel's plays. The draft memoir gave her great pleasure, "rousing parallel memories."[6]

DLS, too, turned to other writing projects as *Busman* thrived. Although Wimsey was more or less retired as a character, DLS had some fun playing around with her most famous creation. She sometimes wrote to her friends, including Muriel and Helen Simpson, in character as Wimsey, even changing her handwriting to fit her alter ego. When the famous cartoonist David Low featured Lord Peter Wimsey in a cartoon, DLS wrote to Muriel in no fewer than four separate handwritings, with separate opinions expressed by herself, Peter, Harriet, and Bunter. Harriet objected to the cartoonist giving her husband "rabbit-teeth"; Peter was alarmed that the cartoon showed him wearing "such checks"; and Bunter, with unexpected sly humor, begged "leave to state my opinion that this is a Low cartoon."[7]

In March 1937, DLS assembled a collection of friends, including Muriel, for a mock inquiry into the Wimsey ancestors. Muriel's special contribution to this "Wimsification" was, naturally, on the Wimseys of Tudor times. Sir Roger Wimsey's life seems to have had a queer subtext. This "delicate & fastidious gentleman," a scholar and a poet, never married, though he and Sir Philip Sidney were "great cronies." Another Tudor Wimsey, Muriel suggested, was actually Shakespeare—or rather, one half of a collaborating duo. This duke of Denver, she argued, worked with the earl of Oxford to write many of Shakespeare's plays. Fresh from her collaboration with DLS, Muriel explained, it was inevitable that she should consider whether these "two gifted youths," Oxford and Denver, so often linked by contemporaries, themselves collaborated. In real life, Muriel was highly skeptical about the theory that Shakespeare was really Edward de Vere, the seventeenth earl of Oxford. As a Wimsey historian, though, she leaped eagerly into the conspiratorial fray, demonstrating her claims with absurd ciphers, symbols, and calculations. DLS sent the published results of her "little Wimsey joke" to D. Rowe for Christmas in 1936. D. Rowe found it all a "lovely jape," and wanted to know: "have none of Peter's school reports or Harriet's early love letters or even Bunter's letters home during the war come to light?"[8]

PERHAPS NATURALLY, AS she renewed her contact with the MAS in the early 1930s, DLS also cultivated a greater degree of connection with Somerville and Oxford. *Gaudy Night*'s fictional college of Shrewsbury is based on Somerville. The characters have echoes of the people DLS knew. Miss De Vine, the historian, suggests aspects of both Mildred Pope and Muriel St. Clare Byrne. DLS, sensibly, denied that she had created any conscious copies of real people in *Gaudy Night*, though she admitted that Miss Barton, with her "feminist and humanitarian views," was based to some extent on Margery Fry, who had been the college librarian before serving as principal from 1926 to 1931. In real life, the Somerville community was ambivalent about the novel. But its portrayal of the life of academic women meant the novel has remained influential, significant, and widely discussed. An academic from Germany told DLS in 1955 that the novel "is highly appreciated by German university women." The mother of Dr. (later Dame) Joan Evans, an Oxford contemporary of the MAS, thought that DLS was "quite the best Somervillian of the younger generation, and read *Gaudy Night* once a year."[9]

Somerville had continued to expand in terms of buildings, though it was limited by Oxford's 1927 decision to restrict the total number of students who could be enrolled through the women's colleges. Helen Darbishire, who had been an English tutor in the MAS's day, took over the leadership in 1931. In 1934, DLS visited Somerville to speak at a dinner celebrating her old French tutor, Mildred Pope, who was leaving to take a position at the University of Manchester. Characteristically, she fussed about the preparations, asking Muriel if a dark blue-gray coat and skirt would be acceptable elements of the required "Full Academical Dress." She didn't relish having to rush a shopping trip for a black suit: "it will be a damned nuisance, me being so outsize."[10]

At the dinner, DLS spoke seriously. For women of her generation, Oxford University had been a distant and rather incomprehensible body, setting exams and providing "the simulacrum of a great tradition which was not ours." They had "rather pathetically" followed that tradition, "hoping that by assiduous make-believe we might somehow end by making the belief come true." Yet it worked, and "a curiously mixed bunch of us went to the Sheldonian to take part in the queerest ceremony of degree-taking that can ever have been held in any University," earning, in rapid succession, not only two degrees, but three sets of academic regalia, the obligation to pay three sets of fees, and the right "to be addressed for the first—& for many of us the last—time by the title: Domina."

Since then, she explained, she had not been much in touch with Oxford life. But although her career had taken her far from the halls of academe, she emphasized the serious importance of a place like Oxford. Young men who had failed to thrive often blamed the university for not preparing them for life. On the other hand, people complained that women, especially, were doing nothing with their university educations, and that "they have only succeeded in making themselves hard-featured, hard-hearted, restless, childless & unhappy." Such complaints were nonsense, DLS argued. For one thing, a university education did a great deal to prepare a person for any sort of work. In the advertising profession, for example, people from Oxford and Cambridge benefited from "the scholar's habit of orderly thinking," an ease with handling words, and the habit of sharing knowledge freely and generously. More importantly, though, Oxford provided a sanctuary for scholars such as Pope. She exemplified the best of Oxford: "the integrity of judgment that gain cannot corrupt, the humility in the face of facts that self-esteem cannot blind; the generosity of a great mind, that is eager to give praise to others; the singleness of purpose that pursues knowledge as some men pursue glory & that will not be contented with the second-hand or the second best."[11]

In 1935, in the midst of writing *Busman's Honeymoon* and *Gaudy Night*, DLS was elected to the chairmanship of the Somerville alumnae organization, the Association of Senior Members. At the same time, Bar was nominated to the committee for the period 1935 to 1937. This organization met twice yearly: a summer meeting held around the time of the Gaudy at Somerville, and a winter meeting held in London just after the new year. Muriel, Bar, D. Rowe, and Susan were all regular attendees of these meetings, particularly the London ones, in the 1930s.[12]

As chairman, DLS sought to link the Association more closely to Somerville and to give it some purpose beyond "the partaking of a cheap tea" and the perpetuation of its own existence. This she achieved through two measures. First, she oversaw some formalizing of the relationship between the Association and the Somerville College council, in particular altering the regulations so that the Association chairman would be elected to the council ex officio and provide official representation on that governing body. As Bar had explained to her, the situation was a delicate one, because the "College rather counts on the Chairman to give them the opinion of members when required," but few members "would want the Old Students to have any power to hold up Council business." Second, DLS initiated what might be imagined as *Gaudy Night* in a bureaucratic manifestation. She introduced the idea at the 1936 Gaudy, arguing that women, too, should benefit from the network of connections spanning professional, political, and social circles that linked alumni of male colleges. As she told Helen Darbishire, "After all—though a good many merry jests have been voiced at the expense of the old school tie, there is something in the idea, if one does not take the thing too sentimentally!" This became a system for linking Somerville alumnae with each other according to shared interests, including a mechanism for allowing graduates to direct inquiries to a central body, which would forward them on to the most appropriate Somervillian. Connected with this was an effort to encourage social gatherings of Somervillians in various places, led by the alumnae. Soon there were plans afoot to start local Somerville organizations in places such as Maidstone and the Leicester-Nottingham area.[13]

The system continued to function after DLS's term as chairman had ended. Late in 1937, the network put her in touch with one of her old Somerville classmates, F. V. Barry. Barry had made a teaching career at Clapham High School, but when that school closed, she was left with an uncertain future and wanted help finding literary work. DLS offered Barry immediate advice and assistance. If she wanted to write children's books, DLS would put her in touch with Basil Blackwell. She could also connect her with Michael Sadleir at Constable, who could put her in touch with the periodical the *Nineteenth Century*. She warned, though, that "none of the high-brow weeklies pay well" and that building a network of literary connections was slow work. Barry, for her part, attended a performance of DLS's newest play.[14]

DLS also gave advice on the advertising business to a recent Somerville graduate in October 1938. In addition to allowing the young woman to use her name when approaching S. H. Benson, DLS offered some general insights.

Advertising firms liked university graduates, but "they will pay more attention to you if you can offer, in addition, a certain amount of worldly experience," whether that was knowledge of "the kind of behaviour expected in
the stately homes of England" or "of how the poor live, which will make
you more sensitive and sympathetic in dealing with such subjects, as how to
make a grand family meal for 4½d. on somebody's butter beans." In 1939,
she was contacted by the writer Marion Müller, née Darbishire. Her husband
was German, and on marrying him, she had lost her British citizenship.
They were, by 1939, desperate to get out of Nazi Germany. DLS was doubtful
about how much help she could be, but she suggested another Somervillian
to contact and also invited Müller to get in touch with DLS's agent and use
her name to establish the connection. DLS had been an effective, original
chairman who fostered new forms of community among Somerville graduates. Even after she left the role, the Association provided MAS members
with an excuse to get together, and DLS seems to have thrown a party the
day after the 1937 meeting.[15]

MURIEL LATER SAID that the most important achievement of "our old *Busman*" was introducing DLS "to the theatre world & theatre people & all that
side of my life, which she took to with a whole heart & really loved." That she
emphatically did. DLS would concentrate increasingly on theater in the years
after *Busman*, producing a remarkable series of plays that staged an intervention in conversations about the status of religion in British life. This work
put her in touch with "theatre people" in general but also, more closely, with
D. Rowe, in particular, who became an important critic for DLS's theatrical
efforts.[16]

DLS had wanted D. Rowe to come see *Busman* in London. For a while,
events conspired against her: opening night was "bang in the middle of
term's last week," and then the next month D. Rowe got the flu and couldn't
"get in to a matinée on my way up to Charis's," as she'd planned. Finally, the
following spring, DLS arranged for D. Rowe and her sister Bena to see *Busman's Honeymoon* from the stalls and to get a tour backstage. Afterward they
visited DLS at her London flat.[17]

From the time of this visit, DLS and D. Rowe developed an ongoing dialogue about the theater. DLS had turned to writing a religious drama, to be
performed in the Canterbury Cathedral chapter house, entitled *The Zeal of*

Thy House. She'd done some market research first, seeing a "Jesuit play" in order "to estimate the chances of religious drama in London." Then, she sent the last remaining typescript copy of *Zeal*, which had "swum up from the deeps of Muriel's house-moving," to D. Rowe, explaining that it was written to suit the chapter house, which had no backstage area to facilitate entrances and exits.[18]

The play was DLS's first full-scale exploration of the link between creative work and religion. It tells the story of an architect, Michael, rebuilding the cathedral who realizes, after a literal fall that disables him permanently, that his sin was not his petty financial crimes nor his sexual affair with a local lady, but his excessive pride in his work. In particular, the play introduces DLS's metaphor between the creative process and the Holy Trinity: the Idea, the Energy, and the Power, which parallel the Father, the Word, and the Spirit. She would continue to develop that metaphor in subsequent work, particularly her essays on religion and creativity.[19]

D. Rowe praised it for its plot, which she said was "based on inexorable logic," joking that being logical was too often, in her region at least, equated with "smelling nasty." She saw Michael's culminating speech on "the three-fold nature of the works of creation" as being in conversation with the "'integrity' motif of 'Gaudy Night.'" That novel had insisted that intellectual and professional integrity were more important than personal loyalty. In *Zeal*, as D. Rowe realized, DLS developed that idea further, arguing that work has its own transcendent value, ignored at one's peril. D. Rowe also admired the play from a technical perspective. The prose, she felt, held a "constant suggestion of rhythm." She was impressed at how DLS had navigated the limitations of the available stage by "stately entrances down the main body" and by parking people, as necessary, on a plinth and steps. Far too many performance spaces posed this trouble, she reflected: "oh the number of amateur performances in which the stage direction should read (exit L, into Hall playground, duck and run round the back of the Hall in the rain for next act)." She asked, too, whether the space between the proposed screens would be large enough for the props and actors awaiting cues, and hoped that the screens themselves would be fixed securely: all sage advice from a seasoned producer.[20]

DLS was grateful for D. Rowe's reply, especially the point about logic. "I do feel that if one has to write a play on a religious subject, the only way to do it is to avoid wistful emotionalism, and get as much drama as one can out of sheer hard dogma." She forgave the chapter house its lack of backstage, since it was built in the fourteenth century, and reassured D. Rowe on the subject of the screens. But she agreed, in general principle, on the subject of inadequate amateur stage accommodation. "Poor Muriel," she explained, had faced dire problems at Bedford College. "In her production of *Tobias*, a black-out could only be obtained by signalling from the back of the hall to a person down a passage, who then waved a handkerchief to a person standing by the switch at the end of another passage. On the occasion when I was there, it was not obtained."[21]

DLS invited Muriel, Bar, and D. Rowe to join her at the theater festival in Canterbury where her play was to be performed. She explained to the organizer that Muriel was, in addition to being her collaborator, "an amateur theatrical producer of considerable experience," while D. Rowe was a producer "at one of the most important amateur theatres in the kingdom." She also invited her friends to a dinner beforehand that featured a brief spoof play: *A Meal in My House, or, A Quotation for Every Occasion: An Irreligious Drama*. Muriel went, but D. Rowe, although she had been looking forward to going, couldn't join them, thwarted this time, she said, by the vicissitudes of cross-country trains and weekend schedules. This was the moment when Charis and her son were staying with her while he convalesced from appendicitis. Perhaps that added to the balance of the fates against the journey. However, she and Charis were both reading the novel version of *Busman's Honeymoon* and, she told DLS, enjoying it "*enormously.*"[22]

DLS was delighted at the play's success. She wrote, with uncharacteristically exuberant punctuation, to Muriel: "I have had a kindly review of *Zeal* in the *New Statesman*!!!!!" The play next enjoyed a stint in London. Muriel saw it there, again, in March 1938. At DLS's request, D. Rowe hung some posters for the production in her Bournemouth theater, in order to bring it "to the notice of any Bournemouth people who may be visiting London at Easter." The play, with its London company, then went on a national tour, which included a stint in Bournemouth at the Palace Court Theatre in March 1939. Conveying the news to DLS, D. Rowe was delighted: "*hurray!*" The Bournemouth Little Theatre Club had its part to play, aside from just hosting—the cast of one of its recent productions chanted the chorus in *Zeal* there. Still, *Zeal* was no *Busman*. DLS had invested her own money in the tour, and in November 1938, she said that although it was "doing very well," it was "not paying back the capital."[23]

DLS worked on other plays, too, in the late 1930s. *The Devil to Pay* re-imagined the Faustus legend and, like *Zeal*, played at Canterbury Cathedral and then in London. While writing it, she complained to D. Rowe that she'd invented a fictional, wise pope for the play, only to be thwarted by historical fact, which provided for a pope "the most flagrantly vicious and corrupt Borgia that ever defiled a family or the Vatican." Once again, D. Rowe regretted missing it in Canterbury, but looked forward to seeing it in London, where she would be staying in Charis's flat; she invited DLS to join her there for a "meal or a sherry or anything."[24]

FOR HER PART, D. Rowe wanted DLS to become more involved in amateur theater. "I want to show you our Little Theatre sometime: it is small but not ill-favoured and definitely our own," she wrote in 1937. In the autumn of 1938, the Bournemouth Seven Years Association invited DLS to come and give a talk, and DLS asked if she could stay with D. Rowe for the night, since "it would be great fun to have a chat." D. Rowe was delighted to agree. "The household is an elastic one with ever-open doors who will welcome you as a brilliant bird of passage." She also asked after Muriel and Bar, referring to them as "the MBs." For the talk itself, D. Rowe booked fifty seats "for all your devotees at school," and plotted to bring DLS to the theater's Green Room Club for drinks afterward.[25]

D. Rowe would have liked to turn this into a professional collaboration. Her idea was to involve DLS in the national amateur theater competitions sponsored by the *News Chronicle*, which saw amateur clubs from around the country put on a chosen play. The Bournemouth club had been very successful in these competitions. In 1938, the play was one written especially for the contest by J. B. Priestley, entitled *Mystery at Greenfingers*. D. Rowe played Miss Tracey, "the avid reader of detective fiction who really knows more about the Greenfingers mystery than anyone else, but who whimsically sets out" to solve the case. DLS planned to attend the performance in London and to meet D. Rowe as well. The Bournemouth Little Theatre Club came first out of 204 entrants, celebrating their triumph back home with a gala dinner and dance. In 1939, the club entered the *News Chronicle* competition again. Although the play this time was set in the present, a club member suggested the club's production be set thirty years earlier. D. Rowe, as

D. Rowe (with gun) in *Mystery at Greenfingers* (BLTC)

producer, took this and ran with it. Her controversial decision was criticized and she herself had doubts about the production, but they took the trophy again. DLS toasted the cast of this production in person in London, and D. Rowe told her that "your presence and speech made the supper party a high spot for the cast."[26]

D. Rowe wondered how a competition like the *News Chronicle*'s could attract a writer of DLS's caliber. She'd been disgusted with Priestley's play, telling DLS that "the real mystery is how he ever came to compose so childishly idiotic a plot." Amateur theater clubs were in perennial need of fresh, good plays, and they were frustrated with their current selection of "(a) good plays, stale. (b) bad plays, unproduced by professionals and with Good Reason. (c) Professionally produced flops." What was needed was a play that could be easily produced and that provided "a *real theme* of interest, good characterization and fool-proof dialogue." Would it be possible, she wondered, for the *News Chronicle* to "foster a sweeping, growing and popular movement" by offering enough money to attract a writer like DLS to write such a play?[27]

In her response, DLS was not encouraging. She had met with someone from the *News Chronicle* about the idea, but warned, "It's *not* an easy proposition: one set, small cast, lashings of females, vigorous action, clearly-drawn characters that don't demand enormous technical range in the performance, *and* a theme equally important & comprehensible to the rustics of Little-Doddering-under-the-Wallop & the sophisticated ladies & gentleman of Highbrow-End Garden City." The chief trouble, though, was not technical but artistic. She could write a play like what D. Rowe demanded, but only if she had "something I really wanted to say in that form." Integrity in work—increasingly, that was DLS's standard, and damn the consequences.[28]

THROUGHOUT THE 1930S, the members of the MAS rebuilt their connections. They spent time with one another, beyond the structures of alumnae meetings and Somerville reunions. Even Charis, recovering slowly from her loss, was brought back into the MAS fold, beyond her deep friendship with D. Rowe. She had lunch with Muriel, for instance, in March 1937, and the following year invited DLS to visit her in Manchester. The MAS exchanged Christmas presents regularly—scarves, lighters, calendars, a writing case. In May 1937, as a "combined Coronation and birthday present," DLS gave Muriel something written by Henry VIII, a rare item that she had purchased in honor of Muriel's work. These tokens of friendship represent something much deeper: the genuine collaboration and intellectual exchange that shaped the work of each of these women in their prime. These renewed connections would also form a bulwark against the approaching cataclysm of another world war.[29]

Part 4

Visions of a New World, 1939–1945

14

WAR BREAKS OUT

U NLIKE WORLD WAR I, WHICH seemed to catch the British public unawares, World War II loomed over the world for months. From late 1938, Muriel found that lectures and programs were canceled or altered for air-raid precautions and war-work preparation. Charis and the Salford Women Citizens' Association began recruiting for the National Service in mid-April 1939. Her eldest, son, Peter had been in the Oxford University Officers' Training Corps from the summer of 1938, and he enlisted in the infantry in July 1939. The war would push the members of the MAS to articulate even more clearly their visions for society and culture, developed over the previous two decades of professional work. It was clear from early on that this conflict would remake Britain in profound ways. The members of the MAS sought to intervene in the debates about that transformation, from the development of new ideas about childhood and socialized medicine to dreaming up a postwar society that would integrate religion and work more ethically than prewar capitalism had done. On a personal level, the war would scramble living situations, pushing some people closer together and creating new distance between others.[1]

Britain officially went to war on September 3, 1939, after the Nazi invasion of Poland. For Mac and DLS, this meant turning energies toward their duties as citizens. Mac joined the Army Officers' Emergency Reserve on September 10, 1939. For her part, DLS sought to offer her services as a lecturer and writer. She arranged a series of talks for the local branch of the Workers' Educational Association that autumn, which would ultimately feature her as well as Gladys Scott Thomson, Helen Simpson, and Muriel St. Clare Byrne.

DLS remarked to the WEA honorary secretary, "I hope you do not mind their being an all-woman team?"[2]

In Bournemouth, the Palace Court Theatre closed for two weeks when war was declared. In the club archives book, there's a poignant heading: "1939–end of war (here's hoping)." The directors soon decided to carry on for the time being, "stressing the value of the organisation of the Club in assisting in the entertaining of H.M. Forces and War charities," though they reduced the number of productions planned for the 1939–1940 season. If an air-raid warning happened during a performance, the audience would be informed from the stage, but the performance would continue; members were advised to remain in the building and seek shelter in the clubroom in the basement if necessary. At D. Rowe's suggestion, the club organized a knitting party, too, to produce things for the troops.[3]

It was immediately clear that air raids on cities would form a part of the conflict. In response to this threat, plans were made across the country to evacuate vulnerable people, especially children, from cities and other likely targets of aerial attack. The scale was vast. In the autumn of 1939, some 3.5 million people evacuated, about 1.5 million of them through the government program; this would be followed by further waves of evacuation in 1940 and 1944. Both Charis and Bar were part of this process, in different ways.[4]

Charis's involvement came through the Greengate Hospital and Open-Air School. This had long been one of the Frankenburgs' main charities. Sydney's parents had been involved, and he had been on the committee from 1914, with Charis joining him from 1925. Adorably, from 1930, their daughter (born in 1928) was an honorary member of the committee; perhaps Charis had brought her along to these meetings, too, so as not to miss her scheduled feedings. Members of the extended Frankenburg family visited Greengate and presented it with gifts on a regular basis. After Sydney's death, Charis took over as chairman of the committee, and her son Peter joined in 1938. D. Rowe began donating annually to the organization in 1937. The hospital was, in every sense, woven into the Frankenburgs' sense of mission.[5]

Greengate was a progressive hospital that aimed to treat rickets in an impoverished district of Salford. The disease was widespread in the industrial north, where pollution blocked out sunshine. Greengate was part of a movement that emphasized diet, fresh air, and sunshine and contributed to the growing understanding of the role played by vitamin D in preventing and curing rickets through light therapy and vitamin supplementation. It was unique, however, in its emphasis on providing education as well as medical treatment. By 1924, it had grown from "a flagged cellar, where texts and bottles are dispensed together" into an institution that championed the idea "that the whole child, not its body only, must be thought of, even in attempting to cure that body." Famed educational theorist Dr. Maria Montessori visited in 1920 to see her methods in operation there.[6]

Effecting a cure in the Salford environment without rupturing family ties was always central to Greengate's mission. In 1927, when Greengate was contemplating expansion, the board of education urged the institution to relocate to a rural setting, leaving the Salford hospital to function as an orthopedic clinic or a day school for "dull and backward children." The committee resisted this suggestion, arguing that Greengate as a whole must remain in Salford in order to fulfill its mission of educating parents as well as children. As Charis put it, "We want to keep the family together, we want to show the mothers what they can do in their own environment."[7]

With air raids looming, however, that principle had to be suspended. At the start of September 1939, forty children from Greengate, together with eight staff and a few other children, were evacuated to Charis's home, Oughtrington Hall. The house was physically transformed: forty-four hooks for waterproof jackets went up outside the billiard room, the porch bell was disconnected "as it was too tempting," the cellars were made gasproof, and the china, silver, and jewelry were stowed in a safe for the duration. The flower borders and the tennis courts became children's gardens. Parents found the transition distressing. One set of parents, visiting after the first few days, insisted on standing where their child couldn't see them, so the child wouldn't become upset. Another couple confessed they had hesitated about evacuation until they heard that it would be to the Frankenburg family.[8]

The children had their own stresses. A week in, one was heard to say, in the midst of quarreling with another, "Well, I hope there is a bloody war, and you haven't got your bloody gas mask!" But Charis tried to provide a semblance of family atmosphere. In late October, she stirred the Christmas puddings "and wished for each of my four and put the shillings in." On Christmas Eve, members of the full Greengate committee came to tea and were entertained by the children doing "a glorified version of their usual games and dances." Her son Peter came home for Christmas and served in the role of Father Christmas for the children.[9]

Bar's school, meanwhile, was evacuated to Berkhamsted, where they joined the Girls High School there. She was in charge of a boardinghouse for some of the students for two difficult terms. She was struck, first of all, by the suffering caused by the evacuation process to the children. As a station-master told her, "It fair turns you over to see them." A six-year-old was found hiding in the bathroom and crying; "I can't bear it another minute," she said. Although agreeing with the argument that evacuation was a monumen-tal social experiment, bridging divides of class and geography, Bar's focus remained on that immediate human pain. "Evacuation," she wrote, "makes one feel as if one had died." The practical upheaval, the social challenges of adapting to a new place, hosts who were sometimes grudging or critical, the constant threat of possible air raids: "well it's not easy to *educate* in these cir-cumstances." And yet, her "predominant impression is of the extraordinary *kindness* of people."[10]

Muriel stayed in London that autumn. She saw Bar for quick visits, and they seem to have found a few days to spend together in Devon in October. Then, Bedford College was evacuated from London to temporary quarters in Cambridge, and Muriel, too, began a more peripatetic existence. They decided to rent out their house at 28 St. John's Wood Terrace, though it was not easy to find a tenant. At the beginning of February 1940 the house stood empty, "nestling prettily beneath the Primrose Hill A.A. [anti-aircraft] guns!" They grappled, too, with the complexities of insuring a dispersed and mobile household. By the summer of 1941, the house was rented to the first in a series of short-term tenants, including a refugee whose rent Muriel and Bar subsidized.[11]

Susan had assisted with the evacuation of Bedford College to Cambridge. In the spring of 1940, however, she fell ill again. She stayed in Cambridge for a while, convalescing with the Cambridge University historian George Trev-elyan and his wife, Janet. George, like Muriel, was a historian who wrote for a wide audience: his 1944 *English Social History* would be one of the best-selling history books of the century. Muriel spent some time with all of them in March—George enjoyed their talks, and Janet was glad to understand Muriel's role in Susan's life better. "And *you* fit in to the picture so admirably now!" she wrote. Susan was improving, "and I shall hope to deliver her to you safe and sound," as soon as possible, Janet wrote, adding, "But we must see how she gets on. She has not yet had *all* her clothes on."[12]

THE PERIOD FROM September 1939 to May 1940 has been described as the "Phoney War," when not much seemed to happen. This came to an end on May 10, with the German invasion of Belgium, the Netherlands, and Luxembourg. Suddenly, a German invasion of Britain seemed an imminent possibility, as British forces were pushed back to the coast of France by the end of May and, famously, evacuated from Dunkirk. For the members of the MAS, as for all Britons, this meant confronting an existential threat. Charis's thoughts were for her daughter and the violence she might face at the hands of an invading force. She asked her doctor about securing a lethal pill, on the grounds that a peaceful death was better for her daughter than the horrors of being attacked and killed by Nazis, but he gently put her off. More practically, perhaps, Susan obtained three tubes of cocaine eye ointment for herself, Muriel, and Bar, to use in case they were bombed and got glass in their eyes.[13]

Muriel and Susan both made new wills in May 1940, which provide a vivid glimpse into their personal lives. Muriel left all of her things to Bar or, if Bar had already died, to Susan. If both Susan and Bar were dead, Muriel directed some money to go to another person "to pay for the keeping of my dog and cat." The MAS was here, too—DLS, Bar, and Susan were joint literary executors, and DLS and D. Rowe were invited to choose a gift for themselves from among Muriel's possessions. Susan left her money to the Trevelyans and her possessions to Muriel to dispose of as she liked—though Susan specified that her letters and papers should be "burnt unread." As the Battle of Britain raged on, pitting the Royal Air Force against the Luftwaffe above the Channel, Susan decided to leave her job with Bedford College and join her friends Caroline Spurgeon and Virginia Gildersleeve in the United States, citing ill health. Muriel became her go-between to Bedford, passing the message that Susan had arrived safely in New York to the college and the Trevelyans as soon as she received the cable.[14]

It became clear, over the summer, that a German invasion of Britain would be prevented for the time being. But the autumn brought the Blitz, the campaign of bombing that targeted British cities and other sites of importance. This brought new terrors and troubles. Muriel and Bar decided that they must evacuate their pets. Muriel telephoned all sorts of possible places and finally found one that would take both cat and dog. There, Bunter visited Timothy daily. "This, we thought, was very touching—the orphans of the storm clinging together," until Muriel and Bar realized that it was in fact because Bunter liked to lick the leftover milk in Timothy's saucer. The plight of their peripatetic pets recurs in their wartime letters. Sometimes Bar brought Bunter to Berkhamsted, and at one point she went "to fetch Bunter for Muriel," and then traveled with him and Timothy by train. The cat "received the adoration of two female porters at Wilton & had the horror of having his nose tickled by an American airman, who had had 3 missions

Muriel and Bar with pets (MSBC 9/3)

the night before & was sleepy in consequence!" They arranged for food to be sent, too—Bar brought herring and milk, and Muriel stored meat in her bath in Cambridge until she could arrange for it to be brought to the dog.[15]

Muriel herself spent parts of the autumn of 1940 with DLS in Witham, paying her some rent. DLS admitted to D. Rowe that she wasn't going to London much, because of the Blitz and Hitler's "nasty habit of dropping things on the line to Town," causing train delays. DLS reported that Muriel found Witham "rather more peaceful than London, though to be sure we get a series of bumps and crashes most nights, but not quite so loudly or so persistently as they do in Town." One time Muriel arrived to find a local drama underway, the result of a bomb that had landed in a neighbor's garden but not gone off. There had been booms in the night, but it was not clear whether it was this bomb (which grew on retelling around the town), or new ones dropped elsewhere. It was all, DLS joked, "confusing as a detective story." The general confusion of the moment is captured, too, in DLS's charming if frustrating postscript to a letter she wrote to Bar: "Muriel's best love—She says she knows she has something to say to you, but can't think what it is."[16]

In Bournemouth, D. Rowe's school was not evacuated. In the shelters during air-raid warnings, she entertained the children with the "serial story of Gervase Piriwin, a small bear." One boy, finding her asleep in the shelter, woke her with the plea, "Auntie Dorothy! I want a story about Gervase Piriwin *rather* quickly." The Bournemouth Little Theatre, too, did its best to carry on. *Busman's Honeymoon* played at the theater in the 1940–1941 season, and DLS was glad to hear it had gone well. Filling the theater was not easy during the Blitz. They offered special discounts to hotel managers who brought parties to the theater, they advertised directly to the civil servants who were evacuated to Bournemouth with their departments, they entertained troops, and they managed to keep their doors open.[17]

Located as it was between Liverpool and Manchester, two major industrial and shipping centers, Charis's Oughtrington Hall experienced many air raids, though nothing worse than broken windows resulted. Charis made careful arrangements to deal with blackout requirements, including a list of all the windows and which staff were responsible for which ones. The children and staff sheltered in the cellars. When the very first air-raid siren sounded, it was "just after elevenses," and one adult suggested that everyone should go to the cellar to find more biscuits. From then on, air-raid sirens were greeted with a general cry of "Sugar-biscuits!" and a rush to the cellars, which came to double as dormitories during the periods of frequent nighttime raids.[18]

Lodging with about ten students in Shenstone Court, the Berkhamsted home of Sir Richard and Lady Cooper, Bar found it difficult to be separated from Muriel as the bombs began to fall. She tried to reason with herself. If Muriel had "copped it at the house," where she was still spending some time, the air-raid patrol would have telephoned Bar. If the railway station had been hit, she'd have heard by rumor. And how likely was it, really, that Muriel had been killed by a bomb in a taxi or on a train? So she told herself "over & over again" lying in bed. "But in spite of all this truth I dissolved into a wet mess when I heard your voice—& feel still as if I had been flogged all over with knotted ropes. I am no heroine."[19]

Bar tried to imagine what was happening in London, piecing it together from rumor and the distant sounds of airplane engines and explosions. She studied the weather: would it be clear enough for airplanes over the Channel, even if it was misty in Berkhamsted? After a bad night of bombing, she consoled herself with the thought, "Whatever that was, it's happened . . . there is no need to fear because the future is already present in the mind of God." Still, she pressed Muriel to leave London, at least for a short respite, such as two nights at Somerville, offering to lend her the money and make arrangements for the cat to be fed. In one of the short stories she wrote during this period, Bar created a character whose experience of fear mirrored her own. That character "lived with naked fear. It ran hotly in her blood, dried her through, beat behind her eyeballs, hung so heavily at her heart that she could scarcely breathe." Yet when her son is badly injured, she must face her fear and finds she is able, at last, to do so, realizing "that the only security in the world lay in love and courage."[20]

The fear and separation made Bar express her feelings for Muriel explicitly. "If I did not know how dear you were to me, my uncontrollable terrors for you since your return to London would have taught me," she wrote. Indeed, if she hadn't "disciplined myself almost to paralysis at the effort not to be possessive about you," she would have been even bolder "in saying how very dear & precious you are & how closely my life is bound up in yours." Bar had undertaken significant emotional work, perhaps as a result of Muriel's relationship with Susan, in overcoming possessiveness, but the war placed a great strain on that commitment to non-possessive love. Bar placed her faith in the importance of Muriel's work, explaining that "the Lisles are a great comfort to me. I think you will be kept to finish them. Like Churchill."[21]

Charis returned to London occasionally in order to see her aging parents, who had refused to evacuate. She had rented a flat in their building, where D. Rowe sometimes stayed too, but limited her visits once bombing started, feeling that, as the sole surviving parent to her own children, she couldn't take extra risks. Her parents' faithful servant Annie Barnard looked after them instead. When Charis's mother died after an extended illness in April 1941, Charis traveled immediately to London.[22]

As it happened, D. Rowe was staying in Charis's London flat at the same time, having taken on warden duty at Paddington, and she arranged for some time off when Charis arrived. Her presence provided Charis with a welcome distraction from the work of dealing with her mother's death as well as getting her father's affairs in order. That first night, Charis and D. Rowe had dinner with Annie Barnard. They had a good time, "all three talking at once most of the time," and D. Rowe showed off her tin hat "and said that she felt exactly like a maggot crawling out of a mushroom." The next evening, the siren went off soon after Charis, D. Rowe, and Annie had gone to bed. All three had the simultaneous thought to get away from the flat's windows, "so Dorothy, Annie, and I brought pillows and eiderdowns . . . into the hall. We sat for a bit and then lay down, Dorothy being half in the bathroom and half out, but we really couldn't sleep very much and after a bit Annie got up and began to make tea. She made us settle down in the kitchen," assuring them that this was the safest place. "She added 'I know a man and his wife who slept in a kitchen like this for weeks until they were bombed out,' and couldn't see why Dorothy and I laughed and laughed."[23]

They ate some tea and cake and, to entertain them, Charis began reading aloud from a sex manual written by her father's former doctor. This doctor had driven Charis up the wall with his shifting stories about fee claims—her own solicitor had praised her attention to detail as she unraveled the issue, saying that "he proposes to call me Lady Peter Wimsey now." Now, as the bombs fell outside, Charis got her revenge. Entitled *Love without Fear*, the doctor's book was, Charis said, the "most revolting" book of sex instruction she'd ever read: "extremely badly written, and full of the most unprofessional self advertisement." The volume was fairly typical of progressive interwar sex advice manuals, emphasizing the need for a husband to learn to bring his wife to orgasm in order to ensure a mutually satisfactory relationship. It's easy to imagine, though, that they found much to giggle about in a book that informed them that, for instance, most women "move their bodies in response to those of their mates" during sex, or that a "masterly touch in her lover is invariably pleasing."[24]

All around them, the Blitz raged, with noise and vibration "like nothing I've ever heard." At one point they all seemed to hear the windows breaking at one end of the flat, though in fact it was the sound of things breaking outside. They were up until 5 a.m., and Charis wired home the next day to let everyone know she was alright. But the return to that undergraduate feeling, staying up late wrapped in blankets on the floor, drinking tea and laughing about sex, insulated her from fear and, for a moment at least, took her back to a time when she had fewer duties and responsibilities. "I had consciously a great feeling of relief that I hadn't these forty children to think of." World War II had brought new burdens of responsibility to Charis, Bar, and D. Rowe as they shepherded children through the terrifying experiences of evacuation and wartime, and all the members of the MAS had faced mortality in a new way. These experiences would push them to ask with a fresh urgency what was required of them as citizens in a new global crisis.[25]

15

SERVICE AND IDENTITY

Ａ

LL THREE OF CHARIS'S SONS—PETER, John, and Miles—served in World War II. D. Rowe's quasi-parental role was especially crucial in these years, and it's clear that all of Charis's children relied on her in various ways. For them, too, the war had an added layer of meaning and complexity. Nazi Germany specifically and violently targeted Jews. For Charis and her children, the war provoked new reflection on their Jewish identity and their connections to larger Jewish communities, now that Sydney was no longer alive to bridge the gap between their hybrid experiences and his Jewish world.

Charis later remembered the period as enormously stressful. In the summer of 1940, her mind occasionally went completely blank, "and I even had to ask where the boys were now." She fainted at a bus stop. Some of this was due to the intense responsibilities she shouldered. When she had a dream that she'd been arrested, "my *only* feeling was profound relief that the whole affair was out of my hands, and that nothing I said or did could have the least effect." She was also overwhelmed by the fact that, having lost her brother and her husband, now her children, too, were in danger. When Ursula had her tonsils out, Charis reacted with uncharacteristic emotion and anxiety, perhaps intensified by the teenager's decision to spend the time leading up to the surgery "playing Chopin's Funeral March over and over on the gramophone!"[1]

Charis was keenly aware of her responsibility as a single parent. She reassured her children about her own health, reporting a slight cold as well as healthy X-ray results in the letters she sent them. More prosaically, she was disappointed in homeopathic pills for hay fever, which turned out to be "a snare and a delusion." She spent a week on holiday in Chester in July 1941 on doctor's advice.[2]

D. Rowe was a consistent friend to Charis, bringing a much needed element of levity and fun on her visits to Oughtrington. Peter joked with D. Rowe about the "convivial evenings" she enjoyed with his mother, "in which we both read books and said, 'Shut up' if anyone spoke." But Charis said they "really had a *lovely* time together, both talking at once." D. Rowe told entertaining stories from the nursing home where Sir Arthur and Louise Marshall were now living. One old lady, seeing D. Rowe tidying her bag, said, "They ought to teach little dogs to do that." Another time, a dog "skipped away one evening with a mouthful of Dorothy's darning silks," and Charis teased her, "He was only trying to live up to the remark of the old lady." It was not all jokes, though. Charis invited a full range of guests to meet D. Rowe: Dr. Langley and his wife, a group of Women Citizens, and some members of the University Women's Association. That Christmastime, D. Rowe and Charis listened together to a broadcast of a radio play that DLS wrote about the nativity, and both admired it. They thought, too, of Charis's youngest son, Miles, when they heard the march of his regiment played on the wireless on New Year's Day.[3]

D. Rowe wrote regularly to each of Charis's three sons wherever they were stationed, and her name recurs frequently in their letters home: they wanted to see her, to hear about her, and to send their news and affection. Closer to home, D. Rowe provided Ursula with mentorship as she navigated the next stage of her education. During one visit, Charis and D. Rowe met Ursula at the veterinary surgery where she was working, and she drove them home in a horse-drawn carriage of some sort. Charis had a short moment when she thought the horse "had pranced on one of the cat-patients," but, luckily, it was only D. Rowe's fur coat. More seriously, D. Rowe and Ursula had "long discussions" about school, examinations, and certificates. At one crucial moment, D. Rowe intervened with the headmistress of Ursula's school. Charis had asked why Ursula hadn't yet been moved up to the senior house but received no real answer. Then D. Rowe, who, Charis said, "is my chief adviser on female education," heard that the headmistress was staying in Bournemouth. She took the opportunity to inform the headmistress "that Ursula belonged to a highly intelligent and intellectual family," noting her grandfather's educational career and her brother John's scholarship. There was no direct reply, but Charis received word that Ursula would be moved to the senior house right away.[4]

Charis had only very limited support, by contrast, from Sydney's family, with whom she had increasingly rocky relations. She had a prickly, on-again, off-again relationship with her sister-in-law Elise and was angry at the fact that her sons mostly avoided military service. Charis's disgust at young people who refused to serve extended beyond her family. The so-called Oxford Group of conscientious objectors made her "absolutely sick." However, she tried to keep up the relationship with Elise, she told her children, "as I think that Daddy would rather I didn't quarrel." Nevertheless, the strained relations created distance between Charis and the wider Frankenburg family.[5]

Being a part-Jewish family in a war against a regime that disproportionately targeted Jewish people, Jewish communities, and Jewish culture was complicated. John and Miles, coming home from the movies, found "Mosley"—presumably referring to Oswald Mosley, the leader of the British Union of Fascists—painted on a wall, and expressed their disgust graphically: "first they spat on each letter and then watered it otherwise!" All three sons volunteered to fight against the Axis powers, and their military service scattered them around the world. Sir Harold Shoobert, a family friend then in India, wrote to Charis in the summer of 1942 expressing his admiration for her sons: "what a great family record! Wouldn't Dobbin and Bill [Sydney] have been proud!"[6]

Peter, the eldest, was the first to go. He was in Egypt by the summer of 1941, taking Arabic lessons in between his duties. The scenes reminded him of D. Rowe's cartoon characters: "tell Dorothy I'm afraid I haven't seen the 'carefree Camel' yet, I've seen a great many camels but they all look a bit worried." He spent time, too, in Palestine, where he was appalled by the commercialization of Christian tourist sites. On the other hand, he compared Tel Aviv favorably with Cairo. While Tel Aviv was "a delightful city, all Jews, very nice, clean and Western," Cairo had been filled with "pimps, touts and filth." Oddly enough, he would see both of his brothers while serving in Egypt: John passed through late in 1941, and Miles in July 1942.[7]

John, the middle son, also left in the summer of 1941. Charis and Miles traveled to his base for a final visit before he left the country, embarking on a long train journey to Bournemouth so that John could say farewell to D. Rowe, too. D. Rowe arrived home just before they had to leave "and was simply thrilled to see us." She took the bus with them back into town and saw them off. "We got back to the hotel after ten, but it had been definitely very well worth while." Something like eight hours of travel for, at most, an hour of visiting, much of it in the bus, and it was still "very well worth while" for all of them—a powerful testament to the significance of the bond.[8]

Miles, the youngest son, enlisted in August 1941. He had to pass a medical exam, which was not entirely straightforward due to an old injury to his knee. But on the day itself he encountered a friend of his father who "crossed out all the deleterious remarks about his knee, and even took the trouble to accompany him to the Chairman of the Board," ensuring that he passed. Later that week, when Miles danced with his sister, Charis was struck by how he moved his hands just like Sydney. While waiting to be old enough to enlist, he became interested in pig breeding, recruiting Ursula as an assistant. As Charis informed Peter, "The aroma from your younger brother and sister is sometimes very potent." When Miles left, Charis gamely took over the collection of pig swill from the neighbors. Miles, meanwhile, went to India as a cadet in the spring of 1942, after a brief visit with his mother in London. His rank, destination, and commission to the Royal Gurkha Rifles were all marks of his talent, reported proudly by his mother. He was curious about his fellow soldiers in India, trying to learn their languages and understand their backgrounds better. Some of them, too, he compared to "Dorothy Rowe's drawings."[9]

When her middle son, John, was taken prisoner by Italian forces in June 1942, Charis reacted in characteristic fashion by seeking out and building community. She joined the Prisoners of War Relatives' Association and began attending meetings. At first, she couldn't find anyone else with relatives in his camp, so she used the same technique that she'd used to get her classmates, including DLS, to Somerville reunions. She obtained the names of the relevant people and wrote to them asking them to come to the very next meeting. Soon she was in touch with other local relatives of prisoners in John's camp. These connections counterbalanced the slow drip of uncertain information, as formal communications and John's letters home arrived only sporadically.[10]

Mussolini resigned on July 25, 1943, and Ursula's governess, Edith "Bonn" Bonnell, and the Greengate hospital matron came to Charis at 11:15 p.m. to tell her the news. D. Rowe, tastelessly, summarized the event thus: "oh what a flop for the big top Wop!" From Sicily, Peter told his mother that he "intends to fetch John for me, also the seat of Mussolini's trousers." As the Allied invasion of Italy progressed, Charis struggled with her anxiety about John. D. Rowe described her state of mind "as balancing an egg in an egg-and-spoon race." In mid-November, Charis finally received a month-old letter from John, reporting that he had been moved to Germany but was alright. He had attempted, unsuccessfully, to escape with two other prisoners. She was pleased, since "if John had not attempted an escape, he would always have felt that he might have pulled it off if he'd tried." In the German prisoner of war camp, John continued his legal studies and passed part of the bar examinations while still a prisoner.[11]

CHARIS'S SONS REFERENCED their Jewish heritage in various ways during the war. Peter had referred approvingly to the Jewish and Western qualities of Tel Aviv, for instance, and Miles reported that the best canteen "is the Jewish Club where all facilities seem to be available." Peter wondered more explicitly, too, about his own Jewishness. As the son of a Jewish man and a non-Jewish woman, he was not automatically Jewish, though he had been raised in the context of an extended Jewish community and family. He asked his mother how he could find out more about Judaism, "as I'm getting increasingly fed up with official Christianity, and also with my own rather indeterminate position. In fact I'm not at all sure that it wouldn't be a very good thing for me to become a performing Jew, but I'd like to know how to find out a bit more about the performance." His brother John, evidently, was also thinking about these matters, though Peter dismissed this with brotherly condescension, suggesting that he was striking a "silly" attitude mainly "to dodge church." But, Peter elaborated to Charis, if he were a practicing Jew he could help Jewish soldiers more easily—implicitly suggesting that conversion would allow him to carry on his father's work. Charis's reply does not survive but it must not have been entirely enthusiastic, since Peter asked her, "What on earth do you mean, 'what about marriage?'" Fighting fascism was one thing; embracing Judaism was another, and Charis evidently believed that conversion had the potential to affect her son's future in negative ways. Indeed, she worried that anti-Semitism could affect them regardless of whether they were fully Jewish. When considering Malvern Girls College for Ursula, she was glad to note that Sir Anderson Montague-Barlow, a "very intimate friend of the Frankenburg family," was chairman of the governors: "anyhow, I don't think there will be any racial trouble there!!"[12]

Charis's father, meanwhile, was in declining health. She spent over a week in London at the end of his life, visiting him daily in the nursing home and trying to soothe him as his mind wandered. When he kept asking for his hat one day, Charis "had a sudden inspiration and said, 'He wants to pray.' So we put a handkerchief on his head and that satisfied him." Despite a lifetime of freethinking Deism, his Jewish heritage was present for him to the end. He was, Charis would say later, "always latently Jewish, whatever he was supposed to be."[13]

So, in a way, was Charis herself. She continued to attend church on significant days such as Christmas and national prayer days, and to conduct herself as a vaguely Anglican Deist. The Greengate children were required to say the Lord's Prayer every night, and Charis adapted the Christian hymn "All People That on Earth Do Dwell" for them, with lyrics that ran, "Oh God who gives us things to eat / And lovely sunshine where we play / Help us to be big, good, and kind / And we'll say Thank You every day." She told them, when they encountered a dead bird, that "the singing part" of the bird had gone to God, and only the body was left behind. This led to a welter of questions about the nature of heaven, including: are there any Germans there? "Yes," said Charis, "but God makes them kind first."[14]

In other ways, Charis positioned herself both inside and outside of Judaism. In February 1944, she wanted some matzo, which she glossed as "Passover cakes." She made a somewhat hazy order and ended up paying a considerable sum for a parcel "about four feet by three feet" and weighing twelve pounds. She was Jewish enough to want matzo at Passover, but not so Jewish that she could obtain it without making a mistake in her order. Charis commented regularly on the Jewish people she encountered in her work as a Salford magistrate. Though her language sometimes jars the modern ear, she generally wrote with sympathy and sometimes pride. Even more strikingly, she translated Jewish culture for her non-Jewish colleagues. Two defendants in a group of eleven-year-olds who'd damaged sewage pipes while digging "were little Jew boys who put on their caps and swore on the Old Testament" before giving remarkably frank evidence. A synagogue caretaker was fined for breaking the blackout because "the electric clock which turned out the lights on the Sabbath had gone wrong!" When the court "gasped in horror" at hearing that a Jewish person had called a Christian neighbor a "shiksa," Charis "was able to explain it to the Bench" as a technical term rather than a slur.[15]

If the situation warranted it, Charis would even claim her own Jewishness. Celebrating the end of her long stint as matron of Greengate in September 1942, she and Bonn went with a friend, nicknamed Beechy, to Manchester and enjoyed coffee and cakes. The celebration was marred by a woman sitting nearby who told them, "All these Jews in here make me sick." They were, she said, "flaunting their fur coats." Charis, whose own fur coat was out of sight, remonstrated gently: surely if you have a fur coat, it would be "more patriotic to wear it than to put it away and to buy a new coat that someone else might need." Even this didn't stop the woman's vitriol. As Charis described it, "Presently I said, mildly, 'Well, you can't expect me to agree with you because I am half-Jewish, and my husband was completely Jewish.' At which point Beechy, who had been simmering for some time, boiled over completely; told her all about my sons, my hospital, and everything else she could think of. Anyhow, the woman will be more careful how she lectures strangers in future." Even as she tried to protect her children, then, Charis willingly embraced her own Jewish background in the face of anti-Semitism.[16]

THROUGH THE SYDNEY Frankenburg British Legion branch, Charis also became more a part of the local Jewish community in her own right during the war. In the spring of 1941, the branch unveiled a plaque to Sydney before an audience of two hundred. Charis, who donated her pension as a war widow to the branch, attended the event. She was treated as an honored and welcomed outsider. The chairman explained to her "that to Jews, the unveiling of a memorial was a sad occasion." Charis herself unveiled the plaque, and then listened to speeches over "an enormous meal of rolls, smoked salmon, cream cheese, and *lots* of chocolate eclairs." She spoke too, telling them she was "trying to continue my husband's good work" and to raise their children to follow his example. A lunch in a private room at the Midland Hotel followed. The veterans, naturally, discussed war, both past and current, but "all seemed very cheerful about the present situation."[17]

At another branch event, this one to raise money for the Greengate Hospital, Charis was again both inside and outside of the Jewish community. Walking into the crowded concert hall, "thick with tobacco smoke and the smell of drinks," Charis was at first afraid she'd be unable to stay. But "very soon I hardly noticed the atmosphere as everybody was so charming." She described the hospital's evacuation to Oughtrington and spoke about the successes it had achieved there. She also spoke about her own children, gently mocking her youngest son for being unwilling to pay for a stamp to write home but having no such compunctions about telephoning her from Scotland, with charges reversed so that Charis paid. "Several different people paused in their laughter to remark, 'The call of the blood.'" Here, the standard interwar English joke about Jewish people as penny-pinchers is softened to an in-joke, used to claim Sydney Frankenburg's son as part of a community. (Charis remembered a similar joke being made about Ursula. She and Sydney had taken her to a Jewish club, where Ursula was given a box of chocolates wrapped in gold. Asked what she would do if they were real gold, she said, "I should sell them," and one of the men there said with delight, "She shows her race.") But if the joke about Miles served to integrate her family into the community, Charis's account of the rest of the night highlights her sense of difference. The next speech, made by a theater manager, was clearly very funny, "but as the funniest were all Jewish jokes I couldn't follow it very well, though the laughter nearly blew the roof off." Accepting the proceeds at the end of the night, Charis thanked everyone and promised to tell her children about everything, including all the jokes, "at least all those that I was able to understand," she added, to fresh gales of laughter. The ambivalence persists to the end of her description: "in fact I had a triumph! The only slight drawback is that I shall feel obliged in future to smile at any peculiar-looking Yidd that I see in the Midland [Hotel], and this may lead to complications."[18]

Nevertheless, Charis's connections with the British Legion and its associated community grew stronger over the course of the war. She had coffee in July 1942 with the chairman of the Sydney Frankenburg branch, who told her that her son's check to the branch "had been written in a Field Service note book, and they are having it photographed." Another of the Legion's leading members, Jack White, also socialized with Charis and assisted the Greengate Hospital. Born in Leeds, White had worked in a waterproofing factory and then served in World War I, earning the Victoria Cross for his bravery. He helped Charis find various necessities for running the hospital in her home, from inexpensive linoleum for the bathroom floors to ribbon for the girls' hair.[19]

Still, Charis was cautious about participating in Jewish politics beyond the local community. She declined an invitation to take part in the

Manchester branch of a national effort to agitate for a Jewish army in Palestine, which was then under British rule. Sydney had opposed such things when he was alive, saying "that Judaism was a religion, not a nationality, and each should be in their own country's army." She admitted that he might have changed his mind in the context of the 1940s, "now that there are so many stateless Jews." Still, she concluded, "I don't feel that I ought to use his name when he felt so strongly on the other side." She consulted a local member of Parliament, Sir Edward Grigg, on the matter, too, and found him opposed for tactical reasons. Arabs would naturally demand the same privilege, "whereas at present they are working in with us & the Jews in *our* Army." Thus, Charis stayed out of the politics around Zionism and a future Jewish state in Palestine. Early in 1943, though, Charis did attend, as a "leading citizen," a meeting at the Manchester Town Hall "to protest against the German treatment of the Jews." There, she enjoyed some lighthearted flirtation with a septuagenarian alderman and spoke with two Jewish men who promised to send money to Greengate. But she recognized the seriousness of the event and the need for unity on this subject. "It was a most impressive meeting, really well done," she wrote, with "representatives of all different religions."[20]

OTHER MEMBERS OF the MAS saw the war as a fight against Nazism, but, like most British people, they did not see it as a fight in defense of the Jews of Europe. Indeed, they sometimes perpetuated anti-Semitic ideas. In 1943, DLS argued, in two letters, that Jewish people were often "bad citizens," marked by a self-conscious sense of difference, though she admitted there were individual exceptions. Bar, too, seems to have believed this. She wrote a piece called "My Solution to the Jewish Problem" around 1943 or 1944, but it does not seem to have survived. She found herself in an awkward situation when invited to visit a Jewish man, who seemed to her "entirely free of the Jewish inferiority complex & highly intelligent." He introduced her to a young Jewish woman, "wholly admirable," who had done air-raid precaution work "all through the Blitz," but he then proceeded to tell this exemplary young woman "rather clumsily my view of the Jew as a bad citizen." Bar was horrified: "I was so overcome with misery that I nearly ran from the room in the middle of the party & finally emerged, feeling I had been scraped with a rake all over." She concluded to DLS, "Oh hell—I had been coping with Jewish disloyalty & discourtesy all week & didn't feel too Christian. . . . Don't go & see him if he asks you." This is a complex scene, and Bar's views aren't entirely clear, though her reliance on anti-Semitic tropes is undeniable. She taught at a school with a large Jewish minority, perhaps explaining, though not excusing, the reference to dealing with "Jewish disloyalty & discourtesy." She seems, here, to have bumped up against the intellectual dishonesty of condemning an entire social group while allowing for a few worthy exceptions, as well as the social embarrassment of having to own up to one's prejudices in front of a member of the stereotyped group.[21]

Charis might have had a certain amount of sympathy with the situation, if not the sentiment, as her wartime writing reflects her own reliance on stereotype and prejudice. She seems never to have seriously questioned her suspicion of Roman Catholics—she hesitated over hiring a Catholic teacher, for instance, though the candidate promised she "wouldn't do any Catholic teaching." Another potential staff member was described as "half-caste," presumably meaning mixed race in some way. Charis was more sympathetic to the "half German refugee" who applied as a nurse, though in this case the matron outright refused to work with her because of her nationality. White Americans, on the other hand, were a source of enduring entertainment. One visiting American was "exactly like a stage American." He wore "white shoes with brown facings," told the children, "Call me Fred," and promised to try to get press coverage for Greengate. In December 1944, Charis asked her handyman, Roberts, "if he knew what Thanksgiving Day was, and he said that he'd asked a Yank in the pub, and this Yank had said that it was to thank God for being born Americans. I said that some people were very easily pleased, and Roberts agreed."[22]

Charis knew that she should do better when it came to black people in Britain. Like other MAS members, she used the phrase "working like a n—" casually, and she related a "funny story" involving a family that refused to billet Jewish soldiers, so were sent two black soldiers instead. The phrasing and dialogue relied on the basest of stereotypes about black Americans. Among the children evacuated with the Greengate Hospital to Oughtrington in 1939 was a black girl. Charis admitted that she was "not very good about the colour bar"—that is, the social taboo against cross-racial interaction— but, when the girl returned home, Charis nevertheless let her "sit on my knee all the way to Salford, and we kissed each other at parting, and she flung her arms round my neck and hugged me!" Charis was such a generous, natural person with children that it's startling to see her hesitate at interacting with a child because of her race.[23]

Her hesitation reflects a larger point about the politics of difference in this era in Britain. Racial and ethnic hierarchies permeated society, even if they were rarely fully acknowledged. The Jewish part of Charis's life remained awkward, ringed with jokes and plausible denial, but nonetheless significant and real. Charis didn't want to endorse her son's possible turn toward Judaism, but she did speak out publicly against anti-Semitism, whether in Germany or Manchester. She walked, in this way, a particularly complicated line: both Jewish and not Jewish, she sought to preserve her own privileges even while, slowly and incompletely, she developed a politics that couldn't accept any bar based on race.

16

THE GREENGATE HOSPITAL

S HELTERING THE GREENGATE HOSPITAL AND Open-Air School in her home provided Charis with an unparalleled chance to put her theories about child development into practice on a scale that was both grand and intimate. In this, she was part of a very particular moment. The evacuation of hundreds of thousands of children across Britain, many of them unaccompanied, created numerous contexts for exploring issues of parental attachment, trauma, and child psychology. Anna Freud and Dorothy Burlingham at the Hampstead War Nurseries, Donald Winnicott with the Government Evacuation Scheme in Oxfordshire, and John Bowlby and Melanie Klein are the most famous examples. This work would transform child psychology by emphasizing, above all, issues of attachment and family context in the development of the child into a healthy adult.[1]

Although Charis remained moderately skeptical about psychoanalysis, she showed, at the Greengate Hospital and as a magistrate working with juvenile delinquents, an increasing interest in questions of child psychology. She fought constantly to ensure that the Greengate patients were not hit or shouted at—linking these practices to emotional disturbances that would manifest as bed-wetting, masturbation, and general unruliness. She sought to recreate a home atmosphere as far as possible and was alive to the importance of family connections. In the courtroom, she emphasized the needs of young people and the importance of a positive, engaged relationship between parent and child, participating in a movement toward more progressive sentencing and treatment of juvenile delinquency.[2]

Housing Greengate Hospital at Oughtrington Hall helped protect the building
from being requisitioned for military use.
It also transformed Charis's daily life. Her
right-hand woman through this period
was her companion and secretary, Ursula's
former governess Edith "Bonn" Bonnell.
Together, they did all sorts of work—she
remembered that they planted "over a hundred cabbages, two hundred cauliflowers, a
hundred and twenty onions," in addition to
housework and knitting twenty-five wool
scarves for troops. All the gardening paid off,

Charis Frankenburg (Wellcome
Collection)

in the form of relative abundance despite ra-
tioning. One morning in 1942 found Charis
in bed dictating a newsletter while consuming a breakfast of "toast, dripping, marmalade, butter, greengage jam, [and] café-au-lait." Inspectors from
the ministries of health and education who visited in December 1939 told
Charis that she "ought to have been a general," based on how well organized
the whole endeavor was. Military leadership was not an option for Charis,
of course, despite her patriotism, but she ran her hospital-school with preci-
sion, authority, and dedication. She recorded the whole operation in family
newsletters circulated to her children and friends, including D. Rowe, which
captured the details of daily life in wartime, from the humorous to the grim,
as well as the larger clashes of ideology and personality.[3]

RUNNING GREENGATE ACCORDING to her principles put Charis in regular
conflict with the rest of the staff, including the matron, the head teacher,
and the teachers and nurses. For various reasons, the institution had four
different matrons and at least five different head teachers during its time at
Oughtrington, a stark contrast to the relative stability of the prewar years.
Out of this upheaval, Charis's approach emerged ever more clearly.

Charis believed that corporal punishment and shouting caused psychological distress and must be replaced with reasonable, nonviolent discipline.
It was, simply, "wrong to inflict pain purposely." She would fight to prevent
corporal punishment throughout the time Greengate was at Oughtrington.

Despite the strength of her views, this was a battle she never entirely won. In June 1942, a mother removed her son after he said a nurse had smacked him. Despite lectures and remonstration, the same nurse confessed later that month to smacking children who wet their beds. To underscore their point, Charis and the matron posted a notice forbidding "all smacking" and warning that it "will be reported to the committee as these children wouldn't be here unless they were delicate." On another occasion, Charis visited a ward at night to deal with two hysterical boys, who, she learned, had been refused a drink of water and then been hit.[4]

Among the negative effects of corporal punishment was, in Charis's view, inappropriate sexual stimulation. Explaining this later in life, she invited her somewhat startled interviewer to consider the significance of "the fact that canes and birch rods are part of the furniture of a brothel." At Greengate, when the matron reported an increase of masturbation among the children under the reign of a particularly violent head teacher, Charis replied, "What do you expect with all this smacking? I told you the two things were connected."[5]

Charis opposed screaming at children, too, suggesting that she was generally against discipline based on frightening them. She criticized one head teacher for her tendency to take a "sergeant-major's voice" when dealing with the children. Seeing the head teacher with her young charges one day, Charis commented, through the drawing room window, on "how lovely it was that she hardly ever had to shout at them now as they were so good." As Charis reported, the teacher "took the hint." It was such an obvious hint that the children took it, too. Digging in a garden bed, Charis overheard one child say to the head teacher, "You mustn't shout at us to-day when Mrs. Frankie can hear you, must you?"[6]

In placing of screaming and smacking, Charis believed in prevention first, and rational discipline where necessary. A boy who had thrown a stone through a window in the summer house was brought to Charis to apologize, and she reasoned with him on the basis of shared values. "He agreed with me that he liked the house and didn't really want" to damage it. Much bad behavior could be prevented by making the children feel at home, rather than institutionalized. Charis praised one head teacher, for instance, who developed new activities to counteract the institutional environment that meant that the children had stopped playing at "shopping, baking, washing, etc. like the usual children of their homes." A visiting official from the Medical

Office of Health praised "the natural un-hospital rough-and-tumble life and atmosphere" that he found there.[7]

Yet, for all the psychological awareness that her approach shows, Charis was impatient with psychoanalytic notions of repression. One teacher took the children on long walks with what Charis felt was inadequate supervision and control, especially in light of the danger of air raids. The problem, Charis felt, was that the teacher "will not realise that their physical safety depends on adequate control which she calls repression." This teacher tried, unsuccessfully, to muster educational theory in her defense. The "approved theory" for educating young children was "skilled neglect," she said. Charis's reply was cutting: "yes, I know; *skilled* neglect." Children needed space, free time, and scope for initiative, but they also needed adequate control.[8]

Charis saw the physical and mental needs of children as inextricably intertwined. She had no patience with teachers who balked at the requirement of being outdoors as much as possible, a crucial element both of the Greengate method of treating rickets with sunshine and of Charis's overall philosophy of child-rearing. She emphasized that the children studied outdoors "even in winter, unless it is actually snowing or raining, when they are in the big room or squash court with windows wide open." Just a few days after the initial evacuation, it gave Charis "great pleasure" to go to the head teacher "and tick her off for leading the entire school indoors for their afternoon rest: she won't do it again."[9]

Greengate was both school and hospital, and Charis argued, too, against divisions and false hierarchies between the nursing and teaching staffs. One head teacher lasted less than two weeks at Oughtrington, after earning Charis's ire for refusing to do anything "not in a teacher's sphere" and insisting on her primacy above the hospital matron. Charis argued that the matron was entitled to make health-related suggestions that could affect how the school ran. She was pleased when another head teacher suggested that nurses and teachers swap some duties, to undo rigid divisions.[10]

These principles pushed Charis into the role of mediator between nursing and teaching staffs, especially between the hospital matron and the head teacher. Disarmingly, she admitted in September 1940, "I find Matron a bit difficult over some things, but, after all, when two middle-aged and autocratic women have to start living together it's pretty good if, at the end of a year, they only occasionally mildly irritate each other." Her management style, too, became increasingly psychologically informed. When the head teacher and the matron were at loggerheads in the spring of 1941, she tried, at first, to be neutral and reasonable. Even though she sympathized with the matron, she put the other side to her when she complained, suggesting possible defenses for the head teacher's behavior. Then, at her wits' end, Charis tried another tactic: bursting into tears, she offered a frank admission of her conflicted feelings. Emotional expression succeeded where a reserved logic had failed. "Matron jumped up, put her arms round me, said she quite understood and would never do it again, and since then she has been quite easy to manage!"[11]

Even as she enforced her agenda, Charis saw herself as a mentor, especially to the young nurses. She admitted that she had a bit of a prejudice against teachers, believing that they were, in general, priggish and selfish, as well as lacking in common sense. D. Rowe, it would seem, was an exception. Perhaps her style of management, based on her own training in hospitals, was simply more familiar to the nurses. One nurse said that "one of the things she likes about Mrs. Frankie is that she is always so nice to you after she's ticked you off."[12]

The hospital took on young women who wanted to be nurses but were too young or inexperienced to get positions at the big hospitals yet. Out of sympathy, she hired a nurse who, at seventeen, was the single mother of a three-year-old. When the young woman became pregnant again, however, she had to leave. In general, though, Charis informally assisted those young employees who became pregnant. She gave them access to the resources they needed, and she even helped to find an adoptive family for one baby. But if Charis was sympathetic with pregnant young women, she did not approve of boldness in looks or conduct. One nurse, who had "plucked eyebrows," was dismissed for staying out all night without informing the matron.[13]

Charis tried, but failed, to be open-minded when it came to the politics of patriotism. When the head teacher position became vacant, Charis convinced the committee to hire a young woman she'd worked with, even though she was a conscientious objector who had refused to register for fire watching in Salford. Her political beliefs caused more trouble than Charis had anticipated. Her fiancé visited and, seeing a portrait of Winston Churchill on the mantelpiece, turned it around with the remark, "This ought to be burnt." Soon, Charis was fed up with the new head teacher. "How these people can eat the food and accept the protection of other people—let others in fact do the dirty work while they keep their own beastly conscience white, has always been beyond me." The head teacher, referred to in Charis's news-letter by this point as the "Conchy Headmistress," resigned after less than a year in the job.[14]

STAFF COULD COME and go. The Greengate committee, on the other hand, grew restive at Charis's dominant influence over the hospital that she now housed. Her battles with the committee suggest that she wanted to move the institution away from a model of amateur charity and toward being a profes-sionalized medical facility. The first conflict was over whether parents in the military should be required to pay a fee for their children being at Greengate, since they received a stipend from the state for that purpose. Charis argued that they should. It would be one thing if the whole institution were simply a charity, free to all. But if money was going to be taken, it had to be taken fairly, including money paid by the state for the maintenance of children. The treasurer opposed her. Parents had often been allowed not to pay, he ar-gued, and men in the military were hardly being overpaid for their sacrifice. The rest of the committee overruled him and sided with Charis.[15]

Charis was resolutely in favor of her nurses and teachers being ad-equately paid and well treated, in line with industry norms and the increasing protections for workers brought in during the war. When the com-mittee tried to save money by skimping on Christmas bonuses and wages at the end of 1941, she was so angry that she threatened to resign. The tactics the committee had chosen seemed designed "to effect a minimum of saving with a maximum of hurt feelings (Dorothy Rowe's phrase!)" and she could not "carry them out with a clear conscience." At the next meeting, despite a heated discussion, her views on salaries carried the day, and she stayed in her position as chairman.[16]

Although she'd won each of these battles, the war was not over. By au-tumn 1942, the committee had divided into pro- and anti-Charis factions. One committee member accused Charis of having "constantly taken advan-tage of what I had been able to do for Greengate to impose my will on the committee." In other words, because she housed the hospital, she could do what she liked, and she knew it. At the next meeting, a month later, Charis asked for a vote of confidence. Her tactic succeeded: all of the committee pres-ent except two voted for her to remain. Over the next few years, she was able to prevail in her views on wages and conditions. In July 1943, the committee agreed to set salaries in accordance with the Rushcliffe report on nurses' salaries. The treasurer even admitted "that sooner or later we should have to adopt this scale, and it would be better to do it now with a good grace." In April 1944, the committee likewise adopted the Hetherington scale of wages and conditions for domestic servants.[17]

In addition to her oversight as chairman of the committee, Charis served as hospital matron on several occasions. The longest stint began in July 1942, after the previous matron retired. Charis and Bonn enjoyed a day of leisure, before, in Bonn's words, Charis took over, "complete in white overalls—which she is longing to don!" Charis rose at 6:30 that morning to be dressed and ready for the children in the bathrooms, and she attended all the meals. Naturally, she undertook a "great deal of re-arranging," replacing the "pure slop" with things like Yorkshire pudding and preventing the nurses from taking more than their fair share of the jam, bacon, and sugar rations. Charis finished her stint as matron at the end of September 1942, after eleven weeks of work, during which she had left Oughtrington only three times, twice for committee meetings and once to take Ursula to the dentist. To ease the transition, Charis gave the new matron some space, though, as she self-deprecatingly admitted, "I made some 'LISTS'!"[18]

As the war continued, it became clear that the central government would, in the postwar era, play a much greater role in education and health care than had previously been the case. Charis took a practical interest in these developments. She loathed red tape and undue deference to officials. In the saga of Greengate's effort to purchase a vegetable-slicing machine, she found a perfect illustration of bureaucratic inefficiency. The purchase order passed through the hands of the Board of Trade, the Ministry of Food, the education authorities in Walsall (by mistake), and finally the Ministry of Health in Manchester before they finally got their slicer. Despite the pleas of her friend at the Ministry, she brought the story to the attention of the *Manchester Guardian*, and her friend "found at least a dozen copies of my little paragraph on her desk the next day."[19]

Charis was ferocious, too, on the professional dignity of midwives, which she felt was threatened by too much bureaucratic oversight. Having fought for greater state recognition of midwives to ensure their ability to earn a living, she now felt that the state had taken too much control. She challenged, for instance, apparent efforts to require Salford midwives to obtain official permission to hold meetings. She thought the younger midwives "who have joined the Municipal Service are not like the old ones, proud of their profession, but just lick the boots of the officials." Indeed, the Salford midwives' association replaced her as president the next year: evidently her irreverent approach to officialdom did not suit their new realities.[20]

None of this blinded Charis to the state's potentially beneficial powers. She continued her work with the Salford Women Citizens' Association during the war, using the opportunities provided by the war to advocate for more women in the police force. Her cousin, Barbara Denis de Vitré, had worked her way up through the police service, becoming the first woman to serve as assistant inspector of constabulary. In 1943, Charis attended a British Hospitals Association meeting as the Greengate representative and heard concerns about the proposed nationalized medical service, which would become the National Health Service after the war and would provide state-subsidized universal access to medical care. While not opposed to it, Charis hoped that there would still be scope for private hospitals to contribute their particular strengths in research and individualized treatment. She continued, in short, to position herself as a particularly socially aware and pragmatic Conservative. When one friend, a communist and consulting doctor at Greengate, told Charis, "For a Conservative you are an astonishingly good democrat," Charis demurred. The "Conservatives are the democratic party," she argued, while "the Labour party is all for Government control and red tape, and the Liberals are all for pious patronising." But as always she wore her politics lightly, making her friend laugh by announcing herself on the telephone as "Comrade Frankenburg." This friend soon claimed Charis as a communist. Charis conceded that, while she didn't share all of her friends' views, "there is more sense in them than one would gather from the papers."[21]

FOLLOWING IN SYDNEY'S footsteps, Charis became a Salford magistrate in January 1938. Overwhelmed by her servants quarreling, DLS commented to Muriel in 1941, "How I should hate to be a magistrate in a poor quarter." Charis, by contrast, thrived. The first women magistrates joined the bench in 1920; they remained rare in 1938, though Charis was sworn in alongside two new female colleagues. Her practical approach and holistic view on family life and society informed her work. She handed tissues to weeping defendants and used her midwifery expertise to assist in cases against putative fathers. In the summer of 1943, a heavily pregnant woman was in court and went into labor. Charis told the other magistrates "that unless they wanted me to practise my profession in open court they'd better bind them over and do it quickly."[22]

Here, more than in the female-dominated spheres of midwifery, birth control, and the Greengate, Charis crossed swords with men who found her too forceful. A local alderman suggested that children should be dealt with by a committee of parents and teachers, not magistrates. Charis and others disagreed, and the alderman said, "It is not Mrs Frankenburg's function to say 'No'"—in other words, she was overstepping her role as a magistrate and venturing into policy where she didn't belong. Later she asked a colleague why the alderman singled her out, and he told her, "Because, my dear, he knows that you are the only strong woman among the magistrates!" Charis was strong, but also quite deliberately charming: "I think I'm the only woman magistrate (except Mrs. Cuddeford) who ever smiles."[23]

She found a steadfast mentor and friend in the stipendiary magistrate, F. Bancroft Turner—the professional who worked alongside the unpaid magistrates like Charis. He called her Frankie, and she called him Bankie. (Charis liked to flirt, in a lighthearted way. A doctor at the Greengate told her, "You undoubtedly have IT as regards children." Coyly, she replied, "Only with children, Doctor?") By the end of the year, they were chatting companionably while Bankie changed from a soft collar to a stiff one to look "more judicial" on the bench. Although he mentored her in the work of the court, Charis held her own against some of his more traditional opinions. One day on the bench, Bankie murmured, "It always makes me laugh when you take your hat off," which she did in order to make the shawl-wearing working-class Salford women feel more equal. He explained that he didn't think women should appear in his court without covering their heads, "any more than you would in church." Charis murmured, "Oh, are you God?"[24]

Soon, Bankie had come to value Charis's judgment and presence on the bench. He told her, "You've got some funny ideas, but it's such a relief to have someone who has any." Yet his ideas were not so far removed from hers. They both embraced the more progressive approach to sentencing and rehabilitation that was then coming to the fore. This drew on the same ideas about child development and the importance of family relationships that Charis used at Greengate. She noted approvingly that Bankie rebuked a father who had beaten his son for stealing, as that "was a *lazy* punishment" compared with the engaged, friendly parenting that would have really changed his son's life. This line became their standard approach. On another occasion, Charis told a mother that she was "asking for trouble" by never allowing her son to have pocket money or go to the cinema.[25]

Charis drew on and contributed to emerging ideas about child psychology and parenting that emphasized attachment and a sense of security. Harsh discipline would terrorize small children and harden juvenile delinquents. What was needed instead, Charis had concluded, was an appeal to reason and a system that prevented bad behavior from taking root in the first place. These ideas have some basis in Charis's earliest work as an expert on child-rearing: the attention to the child's world and the practical outlook on family life are the same. But in the intervening twenty years, it's clear that Charis also took on new ideas. She believed in science, and when science advanced, so did her views. In her work in World War II with Greengate, she was part of that advance, as the mass cultural and social experiment of evacuation produced a new science of child psychology and parental attachment.

17

RUNNING TO STAND STILL

I n Lord Peter Wimsey and Harriet Vane, Muriel and DLS had created an impossible ideal of romance. Real life, and real partnerships, did not run so smoothly. The strain of war laid bare the fault lines of intimate relationships. Muriel, in particular, was running to stand still, balancing multiple jobs and relationships across a country whose routines were disrupted by the war. In a series of remarkable short stories, Bar would describe aspects of her own experience of war and marriage, translating her queer reality into the more acceptable terms of women's magazines. Like them, and like DLS, she concluded that the marital bond was complex and could contain multitudes; it could, and would, endure beyond the vicissitudes of ordinary life. DLS, whose own marriage remained alternately jovial and prickly, increasingly became Bar's confidant in all this, providing the perspective of a good friend who understood what it was to partnered with a temperamental, difficult person.

In an undated poem entitled "Keep Tryst," Muriel wrote about "all the little duties, the hardest tasks of all," which interfere with the pursuit of "the star of a great ambition." For Muriel, the cares of everyday work and making ends meet constantly detracted from the fulfillment of her great goals, whether they were romantic, personal, or intellectual. This was never more true than during these early years of World War II, when she tried to be all things to all people: a teacher, a writer, a researcher, a friend, a partner, and a lover. Her great ambition, professionally, was to be an independent scholar and writer. Her constant battles with bureaucracy, over things like tax assessments and wartime petrol allowances, reflect her struggle to defend that role against the depredations of "little duties" and requirements. She even asked Bedford College to pay her fees by the term as a visiting lecturer, rather than a salary, in order to "safeguard my professional status as an author, & to remain my own employer" for tax purposes.[1]

MURIEL WAS FRANTICALLY busy. After a holiday with Bar in Devon in January 1941, she plunged into a relentless schedule, balancing a variety of teaching duties at Bedford College (still in its wartime home in Cambridge) with her ongoing research and writing. Una Ellis-Fermor, whose classes she was covering at Bedford, told DLS that Muriel was moving so fast "that her features are practically indistinguishable. Yesterday, for instance, she had a rehearsal in one room and a department meeting in the next at the same time and did alternative sentences in each." Muriel's own report to DLS was scarcely less hectic: "I start my day at 9 & finish at about 2pm & rehearse till 10, & then during the worst of the snow had to *cycle*, several miles." Unsurprisingly, perhaps, she got the flu.[2]

Nevertheless, Muriel took on more tutoring hours at Bedford in the following term, leading to the offer of a full-time temporary lectureship beginning in the autumn of 1941. At this, DLS put her foot down and told Muriel that she must get some rest over the summer, even inviting her to come stay in Witham. "You have been rushing about for the last six months; & unless you introduce some sort of stability into your surroundings, you will make yourself ill again & come out in boils & blains & have to sit on a dunghill like Job, scratching yourself with a potsherd & asking God why He has thought fit to afflict you." Muriel needed to take care of herself and her work, and not "let everything go at the call of this, that & the other person." Presumably this arrangement would also have reunited Bar and Muriel, since Bar was also staying with DLS around this time.[3]

Muriel took her friend's advice and spent some time in Essex in July 1941. In August, she went with Bar and the pets to Dorset, where Bunter recovered from minor ailments under their tender care and Timothy brought them the mice and moles he caught. Still, Bar told DLS, "MSB is *very* up & downish." They were soon joined by Susan, who had returned from America, to the dismay of some of her former colleagues. According to Bar, people at Bedford gossiped that Susan was both cowardly and ungrateful. People had taken a lot of trouble to make it possible for her to go, and some said she'd only been trying to get away from the Blitz and was back now that the worst seemed to be over.[4]

Susan returned to Cambridge, where she planned to work as Muriel's secretary, getting books, looking up references, and dealing with correspondence. That autumn, despite the mutterings, Muriel and Susan moved into the Old Rectory in Fen Ditton, several miles outside of Cambridge. Muriel described the house as "*fantastically* like Talboys!" referring to the Elizabethan house rented by Harriet and Peter in *Busman's Honeymoon*.[5]

Judging from asides in their letters, Muriel's friends in this era were aware that both Bar and Susan held significant places in Muriel's life. One signed a letter, "My love always and to Miss Cullis," for example. Another friend sent her "love & all good wishes to you & Bar, & Miss Cullis." The different levels of formality here—Bar versus Miss Cullis—suggest that Susan was not as thoroughly integrated into Muriel's world. A third letter makes this even clearer. This friend asked Muriel to give her love to Bar, before asking, "What's Miss—damn, I've forgotten her name—your Susan anyway, doing now? and where is she?"[6]

There seems to have been general alarm, however, at the plan for Muriel and Susan to live and work together in Cambridge. Muriel got a chastising letter from her friend Gladys Scott Thomson in the late summer or autumn of 1941, and Muriel told DLS that she "just quailed at the very sight of sheets & sheets of something worse than Cross Words, & threw the whole envelope-full to Bar (not *at* Bar): & she read my letter, & reported on the gist thereof." Her Bedford colleague Una Ellis-Fermor, too, was less than pleased. She had been looking forward to seeing a lot of Muriel in Cambridge, and had been "waiting vigilantly for two years to get her the first war vacancy that turned up—but she has gone out to Fen Ditton, five or six miles from here, and has Miss Cullis with her, so I am afraid it will not happen as often as I had hoped." She hinted, though, that the arrangement might be "for the best," at least as far as Muriel's relationship with Susan went: "I found a year in close quarters [with Susan presumably] very illuminating, myself."[7]

The new living arrangements altered the status quo for Bar, Muriel, and Susan: now Susan was the domestic partner, and Bar kept her distance. Bar and Muriel had lunch in late October, but although Muriel was "pathetically anxious" for Bar to go and see the Old Rectory, she refused, for the time being: "I think it much fairer that they should try out the new pattern without interference." Bar finally visited Muriel and Susan in Fen Ditton in January 1942. She arrived on a Thursday, and Susan was away, "but Muriel had a giddy attack on Friday & spent the day in bed." The next day, they spent the morning getting Bar's rations, and then in the afternoon Susan came back. Muriel and Susan, she felt, seemed to talk of little besides "housekeeping & food." For her part, Muriel seemed "more besotted than ever & everything she says underlines S's manifold gifts & graces." Bar was less impressed with Susan, who seemed to her to take the best of everything for herself. She concluded: "I am stiffened in my resolve to refuse to consider a trio."[8]

If the visit was meant as a trial run for a shared household between the three of them, it was, evidently, a failure. Susan had complained to Gladys Scott Thomson about the trials and tribulations of living with Muriel, whose temper she found "almost unbearable at times." Bar admitted that she felt a "mixture of malicious glee & irony & perplexed humility" when she heard this. "I had been really CONVICTED OF SIN for having told Susan in the early days how difficult Muriel was—& to find that she needs to blow off steam—!" More worrying were rumors that Muriel was alienating people at Bedford with complaints about the work and the students. "She *can't* afford to lose that job & it wouldn't be a bad thing if she could keep it after the war." Bar blamed Susan as well as her friend Janet Trevelyan. "They all seem in the circle of a neurotic hell—and I wish I could do something to extricate my poor dear—who isn't neurotic *au fond* I am convinced, & is such a lamb so often."[9]

DLS and, to a lesser extent, Mac provided Bar with a refuge and a friendly ear. Mac gave her a sepia image for her mantelpiece in Berkhamsted, which improved the room's decor greatly. He also painted Bar's portrait. When Christmas came around in 1941, DLS invited both Muriel and Bar. Muriel opted to remain with Susan, and Bar decided to go to Essex. She told Muriel she was "sorry if you minded about my going to D.L.S. for the Christmas holidays," but Muriel needed to accept that she could not "cope any longer with our triangle." Why, she wondered, couldn't Muriel come on her own? Susan would have a house with a telephone and friends nearby, after all. Instead, Bar arrived on DLS's doorstep alone and "looking pretty fagged." She recovered on good food and rest. DLS, Mac, and Bar "contrived to over-eat ourselves in the most seasonable way, the Axis notwithstanding." And Bar took DLS on "two good muddy walks, which doubtless will do me good, though I yawn horribly after them & so does she!" Bar became a regular holiday visitor at DLS's house, with DLS urging her the next year to "come back at Christmas to pay us a nice long Eighteenth-Century visit."[10]

Yet Mac, too, could be mercurial and difficult. His temper was bad enough that DLS specifically looked for servants who would be able to cope with it. In October 1941, DLS told Muriel in mock Elizabethan that "the Master of the House was of a pretty good behaviour, though with a little Tantrum or two to which I paid but little attention." He was especially irritable when she was late coming home from the talks she gave to soldiers in the region. One time, her car broke down on the drive home, and DLS related the whole ensuing argument to Muriel in vivid, comic terms. Mac "said I had been on the binge with the soldiers, and that I was drunk and a liar. So I threw my boots at him and so to bed!" She's paraphrasing the seventeenth-century diarist Samuel Pepys on the boots and the bed, obscuring the reality of her marital troubles with humor. Her letters often dramatized the bickering and disagreement of her marriage for comic effect, leaving unsaid the constant fact that she and Mac were united by argument more than a shared sense of purpose.[11]

BAR AND MURIEL had absorbed Susan into their lives in the 1930s, but by 1941, in the context of wartime upheaval, the old equilibrium was failing and the relationship reached a crisis point. At exactly the same time, Bar began writing and publishing short stories under the pseudonym Anne Elliott, surely in homage to Jane Austen's long-suffering heroine in *Persuasion*. These stories appeared in a variety of middlebrow publications such as *Women's Journal* and *Good Housekeeping*. Like DLS and Muriel, Bar was represented by Nancy Pearn, and she was pleased at the extra income the work brought her.[12]

The stories form a powerful set of meditations on marriage—its constraints and its ability to stretch and reshape itself around the needs and foibles of each couple. One story portrays the engagement of an aristocratic young man and a self-possessed, worldly young woman. They vow to make a "new sort of marriage." Perhaps his mother had been content to provide the harmony to his father's tune, but these two will proceed contrapuntally, exactly like Peter and Harriet. Each partner, Bar insists, must have his or her own interests and desires, and the job of marriage is to bring them into a productive, pleasing relationship with each other.[13]

The question of infidelity animates many of Bar's stories. She's participating, here, in the general reassessment of adultery and marriage that took place after legislation in 1923 allowed women to sue for divorce on the basis of adultery alone. Like other popular writers, she suggests that the bonds of marriage are paramount and that marital love is able to overcome external distractions. She emphasizes the importance of sex, in keeping with the interwar focus on sexual satisfaction as a crucial component to a successful marriage. In "After the Theatre," for example, a wife is toying with infidelity. Her rather selfless doctor husband sends her to Venice as a companion to an aristocratic patient, much as Bar herself had accompanied DLS to that city. There, "almost satiated with beauty," the wife realizes she misses her husband, and she returns home to renew her commitment to him. She asks him to forget "the silly martyred way" she had spoken, as if her life "was one long sacrifice." It wasn't. In fact, his need for her gives her "a field of activity." And she realizes the significance of their physical connection, too. "I've so seldom been away from you, that I didn't realise how much you had given me, as a lover—it's more important than I thought." Devotion and physical connection, here, provide the essence of marriage.[14]

In "Answers to Correspondence," by contrast, time spent apart allows the main character, Elizabeth, to become more independent of her husband. Elizabeth has realized that her husband, Bernard, has taken a lover. "Apart from one or two little stabs of sickness and anger, Elizabeth was surprised to find that she did not care much about the physical side of it." She "had lived among advanced people and had principles about jealousy," understanding that it is not possible to possess the people we love. These phrases call to mind Bar's reference to schooling herself not to be possessive about Muriel. They lived, too, in a context in which women shared their lives with more than one lover—"advanced people," perhaps.

Still, in the story, Elizabeth feels like "a frightful failure." This only changes when the war breaks out. She and Bernard both get evacuated for their work, but to different places, just as Bar was sent to Berkhamsted and Muriel went to Cambridge. At first, Elizabeth "almost felt as if she had died," echoing Bar's profound sense of alienation early on in Berkhamsted. "It was not until the bitter months of the first war winter had been followed by the incredible fears and agonies of a mockingly lovely summer, and the astounding ardours and glories of the Battle of Britain and the Blitz, that she came out of a condition approximating to shell shock." She finds strength, first, in patriotism, and then in her independent life and work. She becomes used to not seeing Bernard, who, she presumes, is spending his leaves with Deirdre, as Muriel spent some of her holidays with Susan.

Then Bernard reaches out with "a very affectionate letter, and rather wistful. Not owning to anything of course. But he'd had 'flu and was sorry for himself." Elizabeth's first reaction is bemusement. "I suppose Deirdre's finished with him. Why should I go back just to slave for him again?" But she feels a "queer ache in her heart," too. She remembers things about him that could easily be about Muriel: "how the slow deliberation with which he put on his horn-rimmed spectacles for example, used to make her bones turn to water." The story ends on an ambivalent note, as a friend advises Elizabeth to go slowly. No fictional story is pure autobiography, but the parallels between Bar's real life and Elizabeth's fictional one suggest that this story conveys some of the emotional complexity of Bar's wartime experience. Accepting Susan was part of what Bar understood as required for an advanced, modern, non-possessive partner. But, as Susan complained about Muriel's neediness and Bar found external validation in her work as a teacher and an author, she began to question the situation.[15]

BY THE SPRING of 1942, Muriel was also getting fed up with her living situation at the Old Rectory with Susan. She struggled to get a petrol allowance that would cover her journeys between Fen Ditton, Cambridge, and London. In June 1942, she cryptically wrote to DLS, "The Rectorial situation becomes more & more untenable." By July, she was packing up and planned to return to 28 St. John's Wood Terrace "for good I hope." Although she continued to travel to Cambridge and teach for Bedford, she could spend more time on the Lisle letters in London. That work had been hindered by the closure of the Public Record Office. In May 1942, however, she negotiated to get access to the papers. Later in the war, when the bombing started again, a "condition of being allowed to work was that when the men in charge rang a bell everyone else had to get under the tables."[16]

The possibility of a domestic trio remained, and Muriel, Bar, and Susan lived together at St. John's Wood Terrace for various stretches of time. Bar struggled with the situation. She "didn't even flinch" when Susan made an officious remark about the cost of milk. But she chafed at the uncertainty about meals—an effort to cook asparagus, for example, was undone by the general chaos about timing and who was doing what. Bar reentered the role of Muriel's helpmeet, while Susan seemed to live a life of relative luxury. One morning, when Bar had just returned from Essex, Susan slept in, "so I got M's breakfast & relit the kitchen fire, which hadn't been properly raked for days. While she floated vaguely about & went off to have her hair done!!" Another time, Susan's arrival meant that Bar could get away to Essex for a few days despite the lack of servants: "she is becoming positively *useful*."[17]

It's no surprise that the tensions of evacuation, mobilization, and large-scale civilian bombing tore at the patches and papered-over joins in these relationships. What's striking is how Bar was able to rely on DLS and the contemporary language of companionate heterosexual marriage to make sense of the challenges of her own situation. In an era in which same-sex relations between men were criminalized and between women were hedged with the threat of scandal, Bar nonetheless found the conceptual tools she needed to see her through a particularly trying set of circumstances. At the same time, DLS and, to a lesser extent, Muriel embarked on their own projects of refashioning the tools of religion and science to make a bid for a better future.

18

BRIDGEHEADS TO THE FUTURE

I N THE LATE 1930S AND early 1940s, DLS became increasingly preoccupied with three related issues: the importance of work in leading an ethical, spiritually satisfying life; the right of women as well as men to that work; and the gap between popular impressions of mild, boring Christianity and what she saw as the religion's real significance. She and Muriel addressed these issues in collaboration, coediting a series of books under the title Bridgeheads that they hoped would spark a general reassessment of the relationship between work and ethics. Here, and in a series of essays, a set of plays, and a memoir, they challenged received wisdom on subjects ranging from gender to Jesus, producing a body of wartime work that was alternately energetically optimistic and devastatingly bleak.

It was also unfailingly democratic. DLS knew that language was "an instrument of power," and should be handled as such. Perhaps even more important, ordinary people needed their own weapons with which to combat the misuse of language. DLS and Muriel developed this idea in a dialogue about education, which DLS adapted into a published essay. More people were literate than ever before, but, at the same time, people were "susceptible to the influence of advertisement and mass-propaganda to an extent hitherto unheard-of and unimagined." To deal with this calamity, she and Muriel proposed a return to the medieval trivium of grammar, dialectic, and rhetoric, in order to give people the tools with which to make sense of the ambiguous language that confronted them.[1]

Such issues were heightened in the context of war, when governments summoned the language of patriotism to their own ends. In keeping with their broadly moderate conservative outlook, the members of the MAS supported the British war effort from a patriotic standpoint. As Charis put it, "I'm not 'my country right or wrong' but I would always give the English the benefit of the doubt." Charis, D. Rowe, and DLS all admired Winston Churchill and what he stood for. In a 1943 essay, DLS cast Churchill as the "Old Nurse—tart, solid, bustling and comfortable" who had rescued the English from "a peevish new-fangled and semi-educated governess" and returned them to their better natures. To Muriel, DLS described Churchill in more masculine terms, as a real Englishman, "gent, scholar, wit, foul-mouthed, bon vivant, & all the rest of it."[2]

DLS tried to intervene in the British wartime conversation at a deeper level, too. When war broke out, a relative asked Muriel, "Is D.L.S. writing madly for the troops. If she hasn't killed Lord Peter, will she give us Lord Peter & Harriet in the secret service with some nice Gaudie Nightie bits about spies, & civil servants, & international chess-men and some sonnets, and a bit more attractive insolence-on-the-Cher." In fact, DLS had applied to the War Office to work in propaganda, and she joined the register for war service compiled by the Society of Authors, Playwrights, and Composers in May 1939 at the Ministry of Labour's request. She was in touch with the Ministry of Information, but disliked their approach and declined, sensibly, the invitation to write a pamphlet on German forgery and police methods. DLS called the Ministry an "overcrowded monkey-house of graft and incompetence." In Muriel's recollection, "A certain gentleman-in-charge interviewed us, & was much too jealous of DLS's powers & prestige to have any use for us!"[3]

DLS did address troops and other groups during the war. She even agreed to autograph national savings certificates at Harrods in July 1940 as part of a national effort, though she was bemused by members of the public who could be "lured into saving their souls and bodies" by a detective writer's signature. In wartime essays that reached a much broader audience, she argued that the English were essentially moderate, just, and good. She celebrated the country both for its insular stability and for its tradition of openness. English people were mongrels, she wrote, and were thus welcoming to foreigners, "provided they come in assimilable numbers and turn into islanders." The English were, moreover, able to expand freely and know themselves, because they were sure of their position in a stable class hierarchy. Most importantly, they had a particular, historic role in resisting European dictators, which they were fulfilling once again in the fight against Nazism.

This sort of thing earned her admiration from distant quarters, including Felix Frankfurter, the United States Supreme Court justice, and W. L. Mackenzie King, the Canadian prime minister. Sending Mackenzie King an autographed book by request, DLS also included a long letter giving him "my usual 'piece' about England." Touched, he rang her up personally. As DLS told Bar, "So we exchanged messages of good will and blessing like a couple of buddies, or statesmen 'saluting' somebody's anniversary, while Mac sat gloomily over the remains of the soup and wondered what all the yattering was about."[4]

BUT WHILE SUCH writing was popular, and perhaps good for morale, it was not at the core of what DLS wanted to do, which was, increasingly, to use the war as an opportunity to rethink fundamental issues. She believed that the conditions of war might foster self-reflection. Generally, one could distract oneself from deeper questions by taking a drive, seeing a film, or even reading a detective novel. In wartime, "cut off from mental distractions by restrictions and blackouts, and cowering in a cellar with a gas-mask under threat of imminent death," such questions could perhaps receive their due.[5]

To achieve this end, DLS, Muriel, and their mutual friend Helen Simpson decided to launch a series of books. The core concept of the series would be creativity as a driving force in the reinvention and rebirth of postwar society. More immediately, they were meant to "give to the people of this country a constructive purpose worth living for and worth dying for." DLS kicked around various possible symbols to represent the series—a seahorse? The "budding wand" from tarot? A phoenix? In the end, they chose a bridgehead, suggesting a fortified position from which progress would be possible. Outlining the setup in 1939, DLS explained that the project was nonsectarian— DLS was Anglican, Simpson Catholic, and Muriel "rather inclined to be anti-organised-religion of any kind." She admitted that it looked "rather absurd for three women, without any very special influence or qualifications, to embark on this kind of programme," but argued that all the best things begin in humble surroundings. Why shouldn't three ordinary women remake the world?[6]

Their plan was disrupted by Simpson's death from illness in 1940. DLS regarded her death as both a personal tragedy and a loss for the project of postwar reconstruction. Nonetheless, DLS and Muriel pursued Bridgeheads, with DLS as general editor and Muriel as organizing secretary of the project. DLS was an active, busy editor. She edited in the midst of bombing, and kept manuscripts in the air-raid shelter, one night putting them all "to bed in the bunk with a hot-water bottle" against the damp, which was, after all, preferable to being burned up. All sorts of literary treasures lived in this snug spot. When Muriel received a request from someone interested in her play *Paul, A Prisoner*, she wrote to DLS: "*of course* my only copy *would* be in your dugout! . . . It is, I believe, in the blue file labelled Lisle Papers!!"[7]

DLS began the series with her own book, *The Mind of the Maker*, which takes on the task of explaining creativity in a theological light. It accomplishes this through an extended analogy between God, as the ultimate creator of the world, and human beings, who find their truest meaning in their own creativity, as expressed through authentic work. The concept of the Trinity is at the heart of this analogy, which links the creative process of Idea, Energy, and Power to the Christian notions of Father, Word (or Son), and Spirit. Both religion and art, DLS argued, are centrally concerned with the act of creation and construction, crucial activities in a world where "the purely analytical approach to phenomena is leading us only further and further into the abyss of disintegration and randomness." Every artist—and thus every worker, if work is understood as an act of creation rather than drudgery—is animated by a drive to realize a central Idea. Fidelity to that Idea is absolutely necessary. "It is a short and sordid view of life that will do injury to the work in the kind hope of satisfying a public demand," DLS argued at the end of the book. Instead, "all workers should behold the integrity of the work," or in other words, work "must be done for God first and foremost."[8]

The book resonated with readers, though some struggled with the religious metaphor at its heart. One said that reading it made her "feel as if I had been living for months in a kind of spiritual gas mask . . . and suddenly I could breathe again." DLS sent a copy to Helen Darbishire, who found herself "rather stumbling at the function of the Holy Ghost in your interpretation, but I see the idea." George Trevelyan found it "full of illumination and wisdom," but balked at the use of the Athanasian Creed, which was, he felt, "much narrower and nastier" than DLS's interpretation gave it credit for.[9]

Una Ellis-Fermor wrote the second Bridgehead, *Masters of Reality*. Like *The Mind of the Maker*, the book is concerned with the need of human beings to exercise their creative force, or imagination, as Ellis-Fermor calls it. Criticizing the modern tendency toward mechanization, she argues that the present-day citizen is overwhelmed by the amount of information constantly spewed forth by broadcasts, megaphones, placards, and advertisements. What was needed was the development of each person's inherent ability to make creative use of the materials at hand. The editorial correspondence about the book illuminates DLS's insistence that the series should be able to speak to a broad public, "an all-round, intelligent, but not specialised public," as DLS put it. In concrete terms, this meant writing concisely and vividly, as well as sympathetically, so that readers could see themselves even in the "bad" characters in the book's central parable. To Muriel, DLS confessed she thought that Ellis-Fermor's style "is better fitted for the writing of earnest tracts than for fiction."[10]

As a project envisioning the future, Bridgeheads aimed to deal with social phenomena across the spectrum of human experience. DLS and Muriel wanted critical books that would take on the pieties and commonplaces of wartime discourse, written by leading thinkers. Dr. G. W. Pailthorpe planned to write a book on *The Social Value of Surrealism*. Denis Browne, Helen Simpson's widower, was meant to write *A New Charter for Medicine*. DLS talked about approaching Storm Jameson, who was, she felt, the only voice then speaking "against the 'peace & security' illusion." Gerry Hopkins was floated as a potential contributor who could write "about the cult of the business man in public affairs." Judging from its title, and Muriel's sympathy with the worker's perspective, her proposed book on *Privilege and Responsibility* might have considered the question of class relations.[11]

The competing demands of war work meant that many of the projected volumes were never finished. Half-jokingly, DLS told Muriel in August 1941 that "the correspondence I have had lately with Miss St. Clare Byrne does not encourage me to hope that *Privilege & Responsibility* will be ready for some little time!" Indeed, it never saw the light of day. DLS and Muriel had high standards. They rejected books for being unoriginal, for being vague, and for being written in a diffuse, cliché-ridden style. One manuscript presented views that chimed with DLS's "more unregenerate reactions," but relied on questionable sources and unscholarly references. If this book was too casual, another was too scholarly, "rather exclusively the book of somebody who is a scientist, rather than a writer." Rejecting a book on the treatment of animals, DLS argued that the subject could only be addressed within Bridgeheads as part of "the whole complicated problem of how far man is justified in subordinating the rest of creation to his use and service, and how far he *can* do so without disturbing the order of nature in a catastrophic way." The goal was always to say something of lasting importance about human beings and their world, rather than scoring particular political points.[12]

The Bridgeheads project pulled DLS's gaze outward, beyond her usual topics and preoccupations. She realized, belatedly, the significance of the British Empire, not as a vague backdrop to English glory, but as a central institution and problem for people around the world. As a younger woman, DLS's rare references to empire had often been laden with metropolitan snobbery and even racism. When Jim Jaeger was considering a job in Australia in 1919, DLS was skeptical that there was any "good journalism to be done" there. Around the same time, reacting to news that a friend had taken a job in Ceylon, she said bluntly, "I hate them black places." By the 1940s, her "usual piece" on England emphasized the value of the empire, its association with liberty, and its reliance on local decisions. She realized now, though, that this wasn't really enough.[13]

In the spring of 1943, DLS outlined a potential Bridgehead book on the subject of empire and the colonies, discussing it with Muriel and then showing a draft to Bar in person. She wanted a book that would "examine the *idea* of British *Imperium*" as a distinct historical phenomenon and as a possible bridgehead toward a postwar world of federated nations. The outline walked an uneasy line between suggesting areas of inquiry and summarizing DLS's own views. She admitted, for instance, "I don't pretend to understand India." Yet she also suggested that Indian nationalists might be going about things backward, demanding independence before they'd proved their capacity for self-government.[14]

Although the Bridgeheads book on empire never materialized, DLS believed that people needed good books through which they could come to terms with the whole question. Advising her old friend Frank Brabant on his draft novel, she argued that he should write a "straight African story, dealing with the actual situation," because "good novels" were more useful than government reports to a British public trying to work out "what in blazes it's doing with all its native responsibilities." Her intellectual curiosity stands awkwardly alongside an ideology that privileged empire and doubted the capacity of nonwhite nations for self-governance. A lifetime of insularity could not be so easily undone, despite DLS's intentions and ambitions.[15]

The Bridgehead series ultimately produced little in the way of books: really just DLS's and Ellis-Fermor's books as companion volumes, with an odd coda in the form of an avuncular book on the parliamentary system for children by A. P. Herbert in 1946. But the project is crucial context for understanding the sheer scope of DLS's intellectual ambition in this decade. It is a useful corrective to the notion that she became narrowly focused on theology. On the contrary, her interests expanded dramatically, from empire to capitalism, from the Trinity to the capacity of human beings to destroy the world. No longer content with providing "recreation for noble minds," she wanted to bring cutting-edge ideas to all sorts of minds and to find redemption for everyone in the value of creative work, broadly defined.[16]

ONE ELEMENT OF this was a growing clarity about the essential equality of women and men as human beings, who deserved an equal chance to do creative, meaningful work. For DLS, this represented a significant transformation. As a young person, she admitted, she had not been involved with social movements, being "just lazy and deeply prejudiced by a Tory Church of England upbringing. And completely self-centred." She hadn't been "a 'feminist'—I didn't have to be," because of the privileges of her life and the relative ease with which women could become authors. DLS certainly ran into difficulties—a proposed talk on the BBC, "Living to Work," was, DLS recalled, rejected partly on the grounds that "our public do not want to be admonished by a woman." But her road to professional success was, she felt, comparatively untroubled by sexism. As a result, DLS realized only slowly how pervasively British society limited women on the grounds of their gender alone.[17]

Muriel's background was different: she understood from a young age that girls and boys were treated very differently. This was difficult for her on the level of abstract justice—boys got the better-made toys for no discernable reason—and on a more personal level, because Muriel identified with masculinity so strongly and thus felt alienated by being treated as a girl. As the bombs fell, Muriel decided to finish the memoir in which she explored the dilemma: "I thought I might not be here another year," she said later. Struggling to place it with a publisher, she asked DLS for help. Their agent, Nancy Pearn, "takes your word, you know—witness her immediate placing of Bar's bit when you told her to place it!" It's hard to imagine that Bar appreciated this framing of events, but Muriel was writing the letter from Berkhamsted, so it's possible Bar saw it and agreed.[18]

Instead, DLS got eminent poet T. S. Eliot to take an interest after they crossed paths at the dentist—as DLS put it later, "I accosted you, so to speak, on the tooth-snatcher's very doorstep." Eliot remembered Muriel as "a great Elizabethan scholar" who was "one of the few human beings connected with the Shakespeare Association" and who "like myself used to smoke French cigarettes." What, he asked, did she smoke now? Something "repellent," DLS replied. Muriel, naturally, was delighted with this; she returned Eliot's compliments and added, "I now smoke John Cotton's Cuba blend—not at all a bad substitute."[19]

Tobacco-related pleasantries aside, Eliot was sympathetic to the particular needs of this book, recognizing that it did not fit into a neat category. DLS suspected he was relieved, too, at its brevity, "since his encounter with you at the Thingummy-bob committee-meetings had rather led him to expect seven volumes or so of Elizabethan research." He made an offer for the book, and both Muriel and Bar were thrilled. Bar, with her own relationship worries on her mind, speculated that Susan would be "frightfully jealous" of how DLS had helped Muriel. More temperately, she added that she was "very very grateful to you on Muriel's behalf for pushing it."[20]

Both the book, published as *Common or Garden Child*, and its author defied categorization. Muriel worried about how to portray her own complex feelings—her identification with her father, her preference for masculine activities—in a way that did justice to the nuances of her experience. One friend, the writer Harold Child, read drafts of the manuscript and assured her: "I don't see any trace of your having 'ought to have been a boy'; but I do see your enormous luck in being a girl with the advantages of being a boy and the power to make use of them; so that you got most of the benefits of both your sexes." Later, he added, "But after so much association with men you must have found it mighty hard to become respectable and ladylike on the outside. Inside, of course, you never did and never will." His comments are generous and telling.[21]

Many women used masculine nicknames and wore masculine attire in interwar Britain, and it could be a sign of modern sophistication rather than an indication of what we might now call lesbian or trans identity. DLS, for instance, often appeared in trousers or with masculine accoutrements, earning Mac's disdain. In claiming two sexes for Muriel, however, Child drew lightly on the sexological and related discourses of the era, which suggested that some people might inhabit a third gender or have differing inherent amounts of masculinity and femininity, and which linked homosexuality with gender deviance, or what was called inversion. He underscores that her story is part of the history of nonbinary genders as well as the history of homosexuality. The newspapers of the era reveled in sensational stories of people who lived as the other sex from the one they'd been assigned at birth, so Muriel would have had at least glancing familiarity with this as an option, though not as one she necessarily would have felt able to exercise even if she'd wanted to. Photographs of Muriel suggest a confident person wearing generally, but not exclusively, masculine clothing. Bar, on the other hand, was glamorous and feminine in her clothing, suggesting that the couple could have been read using the cultural concepts of the masculine female-born "invert" and the "normal woman" turned lesbian, in interwar terms—or as a butch/femme couple, in postwar terms.

Muriel uses none of those terms, nor any of the language about transgender identities that would develop from midcentury. When she asked Child whether her manuscript gave the impression that she thought she ought to have been born a boy, she might have been distancing herself from narratives of cross-gender identification. But Muriel was proud to claim masculinity in other respects, in her clothing and, implicitly, in how she moved through the world. Her words to Child might be better read as something else: a claim for sufficiency, a refusal not of difference but of wistfulness. As Child sympathetically translated it, she didn't need to be born a boy in order to benefit from "both her sexes."[22]

In *Common or Garden Child*, Muriel explores her childhood experiences, evoking vivid emotional states: outrage at the limitations placed on her as a girl, ecstasy as she trailed along with her father, a sense of workmanship and pride using the tools that her grandfather gave her. Reviewers were divided about what, exactly, it said about gender. In *Time and Tide*, Stephen Gwynn called it "a study of the kind of girl who always wanted to be a boy," though one who eventually became "just as feminine a young female as any other." The *Times Literary Supplement* reviewer, perhaps coached by Muriel, praised the book for

Muriel St. Clare Byrne (MSBC 9/3)

being written "with no self-pity of the 'ought to have been a boy' kind." An old school friend wrote, too, delighting in how the book brought back her own memories of Muriel "sitting on a wall in boy's clothes" and wearing short hair "long before it was the fashion to do so." She concluded, "You were not *in the least* 'ordinary' you know!"[23]

WHY, THOUGH, SHOULD only boys get to play with sturdier toys? In a pair of essays written in the summer of 1941, DLS and Muriel argued that gender had become too all-determining of a category in modern life. They had both been irritated by a special issue of the journal *Christendom* that June on the subject of the "emancipated woman." The point, DLS argued to the journal's editor, Maurice Reckitt, was not what women needed or deserved: it was that women were always discussed as women first, whereas men got to be people first.[24]

Muriel and DLS corresponded about their respective essays that summer. Bar weighed in, too. She found DLS's draft article "simply brilliant—*and* sound & profound," reading it "with joyous guffaws several times." On holiday in Devon, she was helpmeet as well as critic, stuck doing the housework while Muriel tried to get some work done on her own draft in between bouts of insomnia. It wasn't all drudgery, though: they went to the beach, where Muriel complained that it was simply too windy to write.[25]

Ultimately, Muriel and DLS maintained that women were human beings, and the social system founded on denying that fact was the real problem. DLS reached for a feline analogy to make the point. "The domestic function of a cat, quâ cat, is to catch mice," she wrote. Whether that was a male or a female cat depended only "on the individual preference for kittens or smells about the house." Producing kittens was only one aspect of a female cat's life, in no way impeding her ability to catch a mouse. In the same way, it was wrong to attempt to limit women to their role as mothers. DLS would never tolerate the notion that women were special in some mysterious way. Such references to a feminine mystique were "poison," as well as being empirically unsound.[26]

In some respects, Muriel echoed DLS's points. It was time, she wrote, to "accept the basic fact that men and women are equally and essentially and primarily human beings." She was more uncompromising, however, in her criticism of patriarchal attitudes, asserting, "Most men feel strongly that the needs and scope of women's lives are not of equal value with theirs." Most of all, she explicitly argued for a social constructionist point of view. She cited scientific authority on the fact that men and women had both masculine and feminine aspects. Given that, the categorization of humans into two sexes was inevitably a bit artificial. Society could only function, she said, if a majority of "the social group described as women" was satisfied. Not "women" but "the social group described as women." She underscored the point—that social gender was different from sexual biology—by closing her article with a line from Harley Granville-Barker's 1910 play, *The Madras House*, which prefigures Simone de Beauvoir: "male and female created He them: but men and women are a long time in the making."[27]

DLS's ARGUMENT ABOUT the importance of creative work was, ultimately, a theological and a spiritual one. As *The Mind of the Maker* suggested, she was increasingly concerned about the status of religion in modern Britain. She was skeptical of the current attention being paid to Christianity: official broadcasts and days of prayer and so on gave one "a haunting feeling that God's acquaintance is being cultivated because He might come in useful." She was aware, too, of her own marginal position within the church— mother to a son born out of wedlock and wife to a divorced man, she did not even attend her parish church regularly. She described her religious conviction as ambivalent, admitting that she was "in love with an intellectual pattern" rather than being a convinced, mainstream, abiding Christian. Significantly, she turned down the offer of an honorary degree in divinity from Lambeth on these grounds, as well as to preserve her freedom as a writer.[28]

Nevertheless, DLS used Christianity in these years to make a series of uncompromising, surprising arguments. Like *The Mind of the Maker*, her broadcasts and essays on Christianity were meant to galvanize the nation, providing them

Dorothy L. Sayers (DLSA)

with the spiritual impulse necessary for the making of a better postwar world. Religion was crucial to this earthly project, DLS argued, because it was invested in the essential goodness of the material world. In a 1940 broadcast, she drew two lessons from the belief that Christ was both entirely human and entirely God: first, that religion is "active, positive, and creative," concerned with doing good in the world; and second, that "matter and the material body are good and not evil." Pushing this further, DLS argued that all "cruelty to God's living children, all greedy exploitation of the world's resources, all waste and destruction, all using of matter for ugly and evil ends," including "bad art" and "dishonest workmanship," amounted to sacrilege.[29]

This led DLS to a more general critique of capitalism. To an audience in Eastbourne in 1942, she argued that work and religion had become too separate, with the result that work was no longer filled with meaning and inherent value. Because modern people had built their society on "Envy and Avarice," they were stuck in an "appalling squirrel-cage of economic confusion." She told the Public Morality Council that the idea of "immorality" had become too narrowly identified with lust. Vindictiveness in war was wrong, too, and so was a gluttonous cycle of ever-expanding production and consumption. She was scathing about her own former industry, which produced "the furious barrage of advertisement by which people are flattered and frightened out of a reasonable contentment into a greedy hankering after goods which they do not really need." She hoped that the war would lead to a permanent, beneficial change. Until then, she warned, "the economic balance-sheet of the world will have to be written in blood."[30]

In her essays, broadcasts, and Bridgehead book, DLS retained some optimism about the future. She took a bleaker view in the cycle of plays on the life of Jesus that she wrote for the BBC, grouped under the title *The Man Born to Be King* and broadcast between December 1941 and October 1942. These were designed to be aired in Children's Hour, building on the success of her earlier nativity play, and were part of the BBC's mission of promoting "Christian and liberal" ideals. But they were no reassuring Sunday school fare. DLS insisted on the raw humanity of the events she portrayed, which led, inevitably, to the conclusion that human beings are capable of extraordinary evil, not occasionally or exceptionally, but as the result of our nature. We must strive for improvement, but we must also recognize that Christianity warns us of our inevitable failure.[31]

As a dramatist, DLS refused to pander to a notional child, citing the authority of Bar as a schoolmistress that "you couldn't pontificate about 'the' school-child at all." By law, Christ could not be portrayed onstage by an actor; the BBC got around this by claiming that reading Christ's words over the air was fundamentally different. DLS gave no quarter to those who might have preferred a less confrontational production. She had her actors speak in modern English, using appropriate modern accents. She refused to censor the language at the crucifixion scene, because "you can't expect crucified robbers to talk like a Sunday-school class," even if it did horrify parents. DLS and her collaborators ultimately "succeeded in shocking ourselves" in rendering a realistic crucifixion. Bar's students, listening in, "just sat together and cried all the time." It was brutal, DLS admitted, but so was Hitler: "and it's just as well people should know that Christianity deals with that kind of thing, and not with merely deprecating the pleasanter sins and urging people to go to church."[32]

The plays were a major success and would continue to draw wide audiences every time the BBC aired them. The members of the MAS were impressed, too. Charis listened to at least two installments, one with Diana Whitwill, another old Somerville friend. Charis wrote to tell DLS how much she liked it: "more power to your elbow!" In December 1941, Bar and Mac listened together to the first play, and both enjoyed it. Bar listened to later installments with her students as well. "MSB said from reading, that the plays had a cumulative effect—oh my goodness she is right." Mac was especially moved by the third installment, which relates the story of a nobleman who asks Jesus to save his son. In DLS's rather deprecating words, Mac gave "a touching impersonation of the 'gruff warrior with tears in his eyes,'" and said if it moved him it would move anyone.[33]

At Somerville, DLS had argued to her parents the necessity of her working out her views on religion using her own mind. Now, she hoped that her plays would invite a similar process among their listeners. She told the woman who cleaned her house that she must never tell her children not to ask questions about religion. Tell them "that you don't know, if you like, and that they must read books about it, or ask somebody who does know. But don't give them the idea that the whole thing will fall to pieces if one starts asking questions."[34]

Yet the ultimate lesson DLS took was a grim one. Religion showed the folly of faith in human progress. Christianity had at its heart "this terrifying drama of which God is the victim and hero." The story of Christ "is the story of how man killed and murdered God; and it is the epitome of all history." This is the essence of original sin, "that seed of corruption" which, DLS argued, "is manifest, not simply in our vices, *but also in our virtues and our ideals.*" Had Jesus lived in the present day, it was not only the Nazis who would have killed him. The internationalists would have, too. Anyone would, because it is our nature to do so.[35]

IF THIS SEEMS unbearably bleak, it is worth remembering that, as she pushed fifty, DLS was watching the world tear itself apart for the second time in her life. Once again, this had profound personal consequences, particularly for Charis. She had learned, to her immense pride, that her youngest son, Miles, had been made an acting captain in January 1944. Five months later, following the news from India closely, Charis hoped "that Miles was with those Gurkhas who sat laughing at the Japanese" after they had escaped their pincer movement and left them to fight each other. In fact, though she didn't know it yet, tragedy had occurred.[36]

Miles Frankenburg was killed in what one official historian described as "perhaps the most tragic" event in the regiment's history. Three platoons were ordered to attack a ridge that had been retaken by Japanese forces. Observing the attack, Miles saw several men from the regiment wounded and one killed. He led a group of men in another effort to take the ridge, but he was killed by enemy fire. By the end of the attempt, nine Gurkha soldiers, including three officers, had been killed and thirty-three wounded. The Japanese remained in control of this particular ridge, though the attacks had been successful in stopping their overall momentum toward the British position in Imphal.[37]

Charis's family newsletters stop abruptly at the end of May 1944; for two months, her lively voice falls silent. In June, Peter told his mother, "I still feel all stirred up inside" whenever he thought of his youngest brother. Ever the list maker, Charis counted and listed the condolences she received: 258 by July 1944. She took comfort, too, in the sheer heroism of Miles's death. When his major wrote to tell her that he was killed "very gallantly leading his Company in a counter-attack," she concluded: "this is as good as it could be." More prosaically, she gave Miles's share of the pigs to Roberts, the cook turned handyman with whom he'd originally shared them.[38]

As a grieving mother, Charis seems to have needed a change, though her responsibilities meant that it couldn't happen immediately. She pushed the Greengate committee to begin making plans for the end of the war and the departure of the hospital from her house. In the meantime, as the hospital treated more patients more quickly, Charis kept working, even taking on another stint as temporary matron, and continuing to advocate for the institution to have a place in the new state-run medical service that was being planned. Thanks to Charis's efforts, when Greengate Hospital returned to Salford in July 1945, the transition was smooth. Here, Charis said, it could once again provide an educational example, showing parents what could be achieved "under their noses and in the next street."[39]

She continued to serve as an authority on the intersection of parenting and public health. Throughout the war, she had spoken to various groups about issues relating to child development, including the Altrincham Girls' High School, where Diana Whitwill was working. In August and September 1944, she gave a series of lectures at Liverpool University as part of a class "of Head Teachers, Probation Officers, Health Visitors, etc., on the subject of What to Teach Parents, and how to get it across." D. Rowe attended one of these lectures and gave Charis "good marks," noting that "there wasn't one er or um!" She also suggested that it was time Charis wrote "a companion volume" to *Common Sense in the Nursery*. In the new, revised edition of that book, Charis cautiously praised the increasing state provision for children in Britain, urging parents to "welcome gladly the skilled help of nurse, clinic, school, State, but allow nobody to 'take over.' Yours is the responsibility—and the reward."[40]

Theirs, also, the pain and anxiety. While she was visiting Charis, D. Rowe sent Peter a reassuring letter about how his mother was holding up. Peter teased Charis, "I liked Dorothy's letter. I enjoy hearing about all your boyfriends." In fact, Charis was anxiously awaiting her children's return from war. In early December 1944, Peter wrote a joyful letter announcing his impending return and asking his mother to make sure that D. Rowe was informed so she could see him as soon as possible, too. He beat his letter back to Britain, calling Charis from nearby Warrington and greeting her with a cheery "Hullo Mum!" His younger brother John returned to England in April 1945, so sick with diabetes that Charis didn't recognize him at first in the hospital. With the help of the ever-faithful Dr. Langley, he recovered.[41]

With three of her four children home safely, Charis left the Manchester area in 1945. She had little connection left with any of Sydney's family, and a move to small-town Oxfordshire returned her to an area with happy childhood memories and nearby relatives of her own. The move also brought her closer to where her children were now studying and working. There, she slowed her pace, retaining only a few public roles and taking time, perhaps, to grieve the double losses of the past decade.[42]

THE WAR'S IMPENDING end also pushed Muriel and Bar to reckon with the status of their relationship. Muriel was unwell in the spring of 1944, taking a rest holiday in Shropshire with, it seems, Bar's financial support. Susan joined her, having resigned her current job to do so. Bar remarked, "It seems in my humble opinion (unasked!) that it simplifies the immediate & complicates the more distant future."[43]

The great question was whether all three of them would live together full-time at 28 St. John's Wood Terrace after Bar returned from evacuation in Berkhamsted. Bar wondered to DLS: "if I go back to 28—which they can't afford without me—how can I ensure not being hounded by the lady?" DLS seems to have offered Bar her own flat on Great James Street as an alternative. Bar told Muriel she "had an option on a flat," without explaining it was DLS's. She wanted Muriel to know that "I meant business," but she didn't want her to "feel there was any sort of conspiracy against her."[44]

Bar's ambivalence muted her fears, even in the midst of the renewed wave of aerial bombardment in 1944, when the new flying "doodle-bug" bombs added a fresh layer of terror. Muriel and Bar's house was directly at risk. After a particularly noisy night, Mac prophesied that "London is probably by now dust & ashes," and DLS asked Muriel and Bar to please "confirm or deny" this, "especially as regards the Terrace." But the debilitating fears of the Blitz were over for Bar. At one point, a scheduled trip from her evacuated school to London was delayed. She was disappointed to lose the chance of seeing Muriel, but refused to "let Hitler influence me." In other words, she would no longer let her fears rule her. Since 1941, she'd grown braver and more independent, and perhaps less certain of where she and Muriel stood with regard to each other. She even considered asking a friend to let her, Bunter, and Timothy visit in August rather than return to London. On the other hand, Muriel helped Bar buy a dress to wear to a friend's wedding in the summer of 1944, suggesting that their connection was not lost.[45]

As the prospect of her school's return to South Hampstead loomed, Bar wondered what would happen. She didn't press to be among the first of the staff to go back, "in the face of MSB's complete lack of enquiries for my return," though she dreaded prolonging her stay in Berkhamsted. Finally, she drew a line in the sand: she would not live with Susan. Bar said she "was terribly sorry about it, that it was quite the horridest situation I had ever been in, & that was saying a good deal—but it was a case of 'Here I stand, I can no other.'" Muriel had what must have been a difficult conversation, and Susan "said in that case she would go." Muriel was still worried about Susan's future, but Bar was more ruthless: "oh well. . . . Susan has two fur coats . . . need one bother?" Susan moved to a cottage in Surrey in February 1945, framing the move in Virginia Woolf's terms: "I had at last to get into a Room of my Own." Muriel facilitated the move, collecting the items that Susan had left with Bedford College. Susan was still a regular visitor to Muriel and Bar's home, and Muriel, at least, visited her in Surrey as well. The wartime experiment in a more integrated cohabitation, however, was over.[46]

WORLD WAR I had altered trajectories for the members of the Mutual Admiration Society, remaking the landscape of possibilities for them at the very start of their careers. World War II, by contrast, broke upon them in their prime. In their mid- to late-forties, they were able to make tangible contributions to the national projects of winning the war and shaping plans for a new, postwar Britain. But it would be entirely misleading to think of the war only in terms of opportunity. The years of bloodshed and bombs wreaked havoc and exacted heavy personal tolls on the MAS, their families, and their communities. Even as they looked forward, they were always aware of the sorrow, suffering, and even evil that were inextricable parts of human life.

Part 5

Masterworks and Legacies, 1946–1988

19

FRIENDSHIPS AND TRIUMPHS

DEATH HAD A WAY OF bringing friends closer. Charis, living in Oxfordshire and then London, reached out to her old friends, rebuilding connections that had grown casual or rote during her life in Manchester. When DLS's husband died, in 1950, she, too, was brought more firmly into the London-based world of Muriel and Bar. This was also an era of retirements and transitions: Charis found a new role as an advocate for women in postwar London, while D. Rowe and Bar both retired from teaching but embraced new creative projects. DLS embarked on her masterful translation of Dante's *Divine Comedy*, a project that offered both theological dimensions and a chance to work on a profoundly popular work of genius. Even as they sustained losses, the MAS saw their bonds grow stronger, fueling these new endeavors.

By the late 1930s, only D. Rowe seemed to link Charis with the rest of the MAS. There wasn't a falling-out, judging from Charis's references to DLS—she was proposed as a visitor to one son's school in 1936, and her books were part of a package Charis sent to another son in the army. But when Charis wrote to congratulate DLS on her wireless play in 1942, she gave her an update on her life since 1939, a clear indication that they were not in close contact. Their friendship reignited after the war. Charis's daughter, Ursula, provided the first spark. When she attended a course at the Essex Institute of Agriculture, DLS and Mac made her welcome at their home. Ursula asked her mother why she'd fallen out of touch with DLS, when she was "quite the nicest woman you know." Charis, accordingly, apologized to DLS for being so out of touch: "I'm *very* sorry, & hope to do much better in future." Perhaps

D. Rowe urged the reconnection, too. She was there when Charis wrote her apologetic letter, and added her own postscript reporting that Ursula "had been greatly thrilled at coming to tea with you."[1]

Soon, Charis and DLS were trading visits and letters once again. Their shared love of pets provided a medium for their return to intimate friendship. Charis sent a sympathetic letter, for example, about the death of one of DLS's chickens. In July 1948, DLS saw Charis when she was in Oxford to speak about Christian aesthetics. Her apology afterward for "any gluttonous behaviour, especially with the raspberries," suggests an idyllic midsummer visit. She also offered the greetings of her cat, Blitz, who promised to "dedicate his next mouse to you." Charis's "little rabbit" replied later that year with Christmas greetings to Blitz. Perhaps, after the staggering experiences of the war, it was easier to reestablish friendship through adorable animal intermediaries.[2]

D. Rowe, whose life was increasingly hectic, was another intermediary. She found that everything "seems to be a little more so" in her postwar life: the school was fuller, Louise and Arthur Marshall were needier, and the theater club was "more booming and consequently more demanding," though also "more fruitful of new and interesting experiments." Still, she visited Charis frequently, if chaotically. "A large parcel, addressed by D.R. to herself & dropping to bits has just come, so I suppose that she will arrive shortly." D. Rowe's presence at Charis's also served as the pretext for wider MAS reunions.[3]

Meanwhile, the usual rounds of weekends, dinners, and holidays shared by the members of the MAS continued. Muriel and Bar were back in Stoke Fleming, Devon, in the summer of 1947. Bar wanted better amenities in the bungalow, which lacked a refrigerator—that postwar sign of modernity. She would find one the next month in Essex, where DLS had bought a brand-new appliance, to Muriel's punning alarm: "the price of your Frig. gives me cold shudders! Talk about freezing assets." Televisions were the other great signifier of modern times, and that autumn *Busman's Honeymoon* had its first television production, to the delight of its authors, who came to watch the final rehearsal.[4]

Christmas usually saw DLS, Mac, Muriel, Bar, and sometimes Susan together. In 1948, Muriel dragged her feet about going with Bar to Essex, feeling anxious about money and generally out of sorts. They went, though, and the two couples seem to have had an excellent time. Muriel and Bar returned to London restored and happier, and suffered only one wrong turn on the drive home, which Bar graciously said "was *probably* my fault." DLS reported that Mac was "still more or less in bed," and her cat Blitz had had a hair ball in her bedroom, "but I seized him at the first choke, & carried him, retching, out into the yard." It must have been a good party.[5]

They would not enjoy many more such evenings as a group. Mac's health had been weakening for a long time, and he died in June 1950. He and DLS had been married for nearly a quarter of a century. Though they'd had difficulties and differences, they'd found ways to make their partnership work. It is not easy to assess the marriage. On the one hand, there's an impression of distance—the separate bedrooms, the decision not to integrate DLS's son or Mac's children from his first marriage into their home or even, really, their lives. Mac's temper casts its shadow. And yet, there are also the manifest signs of connection—Mac's portrait of Bar, for instance, is a testament to Mac's place within DLS's most intimate circles of friendship. Bar came to Essex to help DLS in the immediate aftermath of Mac's death, helping with the cooking as Mac's brother assisted with sorting out Mac's papers. DLS told Muriel, "It will seem very queer without Mac—I shall miss having him to look after, & there will be nobody," she added, to "keep me up to the mark!" She hoped that Muriel would visit soon, or perhaps that the two of them "might go off somewhere & take a little holiday to refresh our minds."[6]

The members of the MAS drew DLS closer in her widowhood. DLS spent a great deal of time with Muriel and Bar, joining them on holidays, visiting London, and lecturing at the Royal Academy of Dramatic Art at Muriel's invitation. In August 1950, there was a proper reunion: Charis, DLS, D. Rowe, and Muriel all gathered at Charis's house in Oxfordshire, where Charis plied them with homemade macaroons. After she'd returned home, DLS sent Charis a tin of golden syrup and some sugar by way of thanks. The sense of sweet connection remained with them, even after they'd departed. The following January, an unusually mild day found D. Rowe and Charis "sitting in the kitchen making macaroons with spring sunshine pouring in; and recalling our happy time all together here last summer."[7]

How did the MAS, in the midst of these visits, discuss things like the loss of a partner or a child, or the significance of their enduring connection? On the page, at least, they turned to cats and dogs. They were probably very well aware of this sublimation: one of Bar's stories concerned the romance between an anxious country spinster and a colonel, narrated entirely through the interactions of his Pekingese, Kai Lung, and her cat, Mr. Darcy. In real life, the deaths of pets provided a particular opportunity to reflect on mortality. D. Rowe's "Epitaph on a Cat (who was always delightful and often good)" prays "that tiny ghost" might find "some gentle mistress" beyond the river Styx. In her Miltonian parody "Pussydise Lost," DLS imagines pet owners as gods. She narrates the bewilderment of a cat praised for killing a mouse but rebuked for killing a songbird: "why are the trees of Paradise / Set round with prohibitions? / The gods, mysterious and all-wise / Impose these strange conditions." But elsewhere, they acknowledged that the relationship was far more intimate. Bar and Muriel sent DLS a notice when their cat, Timothy, died, asking her to "pray for the rudimentary soul of Timothy White died October 24th 1948 of cerebral haemorrhage after a fall from the garage roofs while on an expedition of neighbour dog teasing aged 17½ years." Within a day or so, DLS had written a poem in response. "Timothy in the Coinherence" draws on Charles Williams's notion of "coinherence," or the innate relationship of all life to God. In the poem, DLS suggests that it's difficult to live up to moral standards in relationships with other people. With cats, it's easier. "Meekly we washed his feet, meekly he licked our hands."[8]

Inviting DLS to London for Christmas just six months after Mac's death, Bar made it sound like DLS would be doing her a favor to accept: "though I go all shy at the thought of cooking for you, it would be a special delight for me as it's such ages since I've seen you." DLS didn't come alone; she brought her cat George Macaulay Trevelyan, named after the historian. DLS expressed her gratitude for her friends' hospitality in his voice more clearly than in her own, in a pair of letters addressed to "Auntie Mew & Auntie Purr" and featuring careful feline misspellings. "It was very kind of Auntie Purr and Auntie Susan to let me sleep on their Bedds and Mistress says I am to apologise for giving them so much trubble on Christmas Eve," he wrote in 1951, before wishing all "a purrspurrous New Year."[9]

As THEIR PROFESSIONAL achievements accumulated, the members of the MAS were keenly aware of their debt to Somerville College and, more generally, the movement for women's higher education. In the play she wrote and produced to celebrate Bedford College's centenary in 1949, Muriel made that clear. It features a Muriel stand-in, named Shirley, who is transported by slightly supernatural means to a plane of existence in which she can converse with some of the luminaries of nineteenth-century feminism. She and Florence Nightingale compare their experiences of coming of age in a world with and without women's education. Florence Nightingale recalls, "One 'came of age' to be slowly starved to death, or suffocated." Shirley, on the other hand, benefiting from her university education, had "the time and the freedom" to read and to write and the ability to sell her work and earn a living. She had been able to harness her energy toward her rightful vocation.[10]

In a similar spirit of recognition and gratitude, all the members of the MAS remained stalwart supporters and defenders of Somerville College, the institution that had launched them into their careers. In 1958, Muriel was invited to a three-year term as one of Somerville's guests of the high table— rather than having members of the Association of Senior Members on the governing body, a few of them were instead invited to keep in touch with the college's life through these honorary posts. But the MAS's loyalty was not blind. When some of Somerville's leaders distanced themselves from a university fund-raising appeal, on the grounds that Somerville would not benefit from money spent on the university's ancient buildings, members of the MAS were furious. DLS believed that Somerville's stance revealed a "feminist inferiority complex" as well as a willingness to be mere parasites on the ancient institution rather than full members of it. Even worse, such a move seemed to justify "every doubt expressed in the past as to whether women are capable of anything beyond a local or domestic loyalty, or of entering into and maintaining a great historic tradition." Bar canvassed their friends for support on the issue. Charis's reaction was "milder" than some, but, once Bar had spoken with her, she "quite came up to scratch" and agreed to sign a letter of protest. Comparing the feminism of the late twentieth century with her own youth, Charis argued that the idea of women's citizenship "doesn't have to fight so hard. I think it exists much more strongly surely." In her young adulthood, "we had to fight for it, all the time. We had to fight to be represented on things." Having fought to be recognized as members of Oxford University, the members of the MAS were outraged at the notion of refusing to pay full dues, even if the battle for equality was far from won.[11]

DLS's FINAL GREAT project would be her translation of Dante's *Divine Comedy*. In some ways an idiosyncratic choice, the work nonetheless brought together DLS's passion for language, her complex ideas about religion, and her commitment to literature that is both popular and transcendently good. At Christmas 1944, she asked Bar to read a sample of Dante's epic poem, some of it translated. Despite her trepidation, Bar was impressed: "but this is just like somebody sitting there in an armchair and telling you a story." DLS would use Bar's phrase and her reaction in an article on Dante, part of her larger project to restore Dante's work to ordinary English readers. Visiting Muriel and Bar in February 1945, DLS read her new translation out loud to them, testing rhyme and meter. DLS's version of the "Inferno," simply titled "Hell," came out in 1949, followed by "Purgatory" in 1955, and "Paradise" (finished by her friend Barbara Reynolds) in 1962. DLS's goal was to honor Dante's intention, which was "to be read by the common man and woman, and to distribute the bread of angels among those who had no leisure to read." Her translation aimed to address Dante to the nation's "enormous new reading public," which was "literate, but not (in the old sense of the word) educated." Muriel was "thrilled" as DLS's Dante emerged in print, considering it "a major literary event in the history of our half century." She told DLS, "I don't think there is another person alive who could possibly have brought to the job the combination of qualifications that you do."[12]

Charis returned to living in London in 1951. Over the next twenty years, she would wrap up her Salford work and become a force to be reckoned with in national organizations dedicated to women and families. The Greengate Hospital and Open-Air School closed soon after Charis's resignation in 1957. In the 1960s, though, she worked to revive the project and its remaining funds, handing the resulting sum to the Salford Education Authority in 1970. They, in turn, opened the Greengate Special Nursery School, whose headmistress had assisted at Greengate during World War II as a young helper. Charis was given the honorary title of Freeman of the City of Salford in 1973 "in recognition of her eminent services to Salford in the field of health and social welfare and as a Justice of the Peace of the City," the first woman ever to be so honored. From a gadfly seeking to provoke the city into doing more for women and children, she had become an honored citizen.[13]

Meanwhile, her work as an expert on motherhood continued. Charis served on several committees with the National Council of Women from the mid-1950s, working nearly full-time and giving official evidence on maternity services, juvenile delinquency, and juries. In 1960, she published a new volume on child-rearing, titled *I'm All Right; or, Spoilt Baby into Angry*

Young Man. A revised version of this book was dedicated "to Dorothy Rowe from Somerville with hoops of steel." The title is a play on the so-called angry young men, the generation of young male writers in the 1950s who railed against society. Charis had no patience with the youth culture of anger and disillusionment. More importantly, the book was an impassioned rebuttal of the misuse of "half-understood and ill-digested" psychoanalytic notions of repression, or the "theory that *thwarting* and *inhibiting* warp the character and give rise to *complexes*." The misapplication of such theories spoiled babies and, more seriously, led to increasing rates of crime and social dysfunction, including "violent crime, insensate destruction of property, drunkenness among young people, lawlessness and divorce."[14]

As they entered their sixties, D. Rowe and Bar retired from teaching, due to rules about mandatory retirement age. Bar had been a prominent figure at South Hampstead High School for Girls in the postwar years, helping to facilitate its return from Berkhamsted, reaching the rank of head of English and serving as temporary headmistress for half a term. The school produced *Busman's Honeymoon* in 1950. Although the young woman who played Lord Peter Wimsey "managed to convey a good deal of his whimsical brand of masculine charm," the audience, alas, greeted the love scenes with "adolescent titters." The students were inspired nonetheless. One remembered that "we, of course, read all of the Lord Peter books, learned to drink our coffee black, and dared to use the word 'damn.'" Bar retired in 1954, after thirty-five years at the school. She was well celebrated: DLS gave a speech, the sixth form dedicated their play to her, and there was even a celebratory dinner with a hand-drawn menu featuring a sheep theme (from "Bar" it was a short step to "baa"). Thanking the alumnae club for its gift, Bar signed her letter, "Yours, with more love than I have ever thought it wise to show you!" The school magazine described her as "such a civilized person," dedicated not only to the school but to conversation, the arts, and beauty. "Household management, particularly the higher flights of cookery: her dog Bunter, whom some of us remember, and her enchanting Persian cat Timothy White, with its successor called Toby: travel in France and Italy; Art with a capital A: and of course, literature and the theater, have all contributed to her pleasure in life." Her students and colleagues wished her leisure for more of all of this, "but we at South Hampstead will miss her more than we can say." In retirement, Bar edited new editions, aimed at students, of some of the texts she'd taught: Chaucer, Dorothy Wordsworth's journals, Jane Austen.[15]

By 1954, D. Rowe found herself with the "rocky pre-eminence of Oldest Inhabitant" at the Talbot Heath School, where she was "fostering the illusion that any neglect of duty must be put down to the eccentricities of the Last of the Victorians." She retired in 1957 after forty years. In January 1958, over one hundred alumnae from twenty-seven different years, along with colleagues from around England, gathered together to honor D. Rowe, presenting her with an antique Spode tea service and a Turkish rug. She professed herself deeply moved by this physical manifestation of a female scholarly community: "when I think of the husbands neglected, the children and grandchildren abandoned, planning and journeys undertaken that you might be there, the sense of your kindness and of the reality of your feeling for old schooldays is overwhelming." All the rug and the tea service needed now, she wrote in her letter of thanks, was for members of the alumnae association "to come and place their feet on the rich comfort of the one, while they drink tea from the other."[16]

In her retirement, D. Rowe remained involved with the Bournemouth Little Theatre Club and its Palace Court Theatre. The theater had enjoyed a boom in the immediate postwar years, which allowed them to pay off the remaining debt on the building. The dramatic selection committee, with D. Rowe still at its heart, worked hard, meeting a full fifty-five times during the 1948–1949 season, for instance. Playing Madame Pernelle in *Tartuffe*, D. Rowe celebrated the fact that acting "is a hobby that doesn't abandon you in middle age; if you're sixty-two you get cast for parts of sixty-two, and generally very good parts they are." She continued, too, to produce plays, from Sheridan to Chekhov. Yet by the 1960s, her commitment to great literature had started to seem fusty rather than pioneering in an amateur theater. In 1962, a club "rag" teased her:

> In Dorothy Rowe's Golden Days
> Ever since the Club was founded
> The Classics are the thing to do
> In them I am well grounded.
> And every year I vote Shakespeare,
> Macbeth, and Lear and Hamlet.
> Down with bad language, sex and sin
> Unless it's in iambic.

More seriously, audiences and membership shrank as television grew more popular. The theater was sold in 1970, as the club could no longer afford to run it, though the club itself continues to the present day.[17]

In 1955, Muriel received the Most Excellent Order of the British Empire in recognition of her achievements as a scholar and writer. "I wish all honours were so well-earned," Charis wrote, sending her best wishes to Bar as well. She told D. Rowe about it, and D. Rowe wrote to Muriel with her bemused congratulations: "and *how on earth* I missed it I can't imagine," she said, and "why you didn't, on not getting a whoop from me, write and say, 'You silly ass, *what about it*?' I can imagine even less, but anyhow herewith whoops with knobs and tassels." She felt "a glow in the glory reflected in (a) *all* Somervillians, (b) M.A.S. in particular, (c) our special section of it in special particular, and (d) the Stoke Fleming party as a plus to it all."[18]

Her uncharacteristic shyness about the OBE notwithstanding, Muriel collaborated and corresponded with D. Rowe about the theater throughout the postwar years. In 1948, after a brief visit, D. Rowe wrote to thank Muriel and Bar "for my lovely glimpse of you both—I don't know any two people who remain so exactly the same and begin again when we left off!" D. Rowe spent a great deal of time in her retirement writing up notes on her analysis of Shakespeare. She collaborated, too, with Muriel on a proposed set of film strips about Shakespearean production. Aimed at students, they would provide images of period-appropriate settings and objects to aid in historical understanding.[19]

This was only one of Muriel's many theatrical projects. She was involved with the Society for Theatre Research and reviewed plays at the Old Vic and Stratford, sometimes taking DLS along. She collected a wide range of material for an exhibition for the Arts Council in 1946 on "The History of Shakespearian Production in England." This exhibit was a bit of Cold War cultural propaganda. It was created in collaboration with the theater section of the Society for Cultural Relations with the Soviet Union and traveled to Moscow and Berlin in 1948. Muriel also edited texts related to theater history, including a new edition of four volumes of the *Prefaces to Shakespeare* by Harley Granville-Barker, who, along with William Poel, had revolutionized Shakespeare performance by using knowledge about the Elizabethan original to create compelling modern drama.[20]

As an independent author, editor, and researcher, Muriel continued to hustle. She told her solicitor that she needed to claim her haircuts as a

business expense for tax purposes, because she had to have her hair professionally done in order to attend "the professional meetings, functions, occasions etc. of bodies to which I belong or with which I am associated," in part
in order "to 'sell' myself and my work." This was absolutely necessary. "How
do you think I got those two Exhibition offers or got the influential supporters for the British Academy and Leverhulme grants? (*Not* by sitting on my
arse in the B.M. [British Museum] and the P.R.O. [Public Record Office]!)"[21]

Nevertheless, in the midst of all the mingling and meeting, Muriel kept
working doggedly on the Lisle letters. This epic masterwork was ultimately
published in six volumes by the University of Chicago Press in 1981, with
Queen Elizabeth II among the donors who helped meet the full cost of production. Muriel delighted in telling the story of her life work's denouement
to interviewers: "when the work was done at last, her colossal manuscript
was packed into a battered suitcase, flown first-class across the Atlantic, and
met at the airport by a limousine 'with outriders, in case of kidnappers,' she
says (impossible to tell whether she's joking). Next morning, it went into
production. 'Can you beat that for melodrama?' says Miss Byrne delightedly.
'That's Chicago.'" In real life, things perhaps took a bit longer: in her diary
for April 1, 1977, there is the exciting entry "Bundle for Chicago," followed
some six weeks later by the slightly anticlimactic "Sent Chap. 7."[22]

Muriel emphasized that, in their very ordinariness, the letters illuminate
some of the great historical transformations of their moment. They capture
the origins, in everyday cadences, of "the tremendous outburst of creative
writing at the end of the century which we call Elizabethan literature." On
the level of political history, they suggest a new interpretation of the fall of
the great Tudor politician Thomas Cromwell. And they had lessons for the
present moment. State terrorism and repression were familiar to modern
readers, who had seen "the brutalities of the sixteenth century . . . rivalled
and even exceeded throughout Europe" in the middle of the twentieth.[23]

Muriel's passion, as always, was the quality of human life in all its rich-
ness. "It is moment-to-moment life, sensation, and thought, that is recorded
in them—all the intimate hopes and fears, the trivial preoccupations, the
obstinacies, the generosities; the pettiness, the magnanimity; the foolish-
nesses, the money-troubles, the wire-pulling, the disappointments and
triumphs; all the quirks and oddities, simplicities and complexities of character; the pace, the quality, the pressure, the almost unbelievable dailyness
of life." She emphasized, too, the role of women in what could have been

a story of powerful men. Honor Lisle demonstrated the gap between the ideal of a meek, self-effacing sixteenth-century woman and the reality—a woman "whom men admired, whose friendship they sought and valued, and to whom they turned for sympathy, companionship and advice," not because she was meek but because she was strong.[24]

Muriel explained that the Lisles, as a project, "had the benefit of my youthful energy, and perhaps of mature judgment and experience of life too." In their years of mature judgment, the members of the MAS distilled their expertise—on the Tudors, on child-rearing, on God and popular literature, on theater—and then shared it as broadly as possible. A reporter for the *Observer* visited Muriel in her home office after the publication of *The Lisle Letters*. "The piles of books and papers recede in the twilight; the photographs of Dorothy Sayers and the white cats and other dear friends have become obscured. Even her eyes—bright and alert under the wild white hair—look tired now. But in the fading light from the window, the pile of red and blue books on the desk still glows with life." The ghosts of the MAS are present in Muriel's books, too. In the acknowledgments, she thanks a long list of people, many of them dead by the time of publication. Bar and Susan and DLS are there, as well as Una Ellis-Fermor, T. S. Eliot, George and Janet Trevelyan, and many others. Their work was over, but their legacies lived on.[25]

20

LEGACIES

W HO CAN KNOW THE LAST time they'll see a friend? D. Rowe was in Essex but missed seeing DLS in August 1957, because DLS was stuck in London "sitting on two frightful committees." DLS hoped she'd come again—"I should love to see you." Muriel went to a Detection Club dinner at the Café Royal in October 1957; she had dinner with DLS on October 22, and supper with her on November 14. On December 17, 1957, DLS died suddenly of a heart attack. Muriel's diary records simply, bleakly, "Dorothy died." DLS was only sixty-four when she died, and her public legacy would be shaped by her surviving friends, who had many more years to live.[1]

Muriel traveled to DLS's home in Essex the day after she heard the news. DLS's secretary could not find her will, but Muriel discovered it rapidly "under the lining paper in an otherwise empty drawer." Anthony Fleming arrived the next day, and Muriel officially learned then that DLS had been his mother all along. Was this revelation or confirmation? In any case, Muriel hugged him and said, "Thank God you've come." Over the next week, the two of them spent a great deal of time together, making arrangements for the funeral and the memorial service. Held on January 15, 1958, the service featured the music of Bach, readings by actor Val Gielgud and philosopher Gordon Clark, and a panegyric by C. S. Lewis. Muriel and Anthony forged a lasting bond during those trying weeks, and she would be godmother to his daughter, DLS's granddaughter.[2]

The Dorothy L. Sayers who is available to the modern reader through her published works and archival papers is, in part, the product of the work of the surviving MAS members to manage and preserve her memory. Charis wrote to their Somerville classmates, raising subscriptions in support of a memorial tablet for DLS in the college chapel. Muriel was DLS's literary executor, facilitating, among other things, Barbara Reynolds's completion of the Dante translation. She also handled questions about television and radio rights and read "Timothy in the Coinherence" on the radio in March 1973. Faced with an early proposal for a biography, Muriel talked it over with Anthony, and they demurred, explaining that DLS "had a very strong dislike for biographies undertaken shortly after the death of the subject." Despite their efforts to insist on this point, however, there were biographies published in the 1970s. D. Rowe warned the writer Janet Hitchman that, if Muriel said DLS didn't want to be written about until fifty years after her death, "you cannot discount it as a mere 'theory' but must accept that it is true." Instead, Hitchman published what Muriel called "the unpleasant little Hitchman book," revealing publicly for the first time that DLS had been Anthony's mother.[3]

Muriel pushed back hard at what she saw as misinterpretations and a salacious focus on DLS's personal life. Ralph Clarke, the chairman of the Dorothy L. Sayers Historical and Literary Society, was particularly interested in the claim that the Wimsey books had been cowritten by Mac Fleming and DLS. Muriel had no patience for this idea, nor for the mistaken notion that she and DLS had rewritten *Busman's Honeymoon* to suit their lead actor. She was irritated, too, by Clarke's insinuations that Mac might have been Anthony's birth father, or even that DLS didn't know who the father was. Linking all of these biographical skirmishes is a focus on the men in DLS's life: her status as a mother, her sexual history, and even whether a man was directly or indirectly responsible for her most famous work. For a group of women who had collaborated with DLS throughout her life, this must have been doubly frustrating to witness. It threatened to erase not only DLS's achievements, but the intellectual community that had fostered them. By depositing her letters and papers with libraries, on the other hand, the members of the MAS made it possible for future books on DLS to be written.[4]

Muriel wrote a new will as the one-year anniversary of DLS's death approached, perhaps confronting her own mortality. She left legacies to the Belvedere School and to Somerville College, in both cases to assist young people like herself to further their educations and careers. She also used the will to give Bar essentially the rights of a spouse, as executor, trustee, and main beneficiary. In addition, she provided some money for Susan, who

Muriel (left, standing), Bar (center, standing), and friends, possibly Charis (seated) (MSBC 5/2)

remained an important figure in her life. Susan visited frequently throughout the 1950s and 1960s, while she moved between Sussex, Kent, and, briefly, London. Muriel gave her an oil stove for one chilly dwelling place, a poignant gesture that suggested both a warm intimacy and the fact that Susan had had to opt for a room of her own. Susan's affection for Muriel was undimmed: "I don't seem able to do much about it but I love you always." Susan died in 1968, a few days shy of her eighty-fifth birthday. In her diary, Muriel recorded simply, "S. died," and the next day, "Funeral 12 noon." She sent the obituary notice to the secretary of Bedford College. In her own will, Susan listed "my great friend Muriel St. Clare Byrne" as one of those entitled to select an item out of her books or jewelry.[5]

After Charis moved to London in 1951, it was easier to combine visits and have small MAS reunions. Dinners, teas, and lunches happened at least yearly, and often more frequently. Charis and D. Rowe both came to supper with Bar and Muriel in January 1967, for example, after the Somerville Association of Senior Members meeting. Later that year, Charis had tea with Muriel and Bar again, and Anthony Fleming and his wife came in the early evening. Perhaps Charis finally had the chance to meet DLS's son.[6]

Bar fell ill with an infection on March 2, 1972, aged seventy-seven, and never fully recovered. Muriel cared for her, with some assistance, and brought her to a few events: a memorial service for her former headmistress, a centenary celebration at Westminster Abbey for the Girls' Public Day School Trust. In 1973, Bar suffered

D. Rowe (BLTC)

another infection and was brought by her doctor to a hospital, where she stayed for nearly two weeks before Muriel removed her, convinced that the hospital was neglecting her care. Muriel herself collapsed in March, and Bar had another stint away from home, this time in a Bournemouth nursing home, which left her a "complete wreck." From that time on, she needed nursing care, but was able to see friends and go for short walks. She missed, though, "our normal Christmas dinners with friends." She evidently had some brain difficulty by this point. This "highly intelligent, extremely well-read and brilliant teacher" was now "completely 'confused' most of the time when she wants to speak or communicate with anyone, but is also still perfectly conscious of what she wants to say and is in some respects as shrewd in sizing up a situation as a normal person," in Muriel's assessment. She was adamant about caring for Bar at home rather than sending her back to a hospital or nursing home.[7]

In early 1974, Muriel asked her friends for assistance with the ongoing strains and costs of caring for Bar. Charis arranged for an annual donation of £60. Together, their friends provided nearly £2,000 of additional support over about eighteen months. Muriel continued work on the Lisle letters in between nursing Bar. Charis kept D. Rowe up to date with the news. "And you may be sure," D. Rowe wrote to Muriel in March 1976, "that we think of you both, and feel the deepest concern for all that concerns you."[8]

Aged eighty-one, Bar died on September 8, 1976. In the first month of her bereavement, Muriel would have been occupied with making arrangements and settling Bar's affairs. She put off a request to come speak on DLS in Illinois because of Bar: "I have not had a single moment since her death when I could get down to any of my own work on the Lisle Letters, let alone the possibility and the necessary substance of a DLS lecture; nor have I yet been able to see what my doctor has got to say on the subject, which is, I fear, rather necessary." The stress must have been immense. On October 3, Muriel broke her arm and had to wear a plaster cast for a month; on October 17, she had a migraine. Her solicitor urged her to "tidy up your Will," since the circumstances—Muriel having outlived both Bar and Susan, and having largely completed the Lisle work—"allow for a major simplification." Her final will made provisions for various friends but left the bulk of her estate to Belvedere and Somerville.[9]

Charis retired from the Salford bench at the statutory age of seventy-five in 1967. "'Frankie,' tall, dark and handsome, collects sea horses, newspaper cuttings, and slightly disreputable stories. No do-gooder has ever made me laugh so much," wrote one journalist. "I do look upon death now as a date in my diary," Charis told another. "But I don't really think about it. I'm not afraid of it." And she enjoyed living alone, explaining, "Anyway, I have lots of friends. I'm always writing to them. We ring each other up. We have lunch with each other. We stay with each other."[10]

Indeed they did. From the mid-1970s, Charis, D. Rowe, and Muriel enjoyed making a band of three, the surviving MAS members. Muriel joined D. Rowe at Charis's flat early in 1978, and they worked together on identifying people from old Somerville photographs for an exhibition at the Bodleian Library. In 1979, D. Rowe told Muriel, "I felt just as you did about our 'threesome' and cherish the warmest hopes of more." They were well aware of the limitations of old age, which made everything take so much longer. When Charis fell and cracked a shoulder, D. Rowe ruefully remarked, "What we octogenarians do get up to! (or down on)." But Charis was grateful for her generally good health. She drank lots of coffee and ate "much more toffee and nut-chocolate than is seemly for my age."[11]

By the end of the 1970s, MAS meetings were increasingly replaced by telephone calls or letters. Charis rang, for instance, on Muriel's eighty-fifth birthday, May 31, 1980. D. Rowe hoped Muriel, at least, would be able to attend the Somerville centenary celebrations in 1979, adding, "As I write this I feel frisky enough to say that though I can't get to this one I shall buy a new frock and hat and go to the one in 2079 A.D." Two years later, Muriel attended what was almost certainly her last Somerville College Gaudy.[12]

Muriel needed day and night nursing begining in 1982. The detailed notes kept by her nurses, some of them written on the reverse side of the proofs of *The Lisle Letters*, make alternately touching and heartbreaking reading. At eighty-seven, she was "very bright & cheerful sometimes, can be bad tempered occasionally," which would have come as no surprise to Bar or Susan. Her wish to drink whisky in the evenings bothered some nurses more than others, and her complaints about doctors and money, combined with episodes of collapse and loss of memory, generated more stress. But there were evidently moments of calm in which her life carried on much as it always had. On November 8, 1982, she "worked at desk most of the evening. Cheerful. Enjoyed chop peas potato jelly & cream." Muriel died late in 1983, aged eighty-eight. Neither Charis nor D. Rowe were up to the task of writing part of her obituary.[13]

Charis died in April 1985, aged ninety-three, at a rest home in Berkshire. She divided her estate between her children or their families, and left her body to medical use. This final donation is a fitting gesture from a woman who had dedicated her life to improving the health and well-being of others.[14]

D. Rowe entered a rest home in June 1981 and, in 1985, wrote that she did not "think I shall ever move from it." She died in April 1988, the last surviving MAS member, aged ninety-five. Her will made provisions for her sister Bena and her two nieces, her "first and supreme concern." A codicil, added after Bena's death, gave a small legacy to two local friends, requesting "that the money shall be used for something joyful in their respective gardens in gratitude for our long and happy friendship."[15]

One of the readings at Muriel's funeral was an excerpt from DLS's *The Just Vengeance*. "A universe is extinguished / Every time a soul goes out of it," she had written there.

> We die into something
> As we were born into something; but the act of death,
> Like the act of being born, is an individual matter,
> As thou hast discovered.[16]

CONCLUSION

A s DLS said, birth and death are individual matters. What comes between is not. Charis Frankenburg, Dorothy L. Sayers, Dorothy Rowe, and Muriel St. Clare Byrne lived and worked in a series of communities. One of the most important of these was the long-lasting, tightly knit Mutual Admiration Society. Far more than a self-indulgent praise circle, the MAS was defined from the start by its commitment to honest criticism and the highest artistic and intellectual standards. In its various incarnations over the subsequent decades, it also provided support and inspiration. The MAS pushed DLS to write prose in the first place. Lord Peter Wimsey owes his existence to one MAS member and his marriage to another. Dedicating *Busman's Honeymoon* to Muriel St. Clare Byrne, Marjorie Barber, and Helen Simpson, DLS wrote that they had demonstrated the sort of "friendship of which the female sex is said to be incapable; let the lie stick i' the wall!"[1]

Their friendships spurred dazzlingly diverse careers. They were united, though, in intervening in a very particular cultural debate over the dangers and opportunities of widening literacy. How, especially, to vanquish the specter of mass democracy wrenched toward fascism? The MAS offered one answer, in their insistence that the biggest ideas were the property of every human being. Mass culture could be used for more than selling mustard and politics. Provincial amateur theater deserved cutting-edge staging and interpretation. Working mothers deserved the latest theories on parenting, the most scientific birth control, and the means to raise happy, healthy families. Ordinary readers deserved not only stories of kings and queens, but the most sophisticated analysis of rare documents and the experience of being

put in touch with the realities of daily life in the past. And absolutely everyone deserved the chance to worry out for themselves the biggest questions of
morality, truth, and the nature of the universe. The MAS wanted to put the
tools of learning, which they had won for themselves with such difficulty at
Somerville, into everyone's hands.

The members of the MAS were elitist in many ways. As popularizers and
public intellectuals, they were both democratic and profoundly limited. Like
any universalizing project, the MAS's vision of making serious ideas available to everyone had its own blind spots and boundaries. If the members of
the MAS were not always comfortable with the results of inequality and class
divisions, neither were they dedicated to changing that hierarchy. They frequently ignored the world beyond England, were casually racist, and largely
failed to challenge the rise of anti-Semitism. Yet, in their own ways, they
grappled seriously with the questions posed by modernity.

In a sense, the members of the MAS were among the first beneficiaries
of the democratization of British culture. Oxford degrees, the vote, the right
to sit on juries and serve as magistrates, the practical ability simply to rent a
room of one's own and make one's own way in the world for better and for
worse—they saw all of these things made available to at least some British
women during their young adulthood. They saw, too, the limitations of such
a transformation. Plenty of doors remained closed; plenty of mediocre men
easily achieved what these women fought for but never reached. Restricted
reproductive options meant that DLS had to contort herself to keep her
independence after conceiving outside of marriage. Muriel had profound,
long-lasting romantic relationships with two women, but had to conceal letters and write carefully to prevent scandal, even as she made use of the legal
options at her disposal—such as wills and insurance policies—to protect her
household with Bar.

By the end of World War II, DLS had reached a deeply pessimistic outlook. The message of Christianity, or one of its messages, was that, if God is
among us, we will kill him. No wonder the vivid, sprawling vision of Dante
appealed to her at this juncture. What, finally, is the point of bringing the
best ideas to people, if we are ultimately so essentially wicked that we will
murder transcendent goodness if it's put in front of us? Charis's life, too,
was shaped by the traumas and losses of the two world wars. Writing *I'm
All Right; or, Spoilt Baby into Angry Young Man*, she was frustrated at what
had resulted: a silly, misapplied doctrine of repression that left babies feeling

insecure and produced a selfish, destructive generation. World War II had laid bare the destructive capacity of human beings once again. Never mind, DLS and Charis seemed to conclude. We must simply get on with the work, even while knowing that the human universe tends toward entropy.

And so they all did, retaining that commitment to intellectual integrity and creative work that had defined their careers, and finding joy in everyday life—the dailyness revealed in *The Lisle Letters* and the ordinary joys of spending time with friends. Even at its most starkly realistic, the work of the MAS forms a profoundly optimistic project. It insists that our birthright, as human beings, encompasses the full range of culture, and that even our most quixotic or futile efforts are ennobled, so long as they are defined by that integrity that links head and heart. That integrity is nowhere more evident than in the MAS itself, which united profound intellectual and emotional commitments. Loving one another, they built a kind of family beyond the structures of patriarchy. Offering one another space for reinvention, they helped to change what it meant to be born female in the twentieth century.

ACKNOWLEDGMENTS

This book owes its existence to my own writing communities and friendships. For encouragement and support, I thank Kevin Birmingham, Susanna Bohme, Michell Chresfield, Diana Doty, Jeanne Follansbee, Gabi Gage, Emily Gardel, Simon Jackson, Jill Lepore, Chris Moores, Sarah Morton, Brucie Moulton, David Moulton, Nicole Mushero, Andreas Neumann-Mascis, Megan Kate Nelson, Maxwell Ng, Manu Sehgal, and my colleagues and students in History & Literature at Harvard and in the History Department at Birmingham. Laura Nym Mayhall introduced me to Dorothy L. Sayers. *The Toast*, and Toasties, made me believe this book could happen, as did Nicole Soojung Chung, who introduced me to my incomparable agent Amanda Annis. My thanks are due to all the librarians and archivists I worked with, especially Seona Ford (Dorothy L. Sayers Society), Kate O'Donnell (Somerville), Barry Meehan (Bournemouth), and Laura Schmidt (Wheaton), and to everyone who gave me someplace to stay while researching this book, especially the Cohen/Silfen/Kasdan family, Margaret Gardel, Sally Lewis, and Natasha Ulph. Special thanks to Niamh Coffey, my research assistant, and to the College of Arts and Law at the University of Birmingham and Harvard University for research funding. For allowing me to use their personal papers and memories, thanks to Andrew Belsey, John Collett, Alwyn Ladell, and Elvira Niles. Quotations from Muriel Jaeger are by permission of the Estate of Muriel Jaeger. Quotations from Vera Brittain are by permission of Mark Bostridge and T. J. Brittain-Catlin, literary executors for the Estate of Vera Brittain 1970. Quotations from Janet and George Trevelyan are by permission of the Trevelyan family. Quotations from Dorothy L. Sayers are by permission of the Dorothy L. Sayers Estate. My editors have been brilliant: Sarah Castleton at Corsair, and Leah Stecher and Claire Potter at Basic Books. Deborah Cohen, Maggie Crowley, Elaine Fulton, Matt Houlbrook, Deb Jewison, Mel Larsen, Sharon Marcus, and Zoë Thomas read full drafts and provided invaluable advice and community. Rather like Marjorie Barber, Theadora Fisher has endured the giant bulk and overwhelming personalities of the Mutual Admiration Society in our lives for nearly half a decade: for that, and for absolutely everything, I thank her.

NOTES

ABBREVIATIONS

Balliol: Balliol College
BLTC: Bournemouth Little Theatre Collection
Bodleian: Bodleian Library
Collett: John Collett Personal Collection of Muriel Jaeger's Papers
CRL: Cadbury Research Library
CUB: Charis U. Barnett
CUBFC: Mrs. Charis U. (Barnett) Frankenburg Collection (SC/AO/RG/RC)
CUF: Charis U. Frankenburg
CUL: Cambridge University Library
DLSA: Dorothy L. Sayers Society Archives
FHL: Friends Historical Library of Swarthmore College, PA
GHOASC: Greengate Hospital and Open-Air School Collection
HLS: Harvard Law School Library
Houghton: Houghton Library
MCL: Manchester Central Library Archives and Local Studies
MEWC: Dorothy L. Sayers Collection, Marion E. Wade Center, Wheaton
    College, IL
MSB: Muriel St. Clare Byrne
MSBC: Muriel St. Clare Byrne Collection, Somerville College Library
NA: National Archives
RHUL: Royal Holloway University Library Archives
Smith: Mortimer Rare Books Collection, Smith College
Somerville: Somerville College Archives and Special Collections
Tameside: Tameside Local Studies Library
Wellcome: Wellcome Collection Library
WL: Women's Library

INTRODUCTION

1. "to read aloud": Charis U. Frankenburg, *Not Old, Madam, Vintage: An Autobiography* (Lavenham, UK: Galaxy Press, [1975?]), 62.

2. "Anon, who wrote": Virginia Woolf, *A Room of One's Own* (Chichester: Wiley Blackwell, 2015), 31; Seth Koven, *The Match Girl and the Heiress* (Princeton, NJ: Princeton University Press, 2014), 134, 189; Matt Houlbrook, *Prince of Tricksters: The Incredible True Story of Netley Lucas, Gentleman Crook* (Chicago: University of Chicago Press, 2016).

3. Adrian Bingham, "Cultural Hierarchies and the Interwar British Press," in *Middlebrow Literary Cultures: The Battle of the Brows, 1920–1960*, eds. Erica Brown and Mary Grover (Houndmills, UK: Palgrave Macmillan, 2012), 55; D. L. LeMahieu, *A Culture for Democracy: Mass Communication and the Cultivated Mind in Britain Between the Wars* (Oxford: Clarendon Press, 1988).

4. Victoria Stewart, *Crime Writing in Interwar Britain: Fact and Fiction in the Golden Age* (Cambridge: Cambridge University Press, 2017), 1, 4–5; Melissa Schaub, *Middlebrow Feminism in Classic British Detective Fiction: The Female Gentleman* (Houndmills, UK: Palgrave Macmillan, 2013), vii, 5; Celia Marshik, *At the Mercy of Their Clothes: Modernism, the Middlebrow, and British Garment Culture* (New York: Columbia University Press, 2017), 141; Kate Macdonald and Christoph Singer, eds., *Transitions in Middlebrow Writing, 1880–1930* (Houndmills, UK: Palgrave Macmillan, 2015); Christoph Ehland and Cornelia Wächter, eds., *Middlebrow and Gender, 1890–1945* (Leiden, Netherlands: Brill Rodopi, 2016).

5. "vaguely sympathy-for-labour-&-women" DLS to MSB, 26 Feb. 1940, 424, MEWC; Clarisse Berthezène, *Training Minds for the War of Ideas: Ashridge College, the Conservative Party and the Cultural Politics of Britain, 1929–54* (Manchester, UK: Manchester University Press, 2015); Alison Light, *Forever England: Femininity, Literature and Conservatism between the Wars* (London: Routledge, 1991); Peter Mandler, "Against 'Englishness': English Culture and the Limits to Rural Nostalgia, 1850–1940," *Transactions of the Royal Historical Society* 7 (1997), 155–175.

6. "exceptionally large number": *Observer*, 17 July 1938.

CHAPTER 1: ARRIVING AT OXFORD

1. "daintily served with dispatch": *Oxford Mail*, 22 July 2013; Diary, 11 Oct. 1912, CUBFC.

2. CUB to family, 12 Oct. 1912, CUBFC.

3. "one works after": Postcards, 3/1 MSBC; "a most grisly turmoil": DLS to Godfrey, 11 July 1913, MS308, Smith; M. St. Clare Byrne and Catherine Hope Mansfield, *Somerville College 1879–1921* (Oxford: Oxford University Press, n.d.), 9, 16–18, 33–34; Margaret Birney Vickery, *Buildings for Bluestockings: The Architecture and Social History of Women's Colleges in Late Victorian England* (Newark, DE: University of Delaware Press, 1999), 99.

4. Laura Schwartz, *A Serious Endeavour: Gender, Education and Community at St. Hugh's, 1886–2011* (London: Profile Books, 2011), 5–6; Christine D. Myers, *University Coeducation in the Victorian Era: Inclusion in the United States and the United Kingdom* (New York: Palgrave Macmillan, 2010), 6–7; Carol Dyhouse, *No Distinction of Sex? Women in British Universities, 1870–1939* (London: University College Press, 1995);

Alison Mackinnon, *Love and Freedom: Professional Women and the Reshaping of Personal Life* (Cambridge: Cambridge University Press, 1997); Paul Deslandes, *Oxbridge Men: British Masculinity and the Undergraduate Experience, 1850–1920* (Bloomington: Indiana University Press, 2005), xii, 7.

5. "I'm simply dead sick": DLS to Godfrey, [1913], MS308, Smith.

6. "modest manners": Byrne and Mansfield, *Somerville College*, 15, 66; Pauline Adams, *Somerville for Women: An Oxford College 1879–1993* (Oxford: Oxford University Press, 1996), 55; Vera Brittain, *The Women at Oxford: A Fragment of History* (London: George G. Harrap, 1960); Dyhouse, *No Distinction of Sex?*.

7. Byrne and Mansfield, *Somerville College*, 35.

8. 1901, 1911 censuses; *Barnsley Chronicle*, 2 July 1932, 10.423, DLSA.

9. Frankenburg, *Not Old*, 9, 13, 31.

10. "were awfully good": Israel Schenker, "Familial History of the Tudor Age Is Brought to Life," *Smithsonian* April 1981, PP56/L/1, RHUL; "England and Wales Marriages, 1538–1940," Ancestry.co.uk.

11. T. B. Rowe to John, 6 Feb. 1902, T. B. Rowe Papers Add. 8252/7/9, CUL; Isobel Hurst, "'Maenads Dancing before the Martyrs' Memorial': Oxford Women Writers and the Classical Tradition," *International Journal of the Classical Tradition* 12, no. 2 (Fall 2005): 175.

12. "I apparently cried out": Rowe to Lee, 17 Nov. 1985, 25.859, DLSA; Board of Education Inspection Report, Feb. 1910, ED 109/1812, NA; 1911 census.

13. "Cat O'Mary: The Biography of a Prig," in *Dorothy L. Sayers: Child and Woman of Her Time*, ed. Barbara Reynolds (Swavesey, UK: Dorothy L. Sayers Society, 2002), 36, 91; Muriel Jaeger to Clifford Jaeger, 11 Dec. 1904, Collett.

14. M. St. Clare Byrne, *Common or Garden Child: A Not-unfaithful Record* (London: Faber & Faber Ltd., 1942), 9, 184–187.

15. "as it was an exceptional year": Diary, 27 Mar. 1912, CUBFC; Frankenburg, *Not Old*, 54; *Manchester Guardian*, 29 Mar. 1912.

16. Brittain, Vera, *Testament of Youth: An Autobiographical Study of the Years 1900–1925* (London: Penguin Books, 2005), 105–106; Frankenburg, *Not Old*, 62.

17. "Am discovering so many": Postcards, MSBC 3/1, Somerville; "I have been": CUB to family, 12 Oct. 1912, CUBFC; "practiced the Baton": CUB to family, 16 Oct. 1912, CUBFC; "the most amusing person": CUB to family, 30 Oct. 1912, CUBFC; "dutifully deposited," "two-penny pair of tongs," "the discards": Frankenburg, *Not Old*, 62, 64.

18. DLS to people, n.d., 78a, and DLS to people, [1914?], 80, MEWC; James Brabazon, *Dorothy L. Sayers: The Life of a Courageous Woman* (London: Gollancz, 1981), 42.

19. "four freshers to tea": Diary, 12 Oct. 1912, CUBFC; Diary, 22 Oct., 30 Oct., 6 Nov., 14 Nov. 1912, CUBFC; "wading through the freshers": CUB to family, 3 Nov. 1912, CUBFC; CUB to family, 16 Oct. 1912, CUBFC.

20. "one 'proposed' and Christian names": Frankenburg, *Not Old*, 59; CUB to family, 11 Jan. 1913, 19 Jan. 1913, and Diary, 2 Dec. 1912, 4 Feb. 1913, CUBFC; Vera Farnell, *A Somervillian Looks Back* (Oxford, 1948), 12; "which she hated": Muriel Jaeger, "The Light Touch" (1919), Collett.

21. "flowery chintz": Vera Brittain, *The Dark Tide* (London: Virago, 1999), 26; "into ecstasies," "the prettiest room": CUB to family, Oct. 1912, CUBFC; "an only girl":

Frankenburg, *Not Old*, 57; Postcards, MSBC 3/1, Somerville; "lying on my back": DLS to people [1912?], 65, MEWC; Schwartz, *A Serious Endeavour*, 112–115; Jane Hamlett, "'Nicely Feminine, Yet Learned': Student Rooms at Royal Holloway and the Oxford and Cambridge Colleges in Late Nineteenth-Century Britain," *Women's History Review* 15, no. 1 (2006), 157–158.

22. "a sort of cooperative": CUB to family, 19 Oct. 1913, CUBFC; CUB to family, 17 Nov. 1912, 7 May 1913, CUBFC; "bottled raspberries . . . introduced toasted marsh-mallows . . . closing efforts": Frankenburg, *Not Old*, 58, 64–65; "with a kettle": Brittain, *Testament of Youth*, 106.

23. DLS to people, 7 Nov. 1913, 78a, MEWC; Postcards, MSBC 3/1, Somerville; Diary, 24 Jan. 1913, CUBFC; "rather daunting," "She was, in fact": Frankenburg, *Not Old*, 57–59.

24. "reminded people that bicycles": 15 Oct. 1914 and 28 Mar. 1913, 12 June 1913, 30 Apr. 1914, 18 June 1914, Minutes of College Meetings 1913–1916, Somerville.

25. "was heavy with the fumes": Brittain, *Dark Tide*, 26; "exquisite smoke rings": Muriel Jaeger, "The Light Touch," (1919), Collett; DLS to parents, 1 Dec. 1912, Barbara Reynolds, ed., *The Letters of Dorothy L. Sayers*, vol. 1, *The Making of a Detective Novelist, 1899–1936* (London: Hodder & Stoughton, 1995); Adams, *Somerville for Women*, 127; "a disapproving shopman": Frankenburg, *Not Old*, 57.

26. "craze for untidiness," "fearfully smart," "so tight": DLS to parents, 20 Apr. 1913, Reynolds, *Letters*, vol. 1; "self-conscious in her ungainliness": DLS to Godfrey, [1913], MS308, Smith; "a very tiresome": Brittain, *Women at Oxford*, 135; "wearing a three-inch wide scarlet riband": Farnell, *A Somervillian*, 13.

27. "I suppose there are": Frankenburg, *Not Old*, 69; Farnell, *A Somervillian*, v.

28. "woman-studentish": CUB to family, 26 Oct. 1913 and 8 Mar. 1914, CUBFC; Sarah Aiston, "A Maternal Identity? The Family Lives of British Women Graduates Pre- and Post-1945," *History of Education* 34, no. 4 (2005); Claire Langhamer, *The English in Love: The Intimate Story of an Emotional Revolution* (Oxford: Oxford University Press, 2013), 6; Mackinnon, *Love and Freedom*, 8–9.

29. "Oxford colleges": CUB to family, 22 June 1914 and 19 Jan. 1913, CUBFC.

30. "never says a word": DLS to people, 27 Apr. 1913, 78b, MEWC; "severely iso-lated," "I wandered," "very much surprised . . . he passed me": DLS to Godfrey, 11 July 1913, MS308, Smith.

CHAPTER 2: MUTUAL ADMIRATION SOCIETY ON STAGE AND PAGE

1. "M.A.S. with Miss Middlemore": Diary, 6 Nov. 1912, CUBFC; "some little digs": CUB to family, 14 June 1913 and 24 Nov. 1912, CUBFC; DLS to parents, 19 Nov. 1912, Reynolds, *Letters*, vol. 1; "if we didn't give ourselves": Frankenburg, *Not Old*, 63; "took themselves very seriously": Brittain, *Testament of Youth*, 108.

2. DLS to people, 19 Jan. 1913, 66, MEWC; "prose description of the three men . . . sense of humour": CUB to family, 19 Jan. 1913, CUBFC.

3. CUB to family, 26 Jan. 1913, CUBFC.

4. "a most frightfully" "a shadowy figure": DLS to parents, 26 Jan. 1913, Reynolds, *Letters*, vol. 1; "I believe Jim," "There's something," "only person who was": CUB to family, 26 Jan. 1913, CUBFC; Diary, 24 Jan. 1913, CUBFC.

5. "read a paper": CUB to family, 5 Feb. 1913 and 26 Jan. 1913, CUBFC; "all us vain, sentimental fools": "The Last Castle," "CHG from DLS" (Oxford, 1915), MS308, Smith; Dorothy L. Sayers, *Op. I.*, (Oxford: Blackwell, 1916).

6. "Dorothy Rowe is very clever": CUB to family, 19 Jan. 1913, CUBFC; "deep ethical discussion": CUB to family, 27 Feb. 1913, CUBFC; CUB to family, 3 Nov. 1912, 2 Feb. 1913, CUBFC.

7. "very good at inventing": "D. H. R. Member of Staff" (Bournemouth: Victory Press, [1958]), 4; *The Eagle and the Wolf*, 2/5 MSBC; Byrne, *Common or Garden Child*, 120; "If a grown-up said": "Cat O'Mary," 59.

8. "entrancing society," "very high stiff collars," "I would be all right": Byrne, *Common or Garden Child*, 38, 53, 59, 120–122; "A School Story, or a Runaway Girl from Quoswind School," *Comet*, 2/5 MSBC.

9. "had to dress as a character . . . been to here": CUB to family, 8 June 1913, CUBFC; Susan J. Leonardi, *Dangerous by Degrees: Women at Oxford and the Somerville College Novelists* (New Brunswick, NJ: Rutgers University Press, 1989), 35.

10. "The Pen was completely": DLS to people, [Oct. 1913], 78a, MEWC; "wearing whiskers": Farnell, *A Somervillian*, 35.

11. Diary, 15 Feb. 1913, CUBFC; "dread of something": "Hamlet" notebook, CUBFC; "one roar": CUB to family, 16 Feb. 1913, CUBFC; Frankenburg, *Not Old*, 68.

12. *Fritillary*, March 1914, CUBFC.

13. "Order, order," "I think so": CUB to family, 28 Nov. 1912 and 5 Feb. 1913, CUBFC; Diary, 22 Oct. 1912, 27 Nov. 1912, CUBFC; Frankenburg, *Not Old*, 63; Brittain, *Women at Oxford*, 113; Farnell, *A Somervillian*, 43.

14. "an arresting manner:" *Fritillary*, March 1913; *Fritillary*, December 1912; "look respectable," "educated classes": DLS to people, [22 Feb. 1914?], 79, MEWC; Sarah Wiggins, "Gendered Spaces and Political Identity: Debating Societies in English Women's Colleges, 1890–1914," *Women's History Review* 18, no. 5 (2009), 747.

15. Brittain, *Women at Oxford*, 112; Frankenburg, *Not Old*, 49; Frankenburg Manchester Studies 1045, Tameside; CUB to family, 26 Oct. 1912, CUBFC.

16. "amused us very much": CUB to family, 1 Feb. 1914, and draft speech, CUBFC; "that the reluctance," "so long as it is": *Fritillary*, March 1914.

17. "because we made funny speeches": Frankenburg interview, 8SUF/B/144, WL; Julia Bush, *Women against the Vote: Female Anti-Suffragism in Britain* (Oxford: Oxford University Press, 2007).

18. "behaved as coldly": DLS to people, "Sunday 27th" [1912?], 65, MEWC; "misty theological discussion," "unprofitable argument": DLS to Catherine Godfrey, [1913], MS308, Smith; "after my soul's welfare," "what you have been . . . for myself": DLS to people, March 1914, 79, MEWC.

19. DLS to Godfrey, [1913], MS308, Smith; "whose philosophy": DLS undergraduate notes and essays 1-15 and 1-9, MEWC; G. K. Chesterton, *Heretics* (London: Bodley Head, 1909), 22.

20. "My word!": CUB to family, 3 Nov. 1912, CUBFC; "immensely funny," "believed that there were many": Frankenburg, *Not Old*, 10.

21. Byrne and Mansfield, *Somerville College*, 16–18; Hurst, "Maenads Dancing," 164–167; "often ingenious," "She has no standard," "a power of thinking": Somerville College Reports 1911–1912.

22. "Somebody says they are": CUB to family, 12 Oct 1912, CUBFC; "rather trying," "sniffs violently": 26 Oct. 1912, CUBFC; Somerville College Reports 1911–1912.

23. Somerville College Reports 1911–1912.

24. "manes": DLS undergraduate notes and essays 1-5 and 1-10, MEWC; "symphony on the vowel," "slow mill": "Cat O'Mary," 96–97, 122.

25. DLS undergraduate notes and essays 1-1, 1-2, 1-6; "practically untranslatable," "girl who is": DLS to father, 21 June 1914, 80, MEWC.

26. CUB to family, 27 Feb. 1913, CUBFC.

27. "Working? No": DLS to Godfrey, [1913], MS308, Smith; "a perfect orgie": DLS to Godfrey, 11 July 1913, MS308, Smith; "was still not done": DLS to Jaeger, 22 July 1913, 22, MEWC.

28. CUB to family, 2 Feb. 1913, CUBFC.

29. "far below what she can": Somerville College Reports 1911–1912; Diary, 3–5 and 13 Mar. 1913, CUBFC; CUB to family, 17 June 1913, CUBFC; "Well, Miss Barnett": Frankenburg, Not Old, 62.

30. "Golden Book": CUB to family, 4 Mar. 1913, CUBFC; "It is perfectly glorious": CUB to family, 17 June 1913, CUBFC.

31. "killing manner": DLS to Godfrey, 11 July 1913, MS308, Smith; "desecrated his masculine": DLS to Godfrey, 29 July 1913, MS308, Smith; E. B. Poulton, "Frederick Augustus Dixey, 1855–1935," Obituary Notices of Fellows of the Royal Society 1, no. 4 (December 1935).

32. "quite literally," "tore over," "the enemy," "fell head over ears," "isn't it a killing," "addressed all the assembled": DLS to Godfrey, 29 July 1913, MS308, Smith; "simply bristled": CUB to family, 17 June 1913, CUBFC; DLS to people, June 20, 1913, 78b, MEWC.

33. "home-sick for Oxford": DLS to Godfrey, 11 July 1913, MS308, Smith; "I am not pleased": DLS to Jaeger, 22 July 1913, 22, MEWC; "I cannot get any": DLS to Jaeger, 30 July 1913, 22, MEWC.

34. DLS to Jaeger, 22 July 1913, 22, MEWC.

35. DLS to Jaeger, 30 July 1913, 22, MEWC.

36. "all the first year": CUB to family, 19 Jan. 1913 and 26 Jan. 1913, [May 1913], CUBFC; "something that I": DLS to Godfrey, 29 July 1913, MS308, Smith.

37. "read an awfully good": CUB to family, 21 Oct. 1913, CUBFC; "very cheeky," "will do her good": CUB to family, 2 Nov. 1913, CUBFC; "D. R. has naturally": CUB to family, 3 Nov. 1913, CUBFC.

38. "a psychic story," "two French translations": CUB to family, 21 Nov. 1913, CUBFC; "M.A.S. style": CUB to family, 23 Feb. 1914, CUBFC; Frankenburg, Not Old, 63; 12 June 1913, Minutes of College Meetings, Somerville; Fritillary, November 1913.

CHAPTER 3: UNIVERSITY PASSIONS

1. Judy G. Batson, Her Oxford (Nashville: Vanderbilt University Press, 2008), 154; Byrne and Mansfield, Somerville College, 77; "it was up to us": Frankenburg, Not Old, 59.

2. "ran its course," "in a rather exalted": "Cat O'Mary," 121, 130; "Grey eyes": "To Bianca," MS308, Smith.

3. Brittain, Women at Oxford, 123; Brittain, Testament of Youth, 106; "I will now stop": DLS to people, n.d., 80, MEWC; "burst into tears": DLS to people, [March

1914], 79, MEWC; "at his most": DLS to people, [1914], 80, MEWC; "from Somerville," "H.P.A.," "Of course, the two": DLS to people, [1914], 81, MEWC; "exulted when he threw," "well-known strip-tease": DLS to Cyril Bailey, 23 Sept. 1946, 202, MEWC.

4. DLS to Cyril Bailey, 23 Sept. 1946, 202; DLS to Jaeger, 15 Apr. [1915], 22, MEWC; DLS to Godfrey, 28 July 1914, MS308, Smith.

5. DLS to people, Mar. 1914, 79, MEWC; "what a problem," "I really didn't," "if a woman": DLS to people, [21 Feb. 1915], 84, MEWC; "with a really": DLS to Godfrey, 5 Jan. 1915 and 28 July 1914, MS308, Smith.

6. DLS to parents, 7 Feb. 1915, Reynolds, *Letters*, vol. 1.

7. "To HPA," MS308, Smith.

8. "And for one blissful": Frankenburg interview, 8SUF/B/144, WL; Diary, 16 Nov. 1912, CUBFC; "we have had no bust-up," "I am just": CUB to family, 19 Jan. 1913, CUBFC.

9. "fills us," "so that they": CUB to family, 14 June 1914 and 22 June 1914, CUBFC.

10. Byrne, *Common or Garden Child*, 145, 154, 156–157, 159, 163. Ellipses original.

11. M. St. Clare Byrne, *Aldebaran* (Oxford: Blackwell, 1917), 13, 48–52, 55.

12. M. St. Clare Byrne, "Favete Linguis," in *Oxford Poetry 1917* (Oxford: Blackwell, 1918), 2.

13. Sharon Marcus, *Between Women: Friendship, Desire, and Marriage in Victorian England* (Princeton, NJ: Princeton University Press, 2007); Martha Vicinus, *Intimate Friends: Women Who Loved Women, 1778–1928* (Chicago: University of Chicago Press, 2004); Lesley Hall, "'Sentimental Follies' or 'Instruments of Tremendous Uplift'? Reconsidering Women's Same-Sex Relationships in Interwar Britain," *Women's History Review* 25, no. 1 (2016), 130.

14. "A life without desire": Byrne, *Aldebaran*, 31; "Few friendships," "Veronica": Timothy d'Arch Smith, ed., *The Quorum: A Magazine of Friendship* (New York: Asphodel Editions, 2001), 2, 10, 22.

15. Diary, 8 Feb. 1913; CUB to family, 1 June 1913, CUBFC.

16. "but as he apparently": CUB to family, 23 May 1914 and 11 Jan. 1913, 7 May 1913, CUBFC; "Appalling situation," "I shouldn't be," "roared with laughter": DLS to parents, Nov. 1913, Reynolds, *Letters*, vol. 1.

17. "not bad": DLS to people, 16 Feb. 1913, 66, MEWC; "a sort of mountain-top," "a free & friendly": DLS to people, 2 Nov. 1913, [1913], 78a, MEWC.

18. "some copper-coloured": DLS to people, 2 Nov. 1913, 78a, MEWC; "The king": DLS to people, [1913], 78a, MEWC; "went out with her husband": DLS to people, [Jan. 1914?], 79, MEWC.

19. Corpus Christi College Roll of Honour 1914–1918; "so my 'womanly": DLS to people, 7 June 1913, 78b, MEWC; "he talk a great deal": DLS to people, 9 Feb. [1914], 79, MEWC; DLS to people, [3 May 1914?], 80, MEWC; "he seems to have": DLS to parents, 14 June 1914 and 7 June 1914, Reynolds, *Letters*, vol. 1; DLS to Godfrey, 28 July 1914, MS308, Smith.

20. "family reasons," "favourite theory": CUB to family, 18 Jan. 1914 and 1 Feb. 1914, CUBFC; "exactly the same": CUB to family, 6 June 1914, CUBFC; "one of the three": Frankenburg, *Not Old*, 70; Emily Rutherford, "Arthur Sidgwick's *Greek Prose Composition*: Gender, Affect, and Sociability in the Late-Victorian University," *Journal of British Studies* 56 (January 2017).

21. "says that I am no linguist": CUB to family, 21 June 1914, CUBFC; "the whole of the Anglo Saxon": CUB to family, 12 Oct. 1913, CUBFC; "sufficiently serious-minded": CUB to family, 21 June 1914, CUBFC; "superficially clever": Somerville College Reports 1911–1912.

22. "frivolous": CUB to family, 1 Feb. 1914, CUBFC; "because the refrain": CUB to family, 15 Feb. 1914, CUBFC; "first rate," "Everybody except Jim": CUB to family, 3 May 1914 and 21 June 1914, CUBFC.

23. CUB to family, 21 June 1914, CUBFC.

CHAPTER 4: BATTLEFRONTS

1. "chamber of horrors": Frankenburg interview, 8SUF/B/144, WL; Rowe to Jaeger, 22 Oct. 1933, Collett.

2. DLS to people, [1914], 80, MEWC; "splendid 15th century," "Old England": DLS to Jaeger, 21 Sept. 1914, 22, MEWC; DLS to Godfrey, 28 July 1914, MS308, Smith; Brabazon, *Dorothy L. Sayers*, 52.

3. Frankenburg, *Not Old*, 72–73.

4. WO339/24511, NA; *Denis Oliver Barnett: In Happy Memory. His Letters from France and Flanders October 1914–August 1915* (Privately printed, 1915), vii–viii; Frankenburg, *Not Old*, 20; Frankenburg interview, 8SUF/B/194, WL.

5. "I bought food": Frankenburg interview, 8SUF/B/194, WL; Frankenburg, *Not Old*, 73; *Denis Oliver Barnett*, x; DLS to Jaeger, 21 Sept. 1914, 22; "he looked very nice": DLS to people, 8 Nov. 1914, 81, MEWC; DLS to people, [7 Mar. 1915], 84, MEWC.

6. "The men did": Frankenburg interview, 8SUF/B/144b, WL; Brittain, *Dark Tide*, 37; Byrne and Mansfield, *Somerville College*, 54; Batson, *Her Oxford*, 160; "many of them": Farnell, *A Somervillian*, 42.

7. "we sang 'God Save the King'": DLS to people, 1 Nov. 1914, 81, MEWC; "Heroic Exploit": "The Week on Oxford," 66, MEWC.

8. *Fritillary* December 1914; Frankenburg, *Not Old*, 75; DLS to people, [1914], 81, MEWC; "You should have seen": DLS to parents, 8 Nov. 1914, Reynolds, *Letters*, vol. 1.

9. DLS to Godfrey, 6 Jan. 1915, MS308, Smith; Catriona Pennell, *A Kingdom United: Popular Responses to the Outbreak of the First World War in Britain and Ireland* (Oxford: Oxford University Press, 2012).

10. "Emily's bomb," "It is quite melancholy": DLS to Jaeger, 15 Apr. [1915], 22, MEWC; "new light": Byrne and Mansfield, *Somerville College*, 36–37, 40–41; "Oh, hateful sight": Farnell, *A Somervillian*, 42.

11. "advanced in wisdom": Somerville College Reports 1911–1912; "an awfully nice": Frankenburg, *Not Old*, 63; DLS to people, [Jan. 1915], 84, MEWC; *Aberdeen Daily Journal*, 27 Dec. 1915.

12. "careless attitude," "symbolic and affirmative," "has some very good": *Fritillary*, March 1915; Kristin Ewins, "A History of the *Fritillary*: A Magazine of Oxford Women's Colleges, 1894–1931," *Notes and Queries* 55, no. 1 (2008), 60–64.

13. *The Times*, 3 July 1915; Catherine Kenney, "Sayers [married name Fleming], Dorothy Leigh," *Oxford Dictionary of National Biography*, 3 Sept. 2004; Byrne and Mansfield, *Somerville College*, 81; Anthea Bell, "Dorothy Rowe," in *Somerville College Report and Supplement 1988*; "Goodbye to the Bodley . . .": "Pied Pipings or the Innocents Abroad," going-down songs, CUBFC.

14. Sayers, *Op. I.*, 70–71.

15. "who will be feeling": DLS to Rowe, 8 Oct. 1915, 427, MEWC; DLS to Jaeger, 14 Nov. 1916, 22, MEWC.

16. DLS to Godfrey, 22 Sept. [1915?], MS308, Smith; "a M.A.S. dinner": DLS to Jaeger, 24 Dec. 1916, 22, MEWC.

17. "Good old M.A.S.": DLS to Jaeger, 27 July 1915, 22, MEWC; "charming and undeserved": DLS to Jaeger, 26 Sept. 1915 and 14 Nov. 1916, 22, MEWC; "corresponding in parodies": DLS to Jaeger, 15 Dec. 1915, 22, MEWC; DLS MS-444, MEWC; DLS to Godfrey, 5 Jan. [1915], MS308, Smith; "disbanded, because its first members," "drunk the toast": Muriel Jaeger, "The Light Touch," (1919), Collett.

18. "full powers as": DLS to Jaeger, 11 Apr. 1916, 22, MEWC; Sayers, *Op. I.*

19. "have got nervous breakdown": DLS to Jaeger, 27 July 1915 and 26 Sept. 1915, 22, MEWC; DLS to people, [7 Mar. 1915], 84, MEWC; "the big push": DLS to mother, [June? 1917] and 29 Jan. [1917], 68, MEWC; WO/372/6/36565, NA.

20. "airy apology": DLS to people, 8 Nov. 1914, 81, MEWC; "hate the whole thing": DLS to Jaeger, 26 Sept. 1915, 22, MEWC; WO339/26110, WO/372/7/114691, NA; "robbed him of occasion": Sayers, *Op. I.*, 68.

21. "horrible and indecent": Hugh Sidgwick to Ethel Sidgwick, 16 Dec. 1916 and 18 May 1917; Colin Taylor to Frank Sidgwick, 1 Oct. 1917; "a triumph": Hugh Sidgwick to Frank Sidgwick, 11 Aug. 1916 and 18 Jan. 1917, Sidgwick Letters, Balliol; WO339/52964, NA; Middlemore to Sarah Margery Fry, 5 June 1916, 9 June 1916, L. Add. 1754–1755, CRL.

22. "kind of a mother," "It's all very easy": Middlemore to Sarah Margery Fry, 23 May 1917, L. Add. 1956, CRL; Obituary, Hugh Sidgwick to Ethel Sidgwick, 27 Mar. 1917; "knew suddenly": Middlemore to Frank Sidgwick, 21 Nov. 1917, Sidgwick Letters, Balliol; Andrew Belsey, "Naomi Royde-Smith" 6 July 2017, personal correspondence with the author; Christine von Oertzen, *Science, Gender, and Internationalism: Women's Academic Networks, 1917–1955*, trans. Kate Sturge (New York: Palgrave Macmillan, 2014), 1.

23. "so much of": C. S. Sidgwick to [Frank Sidgwick?], n.d.; "if he realised really": Middlemore to Frank Sidgwick, 21 Nov. 1917, Sidgwick Letters, Balliol.

24. J. H. Nixson Eckersall to C. S. Sidgwick, 22 Sept. 1917; G. H. Peskett to C. S. Sidgwick; "wife-elect": C. S. Sidgwick to [Frank Sidgwick?], n.d., 10 Oct. 1917, 21 Nov. 1917, 12 Jan. 1918; "answer unnecessary": Middlemore to Ethel Sidgwick, 2 Oct. 1917; "From his last written letter": Middlemore to Frank Sidgwick, 21 Nov. 1917, Sidgwick Letters, Balliol; Middlemore to Sarah Margery Fry, 25 Aug. 1917, L. Add. 1757, CRL; *Memoir of Mary Christina Sidgwick, née Coxhead*, ed. Ann Baer (unpublished, 1983), 69, from Andrew Belsey, personal correspondence with the author; WO339/52964, WO/372/18/61777, NA.

25. "rather cold," "can't see the eternal," "I found it," "well, he was done," "I am having": *Denis Oliver Barnett*, 4, 8, 13, 15, 19, 21; "Dear old Sydney," "But we emerged": Frankenburg, *Not Old*, 75.

26. Frankenburg, *Not Old*, 76; "You at home": *Denis Oliver Barnett*, 37, 129, 136, 138.

27. "he sensed an enemy": Frankenburg, *Not Old*, 76; "gas area," "It was for carrying": *Denis Oliver Barnett*, x–xi, 159, 165, 169–70.

28. WO339/24511, NA.

29. "I'm sure if I," "perfectly ripping," "that it rang": DLS to Jaeger, 26 Sept. 1915, 22, MEWC; "I found him": Sayers, *Op. I.*, 38.

30. "in a depressed": DLS to Jaeger, 26 Sept. 1915, 22, MEWC; "lay on the floor," "lest I should," "of course, one can't": DLS to Rowe, 8 Oct. 1915, 427, MEWC.

31. "I just wanted": Frankenburg interview, 8SUF/B/144, WL; "the steady, silent": M. St. Clare Byrne, "And One Fell by the Wayside . . . ", *Oxford Poetry 1918* (Oxford: Blackwell, 1918), 4; Byrne and Mansfield, *Somerville College*, 46–53.

32. Rowe to Lee, 17 Nov. 1985, 25.859, DLSA; "It was the sort of": "D.H.R. Member of Staff," 6; Emily Penrose to Jaeger, 30 June 1916; Margaret McKillop, 12 Nov. 1920, Collett; DLS to people, 30 May [1917], 14 Nov. 1917, 68; DLS to Jaeger, 15 Aug. 1917, 18 Dec. 1917, 25 Apr. 1918, 22, MEWC; Middlemore to Sarah Margery Fry, 6 July 1915, L. Add. 1752, CRL.

33. "My mother, at Burnt Hill": Frankenburg, *Not Old*, 74, 78; "wasn't really a re-spectable": Frankenburg Manchester Studies 1045, Tameside.

34. "through a haze," "I had to steel": Frankenburg, *Not Old*, 79, 81–82, 85; Alison Nuttall, "Midwifery, 1800–1920: The Journey to Registration," in *Nursing and Midwifery in Britain Since 1700*, eds. Annie Borsay and Billie Hunter (Houndmills: Palgrave Mac-millan, 2012), 139–142.

35. "Coloured people were": Frankenburg, *Not Old*, 83; Stephen Bourne, *Black Pop-pies: Britain's Black Community and the Great War* (Stroud, UK: History Press, 2014).

36. Frankenburg, *Not Old*, 87, 89–90.

37. Frankenburg interview, 8SUF/B/194, WL; Edith M. Pye, ed., *War and Its Af-termath: Letters from Hilda Clark, M.B., B.S. from France, Austria and the Near East 1914–1924* (London: Cathedral Press, n.d.), 15–16, 18; Anne Powell, *Women in the War Zone: Hospital Service in the First World War* (Stroud, UK: History Press, 2009), 19, 112–113.

38. "was sent from," "merely told to keep": Frankenburg, *Not Old*, 91–93, 98; "feed them only": Pye, *War and Its Aftermath*, 19, 23.

39. Frankenburg, *Not Old*, 95, 99–100.

40. Frankenburg, *Not Old*, 100, 103; DLS to Godfrey, 28 Nov. [1915?], MS308, Smith.

41. Frankenburg interview, 8SUF/B/194, WL.

CHAPTER 5: TEACH OR MARRY?

1. "Give her a room": Woolf, *Room of One's Own*, 68; "in modern fashion": Muriel Jaeger, *The Man with Six Senses* (Boston: HiLo Books, 2013), 24.

2. "Women have claimed": "British Federation of University Women," December 1920, Sayers Family Papers 1–7, MEWC; von Oertzen, *Science*, 23, 26.

3. Adams, *Somerville for Women*, 31–45; "simply didn't give a chance": Notebook, 3, MSBC.

4. "drifted . . . on the principle": Byrne and Mansfield, *Somerville College*, 85; "he took no further": Frankenburg, *Not Old*, 184.

5. "D.H.R. Member of Staff," 6; E. Medwin to Blanche Rowe, 16 Oct. [1889], T. B. Rowe Papers Add. 8252/15M/1, CUL; Elizabeth Edwards, *A History of Bournemouth: The Growth of a Victorian Town* (Chichester, UK: Phillimore & Co. Ltd., 1981), 86–87; Board

of Education Inspection Reports ED109/1812 (1910), ED109/1813 (1919), ED109/1814 (1928), ED109/1815 (1939), NA.

6. Board of Education Inspection Report ED109/1814 (1928), NA; "I know what it," "If you really," "No one," "Perhaps, for the first": "D.H.R. Member of Staff," 8.

7. "dysentery among the junior": CUF Newsletter, 20 Sept. 1943, MS Eng. c. 7048, Bodleian; Rowe to MSB, 31 Jan. 1938, 25 June 1948, 1/9, MSBC; "added with her familiar": "D.H.R. Member of Staff," 20.

8. "the sight of her": Joy Martin to Hugh Norris, 30 June 2000, 25.863, DLSA; "Oh! I always keep": "D.H.R. Member of Staff," 5, 6, 9, 26–27.

9. "D.H.R. Member of Staff," 13; "could play Juliet," "you lit up our minds": *Old Girls' Chronicle*, March 1958.

10. Bell, "Dorothy Rowe."

11. DLS to Godfrey, 22 Sept. [1915?], MS308, Smith; DLS to Jaeger, 26 Sept. 1915, 27 Mar. 1916, 14 Nov. 1916, 22, MEWC; Darbishire reference 16 Mar. 1916, and Emily Penrose reference, 21 Apr. 1918, 2b/6, MSBC; "willing and punctual": J. B. Lancelot reference, 31 Mar. 1917, 2b/6, MSBC; "know as much": "Labuntur Anni . . . " 7/7, MSBC.

12. WO/372/23/6170, NA; "thorough and interesting": D.C. Kitchee reference, 22 Apr. 1919, 2b/6, MSBC; E. D. Monro reference, Jan. 1920, 2b/6 MSBC; "men didn't want": Janet Watts, "How Muriel Byrne Revealed the Private Life of a Tudor VIP," *Observer*, 21 June 1981, PP56/L/1, RHUL; "November 1917: Entertaining the Troops," *Somerville and the Great War* (blog), 3 Nov. 2017, http://blogs.some.ox.ac.uk/thegreatwar/2017/11/03 /november-1917-entertaining-the-troops/.

13. "patience & sympathy": DLS to Jaeger, 26 Sept. 1915, 22, MEWC; "is going to be": DLS to Godfrey, 19 July [1915] and 22 Sept. [1915?], MS308, Smith.

14. DLS to Godfrey, 28 Nov. [1915?], MS308, Smith.

15. "because my brain," "simply bristles": DLS to Jaeger, 6 Feb. 1916, 22, MEWC; "I had never seen": DLS to Jaeger, 14 Nov. 1916 and 27 Mar. 1916, 5 Aug. 1916, 22, MEWC.

16. "sent a minute," "business details": DLS to Jaeger, 8 Mar. 1917, 22; "no future": DLS to parents, [25 Jan 1917], 68, MEWC.

17. "immoral to take": DLS to Jaeger, 8 Mar. 1917 ("It's"), 22, MEWC; "publishing isn't work": DLS to parents, 13 Feb. 1917, 68, MEWC; "the clank and gurgle": DLS to Rowe, 8 Oct. 1915, and DLS to mother, 5 Feb. 1918, Reynolds, *Letters*, vol. 1; Dorothy L. Sayers, "Fair Erembours," in *Oxford Poetry 1917* (Oxford: Blackwell, 1918), 52–53.

18. "Anything said is better": DLS to Jaeger, 2 Oct. 1918 and 22 Nov. 1918, 22, MEWC; "strange way": DLS to Jaeger, 26 Nov. 1918, 22, MEWC; "'jargon' is responsible": DLS to Jaeger, 11 Jan. 1919, 22, MEWC; Barbara Reynolds, *Dorothy L. Sayers: Her Life and Soul* (London: Hodder & Stoughton, 1993), 100.

19. "gorgeous Whit-week-end," "Tony, Cherub, Jim": DLS to people, 30 May [1917] and 28 Apr. [1917], 68, MEWC; "alas! the Tribal Meeting": DLS to Jaeger, 20 Aug. 1917 and 21 Aug. 1917, 22, MEWC; "amazing woman": DLS to Jaeger, 26 Nov. 1918, 22, MEWC.

20. Frankenburg, *Not Old*, 75–76, 84.

21. "Something's happened": Frankenburg, *Not Old*, 85, 106; WO374/25510, NA.

22. Frankenburg, *Not Old*, 84; "he loved me," "He then said": DLS to mother, 11 June 1917 and [June? 1917], 68, MEWC.

23. "looking like a Good": DLS to mother, 11 July 1917, 68, MEWC; "But could I bring myself": DLS to people, "Trinity X," and 20 Sept. 1917, 68, MEWC; "Oh my dears": DLS to people, 14 Nov. 1917, 68, MEWC; "that you were": Hodgson to DLS, 30 Dec. 1919, Sayers Family Papers 1-3, MEWC; "perfectly graduated series": DLS to people, 2 Jan. 1920, 87, MEWC.

24. WO374/25510, NA; "rather faded," "Then why didn't," "With an exultant": Frankenburg, *Not Old*, 103–104.

25. Frankenburg Manchester Studies 1045, Tameside.

26. "I mumbled something": Frankenburg, *Not Old*, 104–106, 183–184; Marriage certificate, "England and Wales Marriages, 1538–1940," Ancestry.co.uk.

27. "sitting on the open": "D.H.R. Member of Staff," 7; "original, as usual": DLS to Jaeger, 26 Nov. 1918, 22, MEWC; "and I was in Trafalgar": Watts, "Tudor VIP"; Frankenburg, *Not Old*, 108–109; WO374/25510, WO/372/7/146001, NA.

28. "quite sex-ridden," "how much of all": DLS to Jaeger, 22 Dec. 1918, 22, MEWC; "me thinks she is": DLS to Jaeger, 6 April 1919 and 24 Feb. 1919, 22, MEWC; Marriages Registered in January, February and March 1920, Ancestry.co.uk.

29. Dorothy L. Sayers, "Eros in Academe," *Oxford Outlook* 2, no. 1 (June 1919), 111, 115.

30. "foolish thing": DLS to Jaeger, 24 Feb. 1919, 22, MEWC; "How complicated our latter-day": DLS to Jaeger, 2 Oct. 1918, 22, MEWC; "a helpless male": DLS to people, 30 May [1917], 68, MEWC; DLS to parents, [July 1918?], Reynolds, *Letters*, vol. 1.

31. "permanent woman": DLS to father, 22 Jan. 1919, Reynolds, *Letters*, vol. 1; "simply dare not," "that's why they," "a kind of nightmare," "damnable feeling": DLS to mother, 6 June 1919, Reynolds, *Letters*, vol. 1; DLS to Jaeger, 6 Apr. 1919, 22, MEWC.

32. DLS to mother, 30 Jan. 1919, 86, MEWC; "and giving coachings": DLS to people, 19 May 1919, 86, MEWC; "grey eyes radiated," "large pendulous earrings": Eric Whelpton, *The Making of a European* (London: Johnson, 1974), 91, 109, 114–115, 126; "the things you did not say": Dorothy L. Sayers, "Sympathy," in *Oxford Poetry 1919* (Oxford: Blackwell, 1920), 51; Reynolds, *Letters*, vol. 1, 150n1; Reynolds, *Dorothy L. Sayers*, 106.

33. Whelpton, *Making*, 131, 138; Reynolds, *Dorothy L. Sayers*, 108; DLS to Jaeger, 27 June 1919, 22 July 1919, 22, MEWC; DLS to Eric Whelpton, n.d.; DLS to mother, 6 June 1919, Reynolds, *Letters*, vol. 1.

34. "beautiful shoulders": DLS to parents, 2 Nov. 1919, Reynolds, *Letters*, vol. 1; "handsomer than ever," "that does not," "I shall be surprised": DLS to Jaeger, 14 Sept. 1919, 22, MEWC; "she did a great deal": Whelpton, *Making*, 139.

35. "the only person": DLS to parents, 23 Nov. 1919, Reynolds, *Letters*, vol. 1; "that if I find": DLS to parents, 7 Dec. 1919 and 27 Feb. 1920, Reynolds, *Letters*, vol. 1; "He would get on": DLS to people, 11 Apr. 1920, 87, MEWC; Whelpton, *Making*, 157.

36. "black times": DLS to mother, 11 May 1920 and 11 Apr. 1920, 87, MEWC.

CHAPTER 6: DETECTION AND DESPAIR

1. "D. Rowe is with Charis": DLS to Jaeger, 14 Sept. 1919 and 26 Nov. 1918, 19 Dec. 1918, 1 Sept. 1920, 22, MEWC; Sayers Family Papers 1-7, MEWC; DLS to mother, 30 Jan. 1919, 86 MEWC; DLS to mother, 18 Aug. 1920, Reynolds, *Letters*, vol. 1.

2. "discreet packages": DLS to Jaeger, 8 Mar. 1920, 22, MEWC; "the old romance," "Now is the moment": fragment, 22, MEWC; "nice, scratchy," "the Osiris," "the

Oriental": DLS to Jaeger, n.d., 22, MEacWC; "John-James-Peter": DLS to Jaeger, 31 Mar. 1920, 22, MEWC.

3. "obviously, by divine law": DLS to Shrimpton, 11 Apr. 1921, 57, MEWC.

4. "paramount necessity": DLS to parents, 3 Oct. 1920, Reynolds, *Letters*, vol. 1; "Now I couldn't": DLS to mother, 23 July 1920, Reynolds, *Letters*, vol. 1; DLS to parents, 29 Sept. 1919, 86; DLS to Jaeger, 14 Sept. 1919, 22; Cecil Mannering to DLS, 21 Sept. 1920, 50; notes, Sayers Family Papers 1-7, MEWC.

5. Brittain, *Women at Oxford*, 156; *The Times*, 15 Oct. 1920; A. G. Grenfell to Mrs. Jaeger, 4 Oct 1920, Collett; "I want so much": DLS to mother, 18 Aug. 1920, Reynolds, *Letters*, vol. 1.

6. Byrne and Mansfield, *Somerville College*, 69; *The Times*, 15 Oct. 1920; *Manchester Guardian*, 15 Oct. 1920; *Christian Science Monitor*, 8 Nov. 1920; Brittain, *Women at Oxford*, 156.

7. Brittain, *Women at Oxford*, 156; Brittain, *Testament of Youth*, 507–508; *Christian Science Monitor*, 8 Nov. 1920; Brabazon, *Dorothy L. Sayers*, 85.

8. "He announced in such": Frankenburg, *Not Old*, 70.

9. "that slough of despond": Brittain, *Testament of Youth*, 545; DLS to Jaeger, 1 Sept. 1920, 22, MEWC; DLS to mother, 3 Sept. 1920, 14 Dec. 1920, 87, MEWC; DLS to father, 2 Apr. 1921, 88, MEWC; DLS to parents, 11 Apr. 1921, 88, MEWC; "or somebody": DLS to mother, 16 July 1921, 88, MEWC; "what she's doing": DLS to mother, 15 Mar. 1921 and 18 Aug. 1920, Reynolds, *Letters*, vol. 1; DLS to parents, 3 Oct. 1920, 26 Oct. 1920, Reynolds, *Letters*, vol. 1; Sidney Lee, 11 Nov. 1920, Collett; Catherine Clay, *British Women Writers 1914–1945: Professional Work and Friendship* (Aldershot, UK: Ashgate, 2006), 9–10.

10. "Alas! for the good old times": Muriel Jaeger, "What May I Do?" Collett; "hurls fearful inspired": DLS to people, 20 Nov. 1920, 87, MEWC; "surpasses everything else": DLS to mother, 22 Jan 1921, 88, MEWC.

11. "Teaching Record DLS," 6.528, DLSA; "a Master of Arts," "The Permanent Elements": DLS to director, 14 Dec. 1920, 583, MEWC.

12. DLS to Jaeger, 1 Sept. 1920, 22, MEWC; "If you can guess": DLS to mother, 22 Jan 1921, 88, MEWC.

13. "a depressing sight": DLS to parents, [1921] and 3 July 1920, Reynolds, *Letters*, vol. 1; DLS to Jaeger, 2 Oct. 1918, 22, MEWC; DLS to mother, 8 Aug. 1918, 83, MEWC; "I can't help": DLS to parents, [Lent 1921], 88, MEWC; "care much which set": DLS to mother, 26 Oct. 1922, 89, MEWC; "a woman doctor": DLS to parents, 17 Mar. 1922, 89, MEWC.

14. DLS to Jaeger, [1922?], 22, MEWC.

15. "a curious, eccentric-looking": DLS to parents, 7 Dec. 1920, Reynolds, *Letters*, vol. 1.

16. John Cournos, *Autobiography* (New York: G. P. Putnam's Sons, 1935), 191, 197; Donna Krolik Hollenberg, "Art and Ardor in World War One: Selected Letters from H. D. to John Cournos," *Iowa Review* 16, no. 3 (Fall 1986), 125–129, 144n2; David Ayers, "John Cournos and the Politics of Russian Literature in *The Criterion*," *Modernism/modernity* 18, no. 2 (2011), 356; Aldington to Cournos, 6 Apr. 1918; "shameless luxury": Fletcher to Cournos, 1 June 1920, B MS Eng 998.998.3, Houghton; "new woman affair," "You admit": Fletcher to Cournos, 19 Nov. 1920, B MS Eng 998.998.3, Houghton.

17. "lots of parties": DLS to parents, 1 July 1921, 88, MEWC; "I can't get": DLS to mother, 16 July 1921, 88, MEWC.

18. DLS to mother, 27 July 1921, Reynolds, *Letters*, vol. 1; "really want to know": DLS to mother, [1921], 88, MEWC; "Art with a capital": DLS to mother, 8 Nov. 1921, 88, MEWC; "it was a fearful," "tramped half London": DLS to Cournos, 13 Aug. 1925 and 4 Dec. 1924, MS Eng 1074, Houghton.

19. "vulgar little tabby": DLS to mother, 13 June 1922 and DLS to parents, 24 Nov. 1921, Reynolds, *Letters*, vol. 1; "monstrous size": DLS to parents, 13 Nov. 1922, 89, MEWC; "delighted to be able": Rowe to DLS, 17 July 1922, 427, MEWC.

20. Kate Fisher, *Birth Control, Sex, and Marriage in Britain, 1918–1960* (Oxford: Oxford University Press, 2006), 78, 169; Clare Debenham, *Birth Control and the Rights of Women: Post-Suffrage Feminism in the Early Twentieth Century* (London: I. B. Tauris, 2014), 72; Hera Cook, *The Long Sexual Revolution: English Women, Sex, and Contraception, 1800–1975* (Oxford: Oxford University Press, 2004); "for all your talk": DLS to Cournos, 4 Dec. 1924, MS Eng 1074, Houghton; Cournos, *Autobiography*, 101.

21. "on a point": DLS to mother, 18 Jan. 1922, 89, MEWC; DLS to parents, 17 Mar. 1922, 89, MEWC; "deserves something better": DLS to mother, 20 Feb. 1922 and 24 July 1922, Reynolds, *Letters*, vol. 1; "Don't let John": Rowe to DLS, 17 July 1922, 427, MEWC.

22. John Cournos, *The Devil Is an English Gentleman* (New York: Farrar & Rinehart, 1932), 499, 501–502, 507, 513–515, 597.

23. Alfred Satterthwaite, "John Cournos and 'H.D.'," *Twentieth Century Literature* 22, no. 4 (December 1976), 402–403.

24. Dorothy L. Sayers, *Strong Poison* (London: Gollancz, 1941), 29, 59.

25. "so much as sent": DLS to parents, 28 Nov. 1922, 89, MEWC; Fletcher to Cournos, 1 Oct. 1922 [1923], 28 Aug. 1925, B MS Eng 998.998.3; DLS to Cournos, 22 Aug. [1924], MS Eng 1074, Houghton; Hollenberg, "Art and Ardor," 150n7.

26. "such a hopelessly," "but it's too risky": DLS to mother, [November 1921], 88, MEWC; "prevents me from wanting": DLS to mother, 19 Dec. 1921, 88, MEWC; DLS to mother, 20 Feb. 1922, 89, MEWC; DLS to parents, 3 Mar. 1922, 89, MEWC.

27. Rowe to Geoffrey Lee, 17 Nov. 1985, 25.859, DLSA; "to a few," "a few little," "chasing after": DLS to parents, 17 Mar. 1922 and 3 Mar. 1922, 89, MEWC.

28. DLS to father, 4 Apr. 1922, 89, MEWC; DLS to parents, 19 July 1922, 89, MEWC; "guard it with care": Rowe to DLS, 17 July 1922, 427, MEWC; "I am rich!": Rowe to Geoffrey Lee, 17 Nov. 1985, 25.859, DLSA.

29. "a dictum": DLS to mother, 8 Nov. 1921, 88, MEWC; DLS to mother, 8 Dec. 1922, 89, MEWC.

30. Dorothy L. Sayers, *Whose Body?* (London: Gollancz, 1935); Dorothy L. Sayers, *Have His Carcase* (London: Gollancz, 1932); Whelpton, *Making*, 16, 64; Remizov letters, GEN MS Russ 65, Houghton; Janet Hitchman, *Such a Strange Lady: A Biography of Dorothy L. Sayers* (London: New English Library, 1975), 103.

31. "Being half Jewish": Frankenburg to Ralph Clarke, 23 Sept. 1972, 25.852, DLSA; Hitchman, *Such a Strange Lady*, 123–125; Brabazon, *Dorothy L. Sayers*, 124; Lillian S. Robinson, "The Mysterious Politics of Dorothy Sayers," in *At Home and Abroad in the Empire: British Women Write the 1930s*, eds. Robin Hackett, Freda Hauser, and Gay Wachman (Newark, DE: University of Delaware Press, 2009), 223; David Feldman,

"Conceiving Difference: Religion, Race and the Jews in Britain, c. 1750–1900," *History Workshop Journal* 76, no. 1 (October 2013); Sarah Mass, "Sunday Rites or Sunday Rights? Anglo-Jewish Traders and the Negotiability of the Mid-Century Sabbath," *History of Retailing and Consumption* 2, no. 1 (2016).

32. Stefan Schwarzkopf, "Consumer Communication as Commodity: British Advertising Agencies and the Global Market for Advertising, 1780–1980," in *Consuming Behaviours: Identity, Politics and Pleasure in Twentieth-Century Britain*, eds. Erika Rappaport, Sandra Trudgen Dawson, and Mark J. Crowley (London: Bloomsbury, 2015); Ruth Artmonsky, *Designing Women: Women Working in Advertising and Publicity from the 1920s to the 1960s* (London: Artmonsky Arts, 2012), 9; Julia Bigham, "Advertising as a Career," in *Women Designing: Redefining Design in Britain between the Wars*, eds. Jill Seddon and Suzette Worden (Brighton, UK: University of Brighton, 1994), 20–22; "under the impression": DLS to mother, 6 Nov. 1922, 89, MEWC.

33. "energy and rush": DLS to parents, 28 Nov. 1922 and 14 Aug. 1922, 89, MEWC; "exhausted with trying": DLS to parents, 24 May 1922, Reynolds, *Letters*, vol. 1; "all lies from beginning": DLS to parents, 1 June 1922 and 15 June 1922, Reynolds, *Letters*, vol. 1.

34. Dorothy L. Sayers, *Murder Must Advertise* (London: Gollancz, 1933); *The Recipe-Book of the Mustard Club: A Treasury of Delectable Dishes, Both New and Old, in the Right Tradition of Good English Cookery* (Norwich, UK: J. & J. Colman, n.d.); Hitchman, *Such a Strange Lady*, 69–71; Brabazon, *Dorothy L. Sayers*, 135; "with pleasure going up": MSB to Hitchman, 9 June 1967, 25.367, DLSA; DLS to Shrimpton, 13 Nov. 1925, 56.

35. "an absolutely rock-bottom," "literary intellect," "all about cars": DLS to mother, 18 Dec. 1922, Reynolds, *Letters*, vol. 1; Barbara Reynolds, "Particulars of the Birth of John Anthony," in Reynolds, *Letters*, vol. 1, 439–441.

36. DLS to parents, 26 Jan. 1923, 90, MEWC; DLS to mother, 8 Jan. 1923, 90, MEWC; "damned unsporting": DLS to mother, 15 Feb. 1923, Reynolds, *Letters*, vol. 1.

37. DLS to Cournos, 25 Jan. 1925, MS Eng 1074, Houghton.

38. DLS to Cournos, 27 Oct. 1924, MS Eng 1074, Houghton.

39. DLS to parents, 23 Nov. 1919, 7 Dec. 1919, 3 July 1920, 18 Aug. 1920, Reynolds, *Letters*, vol. I; "I had to re-write": DLS to mother, 22 Jan. 1924, Reynolds, *Letters*, vol. 1; Adèle to DLS, 20 Sept. 1920, 50, MEWC; DLS to mother, 8 Dec. 1922, 89, MEWC; Pat Thane and Tanya Evans, *Sinners? Scroungers? Saints? Unmarried Motherhood in Twentieth-Century England* (Oxford: Oxford University Press, 2012), 41–42.

40. "congratulated on looking": DLS to Cournos, 27 Oct. 1924, MS Eng 1074, Houghton; DLS to mother, 17 Mar. 1923, MEWC; Thane and Evans, *Sinners?*, 2.

41. Reynolds, "Particulars," 439–440.

42. "Perhaps I should say": Rowe to Ralph Clarke, 2 Sept. 1976, 25.848, DLSA; "the penalties for giving false": Rowe to DLS, 2 Jan. [1939], 427, MEWC; Brabazon, *Dorothy L. Sayers*, 174; Nadja Durbach, "Private Lives, Public Records: Illegitimacy and the Birth Certificate in Twentieth-Century Britain," *Twentieth Century British History* 25, no. 2 (2014).

43. "a good start," "struggle": DLS to Shrimpton, 27 Jan. 1924, Reynolds, *Letters*, vol. 1; "Suggested food": Note, Sayers Family Papers 1-22, MEWC.

44. "truly magnificent": DLS to Cournos, [5?] Feb. 1925, MS Eng 1074, Houghton; "behave pretty callously": DLS to Cournos, 4 Dec. 1924, MS Eng 1074 Houghton; "unaccustomed to success," "might not be able": "Cat O'Mary," 140–141.

45. Reynolds, "Particulars," 440; Deborah Cohen, *Family Secrets: The Things We Tried to Hide* (London: Penguin, 2014), 115, 125.

46. DLS to people, 8 Jan. 1918, 83; DLS to Shrimpton, 7 Mar. 1919, 53; DLS to Shrimpton, 11 Apr. 1921, 31 Dec. 1921, 7 June 1922, 57, MEWC; Brabazon, *Dorothy L. Sayers*, 22–26.

47. "won't have any," "extremely healthy," "for some years": DLS to Shrimpton, 1 Jan. 1924, Reynolds, *Letters*, vol. 1; "sturdy little boy": DLS to Shrimpton, 6 Jan. 1924, Reynolds, *Letters*, vol. 1.

48. "I won't go into," "It would grieve": DLS to Shrimpton, 27 Jan. 1924, Reynolds, *Letters*, vol. 1; "it can't be helped": DLS to Shrimpton, [February 1924], Reynolds, *Letters*, vol. 1; DLS to Shrimpton, 6 Feb. 1924, 55, MEWC.

49. "great relief": DLS to Shrimpton, 1 Feb. 1924, 55, MEWC; "all charmed": DLS to Shrimpton, 6 Feb. 1924, 55, MEWC; "elephant-flaps": DLS to Shrimpton, 21 Feb. 1924, 55, MEWC; DLS to mother, 25 Aug. 1924, 91, MEWC; DLS to Shrimpton, n.d., 51, MEWC.

50. "little woolly jacket," "grown elvish": DLS to Shrimpton, 10 Apr. 1924, 55, MEWC; "Poor little J. A.": DLS to Shrimpton, 29 Apr. 1924, 55, MEWC; "worry and embarrassment," "being sympathized," "As it is": DLS to Shrimpton, 2 May 1924, 55, MEWC; DLS to mother, 30 Apr. 1924, 91, MEWC.

51. "go to hell," "mechanically-mind," "I'm so bored": DLS to Shrimpton, 2 May 1924 and 1 Mar. 1924, 55, MEWC; Reynolds, *Letters*, vol. 1, 214; "It frightens me": DLS to Cournos, 22 Feb. 1925 and 25 Jan. 1925, MS Eng 1074, Houghton.

52. "would be sorry," "can, if necessary": DLS to mother, 28 Apr. 1925, 92, MEWC; "shove J.A. off": DLS to Shrimpton, 15 Apr. 1925, 56, MEWC; "an old college friend": DLS to Shrimpton, 20 Apr. 1925, 56, MEWC.

53. "one may as well," "a kind of literary," "moulded into," "overborne": DLS to Cournos, 13 Aug. 1925 and 29 June 1925, MS Eng 1074, Houghton.

54. "Marrying a highbrow," "I have a careless rage": DLS to Cournos, 25 Jan. 1925, n.d. and 25 Jan. 1925, MS Eng 1074, Houghton.

55. Dorothy L. Sayers, *Clouds of Witness* (London: Gollancz, 1935); "to feel the engine": DLS to Cournos, 13 Aug. 1925 and 28 Mar. 1925, MS Eng 1074, Houghton; DLS to Shrimpton, 27 Apr. 1925, 56, MEWC; "come & set up": DLS to people, 23 Dec. 1925, 92, MEWC; DLS to mother, 17 Dec. 1925, 92, MEWC.

56. "The Memories of Muriel St. Clare Byrne," 6.666, DLSA; Brabazon, *Dorothy L. Sayers*, 114–115; WO339/1408, NA.

57. Atherton Fleming, *How to See the Battlefields* (London: Cassell & Co. Ltd., 1919); Divorce Court Files, J77/1465/5172, J77/1964/1486, J77/2083/5253, NA; Caitríona Beaumont, *Housewives and Citizens: Domesticity and the Women's Movement in England, 1928–64* (Manchester, UK: Manchester University Press, 2014), 71; Hannah Charnock, "'A Million Little Bonds': Infidelity, Divorce and the Emotional Worlds of Marriage in British Women's Magazines of the 1930s," *Cultural and Social History* 14, no. 3 (2017), 365; Ann Schreurs statement, 4, MSBC.

58. Brabazon, *Dorothy L. Sayers*, 117; "The Memories of Muriel St. Clare Byrne," 6.666, DLSA.

59. Martin Edwards, *The Golden Age of Murder* (New York: HarperCollins, 2015).

60. Dorothy L. Sayers, ed., *Great Tales of Detection* (London: Dent, 1984), vii–viii.

61. "Do you promise": Brabazon, *Dorothy L. Sayers*, 144; "Avoid use of homicidal lunatics": Curriculum Vitae, 613, MEWC.

62. Stewart, *Crime Writing*, 8; "which it is his business": DLS to George Orwell, 29 Apr. 1946, 27, MEWC.

63. "drugged and doped": "The Union Debate," *Oxford Magazine*, 14 Nov. 1935, 10.424, DLSA.

64. "I can't write": DLS to Cournos, [5?] Feb. 1925, MS Eng 1074, Houghton; "over-intellectualized," "with a serious": Sayers, *Great Tales*, xii–xiii; "Importance of Being Vulgar," *Daily Telegraph*, 13 Feb. 1936, 12.78, DLSA.

CHAPTER 7: PROFESSIONAL MOTHERHOOD

1. "I do rather": Frankenburg Manchester Studies 1045, Tameside.

2. Frankenburg, *Not Old*, 116–117; Bill Williams, *Sir Sidney Hamburger and the Manchester Jewry: Religion, City and Community* (London: Valentine Mitchell, 1999), 62–63; Jewish Social Services (Greater Manchester), *They Came from the Haim: A History of Manchester Jewry from 1867* (Manchester, UK: Jewish Social Services, 1995), 1925; William D. Rubinstein, ed., *The Palgrave Dictionary of Anglo-Jewish History* (Houndmills, UK: Palgrave Macmillan, 2011), 292.

3. "for a joke," "she said": Frankenburg interview, 8SUF/B/144, WL; "weren't getting a fair deal": Frankenburg Manchester Studies 1045, Tameside; *Manchester Guardian*, 27 Jan. 1933; *Manchester and Salford Woman Citizen*, 21 Mar. 1932; Frankenburg, *Not Old*, 121–122.

4. Frankenburg, *Not Old*, 109, 111, 119.

5. "when it was inconvenient," "it's helped me": Frankenburg interview, 8SUF/B/144, WL; "really were labelled," "in a good God": Frankenburg Manchester Studies 1045, Tameside; "half Jewish": Frankenburg to Ralph Clarke, 23 Sept. 1972, 25.852, DLSA.

6. Frankenburg interview, 8SUF/B/144, WL; Rubinstein, *Dictionary*, 54; "must be treated": P. A. Barnett, *Common Sense in Education and Teaching: An Introduction to Practice* (London: Longmans, Green, & Co., 1901), 3, 35.

7. "horrified at the way," "to be so very": Frankenburg interview, 8SUF/B/144, WL; "an entertaining handbook": Frankenburg, *Not Old*, 10–11; "less pleasant": P. A. Barnett, *The Little Book of Health and Courtesy: Written for Boys and Girls*, 2nd ed. (London: Longmans, Green, & Co., 1906), 6, 9, 14.

8. "be cheerful": Barnett, *Little Book*, 24; "Baby Bear said," "made more harmful": Frankenburg, *Not Old*, 11–12, 185; Frankenburg interview, 8SUF/B/144, WL.

9. "like a charwoman": Frankenburg interview, 8SUF/B/144, WL; Alice Reid, "Infant Feeding and Child Health and Survival in Derbyshire in the Early Twentieth Century," *Women's Studies International Forum* 60 (2017), 118; "was her business" Frankenburg, *Not Old*, 111–112, 128.

10. "the inclination of the branch": *Manchester Guardian*, 15 May 1943.

11. Frankenburg, *Not Old*, 117–118.

12. Jane Lewis, *The Politics of Motherhood: Child and Maternal Welfare in England, 1900–1939* (London: Croom Helm, 1980); Francesca Moore, "Governmentality and the Maternal Body: Infant Mortality in Early Twentieth-Century Lancashire," *Journal of Historical Geography* 39 (2013), 55, 67; Reid, "Infant Feeding," 111; Trudi Tate, "King

Baby: Infant Care into the Peace," in *The Silent Morning: Culture and Memory after the Armistice*, eds. Trudi Tate and Kate Kennedy (Manchester, UK: Manchester University Press, 2013), 115; "People really don't": DLS to Shrimpton, 31 Oct. 1924, 55, MEWC; *Manchester Guardian*, 31 Dec. 1925; "Methodical parents": Peter to Charis, 29 Sept. 1932, MS Eng. c. 7043, Bodleian.

13. Tate, "King Baby," 117, 120–121; Cathy Unwin and Elaine Sharland, "From Bodies to Minds in Childcare Literature: Advice to Parents in Inter-war Britain," in *In the Name of the Child: Health and Welfare*, ed. Roger Cooter (London: Routledge, 1992), 178.

14. "deliberate and persistent," "patting, rocking": Mrs. Sydney Frankenburg, *Common Sense in the Nursery* (London: Christophers, 1922), 137, 151; Unwin and Sharland, "From Bodies to Minds," 180.

15. "silly slander": Frankenburg, *Not Old*, 128; "bad old superstition," "Feminists can": Mrs. Sydney Frankenburg, *Common Sense in the Nursery*, rev. ed. (London: Jonathan Cape, 1934), 111; Mary Abbott, *Family Affairs: A History of the Family in Twentieth-Century England* (London: Routledge, 2003); Laura Tisdall, "Education, Parenting and Concepts of Childhood in England, c. 1945 to c. 1979," *Contemporary British History* 31, no. 1 (2017), 33.

16. "Children should be": Frankenburg, *Common Sense* (1922), 5; Linda Bryder, "'Wonderlands of Buttercup, Clover and Daisies': Tuberculosis and the Open-Air School Movement in Britain, 1907–39," in *In the Name of the Child: Health and Welfare, 1880–1940*, ed. Roger Cooter (London: Routledge, 1992), 79, 86; "felt overboots," "a small electric fire": *Guardian*, 9 Apr. 2011; Charis U. Frankenburg, *Common Sense in the Nursery*, rev. ed. (Harmondsworth, UK: Penguin, 1946), vii; Peter to Charis, 27 Jan. 1929; Peter to Charis and Sydney, 18 Oct. 1931, MS Eng. c. 7043, Bodleian.

17. *Manchester Guardian*, 26 July 1930; "on the principle," "until he could": *Manchester Guardian*, 17 Nov. 1932; "obedience and self-control," "Do I need an umbrella": Frankenburg, *Not Old*, 113.

18. Unwin and Sharland, "From Bodies to Minds," 186; *Manchester Guardian*, 9 Apr. 1926; "undesirable handling": Frankenburg, *Common Sense* (1922), 167–169; "something wrong," "not a socially": Frankenburg, *Common Sense* (1934), 150, 154, 157–159.

19. Frankenburg, *Common Sense* (1934), 162.

20. "the importance of personal": Frankenburg, *Common Sense* (1946), v; "sometimes said, 'You go away'": Frankenburg, *Not Old*, 114.

21. *Manchester and Salford Woman Citizen*, Dec. 1938, Jan. 1939; "are within reach": Frankenburg, *Common Sense* (1946), xi; *Manchester Guardian*, 16 Dec. 1932; "adult tools": *The Times*, 8 Jan. 1955.

22. *The Times*, 28 Apr. 1954; Charis U. Frankenburg, *Latin with Laughter* (London: William Heinemann Ltd., 1934), 7.

23. Frankenburg, *Latin*, 18–19, 43.

24. Frankenburg, *Latin*, 9–10.

25. Susan Pedersen, "The Women's Suffrage Movement in the Balfour Family," Ben Pimlott Memorial Lecture, University College London, 3 July 2018.

26. Sally Alexander, "Primary Maternal Preoccupation: D. W. Winnicott and Social Democracy in Mid-Twentieth-Century Britain," in *History and Psyche: Culture, Psychoanalysis, and the Past*, eds. Sally Alexander and Barbara Taylor (New York: Palgrave Macmillan, 2012), 166.

27. Hunter, "Midwifery, 1920–2000," 153; Frankenburg, *Not Old*, 123–124.

28. Frankenburg, *Not Old*, 111; "then I was a midwife": Frankenburg Manchester Studies 1045, Tameside.

29. "because if a woman": Frankenburg interview, 8SUF/B/144, WL; Johanna Alberti, *Beyond Suffrage: Feminists in War and Peace, 1914–1928* (Houndmills, UK: Palgrave Macmillan, 1989), 133–134; "do not regard the provision": *Manchester Guardian*, 27 Jan. 1926; Debenham, *Birth Control*, 7–8.

30. CUB to family, 10 May 1914, CUBFC; Notes, SA/FPA/A14/29 354, Wellcome; *First Annual Report of the Manchester, Salford, and District Mothers' Clinic 1926–1927*, MCL; "we just went around": Frankenburg Manchester Studies 1045, Tameside; *Manchester Guardian*, 2 Mar. 1926; Frankenburg, *Not Old*, 134; *Only Eight Failures: Report on First 1212 Cases at the Manchester, Salford, and District Mothers' Clinic for Birth Control* 15, SA/FPA/A14/29 354, Wellcome; "a lovely smell": Frankenburg interview, 8SUF/B/144, WL.

31. Frankenburg, *Not Old*, 135; Debenham, *Birth Control*, 175, 188–189; *Only Eight Failures*, 8, 15; "always a married woman," "Great care," "who instructs her": *First Annual Report*, 7–8, MCL; Fisher, *Birth Control, Sex, and Marriage*, 34.

32. Frankenburg interview, 8SUF/B/144, WL.

33. Frankenburg, *Not Old*, 136; "doubtful about it," "she was converted": Frankenburg interview, 8SUF/B/144, WL; Debenham, *Birth Control*, 61; "an extremely vulgar speech," "boiling over": CUF newsletter, 7 Apr. 1941 and 3 Nov. 1941, MS Eng. c. 7045-6, Bodleian; *They Came from the Haim*, 1941; Rubinstein, *Dictionary*, 549.

34. Frankenburg, *Not Old*, 136; "used to come": Frankenburg Manchester Studies 1045, Tameside; *First Annual Report*, 7; *Third Annual Report of the Manchester, Salford, and District Mothers' Clinic*, MCL.

35. Debenham, *Birth Control*, 122–129; "which aims at the improvement," "their sisters," "rise up in arms": *Manchester Guardian*, 22 Mar. 1926; "under the patronage": *Catholic Herald*, 27 Mar. 1926; "thrust back into": *Catholic Federationist*, December 1926.

36. *Catholic Herald*, 17 Apr. 1926.

37. "German-Jewish name," "those over-dressed, well-fed": Notes on R. Catholic Papers, SA/FPA/A14/29 354, Wellcome; Frankenburg, *Not Old*, 137; Debenham, *Birth Control*, 105–106; "I must have been": Frankenburg Manchester Studies 1045, Tameside.

38. "Her health had suffered": Notes on Women's Meetings, "The Christian and Birth Control," SA/FPA/A14/29 354, Wellcome.

39. "At the protest," "We were told": Frankenburg, *Not Old*, 137; "You had to, you know": Frankenburg interview, 8SUF/B/144, WL.

40. "all political parties": Notes on mother and child welfare work, Notes on Women's Meetings, SA/FPA/A14/29 354, Wellcome; "generous comments," "this was a graphic illustration": Frankenburg, *Not Old*, 138–140; *First Annual Report*, 9; "considerably less opposition": *Second Annual Report of the Manchester, Salford, and District Mothers' Clinic 1927–1928*, 10, MCL.

41. Frankenburg, *Not Old*, 123, 139–140.

42. "be purer," "the proper information": Frankenburg Manchester Studies 1045, Tameside; "be called a whorehouse": Frankenburg interview, 8SUF/B/144, WL; Frankenburg, *Not Old*, 134.

43. "lest our Caesar's wife": *Only Eight Failures*, 11; "we had awful scenes": Franken-burg Manchester Studies 1045, Tameside; "those who were frantically experimenting": Frankenburg, *Not Old*, 135; Beaumont, *Housewives and Citizens*, 88.

44. "being very careful," "incomplete intercourse": *Second Annual Report*, 8; *First Annual Report*, 5–6, MCL; Beaumont, *Housewives and Citizens*, 85; Fisher, *Birth Control, Sex, and Marriage*, 36–37; Claire L. Jones, "Under the Covers? Commerce, Contracep-tives and Consumers in England and Wales, 1880–1960," *Social History of Medicine* 29, no. 4 (2015).

45. Frankenburg, *Not Old*, 135–136; *First Annual Report*, 6, MCL; "a baby every time": Notes on Women's Meetings, SA/FPA/A14/29 354, Wellcome.

46. "that awful story": Frankenburg interview, 8SUF/B/144, WL; "inadequate housing," "profound sense": *First Annual Report*, 7, MCL; "You cannot expect": "Ma-ternity Training," *Leeds Mercury*, 27 Jan. 1926; "man's job to earn": Notes on Women's Meetings, SA/FPA/A14/29 354, Wellcome.

47. *First Annual Report*, MCL.

48. "It is really splendid": DLS to mother, 30 Jan. 1919, 86, MEWC; Jaeger, *Man with Six Senses*, 21, 134; Leonardi, *Dangerous by Degrees*, 110–127; Brian Stableford, *Scientific Romance in Britain, 1890–1950* (London: Fourth Estate, 1985), 267.

49. *Second Annual Report*, MCL; notes on xeroxing, *Only Eight Failures*, 6, SA/FPA/ A14/29 354, Wellcome; Debenham, *Birth Control*, 24–25, 103.

50. *Only Eight Failures*, 3–7, 9, 11.

51. D. Cross, 19 May 1933; Minutes, 25 May 1933, 22 June 1933, U383/CO1/AM4; Minutes, 27 Apr. 1933, 25 May 1933, 22 June 1933, U383/AM2 GHOASC.

52. "innuendo," "accorded greater consideration," "maternity welfare": *Manchester and Salford Woman Citizen*, 15 Feb. 1927 and 24 Sept. 1926, 20 Mar. 1931; Beaumont, *Housewives and Citizens*, 3, 81; Debenham, *Birth Control*, 50–52.

53. *Manchester and Salford Woman Citizen*, 28 Oct. 1929.

54. "contrary to the Ministry": *Manchester and Salford Woman Citizen*, 15 June 1927; *Second Annual Report*, 8, MCL; "Campbell, Dame Janet Mary (1877–1954)," *Oxford Dictionary of National Biography*, 25 May 2006.

55. Beaumont, *Housewives and Citizens*, 83; Fisher, *Birth Control, Sex, and Mar-riage*, 30; *Manchester and Salford Woman Citizen*, 16 Apr. 1930; *Only Eight Failures*.

56. Fisher, *Birth Control, Sex, and Marriage*, 149–151; Beaumont, *Housewives and Citizens*, 82; Debenham, *Birth Control*, 81; *Manchester Guardian*, 16 May 1934, 22 May 1939; Manchester, Salford, and District Family Planning Clinic, *The Non-Persistent Patient* [1955?], SA/FPA/A14/29 354, Wellcome; Minutes, 20 Jan. 1939, U383/AM3, GHOASC; Manchester, Salford and District Mothers' Clinic, *Annual Report* (1954), MCL.

57. "And don't forget": CUF newsletter, 6 Jan. 1941, MS Eng. c. 7045, Bodleian; Tania McIntosh, *A Social History of Maternity and Childbirth: Key Themes in Maternity Care* (London: Routledge, 2012), 45, 47; *Manchester and Salford Woman Citizen*, 15 Feb. 1926.

58. McIntosh, *A Social History*, 52, 64; *Manchester and Salford Woman Citizen*, February 1935; *Manchester Guardian*, 28 Nov. 1934; "that childbirth is," "the centre of interest": Frankenburg, *Not Old*, 85, 128–129; "I always said," "is a normal pain": Fran-kenburg Manchester Studies 1045, Tameside.

59. *Manchester and Salford Woman Citizen*, 19 Dec. 1930, 20 Jan. 1931, 20 Feb. 1931, 20 Mar. 1931; "idiotic," "a hot cup of tea": Frankenburg interview, 8SUF/B/144, WL; Gwenith

Siobhan Cross, "'A Midwife at Every Confinement': Midwifery and Medicalized Childbirth in Ontario and Britain, 1920–1950," *Canadian Bulletin of Medical History* 31, no. 1 (2014), 147; Frankenburg, *Not Old*, 128; "a bit too sold": Frankenburg Manchester Studies 1045, Tameside; "misguided:" *Guardian*, 5 Aug. 1964; McIntosh, *A Social History*, 49–50.

60. Frankenburg, *Not Old*, 126, 131; "should co-operate with other organisations": *Manchester and Salford Woman Citizen*, February 1935.

61. Frankenburg, *Not Old*, 130–132; Cross, "A Midwife," 141, 143; *Manchester Guardian*, 10 July 1931, 25 July 1936; "the man who got me the seat": Frankenburg Manchester Studies 1045, Tameside; Hunter, "Midwifery, 1920–2000" 154–155; McIntosh, *A Social History*, 45–46, 69–70.

62. Frankenburg, *Not Old*, 130; *Midwives Chronicle and Nursing Notes*, August 1973, SA/FPA/A14/29 354, Wellcome; "avoid an atmosphere": *Manchester Guardian*, 16 June 1936, 15 Feb. 1943, 14 Dec. 1943.

63. David Thackeray, "At the Heart of the Party? The Women's Conservative Organisation in the Age of Partial Suffrage, 1914–28," Clarisse Berthezène, "The Middlebrow and the Making of a 'New Common Sense': Women's Voluntarism, Conservative Politics and Representations of Womanhood," and Julie V. Gottlieb, "Modes and Models of Conservative Women's Leadership in the 1930s," in *Rethinking Right-Wing Women: Gender and the Conservative Party, 1880s to the Present*, eds. Clarisse Berthezène and Julie V. Gottlieb (Manchester, UK: Manchester University Press, 2018), 49, 55, 89–103, 107, 109; David Thackeray, *Conservatism for the Democratic Age: Conservative Cultures and the Challenge of Mass Politics in Early Twentieth Century England* (Manchester, UK: Manchester University Press, 2013); Light, *Forever England*; Ross McKibbin, *The Ideologies of Class: Social Relations in Britain, 1880–1950* (Oxford: Clarendon Press, 1990), 259–293; Frankenburg, *Not Old*, 123.

64. "old feudal idea": Frankenburg Manchester Studies 1045, Tameside; "forest of arms," "Now, hands up": Frankenburg, *Not Old*, 143; Berthezène, "The Middlebrow," 112; "the dirtiest trick," "And a few days": Frankenburg interview, 8SUF/B/144, WL.

65. Frankenburg interview, 8SUF/B/144, WL; "said I was," "I wasn't a real lady," "I've had some funny": Frankenburg Manchester Studies 1045, Tameside; "caricature of my city": *Manchester and Salford Woman Citizen*, 20 Sept. 1933; "the calm effrontery": *Manchester and Salford Woman Citizen*, 20 Nov. 1933.

CHAPTER 8: SLEEPLESS NIGHTS

1. Notes on Munday, 7/3, Certificate, Oct. 1917, 2a/4, Emily Penrose, 21 Apr. 1918, 2b/6, MSBC; [Anthony Munday], *John a Kent and John a Cumber* (Oxford: Printed for the Malone Society at Oxford University Press, 1923), ix.

2. Curriculum Vitae, Marjorie M. Barber, 5/4, MSBC; "Good morning," "I am going," "I think everyone": Elvira Niles to author, 25 Apr. 2018; "an inspiration," "probably a frustrated actress": Miriam Karlin, *Some Sort of a Life* (London: Oberon Books, 2007); "Miss M. M. Barber," *South Hampstead High School Magazine* 68 (1954).

3. Alfred W. Pollard and Marjorie M. Barber, *Chaucer's Canterbury Tales: The Pardoner's Tale* (London: Macmillan, 1929); "What was the Elizabethan," "the feminist movement": Marjorie M. Barber, *Classified Questions in English Literature* (London: Sidgwick & Jackson Ltd., 1928), 9, 16, 64; "virgin motherhood," "After all": "A Livelier Iris," 14, 5/6 MSBC.

4. Darbishire to MSB, 21 Jan. 1921, 1/3; H. Goodman reference, 11 Apr. 1918, 2b/6, MSBC; W. P. Ker reference, 24 June 1920, 2b/6, MSBC; Percy Simpson reference, 30 Jan. 1920, 2b/6, MSBC; "in the teeth": Darbishire reference, 22 Mar. [1920], 2b/6, MSBC; "Muriel St. Clare Byrne 1894–1983," *Somerville College Report and Supplement 1982*.

5. Percy Simpson to MSB, 20 Jan. 1920, 2b/6; Will addition, 21 July 1964, 2a/4, MSBC.

6. Darbishire to MSB, 21 Jan. 1921, 1/3, MSBC.

7. Darbishire to MSB, 5 Feb. 1921, 1/3, MSBC.

8. Probate 1923, Artemisia Desdemona Byrne, Ancestry.co.uk; Invoice, 1 Aug. 1923, 2a/1; Certificate, 28 Mar. 1923; Kenneth Barnes to MSB, 17 Oct. 1923, 2a/4, MSBC; "Muriel St. Clare Byrne 1894–1983"; "Arrangements in the Department of English Literature for the Easter Term 1937," D402, RHUL; "for her stylish delivery": K. Tillotson, "Muriel St Clare Byrne and Bedford College," January 1984, PP56/A/6/6, RHUL.

9. Diaries, 2c/8, MSBC; Anne Witchard, "Sink Street: The Sapphic World of Pre-Chinatown Soho," in *Sex, Time and Place: Queer Histories of London, c. 1850 to the Present*, eds. Simon Avery and Katherine M. Graham (London: Bloomsbury, 2016), 221; Judith R. Walkowitz, *Nights Out: Life in Cosmopolitan London* (New Haven, CT: Yale University Press, 2012); Matt Houlbrook, *Queer London: Perils and Pleasures in the Sexual Metropolis, 1918–1957* (Chicago: University of Chicago Press, 2005).

10. "stretched as far," "the casual arrangement": "Aquarium," 5/6 MSBC; Deborah Cohen, *Household Gods: The British and Their Possessions* (New Haven, CT: Yale University Press, 2009); Matt Cook, *Queer Domesticities: Homosexuality and Home Life in Twentieth-Century London* (Houndmills, UK: Palgrave Macmillan, 2014).

11. "the luckiest cat," "You're lucky": Marjorie M. Barber, "To Michael," 30 Jan. 1925, 5/4, MSBC; "stomach trouble": *Hints to Cat Lovers* (London: A. F. Sherley & Co., 1925), 5/3, MSBC.

12. Anna Clark, *Alternative Histories of the Self: A Cultural History of Sexuality and Secrets, 1780–1917* (London: Bloomsbury, 2017); Laura Doan and Jane Garrity, eds., *Sapphic Modernities: Sexuality, Women and National Culture* (New York: Palgrave Macmillan, 2006); Laura Doan, *Disturbing Practices: History, Sexuality, and Women's Experiences of Modern War* (Chicago: University of Chicago Press, 2013); Koven, *The Match Girl*, 138–139, 244–245; Mo Moulton, "*Bricks and Flowers*: Representations of Gender and Queer Life in Interwar Britain," in *British Queer History: New Approaches and Perspectives*, ed. Brian Lewis (Manchester, UK: Manchester University Press, 2013).

13. Caroline Derry, "Lesbianism and Feminist Legislation in 1921: the Age of Consent and 'Gross Indecency between Women,'" *History Workshop Journal* (2018); Jodie Medd, *Lesbian Scandal and the Culture of Modernism* (Cambridge: Cambridge University Press, 2012), 3–4, 197.

14. Hall, "Sentimental Follies," 131, 137; Barbara Reynolds to Christopher Dean, 13 Oct. 2000, 25.222; 23 Oct. 2000, 25.220; 1 Oct. 2000, 25.217, DLSA; Dorothy L. Sayers, *Unnatural Death* (London: Gollancz, 1935); Sayers, *Strong Poison*; Dorothy L. Sayers, *The Five Red Herrings* (London: Gollancz, 1931); Leonardi, *Dangerous by Degrees*, 64–78; "inverts make me": Barbara Reynolds, "'Dear Jim . . . ' The Reconstruction of a Friendship," *Seven: An Anglo-American Literary Review* 17 (2000), 56; Anna Kisby, "Vera 'Jack' Holme: Cross-Dressing Actress, Suffragette and Chauffeur," *Women's History Review* 23, no. 1 (2014), 132.

15. "the sanest, most generous," "associated with rackety": Muriel Jaeger, *Retreat from Armageddon* (London: Duckworth, 1936), 39–41; Muriel Jaeger, *Experimental Lives from Cato to George Sand* (London: G. Bell & Sons, 1932), 183.

16. "the very ardour": notebook, 3, MSBC; "your hair, just stirring": M. St. Clare Byrne, "Devachan," 7c, MSBC; "inconsistent," "ostracize the love-perversions": M. St. Clare Byrne, *Cash Down*, 7d, MSBC; "your hand, slender": M. St. Clare Byrne, "The Bee," 7d, MSBC; "If I owned the earth": M. St. Clare Byrne, Untitled, 7d, MSBC; "I only know I loved her": Marjorie Barber, "Sonata," (1923), 5/4, MSBC: "Half of me": Marjorie Barber, "Once upon a time," 5/4, MSBC; "A golden spell": Marjorie Barber, "The City Beautiful" (1924), 5/4, MSBC.

17. "I had the gadzookery": Byrne, *Common or Garden Child*, 114–115; "continuous help": M. St. Clare Byrne, *Elizabethan Life in Town and Country* (London: Methuen & Co. Ltd., 1925), v.

18. Billie Melman, *The Culture of History: English Uses of the Past 1800–1953* (Oxford: Oxford University Press, 2006), 187–188, 195; Peter Mandler, *History and National Life* (London: Profile Books, 2002), 61; "a naturally gifted": Byrne, *Elizabethan Life*, 2.

19. "the daily life": Byrne, *Elizabethan Life*, v, 11, 129, 144–145, 243, 265; Laura Carter, "The Quennells and the 'History of Everyday Life' in England, c. 1918–69," *History Workshop Journal* 81, no. 1 (April 2016).

20. "thick-headed," "they say commonly": M. St. Clare Byrne, ed., *The Elizabethan Home: Discovered in Two Dialogues by Claudius Hollyband and Peter Erondell*, 2nd ed. (London: Cobden-Sanderson, 1930); "superstition and fact": M. St. Clare Byrne, ed., *The Elizabethan Zoo: A Book of Beasts Both Fabulous and Authentic* (London: Frederick Etchells & Hugh Macdonald, 1926), vii.

21. "An Elizabethan portrait": "How the Money Went," 7/6, MSBC; "The historian to whom the ordinary": *Sunday Times*, 17 Nov. 1935, 7/7, MSBC.

22. Laura Carter, "Women Historians in the Twentieth Century," in *Precarious Professionals: Gender, Identity and Social Change in Modern British History*, eds. Heidi Egginton and Zoë Thomas (London: Institute for Historical Research, 2019); "left us a bundle": "The Mother of Francis Bacon"; "vigorous, masterful women": "The First Lady Burghley," 7/6, MSBC.

23. M. St. Clare Byrne, ed., *The Letters of King Henry VIII: A Selection, with a Few Other Documents* (London: Cassell & Co. Ltd., 1936), ix; "We invite our fate," "the lost moment": M. St. Clare Byrne, ed., *The Lisle Letters*, vol. I (Chicago: University of Chicago Press, 1981), 2; K. Tillotson, "Muriel St. Clare Byrne and Bedford College," January 1984, PP56/A/6/6 RHUL; "I must say": Byron Rogers, "The Letters from Lord Lisle," *Telegraph Sunday Magazine*, 10.538, DLSA.

24. Mandler, *History*, 51–52; Michael Saler, *The Avant-Garde in Interwar England: Medieval Modernism and the London Underground* (Oxford: Oxford University Press, 1999), viii.

CHAPTER 9: DEPARTURES AND REUNIONS

1. "England and Wales National Probate Calendar (Index of Wills and Administrations) 1858–1966," Ancestry.co.uk; Passenger manifest for Yorkshire (Bibby Line), embarked 10 Dec. 1925; Passenger manifest for M.S. Sibajak, Rotterdam Lloyd Royal

Dutch Mail, departing 16 Dec. 1938; *The Times*, 22 Dec. 1928, 22 Mar. 1933, 24 May 1960.

2. *Bryn Mawr College Calendar Graduate Courses* 1921 and 1922; Middlemore to Aydelotte, 17 June [1922]; Aydelotte to Middlemore, 16 Oct. 1923; Aydelotte to Herman Ames, 9 Oct. 1923; Aydelotte Papers, FHL; *Phoenix* (Swarthmore College), 19 Sept. 1922.

3. "they are giving something": *Phoenix* (Swarthmore College), 15 Apr. 1924 and 10 Jan. 1928, 12 May 1925, 12 Jan. 1926, 29 Sept. 1925, 1 May 1923, 7 Nov. 1922; Ancestry. co.uk, ship's manifest, Andania (Cunard Line), departing Aug. 26, 1923; "kitchen maid of unbeautiful aspect": *College News* (Bryn Mawr), 22 Mar. 1922; "To comb her hair": *The Halcyon* (Swarthmore College yearbook), 1924, 306.

4. Harold Goddard to Aydelotte, 22 Apr. 1926, Aydelotte Papers, FHL; "I am so very sorry": Middlemore to Aydelotte, 28 July [1926] and 15 May [1927] Aydelotte Papers, FHL; Aydelotte to Middlemore, 17 Aug. 1926, 4 May 1927, Aydelotte Papers, FHL; "affectionate thanks": Middlemore to Goddard, 10 Apr. 1928, Aydelotte Papers, FHL; *Phoenix* (Swarthmore College), 27 Apr. 1926, 4 May 1926, 11 May 1926, 1 Sept. 1926, 21 Sept. 1926, 22 May 1928; Ancestry.co.uk, ship's manifest, Majestic (White Star Line), arriving 11 June 1926; Passenger manifest, New York to Plymouth on Rijndam (Holland America Line), arriving 16 July 1928.

5. "Certified Copy of an Entry of Death," 18 July 1931, Amphilis Throckmorton Middlemore, certified at the General Register Office, 1 May 2012; Amphilis T. Middlemore, last will and testament, 25 Apr. 1929, proved 20 Oct. 1931; "a delightful person": Frankenburg interview, 8SUF/B/144, WL.

6. DLS to people, 18 Sept. 1922, 8 Oct. 1922, 89 MEWC; "does like pigs": Rowe to DLS, 17 July 1922, 427, MEWC; DLS to Ivy, 13 Aug. 1924, 55, MEWC; "If it had not been": Sayers, *Whose Body?*; DLS to mother, 25 Aug. 1924, Reynolds, *Letters*, vol. 1.

7. "Jim Jaeger is writing": Sayers to mother, 17 Dec. 1925, 92, MEWC; Leonard Woolf to Jaeger, 28 Sept. 1925, Collett; "who was rather that way": quoted in Reynolds, "Dear Jim," 55–57.

8. Jaeger, *Man with Six Senses*, 12–13; M. Jaeger, *The Question Mark* (London: Hogarth Press, 1926); Leonardi, *Dangerous by Degrees*, 110; Stableford, *Scientific Romance*, 252–254.

9. Draft Curriculum Vitae in *Before Victoria*, by Muriel Jaeger (London: Chatto & Windus, 1956), Collett; Frances Phillips to Jaeger, 22 Nov. 1932, Collett; J. F. Fern to Jaeger, 7 Oct. 1932, Collett; David Higham to Jaeger, 15 Aug. 1935, Collett; "analytical Detective Story": Alan Harris to Jaeger, 22 Jan. 1937 and 19 May 1933, Collett; Muriel Jaeger, "Murder at Hangerden," Collett; Muriel Jaeger, *Hermes Speaks* (London: Duckworth, 1933); Stableford, *Scientific Romance*, 267.

10. "Monthly Fixture Card," Feb. 1933, BLTC; "One's friends are quick": Muriel Jaeger, *The Sanderson Soviet: A Comedy in Three Acts* (London: Samuel French, 1934), 13–14; Rowe to Jaeger, 25 June 1933, 22 Oct. 1933, 6 July 1935, Collett.

11. "first reader": Jaeger, *Before Victoria*; Muriel Jaeger, last will and testament, 8 Nov. 1967, proved 15 Apr. 1970; Elizabeth J. Morse, "Jaeger, Muriel," *Oxford Dictionary of National Biography*, 23 Sept. 2004.

12. "very close to her heart": DLS to mother, 2 Mar. 1925, 92, MEWC; Brabazon, *Dorothy L. Sayers*, 141.

13. Brabazon, *Dorothy L. Sayers*, 151; "By the way, many thanks": DLS to Frankenburg, 5 Mar. 1929, 437, MEWC; Helena Wright, *The Sex-Factor in Marriage: A Book for Those Who Are or Are About to Be Married* (London: Noel Douglas, 1930).

14. DLS to Frankenburg, 5 Mar. 1929, 437, MEWC.

15. "Somerville College Jubilee," 3/1, MSBC.

16. Dorothy L. Sayers, *Gaudy Night* (London: Gollancz, 1935), 326, 331.

17. Diaries, 1929–31, 2c/8, MSBC.

18. "the right kind of oil-stove"": M. St. Clare Byrne, "The Heart Stood Up," 7/6 MSBC; Diaries, 1929, 1931–1933, 2c/8 MSBC.

19. "Never do I forget": Rowe to MSB, 20 June 1979, 4/3, MSBC; Dorothy Rowe, "Record E.489 (Chorale from Cantata No. 147, Bach)," Aug. 1929, 8/4 MSBC.

20. List, 8/4 MSBC.

21. Dorothy Rowe, "Raphael's 'Michael'," 8/4 MSBC; Dorothy Rowe, "twelve steps above": "In the National Gallery," 8/4 MSBC; "How many days": Dorothy Rowe, "For a Diary," 8/4 MSBC.

22. "book-lined groove": M. St. Clare Byrne, "The Student of Literature," 7d MSBC; "I would build you": M. St. Clare Byrne, "Song and Ship," 7d, MSBC.

23. Marjorie Barber, "Lucifer: a Moral Tale," 5/4, MSBC.

24. "The Memories of Muriel St. Clare Byrne," 6.666, DLSA.

25. "full of Scotch scenery": DLS to MSB, 30 Oct. 1930, 185b, MEWC; Diaries 1928, 1930 2c/8 MSBC.

26. DLS to Pearn, 30 Apr. 1934, MS308, Smith; DLS to MSB, [1934?], 629, MEWC; DLS to MSB, 26 Apr. 1934, 185b, MEWC; "Her book may be meant": "A Study of Henry VIII," *Sunday Times*, 7/7 MSBC; Diaries 1933–1935, 2c/8, MSBC; "Love to you both": Violet (no last name) to MSB, 6 Feb. 1934, 1/9, MSBC.

27. Diary, 1932, 2c/8 MSBC; "if you are still": DLS to MSB, 27 May 1933, 185b, MEWC; "various culinary & domestic": DLS to MSB, 13 Jan. 1934, 185b, MEWC; "no need to hasten": DLS to MSB, 27 Oct. 1934, 185b, MEWC; "Mistresse Byrne": DLS to MSB, 10 Oct. 1934, 185b, MEWC; DLS to MSB, 20 Mar. 1933, 30 Apr. 1934, 185b, MEWC.

28. "paradoxical as it may seem": Dorothy L. Sayers, *Strong Meat* (London: Hodder & Stoughton, 1939), 13; "when we were all": Rowe to Geoffrey Lee, 17 Nov. 1985, 25.859; "youth was a worrying": "Life Begins at 40, Says Miss Sayers," *Hampstead and Highgate Express* [1954?] 10.427, DLSA; "my follies": Dorothy Rowe, "Forgiveness," 8/4 MSBC; "Youth gone?": Dorothy Rowe, "Youth Gone," 8/4 MSBC.

CHAPTER 10: SUBVERSIVE SPINSTER

1. "one need not": *Baby Spot*, June 1938, BLTC.

2. "brought up without": DLS to Maurice Reckitt, 19 Nov. 1941; Barbara Reynolds, *The Letters of Dorothy L. Sayers*, vol. 2, *From Novelist to Playwright, 1937–1942* (Swavesey, UK: Dorothy L. Sayers Society, 1997); Lisa Regan, *Winifred Holtby's Social Vision: "Members One of Another"* (London: Pickering & Chatto, 2012), 4–5.

3. DLS to mother, 15 Feb. 1923, 90; Rowe to DLS, 27 Dec. 1937, [24?] Apr. 1938, 427, MEWC; CUF newsletter, 19–20 Apr. 1941, 9 May 1942, MS Eng. c. 7045-7, Bodleian.

4. "is qualified to put": "D.H.R. Member of Staff," 20; Talbot Heath, "Anthea Bell Talks about Dorothy Rowe," 24 Sept. 2014, https://vimeo.com/107024493; "you would have approved": Rowe to DLS, 2 Jan. [1939] and 27 Dec. 1937, 427, MEWC.

5. "a particularly crude": "Bournemouth Little Theatre Club," 6.669, DLSA; Keith Rawlings, *The Bournemouth Little Theatre Club 1919–2007* (Bournemouth, 2007), 2; "Bournemouth Little Theatre Club," 6.669, DLSA.

6. Claire Cochrane, *Twentieth-Century British Theatre: Industry, Art and Empire* (Cambridge: Cambridge University Press, 2011), 71, 74–75, 109; Michael Dobson, *Shakespeare and Amateur Performance: A Cultural History* (Cambridge: Cambridge University Press, 2011), 18, 105; "Bournemouth Little Theatre Club," 6.669, DLSA; Annual reports July 1924, June 1930, brochure Sept. 1929, BLTC; "full of lovely": DLS to parents, 31 Oct. 1920, Reynolds, *Letters*, vol. 1.

7. CUF newsletter, 19–20 Apr. 1941, MS Eng. c. 7045, Bodleian.

8. "Palace Court Theatre Celebrates Its 21st Birthday," *Echo*, [Dec. 1951]; Annual General Meetings 24 June 1929, 25 June 1928, 6 July 1936; *Annual Report* June 1926, BLTC; "Well, perhaps they do not": "Bournemouth Little Theatre Club," 6.669, DLSA.

9. Annual reports, 1926–1939, BLTC; "than that of any similar": *Times and Directory*, 2 Nov. 1929, BLTC; "a central home": "Preliminary Report of the Commission to investigate the 'Little Theatre' Project," BLTC.

10. Cochrane, *British Theatre*, 131–135; Katharine Cockin, *Edith Craig and the Theatres of Art* (London: Bloomsbury, 2017); Dobson, *Shakespeare*, 106–107; Articles of Association, Bournemouth Little Theatre Limited, BLTC; *BLT Annual Report*, 6 June 1930, BLTC; clippings Aug. 1930, "Schedule for Foundation Stone Laying Ceremony," 6 Dec. 1930, BLTC; "LUCK TO THE THEATRE": telegram 15 June 1931, BLTC.

11. "without being luxorious": *Everyman*, 25 June 1931, BLTC; *Times and Directory*, 13 June 1931, BLTC; Keith Rawlings, *Just Bournemouth* (Stanbridge, UK: Dovecote Press, 2005), 43.

12. "They were building their own": "Bournemouth's Little Theatre Opens Its Doors," [*Echo*], 15 June 1931, BLTC; "the value of personal expression": "Another Theatric Garden Party," [*Echo*?], [August 1931?], BLTC; "mass production methods": C. B. Purdom, "Bournemouth's Little Theatre," *Everyman*, 25 June 1931, BLTC.

13. "Extraordinary General Meeting Report," 5 Apr. 1933, BLTC; *Daily Telegraph*, 23 June 1932, BLTC; Leslie Goodwin to members, 28 Sept. 1932, BLTC; "Bournemouth Little Theatre Club," [1934?], BLTC; *Baby Spot*, April 1935, June 1934, BLTC; *Annual Report*,1 June 1935, BLTC; Annual General Meetings, 21 July 1937, 7 July 1939, BLTC; *News Chronicle*, 19 Jan. 1938, BLTC.

14. Cochrane, *British Theatre*, 117.

15. "offered realistic tragedy": H. Mallam-Williams, "The Selection Committee Replies," *Spotlight*, June 1930, BLTC; "Let us, in the name": Leslie Reid, "Emma," *Baby Spot*, January 1938, BLTC; Cochrane, *British Theatre*, 122.

16. "the audience can take": Rowe to Jaeger, 25 June 1933, Collett; "The damnable thing": Rowe to Jaeger, 6 July 1935, Collett.

17. Hugh Norris and Eileen Rawlings, "Dorothy Rowe, BLTC and *Diana of Dobson's*," *Bournemouth Little Theatre News*, November 2009; "loud and continuous": clipping, "Diana of Dobson's," BLTC; Program, *Diana of Dobson's*, 7 Feb. 1920, BLTC; Program, *A Bill of Divorcement*, 15–17 Oct. 1925, BLTC.

18. "all very slick": *Annual Report June 1926*; "a wonderful feat": *Baby Spot*, March 1932, BLTC; "one of the outstanding," "a long scene": *Baby Spot*, May 1936, BLTC; *Baby Spot*, April 1935, April 1936, BLTC; "the majority," "the carefully": clipping, "Little Theatre. 'Bulldog Drummond,'" BLTC; Program, *St. Joan*, 31 Mar.–7 Apr. 1936, BLTC.

19. Dorothy Rowe, "Noah," *Baby Spot*, May 1938, BLTC.

20. "Bournemouth Dramatic Club at Its Best," *Bournemouth Graphic*, BLTC.

21. Clipping, "Jane Austen's 'Emma,'" BLTC; "a fresh and entirely," "In times past": Dorothy Rowe, "The Importance of Being Earnest," *Baby Spot*, March 1938, BLTC.

22. "Do you think": Barber, *Classified Questions*, 25; "the modern clothes Hamlet": DLS to mother, 4 Sept. 1925, 92, MEWC; "as a play": M. St. Clare Byrne, "Introduction to the Illustrations," in *Prefaces to Shakespeare*, vol. 1., *Hamlet*, ed. Harley Granville-Barker (London: B. T. Batsford, 1963), xxi; M. Clare Byrne, introduction to *A History of Shakespearean Production* (London: Arts Council of Great Britain and the Society of Cultural Relations with the Soviet Union, 1948–1949), 2.

23. "almost ultra-modern": clipping, "Sheridan Up to Date," BLTC; Program, *The School for Scandal*, 21–25 Mar. 1933, BLTC; "period," "coloured tights," "always dressed," "played today," "how much more": "In Modern Dress," *Baby Spot*, Mar. 1933, BLTC.

CHAPTER 11: THE PROBLEM OF MARRIAGE

1. Teri Chettiar, "Treating Marriage as 'The Sick Entity': Gender, Emotional Life, and the Psychology of Marriage Improvement in Postwar Britain," *History of Psychology* 18, no. 3 (2015); Langhamer, *The English in Love*; Simon Szreter and Kate Fisher, *Sex Before the Sexual Revolution: Intimate Life in England 1918–1963* (Cambridge: Cambridge University Press, 2010), 56; Ann Rea, "From 'Free Love' to *Married Love*: Gender Politics, Marie Stopes, and Middlebrow Fiction by Women in the Early Nineteen Twenties," in *Aftermaths of War: Women's Movements and Female Activists, 1918–1923*, eds. Ingrid Sharp and Matthew Stibbe (Leiden, Netherlands: Brill, 2011); T. B. Rowe to Blanche Hanbury, [March 1887], MS Add. 8252/4/3, T. B. Rowe Papers, CUL; Blanche Hanbury to T. B. Rowe, 2 Aug. [1888], 11 Aug. 1888, [22–23 Aug. 1888], MS Add. 8252/3/15, 17, 23, T. B. Rowe Papers, CUL.

2. WO374/25510, NA; "He was able": Frankenburg, *Not Old*, 119–120.

3. Minutes, 28 Feb. 1935, 28 Mar. 1935, 2 May 1935, 23 May 1935, 27 June 1935, 25 July 1935, 26 Sept. 1935, 24 Oct. 1935, 28 Nov. 1935, U383/AM3, GHOASC; "desperately ill": Frankenburg, *Not Old*, 120–121.

4. Peter to Charis and Sydney, 7 Oct. 1935, MS Eng. c. 7043, Bodleian; Frankenburg, *Not Old*, 121.

5. "improve my handwriting": Peter to Charis and Sydney, 5 Nov. 1935 and 20 Oct. 1935, 4 Nov. 1935, MS Eng. c. 7043, Bodleian; Frankenburg, *Not Old*, 121.

6. Frankenburg, *Not Old*, 122, 151; Minutes, 28 Nov. 1935, U383/AM3, GHOASC; *Manchester Guardian*, 7 Dec. 1935.

7. "difficult to write," "Doubtless God," "useful caution," "always a source": Frankenburg, *Not Old*, 111, 122, 149; *Manchester Guardian*, 31 Dec. 1935.

8. "short speech," "I want you," "especially adapted": Frankenburg, *Not Old*, 122, 151; *Manchester Guardian*, 25 Nov. 1935; Minutes, 19 Dec. 1935, U383/AM3, GHOASC.

9. Annual General Meeting, 6 July 1936, BLTC; Frankenburg, *Not Old*, 152; Minutes, 21 Apr. 1937, 26 May 1937, 16 June 1937, 20 Oct. 1937, U383/AM3, GHOASC.

10. Frankenburg, *Not Old*, 152; Minutes, 21 Oct. 1938, 25 Nov. 1938, U383/AM3, GHOASC; "Do, Mum": Peter to Charis, 18 Nov. 1938, MS Eng. c. 7043, Bodleian; "You seem to be": Peter to Charis, 26 Feb. 1939, MS Eng. c. 7043, Bodleian.

11. DLS to Stocks, 8 Sept. 1947, 158, MEWC.

12. "I believe that when women": Stocks to DLS, 9 Sept. 1947, 158, MEWC; Hall, "Sentimental Follies," 138–139.

13. Brabazon, *Dorothy L. Sayers*, 116; Rowe to Ralph Clarke, 2 Sept. 1976, 25.848; "The Memories of Muriel St. Clare Byrne," 6.666, DLSA; DLS to MSB, 18 Dec. 1935, 187, MEWC; DLS to M. E. Roberts, 4 July 1936, 420a, MEWC; "married or not": Curriculum Vitae, 613, MEWC; DLS to MSB, 29 Apr. 1933, 22 Mar. 1934, 185b, MEWC.

14. "No wonder a man": Dorothy L. Sayers, *The Unpleasantness at the Bellona Club* (London: Gollancz, 1935), 54–55; Brabazon, *Dorothy L. Sayers*, 147; Ariela Freedman, "Dorothy Sayers and the Case of the Shell-Shocked Detective," *Partial Answers: Journal of Literature and the History of Ideas* 8, no. 2 (June 2010), 372; Monica Lott, "Dorothy L. Sayers, the Great War, and Shell Shock," *Interdisciplinary Literary Studies* 15, no. 1 (2013), 114.

15. [Atherton Fleming], *Gourmet's Book of Food and Drink* (London: Bodley Head, 1933).

16. "the tour that we took," "about ten," "the subject was never": MSB to Ralph Clarke, 4 Sept. 1976, 25.801, DLSA; Diary 1933, 2c/8, MSBC.

17. "Cat O'Mary," 155.

18. "impossible temperament," "the mere fact," "one can do": DLS to John Anthony Fleming, 7 Nov. 1948, Barbara Reynolds, *The Letters of Dorothy L. Sayers*, vol. 3, *A Noble Daring, 1944–1950* (Swavesey, UK: Dorothy L. Sayers Society, 1998); "What can I do": "The Memories of Muriel St. Clare Byrne," 6.666, DLSA.

19. M. St. Clare Byrne, "Two Silences," 7d, MSBC.

20. M. St. Clare Byrne, "No Villain Need Be," 7c, MSBC.

21. Diaries 1928, 1931–1932, 2c/8, MSBC; M. St. Clare Byrne and Gladys Scott Thomson, *My Lord's Books* (London: Sidgwick & Jackston, Ltd., [1932?]).

22. Byrne, *King Henry VIII*, xix.

23. Diary 1931, 2c/8, "A Walk Easter 1926," 5/2, MSBC; von Oertzen, *Science*, 3; "Copies of Documents Relating to Old Postman's Cottage, Alciston, and Professor Caroline Spurgeon," NA, http://discovery.nationalarchives.gov.uk/details/r/8b69aa2f-2d49-4ac1-8a31-d043c66bc443; Clay, *British Women Writers*, 12; Cockin, *Edith Craig*; "The History of Smallhythe Place," www.nationaltrust.org.uk/smallhythe-place/features/the-history-of-smallhythe-place; Kisby, "Vera 'Jack' Holme," 134.

24. Cullis to Olive Monkhouse, 22 Mar. 1931, D352, RHUL; Cullis to secretary, 2 Nov. 1931, D352, RHUL.

25. WO/372/23/9728, NA; Cullis to Margaret Tuke, 7 May 1923, D352, RHUL; Report, 3 Mar. 1931, D352, RHUL; Secretary to Cullis, 5 Mar. 1931, D352, RHUL; Minutes, 13 Mar. 1934, D352, RHUL.

26. Program, *The Cradle Song* preceded by *Very Well Then, Curtain*, 10–11 Feb. 1933, 5/1, MSBC; "head a little," "the lights from above": fragment, postmarked 8 July 1933, 1/6, MSBC; "realised that you like," "an old fool": Cullis to MSB, postmarked 25 Sept. 1933, 1/6, MSBC.

27. Diary 1933, 2c/8, MSCB; "Another Forest Fire": Cullis to MSB, 1933, 1/6, MSBC; "one day I shall": Cullis to MSB, "Trelusa, Thursday" [1933], 1/6, MSBC.

28. Cullis to MSB, 1933, 1/6, MSBC.

29. Cullis to MSB, postmarked 8 July 1933, 1/6, MSBC.

30. "to pretend, or act": Cullis to MSB, "Trelusa, Thursday" [1933], 1/6, MSBC; "the other you": Cullis to MSB, postmarked 21 Sept. 1933, 1/6, MSBC.

31. "a gift from the gods," "a shake," "And I could": Cullis to MSB, postmarked 8 July 1933, 1/6, MSBC; Cullis to MSB, 1933, 1/6, MSBC.

32. "was the ghost," "instead of the usual," "till we meet": Cullis to MSB "Trelusa, Thursday" [1933], 1/6, MSBC; "and you shall": Cullis to MSB, postmarked 14 Sept. 1933, 1/6, MSBC; "keep my evenings": Cullis to MSB, postmarked 21 Sept. 1933, 1/6, MSBC.

33. Cullis to MSB, postmarked 25 Sept. 1933, 1/6, MSBC.

34. Cullis to MSB, postmarked 7 Dec. 1933, 1/6, MSBC; "Love to Bar": Cullis to MSB, 16 Sept. 1935, 1/6, MSBC.

35. "so curtailed," "more sunshine": Cullis to MSB, postmarked 5 Nov. 1934, 1/6, MSBC; Diaries 1934–1936, 2c/8, MSBC; Program, *Tobias and the Angel*, 14–15 Feb. 1936, 5/1, MSBC.

36. Secretary to Cullis, 17 Dec. 1937, D352, RHUL; "I am so awfully sorry": DLS to MSB, 13 Sept. 1937, 187, MEWC.

37. "almost like being able," "a sense of companionship": Cullis to MSB, 17 Nov. [1937], 1/6, MSBC; "grimly grasping": Cullis to MSB, 22 Nov. [1937], 1/6, MSBC.

38. Cullis to MSB, 14 Dec. 1937, 9 Jan. 1938, 16 Jan. 1938, 8 Mar. [1938], 1/6, MSBC; "really attractive," "Those things": Cullis to MSB, 11 Jan. 1938, 1/6, MSBC.

39. Cullis to MSB, 30 Nov. 1937, 1/6, MSBC.

40. "You have I think": Cullis to MSB, 16 Jan. 1938, 1/6, MSBC; "has grown": Cullis to MSB, 20 Dec. 1937, 1/6, MSBC; "very ambivalent," "If my friends": Cullis to MSB, 21 Mar. [1938], 1/6, MSBC.

CHAPTER 12: DOES IT PLEASE YOU?

1. "women and love stories": Curriculum Vitae, 613, MEWC; "getting a bit," "growing older": DLS to MSB, 30 Oct. 1930, 185b, MEWC; Brittain Bright, "The Maturity of Lord Peter Wimsey and Authorial Innovation Within a Series," in *Serial Crime Fiction: Dying for More*, eds. Jean Anderson, Carolina Miranda, and Barbara Pezzotti (Houndmills, UK: Palgrave Macmillan, 2015); Stewart, *Crime Writing*, 102.

2. Sayers, *Have His Carcase*.

3. "female gigolos," "I daresay," "Nobody else": DLS to Frankenburg and Rowe, n.d., 437, MEWC; "left me with increased," "the world's boob": Rowe to MSB, 9 Jan. [1937?], 1/9, MSBC.

4. Sayers, *Murder Must Advertise*; Dorothy L. Sayers, *The Nine Tailors* (London: Gollancz, 1934); Freedman, "Shell-Shocked Detective"; Angela K. Smith, "How to Remember: War, Armistice and Memory in Post-1918 British fiction," *Journal of European Studies* 45, no. 4 (2015), 308–309; Ralph E. Hone, *Dorothy L. Sayers: A Literary Biography* (Kent, OH: Kent State University Press, 1979), 39, 63.

5. "Lord P. says": DLS to Frankenburg and Rowe, n.d., 437, MEWC.

6. Drafts and clippings of reviews, 7/7, MSBC.

7. "Oh, I'm just crazy": M. St. Clare Byrne, "All at Sea," 7c, MSBC; M. St. Clare Byrne, *Cash Down*, 7d, MSBC.

8. M. St. Clare Byrne, *Paul, a Prisoner*, 7c, MSBC.

9. "what it means": Cullis to MSB, "Trelusa, Thursday" [1933], 1/6, MSBC; Cullis to MSB, postmarked 21 Sept. 1933, 14 Sept. 1933, 1/6, MSBC; Violet (no last name) to MSB, 6 Feb. 1934, 1/9, MSBC; Charlotte (no last name) to MSB, n.d., 7e, MSBC.

10. M. St. Clare Byrne, "England's Elizabeth," 7c, MSBC; "a work of great," "harboured a genius": Cullis to MSB, postmarked 20 Apr. 1935, 1/6, MSBC; "I think Miss Byrne": Cullis to MSB, postmarked 21 Apr. 1935, 1/6, MSBC; Posters, 5/1, MSBC; *Evening Standard*, 5 Nov. 1936, 12.20, DLSA; Cockin, *Edith Craig*; *The Times*, 1 Oct. 1928.

11. "what no jury": *The People*, 2 Oct. 1932, 7e, MSBC; *The Times*, 10 Oct. 1932; M. St. Clare Byrne *Well, Gentleman . . . ?*, and Program, *Well, Gentleman . . . ?*, 9 Oct. 1932, 7e, MSBC.

12. "a detective thriller": Jaeger, *Hermes Speaks*, 132; "that's where the money": DLS to parents, [17?] Aug. 1923, 90, MEWC; "in Ur of the Chaldees": DLS to MSB, 29 Apr. 1933, 185b, MEWC; M. St. Clare Byrne, "Theatre-Going a Hundred Years Ago," 7/7, MSBC; M. St. Clare Byrne, "Double—and Quits!" 7d, MSBC.

13. Diary 1935, 2c/8, MSBC; "about this play," "mapped": MSB to Ralph Clarke, 4 Sept. 1976, 4/4, MSBC; "proprietary," "new versions": MSB to Janet Hitchman, 21 July 1967, 25.370, DLSA.

14. Elvira Niles to author, 25 Apr. 2018; Memorial for Graham Brooke Barber, 5/3, MSBC. I am indebted to Theadora Fisher for the point about the physical resemblance. For an alternate queer reading, see Marya McFadden, "Queerness at Shrewsbury: Homoerotic Desire in *Gaudy Night*," *Modern Fiction Studies* 46, no. 2 (Summer 2000).

15. "honest 50-50": MSB to Hitchman, 21 July 1967, 25.370, DLSA; "murder-machine": DLS to MSB, 14 Feb. 1935, 185b, MEWC; DLS to MSB, 6 Mar. 1935, 185b, MEWC; "Your partner in guilt": DLS to MSB, 16 Feb. 1935, 424, MEWC; "What about 4 acts": DLS MS-38, MEWC; DLS MS-17, MS-33, MEWC; Diary 1935, 2c/8, MSBC; MSB to Ralph Clarke, 4 Sept. 1976, 4/4, MSBC.

16. *Evening Standard*, 5 Nov. 1936, 12.20, DLSA.

17. "I find it": DLS to MSB, 16 Feb. 1935, 424, MEWC; "if you think": DLS to MSB, 15 Mar. 1935, 185b, MEWC.

18. "undoubtedly," "This won't worry," "the audience are not": DLS to MSB, 15 Mar. 1935, 185b, MEWC; "With your help": MSB to DLS, [Mar. 1935], 424, MEWC.

19. DLS to MSB, 15 Mar. 1935, 185b, MEWC; "worked over Act II": MSB to DLS, [Mar. 1935], 424, MEWC.

20. "the complete sincerity": Dorothy L. Sayers and M. St. Clare Byrne, *Busman's Honeymoon: A Detective Comedy in Three Acts* (London: Gollancz, 1937), 8; "I don't think": DLS to MSB, 16 Feb. 1935, 424, MEWC; "Why can't I": DLS to MSB, n.d., 629, MEWC.

21. Character sketches, DLS MS-30, MEWC; Sayers and Byrne, *Busman's Honeymoon: A Detective Comedy*, 108.

22. "Tell Bar," "the old boy," "But if it really": DLS to MSB, 15 Mar. 1935, 185b, MEWC; "I feel sure": MSB to DLS, [Mar. 1935], 424, MEWC.

23. "except for the infernal," "We have come": DLS to MSB, 6 Mar. 1935, 185b, MEWC; "I think that," "which is bound," "Please don't mind": DLS to MSB, 30 Mar. 1935, 186, MEWC.

24. "It will have to be": DLS to MSB, n.d., 629, MEWC; "I have made": DLS to MSB, 14 Apr. 1935, 186, MEWC; "curious and (to me)," "I don't want": 1 Apr. 1935, 186, MEWC; "What kind of life": Sayers and Byrne, *Busman's Honeymoon: A Detective Comedy*, 118–119.

25. "dreadfully contrite": MSB to DLS, [Mar. 1935], 424, MEWC; "Curse this ruddy": DLS to MSB, 15 Apr. 1935, 186, MEWC; "Peter must be": DLS to MSB, 1 Apr.

1935, 186, MEWC; "gloomy," "everything is bound": DLS to MSB, 7 Apr. 1935, 186, MEWC; "What I should have done": DLS to MSB, 2 Apr. 1935, 186, MEWC; "I must try": DLS to MSB, 17 Apr. 1935, 186, MEWC; "cursing continually": DLS to Una Ellis-Fermor, 6 Dec. [1940?], 441b, MEWC.

26. "the world's most awkward," "both so touchy": DLS to MSB, 24 June 1935, 186, MEWC; "for whereas our late": DLS to MSB 19 Aug. 1935, 186, MEWC.

27. DLS to MSB, 8 Sept. 1935, 187, MEWC.

28. "Life isn't long": DLS to MSB, 24 June 1935, 186, MEWC; "the kind of thing": DLS to MSB, 2 Apr. 1935, 186, MEWC; "Anything you decide": DLS to MSB, 9 May 1935, 186, MEWC.

29. DLS to MSB, 22 Aug. 1935, MEWC.

30. "the perfect Peter," "is BROKEN": DLS to MSB, 6 Mar. 1935, 185b, MEWC; "rather frightens me": Haddon to MSB, 31 May 1935, 186, MEWC; "to meet Ridley": DLS to MSB, 15 Apr. 1935, 186, MEWC; Reynolds, *Dorothy L. Sayers*, 299.

31. MSB to Ralph Clarke, 4 Sept. 1976, 4/4, MSBC; "struggling with the," "nobody could": DLS to MSB, 18 Dec. 1935, 187, MEWC.

32. Dorothy L. Sayers, *Busman's Honeymoon: A Love Story with Detective Interruptions* (London: Gollancz, 1937), 10, 20; Timothy Willem Jones, "Love, Honour and Obey? Romance, Subordination and Marital Subjectivity in Interwar Britain," in *Love and Romance in Britain, 1918–1970*, eds. Alana Harris and Timothy Willem Jones (Houndmills, UK: Palgrave Macmillan, 2015), 124, 134–136; Lucy Delap, "Conservative Values, Anglicans and the Gender Order in Inter-War Britain," in *Brave New World: Imperial and Democratic Nation-Building in Britain Between the Wars*, eds. Laura Beers and Geraint Thomas (London: Institute of Historical Research, 2011), 156–159.

33. Rowe to MSB, 30 Apr. 1936, 424, MEWC.

34. "secured a bungalow," "in a good": Barber to DLS, 23 Aug. [1936], 423b, MEWC; "the thing," "that you and Muriel": DLS to Barber, 24 Aug. 1936, 423b, MEWC; MSB to Ralph Clarke, 4 Sept. 1976, 4/4, MSBC.

35. MSB to Ralph Clarke, 4 Sept. 1976, 25.801, DLSA.

36. Diary 1936, 2c/8, MSBC; MSB to Ralph Clarke, 4 Sept. 1976, 25.801, DLSA; "fraught with an appalling," "What kind of life": DLS to Maurice Browne, 31 Dec. 1936, Reynolds, *Letters*, vol. 1.

37. "There was a bit," "I really do not": DLS to MSB, 4 Jan. 1937, 187, MEWC; Robinson, "Mysterious Politics," 228; Marshik, *At the Mercy of their Clothes*, 127, 137–139; K. D. M. Snell, "A Drop of Water from a Stagnant Pool? Inter-war Detective Fiction and the Rural Community," *Social History* 35, no. 1 (2010), 30; Alison Light, *Mrs. Woolf and the Servants: An Intimate History of Domestic Life in Bloomsbury* (New York: Bloomsbury Press, 2008); Lucy Delap, "Kitchen Sink Laughter: Domestic Service Humor in Twentieth-Century Britain," *Journal of British Studies* 49 (July 2010).

CHAPTER 13: WHAT THE BUSMAN WROUGHT

1. "as an unrehearsed": MSB to Ralph Clarke, 4 Sept. 1976, 25.801; MSB to Hitchman, 21 July 1967, 25.370, DLSA; [Higham] to MSB, 30 Dec. 1936, 268; DLS (secretary) to H. Brown, 22 Oct. 1954, 319, MEWC; DLS to Barber, 17 July 1937, Reynolds, *Letters*, vol. 2; DLS to Pearn, 30 Sept. 1937, MS308, Smith.

2. "was graciously patronised": "The Tales of Timothy and Toby," 4/3, MSBC; "one of the lost," "We've got a cat," "The cat never": M. St. Clare Byrne, "Those Scotch

Dogs," *Housewife*, November 1940, 7/7, MSBC; Rowe to MSB, 9 Jan. [1937?], 1/9; Diary 1937, 2c/8; MSB, 5 Dec. 1951, 5/2, MSBC.

3. DLS to Barber, 17 July 1937, Reynolds, *Letters*, vol. 2; "at demi-pension": Barber to DLS, 19 July [1937], 423b, MEWC; "asks humbly intelligent": Barber to MSB, n.d., 5/1, MSBC; Dorothy L. Sayers, *Love All* (Perth, Scotland: Tippermuir Books, 2015).

4. "not poisoning your," "presents": DLS to MSB and Barber, 8 Sept. [1937] 186, MEWC; "It is true": DLS to MSB, [1937], 13 Sept. 1937, 187, MEWC.

5. "Well, let's try," "that Busman is": DLS to MSB, 13 Sept. 1937 and 20 Oct. 1937, 187, MEWC; Diary 1937, 2c/8, MSBC.

6. "sabbatical," "necessary mainly": MSB to unknown, 1 Feb. 1940, 1/7, MSBC; "rousing parallel": Rowe to MSB, 9 Jan. [1937?] and 31 Jan. 1938, 1/9, MSBC.

7. "rabbit-teeth," "such checks," "leave to state": DLS to MSB, 2 May 1936 and 18 Dec. 1935, 26 Jan. 1936, 187, MEWC.

8. Brabazon, *Dorothy L. Sayers*, 158; DLS to C. W. Scott-Giles, 25 Mar. 1936, Reynolds, *Letters*, vol. 1; "delicate & fastidious," "two gifted youths": [MSB], "Wimsification in the Eliz. Manner," 4/2, MSBC; M. St. Clare Byrne, reviews of books by Percy Allen (15 Oct. 1931), Gerald H. Rendall (22 May [no year]), 7/7, MSBC; "little Wimsey joke": DLS to Rowe, 21 Dec. 1936, 28 Dec. 1937, 427, MEWC; "lovely jape," "Have none": Rowe to DLS, 24 Dec. [1936], 427, MEWC.

9. "feminist and humanitarian": DLS to H. F. Rubenstein, 18 Oct. 1946, 163, MEWC; "is highly appreciated": Else Kaufmann to DLS, 1 Aug. 1955, 163, MEWC; Adams, *Somerville for Women*, 61; "quite the best": Joan Evans to MSB, 23 Feb. 1975, 4, MSBC; Schaub, *Middlebrow Feminism*; Siobhan Chapman, "Towards a Neo-Gricean Stylistics: Implicature in Dorothy L. Sayers's *Gaudy Night*," *Journal of Literary Semantics* 41, no. 2 (2012); Robinson, "Mysterious Politics"; Ann K. McClellan, *How British Women Writers Transformed the Campus Novel: Virginia Woolf, Dorothy L. Sayers, Margaret Drabble, Anita Brookner, Jeanette Winterson* (Lewiston, NY: Edwin Mellen Press, 2012), 103–105, 139–140.

10. Pauline Adams to Christopher Dean, 28 Jan. 2003, 25.422, DLSA; Farnell, *A Somervillian*, 59–64; "Full Academical," "It will be": DLS to MSB, 11 June 1934, 185b, MEWC.

11. "A Toast to Oxford" [1934], DLS MS-221, MEWC.

12. Agenda, 22 June 1935, and other papers, 425, MEWC; Diaries, 2c/8, MSBC.

13. "the partaking": DLS to Mildred Pope, 14 Jan. 1936, ASM papers c. 1934–1937, Somerville; "After all—though": DLS to Darbishire, 8 June [1936], ASM papers c. 1934–1937, Somerville; DLS to Gladys Scott Thomson, 4 Jan. 1937, ASM papers c. 1934–1937, Somerville; Chairman's report, 425; "College rather counts": Barber to DLS, 30 June 1935, 423b; E. Sears to DLS, 1 July 1936, and DLS to Sears, 3 July 1936, 420a, MEWC.

14. A. K. Lewis to DLS, 8 Dec. 1937, and DLS to Lewis, 15 Dec. 1937, 420a, MEWC; "none of the high-brow": DLS to F. V. Barry, 3 Jan. 1938 and 15 Dec. 1937, 420a, MEWC; Barry to DLS, 12 Apr. [1938], 420a, MEWC.

15. "they will pay": DLS to Hilary Brett-Smith, 3 Oct. 1938, 420a, MEWC; Marion Müller to DLS, 19 Feb. 1939 and DLS to Müller, 7 Mar. 1939, 420b, MEWC; Sylvia Stuart to DLS, 21 Feb. 1939, and DLS to Stuart, 7 Mar. 1939, 420b, MEWC; Diaries 1937–1939, 2c/8, MSBC.

16. MSB to Janet Hitchman, 21 July 1967, 25.370, DLSA.

17. "bang in the middle," "get in to": Rowe to DLS, 24 Dec. [1936] and 15 Apr. [1937], 427, MEWC.

18. "to estimate the chances": DLS to MSB, [1937], 187, MEWC; "swum up from": DLS to Rowe, 15 Apr. [1937], 427, MEWC.

19. Dorothy L. Sayers, "The Zeal of Thy House," in *Famous Plays of 1938–1939* (London: Gollancz, 1939), 92–93.

20. Rowe to DLS, 22 Apr. 1937, 427, MEWC.

21. DLS to Rowe, 25 Apr. 1937, 427, MEWC.

22. "an amateur theatrical producer," "at one of the most": DLS to Margaret Babington, 18 May 1937, Reynolds, *Letters*, vol. 2; "Zeal," 1–16, MEWC; "enormously": Rowe to DLS, 16 June 1937 and 16 May 1937, 427, MEWC; DLS to Rowe, 24 June 1937, 427, MEWC; Diary 1937, 2c/8, MSBC.

23. Diary 1938, 2c/8, MSBC; "I have had a kindly": DLS to MSB, 13 Sept. 1937, 187, MEWC; "to the notice": DLS to Rowe, 31 Mar. 1938, 427, MEWC; "Hurray": Rowe to DLS, 15 Mar. 1939 and 3 Apr. 1938, 6 Mar. 1939, 427, MEWC; "doing very well": DLS to H. C. Escreet, 22 Nov. 1938, 420a, MEWC; Directors Meeting, 13 Mar. 1939, BLTC.

24. Dorothy L. Sayers, *The Devil to Pay* (London: Gollancz, 1939); "the most flagrantly": DLS to Rowe, [1939], 427, MEWC; "meal or a sherry": Rowe to DLS, 13 July 1939, 427, MEWC.

25. "it would be": DLS to Rowe, 18 Oct. 1938, 427, MEWC; "I want to show": Rowe to DLS, 22 Apr. 1937, 427, MEWC; "the household is," "the MBs": Rowe to DLS, 19 Oct. 1938, 427, MEWC; "for all your": Rowe to DLS, 5 Nov. 1938, 427, MEWC.

26. Program, *Mystery at Greenfingers*, 17–22 Jan. 1938, BLTC; "the avid reader": clipping, "A Priestley Play," BLTC; Annual General Meetings, 20 July 1938, 7 July 1939, BLTC; Invitation and program 16 Feb. 1938, BLTC; *Baby Spot*, March 1938, January 1939, February 1939, BLTC; DLS to Rowe, 28 Dec. 1937, 427, MEWC; "your presence and speech": Rowe to DLS, 19 Jan. 1939 and 2 Jan. [1939], 427, MEWC.

27. "the real mystery": Rowe to DLS, 27 Dec. 1937, 427, MEWC; "(a) good plays," "a real theme," "foster a sweeping": Rowe to DLS, 19 Jan. 1939, 427, MEWC.

28. DLS to Rowe, [1939], 427, MEWC.

29. Rowe to MSB, 9 Jan. [1937?], 1/9, MSBC; Diaries 1935, 1937–1938, 2c/8, MSBC; Frankenburg to DLS, 2 Mar. 1938, 437, MEWC; Rowe to DLS, 2 Jan. [1939], 427, MEWC; "combined Coronation": DLS to MSB, 20 May 1937, 187, MEWC.

CHAPTER 14: WAR BREAKS OUT

1. MSB to [accountant?], 21 Oct. 1939, 1/7, MSBC; Frankenburg, *Not Old*, 159; Peter to Charis, 27 June 1938, 11 Nov. 1938, MS Eng. c. 7043, Bodleian.

2. WO339/1408, NA; "I hope you": DLS to Albert Coutts, 11 Nov. 1939, 362, MEWC.

3. Archives 1937–1940, BLTC; "stressing the value": Minutes, 11 Sept. 1939 and 4 Sept. 1939, 26 Feb. 1940, BLTC; Program, *Winter Sunshine*, BLTC.

4. Michal Shapira, *The War Inside: Psychoanalysis, Total War, and the Making of the Democratic Self in Postwar Britain* (Cambridge: Cambridge University Press, 2013), 59–60.

5. Official reports, 1914, 1925, 1936–1945, U383/01, GHOASC; Minutes, 27 Sept. 1928, 20 Feb. 1930, 28 Sept. 1933, U383/AM2, GHOASC; Minutes, 22 Oct. 1931, 25 June

1936, U383/CO1/AM3, GHOASC; Sign-in sheets, reports, 24 Oct. 1927, 28 May 1933, 23 Jan. 1934, U383/CO1/01, GHOASC; Frankenburg Manchester Studies 1045, Tameside.

6.   Roger Cooter, *Surgery and Society in Peace and War: Orthopaedics and the Organization of Modern Medicine, 1880–1948* (Houndmills, UK: Palgrave Macmillan, 1993), 40–41, 44, 53, 61, 161, 175; Frances Rachel Frankenburg, *Vitamin Discoveries and Disasters: History, Science, and Controversies* (Santa Barbara, CA: Praeger, 2009), 96–101; Bryder, "Wonderlands of Buttercup," 72–95; Rod Parker-Rees and Jenny Willan, *Early Years Education: Major Themes in Education* (London: Routledge, 2006), 94n8; "a flagged cellar": *Manchester and Salford Woman Citizen*, 15 June 1924; *Manchester City News*, 13 Jan. 1920, U383/Z2, GHOASC.

7.   Report of interview, 20 Sept. 1927, U383/AM2, GHOASC; *Manchester and Salford Woman Citizen*, 15 May 1927; "we want to keep": Frankenburg Manchester Studies 1045, Tameside.

8.   Minutes, 17 Feb. 1939; D. Cross, 18 Oct. 1939, U383/AM3, GHOASC; "as it was too": CUF newsletter, 14 Sept. 1939 and 4 Sept. 1939, 23 Oct. 1939, MS Eng. c. 7045, Bodleian.

9.   "Well, I hope": CUF newsletter, 8 Sept. 1939, MS Eng. c. 7045, Bodleian; "and wished": CUF newsletter, 22 Oct. 1939, MS Eng. c. 7045, Bodleian; "a glorified version": CUF newsletter, 26 Dec. 1939, MS Eng. c. 7045, Bodleian; clipping, *Manchester Evening News*, 23 Dec. 1939, MS Eng. c. 7045, Bodleian; Peter to Charis, 31 Dec. 1939, MS Eng. c. 7044, Bodleian.

10.   "It fair turns," "I can't bear," "Evacuation makes one," "Well, it's not," "predominant impression": Barber to DLS, [1939], 423b, MEWC; "Miss M. M. Barber," *South Hampstead High School Magazine* 68 (1954).

11.   1939 Diary, 2c/8, MSBC; "nestling prettily": MSB to unknown, 1 Feb. 1940, 1/7, MSBC; MSB to insurance, 7 Nov. 1940, 5/2, MSBC; Scrap, Barber to MSB, n.d., 5/1, MSBC; MSB to Olive Monkhouse, [7 July 1941], D402, RHUL; MSB to DLS, 5 Oct. [1941], 422a, MEWC.

12.   Cullis to Olive Monkhouse, 22 Jan. 1940, and Monkhouse to Cullis, 8 Mar. 1940, D352, RHUL; Mandler, *History*, 71; "And you fit": Janet Trevelyan to MSB, 11 Mar. 1940, 1/8, MSBC.

13.   Frankenburg, *Not Old*, 159; Cullis to MSB, 23 May 1940, 1/6, MSBC.

14.   "to pay for": MSB, will, 31 May 1940, 2a/4, MSBC; "burnt unread": Cullis to MSB, 23 May 1940, 1/6, MSBC; George Trevelyan to MSB, 5 Oct. 1940, 1/8, MSBC; Note, 7 Oct. 1940, and Cullis to principal, 16 Aug. 1940, D352, RHUL.

15.   "This, we thought": M. St. Clare Byrne, "Those Scotch Dogs," *Housewife*, Nov. 1940, 7/7, MSBC; Barber to MSB, 11 July [no year], 5/1, MSBC; "to fetch," "received the adoration": Barber to DLS, n.d., 423a, MEWC; "Muriel St. Clare Byrne 1894–1983," *Somerville College Report and Supplement 1982*.

16.   1941 Diary, 2c/8, MSBC; "nasty habit of dropping": DLS to Rowe, 6 Jan. 1941, 427, MEWC; "rather more peaceful": DLS to W. W. Greg, 18 Oct. 1940; "confusing," "Muriel's best love": DLS to Barber, 11 Nov. 1940, Reynolds, *Letters*, vol. 2.

17.   "serial story," "Auntie Dorothy!": "D.H.R. Member of Staff," 7; DLS to Rowe, 6 Jan. 1941, 427, MEWC; "Members Only 1940–1946," BLTC; Annual General Meetings, 17 Aug. 1942, 21 Aug. 1944, BLTC; Minutes, 28 Oct. 1940, 25 Nov. 1940, 10 Mar. 1941, BLTC.

18. "just after": CUF newsletter, 18 Nov. 1939 and 11 Sept. 1939, 14 Sept. 1939, 7 May 1941, MS Eng. c. 7045-6, Bodleian; "Sugar-biscuits": Frankenburg, *Not Old*, 154.

19. Curriculum Vitae, Marjorie M. Barber, 5/4, MSBC; "Miss M. M. Barber," *South Hampstead High School Magazine* 68 (1954); "copped it," "over & over," "But in spite": Barber to MSB, n.d., 5/1, MSBC.

20. "Whatever that was": Barber to MSB, n.d., 5/1, MSBC; "lived with naked fear," "that the only": Marjorie Barber, "Seven Swords," 5/6, MSBC.

21. Barber to MSB, n.d., 5/1, MSBC.

22. CUF newsletter, 3 June 1940, 14 Apr. 1941, 19–20 Apr. 1941, MS Eng. c. 7045-6, Bodleian; Frankenburg, *Not Old*, 151, 159–160.

23. CUF newsletter, 19–20 Apr. 1941, MS Eng. c. 7046, Bodleian.

24. "he proposes": CUF newsletter, 14 Apr. 1941, MS Eng. c. 7046, Bodleian; "extremely badly written": CUF newsletter, 19–20 Apr. 1941, MS Eng. c. 7046, Bodleian; "move their bodies": Eustace Chesser, *Love Without Fear: A Plain Guide to Sex Technique for Every Married Adult* (London: Rich & Cowan Medical Publications, 1941), 52, 66; Marcus Collins, *Modern Love: An Intimate History of Men and Women in Twentieth-Century Britain* (London: Atlantic Books, 2003); Chettiar, "Treating Marriage," 273; Langhamer, *The English in Love*, 49.

25. CUF newsletter, 19–20 Apr. 1941, MS Eng. c. 7046, Bodleian.

CHAPTER 15: SERVICE AND IDENTITY

1. "and I even had": CUF newsletter, 26 Aug. 1940, MS Eng. c. 7045, Bodleian; "playing Chopin's Funeral March": 26 Jan. 1942, MS Eng. c. 7047, Bodleian; "my only feeling": Frankenburg, *Not Old*, 160, 185.

2. "a snare": CUF newsletter, 25 June 1941 and 16 Oct. 1939, 7 May 1941 5 July 1941, MS Eng. c. 7045-6, Bodleian.

3. CUF newsletter, 7 Sept. 1940, MS Eng. c. 7045, Bodleian; "convivial evenings": CUF newsletter, 9 June 1943, MS Eng. c. 7046, Bodleian; "really had," "They ought to": CUF newsletter, 17 June 1943 and 28 Sept. 1943, MS Eng. c. 7048, Bodleian; "skipped away": CUF newsletter, 31 Dec. 1943 and 6 Jan. 1944, MS Eng. c. 7048, Bodleian; Rowe to DLS, 2 Jan. [1943?], 427, MEWC.

4. "had pranced on": CUF newsletter, 28 Sept. 1943 and 4 Sept. 1943, MS Eng. c. 7048, Bodleian; "long discussions," "is my chief," "that Ursula": CUF newsletter, 20 Sept. 1943, MS Eng. c. 7048, Bodleian.

5. Explanatory note, MS Eng. c. 7044, Bodleian; "absolutely sick": CUF newsletter, 10 Oct. 1941, MS Eng. c. 7046, Bodleian; "as I think": CUF newsletter, 22 June 1942, MS Eng. c. 7047, Bodleian.

6. "first they spat": CUF newsletter, 14 Apr. 1941, MS Eng. c. 7046, Bodleian; "What a great": CUF newsletter, 6 June 1942, MS Eng. c. 7047, Bodleian.

7. Explanatory note, MS Eng. c. 7044, Bodleian; "Tell Dorothy": Peter to Charis, 9 July 1941, MS Eng. c. 7044, Bodleian; "a delightful city": Peter to Charis, 19 Oct. [1942?] and 19 Jan. 1941, 14 Feb. 1941, 12 June 1941, 27 Nov. 1941, MS Eng. c. 7044, Bodleian.

8. CUF newsletter, 9 June 1941, MS Eng. c. 7046, Bodleian.

9. "crossed out all": CUF newsletter, 8 Aug. 1941, MS Eng. c. 7046, Bodleian; "The aroma from": CUF newsletter, 7 May 1941 and 27 Aug. 1941, 21 Apr. 1942, 28 Apr. 1942,

MS Eng. c. 7046-7, Bodleian; "Dorothy Rowe's": CUF newsletter, 3 May 1943 and 7 Jan. 1943, 4 Mar. 1943, MS Eng. c. 7048, Bodleian; Frankenburg, *Not Old*, 161.

10. Frankenburg, *Not Old*, 160; CUF newsletter, 21 Sept. 1942, 9 Nov. 1942, 14 Dec. 1942, 23 Mar. 1943, 3 May 1943, 13 July 1943, MS Eng. c. 7047-8, Bodleian.

11. Peter to Charis, 21 July 1943, MS Eng. c. 7044, Bodleian; "Oh what a flop": CUF newsletter, 2 Aug. 1943, MS Eng. c. 7048, Bodleian; "intends to fetch": CUF newsletter, 13 Aug. 1943, MS Eng. c. 7048, Bodleian; "as balancing": CUF newsletter, 20 Sept. 1943 and 15 Nov. 1943, MS Eng. c. 7048, Bodleian; "if John had not": CUF newsletter, 7 Dec. 1943 and 6 Jan. 1944, 8 Feb. 1944, MS Eng. c. 7048, Bodleian; Frankenburg, *Not Old*, 160.

12. "as I'm getting": Peter to Charis, 8 Dec. 1940, MS Eng. c. 7044, Bodleian; "silly," "What on earth": Peter to Charis, 19 Dec. 1940, MS Eng. c. 7044, Bodleian; "very intimate," "Anyhow, I don't think": CUF newsletter, 6 Dec. 1940, MS Eng. c. 7045, Bodleian; "is the Jewish Club": CUF newsletter, 30 June 1942, MS Eng. c. 7047, Bodleian.

13. "had a sudden": CUF newsletter, 3 Nov. 1941 and 16 Aug. 1941, 14 Oct. 1941, MS Eng. c. 7046, Bodleian; "always latently Jewish": Frankenburg interview, 8SUF/B/144, WL; Frankenburg, *Not Old*, 160.

14. "the singing part," "Yes, but God": CUF newsletter, 4 Sept. 1941 and 26 Dec. 1939, 22 June 1942, 5 Sept. 1942, 20 Oct. 1943, MS Eng. c. 7045-8, Bodleian; "Oh God who gives us": CUF newsletter, 4 Mar. 1944, MS Eng. c. 7048, Bodleian.

15. "were little Jew boys": CUF newsletter, 18 Nov. 1939, MS Eng. c. 7045, Bodleian; "gasped in horror," CUF newsletter, 6 July 1940, MS Eng. c. 7045, Bodleian; "the electric clock": CUF newsletter, 29 Oct. 1942, MS Eng. c. 7047, Bodleian; "Passover cakes," "about four feet": CUF newsletter 21 Feb. 1944, MS Eng. c. 7048, Bodleian.

16. CUF newsletter, 12 Oct. 1942, MS Eng. c. 7047, Bodleian.

17. CUF newsletter, 7 Apr. 1941, MS Eng. c. 7046, Bodleian.

18. "thick with tobacco," "very soon," "Several different," "but as the funniest," "at least all," "In fact I had": CUF newsletter, 4 Feb. 1942, MS Eng. c. 7047, Bodleian; "I should sell": Frankenburg interview, 8SUF/B/144, WL.

19. "had been written": CUF newsletter, 14 July 1942 and 23 Feb. 1942, 21 Sept. 1942, MS Eng. c. 7047, Bodleian; Rubinstein, *Dictionary*, 1029.

20. "that Judaism was," "now that there," "I don't feel," "whereas at present": CUF newsletter, 14 Dec. 1942, MS Eng. c. 7047, Bodleian; "to protest against," "It was a most": CUF newsletter, 7 Jan. 1943, MS Eng. c. 7048, Bodleian.

21. Brabazon, *Dorothy L. Sayers*, 216; Pearn to Barber, 4 Feb. 1944, 5/6, MSBC; "entirely free," "wholly admirable," "I was so overcome": Barber to DLS, 17 Oct. [no year], 423a, MEWC.

22. "half-caste": CUF newsletter, 7 June 1940, MS Eng. c. 7045, Bodleian; "half German": CUF newsletter, 24 June 1940, MS Eng. c. 7045, Bodleian; "exactly like a stage American": CUF newsletter, 16 Aug. 1941, MS Eng. c. 7046, Bodleian; "wouldn't do any": CUF newsletter, 4 Mar. 1944, MS Eng. c. 7048, Bodleian; "if he knew": CUF newsletter, 2 Dec. 1944, MS Eng. c. 7048, Bodleian.

23. "not very good about the colour bar": CUF newsletter, 14 July 1941 and 2 Oct. 1939, 14 Oct. 1941, MS Eng. c. 7045-6, Bodleian; Caroline Bressey, "Geographies of Belonging: White Women and Black History," *Women's History Review* 22, no. 4 (2013); Kennetta Hammond Perry, *London Is the Place for Me: Black Britons, Citizenship, and the Politics of Race* (Oxford: Oxford University Press, 2015).

CHAPTER 16: THE GREENGATE HOSPITAL

1. Angela Davis, *Pre-school Childcare in England, 1939–2010: Theory, Practice and Experience* (Manchester, UK: Manchester University Press, 2015), 26, 37–38, 45; Shapira, *War Inside*, 1, 6–7, 15–16.

2. Shapira, *War Inside*, 140–141; Anne Logan, *Feminism and Criminal Justice: A Historical Perspective* (Houndmills, UK: Palgrave Macmillan, 2008), 67–70.

3. "ought to have been": CUF newsletter, 8 Dec. 1939, MS Eng. c. 7045, Bodleian; "toast, dripping, marmalade": CUF newsletter, 30 May 1942 and 24 Feb. 1941, 3 Mar. 1941, 30 May 1942, 28 July 1942, MS Eng. c. 7046-7, Bodleian; "over a hundred cabbages": Frankenburg, *Not Old*, 159.

4. "wrong to inflict" Frankenburg Manchester Studies 1045, Tameside; "all smacking," "will be reported": CUF newsletter, 22 June 1942 and 17 Aug. 1940, 29 Oct. 1940, 5 July 1941, 6 June 1942, 30 June 1943, MS Eng. c. 7045-8, Bodleian; John Stewart, *Child Guidance in Britain, 1918–1955: The Dangerous Age of Childhood* (New York: Routledge, 2016).

5. "the fact that canes": Frankenburg Manchester Studies 1045, Tameside; "What do you expect": CUF newsletter, 14 July 1941, MS Eng. c. 7046, Bodleian.

6. CUF newsletter, 19 May 1942, MS Eng. c. 7047, Bodleian.

7. "He agreed with me": CUF newsletter, 22 Oct. 1939, MS Eng. c. 7045, Bodleian; "shopping, baking, washing": CUF newsletter 27 Sept. 1941, MS Eng. c. 7046, Bodleian; "the natural un-hospital": CUF newsletter, 24 Aug. 1942, MS Eng. c. 7047, Bodleian; Davis, *Pre-school Childcare*, 62.

8. "approved theory," "Yes, I know": CUF newsletter, 17 Nov. 1941 and 14 Oct. 1941, MS Eng. c. 7046; "will not realise": CUF newsletter, 9 Jan. 1942, MS Eng. c. 7047, Bodleian.

9. "even in winter": "Points to Note," May 1941, U383/AM3, GHOASC; "great pleasure": CUF newsletter, 4 Sept. 1939, MS Eng. c. 7045, Bodleian.

10. D. Cross, 18 Oct. 1939, and "Points to Note," May 1941, U383/AM3, GHOASC; "not in a teacher's": CUF newsletter, 4 Sept. 1939 and 4 Sept. 1941, MS Eng. c. 7045-6, Bodleian; Frankenburg, *Not Old*, 155.

11. "I find Matron": CUF newsletter, 10 Sept. 1940, MS Eng. c. 7045, Bodleian; "Matron jumped up": CUF newsletter, 14 Apr. 1941, MS Eng. c. 7046, Bodleian.

12. "one of the things": CUF newsletter, 14 Dec. 1942 and 30 June 1942, 8 Nov. 1944, MS Eng. c. 7047-8, Bodleian.

13. Frankenburg, *Not Old*, 155; "plucked eyebrows": CUF newsletter, 24 June 1940 and 19 Mar. 1940, 6 Apr. 1940, 6 Dec. 1940, 23 Feb. 1942, MS Eng. c. 7045-7, Bodleian.

14. "This ought to be": CUF newsletter, 17 June 1943 and 23 Mar. 1943, MS Eng. c. 7048, Bodleian; "How these people": CUF newsletter, 26 Aug. 1943 and 2 Aug. 1943, MS Eng. c. 7048, Bodleian; "Conchy Headmistress": CUF newsletter, 21 Feb. 1944, MS Eng. c. 7048, Bodleian.

15. Minutes, 9 July 1941, 10 Sept. 1941, 15 Oct. 1941, U383/AM3, GHOASC; CUF newsletter, 19 Sept. 1941, 14 Oct. 1941, MS Eng. c. 7046, Bodleian.

16. Minutes, 5 Aug. 1941, 21 Jan. 1942, U383/AM3, GHOASC; "to effect a minimum": CUF newsletter, 26 Jan. 1942 and 23 Feb. 1942, MS Eng. c. 7047, Bodleian.

17. "constantly taken advantage": CUF newsletter, 29 Oct. 1942 and 24 Nov. 1942, 2 Aug. 1943, MS Eng. c. 7047-8, Bodleian; "that sooner or later": Minutes, 20 July 1942 and

18 Apr. 1944, U383/AM3, GHOASC; Billie Hunter, "Midwifery, 1920–2000: The Reshaping of a Profession," in *Nursing and Midwifery in Britain since 1700*, eds. Annie Borsay and Billie Hunter, 157.

18. Minutes, 17 June 1942, U383/AM3, GHOASC; "complete in white overalls": CUF newsletter, 14 July 1942 and 22 June 1942, MS Eng. c. 7047, Bodleian; "great deal": CUF newsletter, 28 July 1942, MS Eng. c. 7047, Bodleian; "I made some": CUF newsletter, 12 Oct. 1942, MS Eng. c. 7047, Bodleian.

19. CUF newsletter, 28 July 1942, MS Eng. c. 7047, Bodleian.

20. "who have joined": CUF newsletter, 8 Apr. 1944 and 10 Feb. 1943, MS Eng. c. 7048, Bodleian.

21. "For a Conservative," "Conservatives are," "Comrade Frankenburg": CUF newsletter, 22 July 1941 and 7 Oct. 1939, 19 Oct. 1939, 2 Aug. 1941, MS Eng. c. 7045-6, Bodleian; "there is more": CUF newsletter, 14 Oct. 1941 and 1 Dec. 1941, 21 Apr. 1942, 6 June 1942, 24 Aug. 1942, 5 Sept. 1942, 29 Oct. 1942, 23 Mar. 1943, 3 May 1943, 15 May 1944, MS Eng. c. 7046-8, Bodleian; Logan, *Feminism and Criminal Justice*, 15; Frankenburg, *Not Old*, 144.

22. Logan, *Feminism and Criminal Justice*, 1; *Manchester and Salford Woman Citizen*, Feb. 1938; "How I should hate": DLS to MSB, 16 Nov. 1941, 422a, MEWC; Frankenburg, *Not Old*, 144–146, 152; "that unless they wanted": CUF newsletter, 2 Aug. 1943, MS Eng. c. 7048, Bodleian.

23. "It is not," "Because, my dear": CUF newsletter, 22 July 1941, MS Eng. c. 7046, Bodleian; "I think I'm the only": CUF newsletter, 9 Jan. 1942, MS Eng. c. 7047, Bodleian.

24. "You undoubtedly," "Only with children": CUF newsletter, 13 Aug. 1942, MS Eng. c. 7047, Bodleian; "more judicial": CUF newsletter, 1 Dec. 1941, MS Eng. c. 7046, Bodleian; "It always make," "any more," "Oh, are you": CUF newsletter, 30 May 1942, MS Eng. c. 7047, Bodleian.

25. "You've got some": CUF newsletter, 18 Nov. 1939, MS Eng. c. 7045, Bodleian; "was a lazy": CUF newsletter, 31 Mar. 1941, MS Eng. c. 7046, Bodleian; "asking for trouble": CUF newsletter, 7 May 1941, MS Eng. c. 7046, Bodleian.

CHAPTER 17: RUNNING TO STAND STILL

1. "all the little": M. St. Clare Byrne, "Keep Tryst," 7d, MSBC; MSB to unknown, 1 Feb. 1940, 1/7, MSBC; MSB to Laurence Harbottle, 1 Dec. 1968, 5/5, MSBC; Stenson Cook to MSB, 15 May 1942, 5/2, MSBC; "safeguard my professional status": MSB to Olive Monkhouse, 18 Nov. 1941, D402, RHUL.

2. Secretary to MSB, 19 Dec. 1940, and MSB to Monkhouse, 7 Feb. 1941, D402, RHUL; "that her features": Ellis-Fermor to DLS, 23 Jan. 1941, 441b, MEWC; "I start my day": MSB to DLS, [Jan. 1941], 424, MEWC; DLS to Rowe, 6 Jan. 1941, 427, MEWC.

3. Secretary to MSB, 21 Mar. 1941, 27 Mar. 1941, 14 July 1941, D402, RHUL; MSB to Monkhouse, 26 Mar. 1941, 28 Mar. 1941, 16 June 1941, D402, RHUL; F.P. Wilson to Monkhouse, 29 Mar. 1941, D402, RHUL; "You have been rushing," "let everything go": DLS to MSB, 19 June 1941, 187, MEWC.

4. MSB to Monkhouse, [7 July 1941], D402, RHUL; MSB to DLS, 4 Aug. 1941, 424, MEWC; "MSB is very": Barber to DLS, 18 Aug. 1941 and 13 Jan. 1942, 423a, MEWC.

5. MSB to DLS, [1941], and DLS to MSB, 8 Oct. 1941, 424, MEWC; Cullis to DLS, 4 Feb. 1942, 296, MEWC; "fantastically like Talboys": MSB to DLS, 29 Sept. 1941, 422a, MEWC.

6. "My love always": Helen (no last name) to MSB, 23 Dec. (no year), 1/8, MSBC; "love & all good wishes": Mabella (no last name) to MSB, 21 Sept. 1942, 1/9, MSBC; "What's Miss": Hazel (no last name) to MSB, 16 Mar. 1943, 1/9, MSBC.

7. "just quailed": MSB to DLS, [1941], 424, MEWC; "and have been waiting": Ellis-Fermor to DLS, 4 Oct. [1941], 441a, MEWC; "for the best," "I found": Ellis-Fermor to DLS, 11 Oct. 1941, 441a, MEWC.

8. "pathetically anxious," "I think it": Barber to DLS, Oct. [1941?], 423b, MEWC; "but Muriel had," "housekeeping," "more besotted," "I am stiffened": Barber to DLS, 13 Jan. 1942, 423a, MEWC; Diary, 1941, 2c/8, MSBC.

9. Barber to DLS, n.d., 423b, MEWC.

10. Barber to DLS, 13 Jan. 1942, 423a, MEWC; DLS to Barber, 26 Oct. 1942, 422a, MEWC; "looking pretty fagged," "contrived to over-eat," "two good muddy walks": DLS to MSB, 26 Dec. 1941, 422a, MEWC; DLS to MSB, 15 Oct. 1941, 185a, MEWC; "sorry if you minded," "cope any longer": Barber to MSB, n.d., 5/1, MSBC; "come back at Christmas": DLS to Barber, 22 Sept. 1942, Reynolds, *Letters*, vol. 2.

11. DLS to MSB, 15 Aug. 1941, 187, MEWC; "the Master of the House": DLS to MSB, 15 Oct. 1941, 185a, MEWC; "said I had been": DLS to MSB, 16 Nov. 1941, 422a, MEWC.

12. Jane Austen, *Persuasion*, ed. Marjorie M. Barber (London: Macmillan, 1963), xiv; Barber to DLS, 17 Oct. [no year], 423a, MEWC; Curriculum Vitae Marjorie Barber, 5/4; Pearn, Pollinger, and Higham to Barber, 19 Feb. 1946, 5/6, MSBC.

13. Marjorie Barber, "To Love and to Cherish," 5/6, MSBC.

14. Charnock, "A Million Little Bonds," 363–363, 375–376; Chettiar, "Treating Marriage," 273; Marjorie Barber, "After the Theatre," 5/6, MSBC.

15. Marjorie Barber, "Answers to Correspondence," 5/6, MSBC.

16. MSB to [accountant?], 21 Oct. 1939, 1/7, MSBC; H. W. Harvey, 9 June 1942, 5/2, MSBC; "the Rectorial situation": MSB to DLS, [June 1942], 422a, MEWC; "for good I hope": MSB to DLS, [1942?], and DLS to MSB, 15 June 1942, 422a, MEWC; F. P. Wilson to MSB, 16 Jan. 1943, D402, RHUL; MSB to Monkhouse, 12 Oct. 1944 and 18 June 1945, D402, RHUL; "condition of being allowed": Schenker, "Familial History," RHUL; MSB to Sir Charles Hilary Jenkinson, 13 May 1942, PRO30/75/1, NA.

17. "didn't even flinch," "so I got M's breakfast": Barber to DLS, n.d., 423a, MEWC; "she is becoming": Barber to DLS, 3 Sept. [1941?], 423a, MEWC.

CHAPTER 18: BRIDGEHEADS TO THE FUTURE

1. "an instrument of power": Dorothy L. Sayers, *Unpopular Opinions* (London: Gollancz, 1946), 57; "susceptible to the influence": Dorothy L. Sayers, *The Lost Tools of Learning: Paper Read at a Vacation Course in Education, Oxford 1947* (London: Methuen, 1948), 3, 10.

2. "I'm not 'my country'": Frankenburg interview, 8SUF/B/144, WL; "Old Nurse": Sayers, *Unpopular Opinions*, 103–104; "gent, scholar, wit": DLS to MSB, 20 Aug. 1941, 185a, MEWC.

3. "Is D.L.S. writing": Emily (no last name)to [MSB and Barber], n.d., 1/9, MSBC; "A certain gentleman-in-charge": MSB annotations on Ralph Clarke to MSB, 8 Dec. 1980, 4/4, MSBC; DLS to D. Kilham, 14 May 1939, 364, MEWC; DLS to Graham Greene, 26 July 1940, 7 Aug. 1940 and Greene to DLS, 2 Aug. 1940, 365, MEWC; "overcrowded monkey-house": DLS to J. H. Oldham, 2 Oct. 1939, Reynolds, *Letters*, vol. 2.

4. DLS to W.E. Salt, 7 Feb. 1941, 362, MEWC; E. Flinn to DLS, 5 May 1942, 362, MEWC; W. Buchanan-Taylor to DLS, 11 July 1940, 364, MEWC; "lured into saving": DLS to Buchanan-Taylor, 14 July 1940, 362, MEWC; DLS to Barber, 26 Oct. 1942, 422a, MEWC; "provided they come": Sayers, *Unpopular Opinions*, 62, 64, 67, 72; Felix Frankfurter to Estelle Frankfurter, 19 Aug. [1941], Felix Frankfurter Letters 2/2, HLS; "my usual 'piece,'" "So we exchanged": DLS to Barber, 22 June 1944, Reynolds, *Letters*, vol. 3.

5. Sayers, *Unpopular Opinions*, 17.

6. *Manchester Guardian*, 1 Aug. 1941; "rather inclined," "rather absurd": DLS to J. H. Oldham, 2 Oct. 1939, Reynolds, *Letters*, vol. 2; DLS to Maurice Reckitt, [June 1941?], Reynolds, *Letters*, vol. 2; DLS to Ellis-Fermor, 5 Mar. 1942, 441a, MEWC; DLS to MSB, 1 Mar. 1941, 187, MEWC; "give the people": Brabazon, *Dorothy L. Sayers*, 278.

7. DLS to W. W. Greg, 18 Oct. 1940, Reynolds, *Letters*, vol. 2; "to bed in the bunk": DLS to Ellis-Fermor, 12 Dec. 1940, 441b, MEWC; "of course my only": MSB to DLS, n.d., 422a, MEWC.

8. Dorothy L. Sayers, *The Mind of the Maker* (New York: HarperCollins, 1987), 181, 225.

9. MSB to E. V. Rieu, 26 Mar. 1941, 19, MEWC; Charles Williams to DLS, 23 June 1941, 296, MEWC; "rather stumbling": Darbishire to DLS, 12 July 1941, 296, MEWC; "full of illumination": George Trevelyan to MSB, 2 July 1941, 297, MEWC; "feel as if I had been": Unknown to MSB, n.d., 7/1 MSBC.

10. Una Ellis-Fermor, *Masters of Reality* (London: Methuen, 1942), vii, 13–15, 129; "an all-round, intelligent": DLS to Ellis-Fermor, 6 Dec. [1940?] and 26 Sept. 1941, 12 Dec. 1940, 441b, MEWC; DLS to MSB, 1 Mar. 1941, 187, MEWC; "is better fitted": DLS to MSB, 29 Jan. 1941, 424, MEWC.

11. Barber to DLS, n.d., 423b, MEWC; DLS to MSB, 20 Aug. 1941, 15 May 1942, 185a, MEWC; "against the 'peace & security'": DLS to MSB, 1 Mar. 1941, 187, MEWC; MSB to DLS, [1942]; "about the cult": DLS to MSB, 16 Nov. 1941, 422a, MEWC; folder 296, MEWC; MSB to unknown, 1 Feb. 1940, 1/7, MSBC.

12. "the correspondence I have had": DLS to MSB, 22 Aug. 1941 and 15 May 1942, 20 Aug. 1941, 8 Nov. 1941, 185a, MEWC; "more unregenerate reactions": DLS to MSB, [1942], 629, MEWC; "rather exclusively the book": DLS to [Cora Hodgson?], 5 May 1942, 297, MEWC; MSB to DLS, [1942?], 422a, MEWC; "the whole complicated problem": DLS to MSB, 24 Nov. 1942 and 15 June 1942, 26 Dec. 1941, 422a, MEWC.

13. "good journalism to be done": DLS to Jaeger, 30 Sept. 1919, 22, MEWC; "I hate them": DLS to mother, 16 July 1921, 88, MEWC; Sayers, *Unpopular Opinions*, 64.

14. DLS to MSB, 27 Apr. 1943, 297, MEWC; "examine the idea," "I don't pretend": [DLS], "Imperial Commonwealth," 297, MEWC.

15. DLS to Brabant, 10 Aug. 1944, 27, MEWC.

16. A. P. Herbert, *The Point of Parliament* (London: Methuen, 1946).

17. "just lazy and deeply prejudiced," "a 'feminist'": DLS to Maurice Reckitt, 12 July 1941, Reynolds, *Letters*, vol. 2; "our public do not": Sayers, *Unpopular Opinions*, 7.

18. "I thought I might": Janet Watts, "How Muriel Byrne Revealed the Private Life of a Tudor VIP," *Observer*, 21 June 1981, PP56/L/1, RHUL; Bill (no last name) to MSB, 30 June 1941, 297, MEWC; "takes your word": MSB to DLS, n.d., 424, MEWC.

19. "I accosted you": DLS to T. S. Eliot, 16 Oct. 1941, Reynolds, *Letters*, vol. 2; "a great Elizabethan," "repellent": DLS to MSB, 2 Aug. 1941, 424, MEWC; "I now smoke": MSB to DLS, [1941], 424, MEWC.

20. "since his encounter": DLS to MSB, 15 Aug. 1941, 187, MEWC; "frightfully jeal-ous," "very very grateful": Barber to DLS, 8 Nov. [1941], 423a, MEWC.

21. "I don't see any trace": Harold Child to MSB, 4 Mar. [1941], 7/1, MSBC; "But after so much": Child to MSB, 28 Mar. 1941, 7/1, MSBC.

22. Brabazon, *Dorothy L. Sayers*, 111; DLS to MSB, 8 Aug. 1941, 187, MEWC; Alison Oram, *Her Husband Was a Woman! Women's Gender-Crossing in Modern British Popu-lar Culture* (London: Routledge, 2007); Anjali Arondekar, "In the Absence of Reliable Ghosts: Sexuality, Historiography, South Asia," *differences* 25: 3 (2014), 98–122.

23. "a study of the kind": Stephen Gwynn, "A Foursome of Memories," *Time and Tide*, 20 June 1942, 7/1, MSBC; "with no self-pity": "Unconventional Child," *Times Lit-erary Supplement*, 14 June 1942, 7/1, MSBC; "sitting on a wall," "you were not": Maud Burton (Winter) to MSB, 22 Mar. 1946, 1/9, MSBC.

24. DLS to Maurice Reckitt, 12 July 1941, Reynolds, *Letters*, vol. 2.

25. MSB to DLS, 4 Aug. 1941, [1941], 424, MEWC.

26. Sayers, *Unpopular Opinions*, 106–121; "the domestic function," "on the indi-vidual": DLS to Maurice Reckitt, 19 Nov. 1941, Reynolds, *Letters*, vol. 2; DLS to H. M. Felkin, 11 Mar. 1949, 158, MEWC; "poison": DLS to C. W. Campbell, [10?] Sept. 1947, 158, MEWC.

27. M. St. Clare Byrne, "'Emancipated' Woman and Vocation: Female or Human?" 7/7, MSBC.

28. "a haunting feeling": Dorothy L. Sayers, *The Other Six Deadly Sins: An Address Given to the Public Morality Council at Caxton Hall, Westminster, on October 23, 1941* (London: Methuen, 1943), 19; "in love with an intellectual": quoted in Peter Webster, "Archbishop Temple's Offer of a Lambeth Degree to Dorothy L. Sayers," in *From the Reformation to the Permissive Society: A Miscellany in Celebration of the 400th Anniversary of Lambeth Palace Library*, eds. Melanie Barber, Stephen Taylor, Gabriel Sewell (Wood-bridge: Boydell Press, 2010), 569.

29. Dorothy L. Sayers, *The Christ of the Creeds and Other Broadcast Messages to the British People during World War II* (Hurstpierpoint, UK: Dorothy L. Sayers Society, 2008), 37, 41.

30. "Envy," "appalling squirrel-cage": Dorothy L. Sayers, *Why Work?* (London: Methuen, 1942), 3; "immorality," "the furious barrage": Sayers, *Other Six Deadly Sins*, 3–5, 8, 10; "the economic balance-sheet": Sayers, *Unpopular Opinions*, 12.

31. Dorothy L. Sayers, *The Man Born to Be King* (London: Gollancz, 1943); "Chris-tian and liberal": Daniel S. Loss, "The Institutional Afterlife of Christian England," *Jour-nal of Modern History* 89 (June 2017), 293.

32. "you couldn't pontificate": DLS to James Welch, 11 Jan. 1941, Reynolds, *Letters*, vol. 2; "succeeded in shocking": DLS to Barber, 22 Sept. 1942, Reynolds, *Letters*, vol. 2; "you can't expect": DLS to Val Gielgud, 18 Aug. 1942, Reynolds, *Letters*, vol. 2; "just sat together": DLS to Val Gielgud, 22 Sept. 1942, Reynolds, *Letters*, vol. 2; Melissa Dinsman, *Modernism at the Microphone: Radio, Propaganda and Literary Aesthetics during World War II* (London: Bloomsbury, 2015); Alex Goody, "Dorothy L. Sayers's *The Man Born to Be King*. The 'Impersonation' of Divinity: Language, Authenticity and Embodiment," in *Broadcasting in the Modernist Era*, eds. Matthew Feldman, Erik Tonning, and Henry Mead (London: Bloomsbury, 2014).

33. J. W. Welch to DLS, 21 Apr. 1945, 458, MEWC; "more power to your elbow": Frankenburg to DLS, 1 Feb. 1942, 437, MEWC; "MSB said from reading": Barber to DLS,

15 Feb. 1942, 423a, MEWC; CUF newsletter, 26 Jan. 1942, MS Eng. c. 7047, Bodleian; "a touching impersonation": DLS to Val Gielgud, 8 Feb. 1942 and 22 Dec. 1941, Reynolds, *Letters*, vol. 2.

34. DLS to Barber, 26 Oct. 1942, 422a, MEWC.

35. "this terrifying drama": Dorothy L. Sayers, *The Greatest Drama Ever Staged* (London: Hodder & Stoughton, 1938), 14; "is the story," "that seed," "is manifest": Sayers, *Christ*, 77–78, 81.

36. "that Miles was with": CUF newsletter, 28 May 1944 and 15 Jan. 1944, MS Eng. c. 7048, Bodleian.

37. "perhaps the most tragic": J. N. Mackay, *A History of the 4th Prince of Wales's Own Gurkha Rifles*, vol. 3, *1938–1948* (London: William Blackwood & Sons Ltd., 1952), 192–193; Harold James and Denis Sheil-Small, *The Gurkhas* (London: Macdonald, 1965), 218.

38. "I still feel all": Peter to Charis, 15 June 1944 and 7 Aug. 1944, MS Eng. c. 7044, Bodleian; "very gallantly," "This is as good": CUF newsletter, 31 July 1944 and 4 July 1944, MS Eng. c. 7048, Bodleian.

39. CUF newsletter, 4 July 1944, 31 July 1944, 6 Oct. 1944, 14 Oct. 1944, 2 Dec. 1944, MS Eng. c. 7048, Bodleian; Minutes, 16 Jan. 1945, 17 Apr. 1945, U383/AM3, GHOASC; 1943–1944 official report, U383/05, GHOASC; Frankenburg, *Not Old*, 157; "under their noses": *Manchester Guardian*, 27 Nov. 1945.

40. "of Head Teachers": CUF newsletter, 4 July 1944, MS Eng. c. 7048, Bodleian; "good marks," "a companion volume": CUF newsletter, 21 Sept. 1944, MS Eng. c. 7048, Bodleian; CUF newsletter, 21 May 1941, 13 June 1941, 12 Mar. 1942, 30 June 1942, 7 Jan. 1943, 13 Aug. 1943, 28 May 1944, 8 Sept. 1944, MS Eng. c. 7046-8, Bodleian; *Manchester Guardian*, 2 Dec. 1939; "welcome gladly the skilled help": Frankenburg, *Common Sense* (1946), vi.

41. "I liked Dorothy's": Peter to Charis, 5 Sept. 1944 and 3 Dec. 1944, MS Eng. c. 7044, Bodleian; "Hullo Mum": CUF newsletter, 26 Dec. 1944, MS Eng. c. 7048, Bodleian; Frankenburg, *Not Old*, 160.

42. Explanatory note, MS Eng. c. 7044, Bodleian; Frankenburg, *Not Old*, 157.

43. "It seems in my humble opinion": Barber to MSB, 9 Apr. 1944 and 14 Mar. 1944, 5/1, MSBC; MSB to Olive Monkhouse, 21 Mar. 1944, D402, RHUL.

44. Barber to DLS, 2 June [no year], 423a, MEWC.

45. "London is probably": DLS to MSB and Barber, 8 Mar. 1945, 185a, MEWC; "let Hitler influence": Barber to MSB, [1944], 5/1, MSBC.

46. "in the face": Barber to DLS, n.d., 423a, MEWC; "was terribly sorry," "said in that case," "Oh well": Barber to DLS, 12 Jan. 1944, 423a, MEWC; "I had at last": Cullis to Olive Monkhouse, 14 Feb. 1945 and 21 Feb. 1945, D352, RHUL; Monkhouse to Cullis, 16 Feb. 1945 and Secretary to MSB, 19 Feb. 1945, D352, RHUL; Diary 1945, 2c/8, MSBC.

CHAPTER 19: FRIENDSHIPS AND TRIUMPHS

1. Peter to Charis, 1 Mar. 1936, MS Eng. c. 7043, Bodleian; CUF newsletter, 3 Nov. 1943, MS Eng. c. 7048, Bodleian; "quite the nicest" "I'm very sorry,": Frankenburg to DLS, 28 Dec. 1946 and 1 Feb. 1942, 437, MEWC; "had been greatly thrilled": Rowe to DLS, [Jan. 1947], 427, MEWC; Frankenburg, *Not Old*, 163.

2. "little rabbit": Frankenburg to DLS, 20 Dec. 1948 and 19 May 1947, 20 Aug. 1947, 21 May 1948, 437, MEWC; "any gluttonous behavior," "dedicate his next": DLS to Frankenburg, [1948] and 6 Aug. 1947, 437, MEWC.

3. "seems to be," "more booming": Rowe to DLS, 26 Dec. 1947, 427, MEWC; "A large parcel": Frankenburg to DLS, 20 Aug. 1947 and 20 Dec. 1948, 437, MEWC.

4. Diaries 1947–1949, 2c/8, MSBC; DLS to MSB, 8 Aug. 1947, 13 Aug. 1947, 185a, MEWC; "The price of your Frig.": MSB to DLS, [1947], 422a, MEWC.

5. "was probably my fault": Barber to DLS, [Dec. 1948] and 28 Dec. 1945, [1948?] , 423a, MEWC; MSB to DLS, 28 Dec. 1947, 422a, MEWC; MSB to DLS, [December 1948], 422b, MEWC; "still more or less," "but I seized": DLS to MSB, 2 Jan. 1949, 422b, MEWC; Diary 1948, 2c/8, MSBC.

6. Barber to DLS, 18 June 1950, 423a, MEWC; "It will seem," "might go off": DLS to MSB, 12 June 1950, 422b, MEWC.

7. Frankenburg to DLS, 1 Sept. 1950, 437, MEWC; DLS to MSB, 23 Nov. 1954, 185a, MEWC; MSB to DLS, n.d., 422b, MEWC; DLS to MSB, 11 Feb. 1953, 422b, MEWC; Secretary (DLS) to MSB, 21 May 1951, 514, MEWC; "sitting in the kitchen": Rowe to MSB, 7 Jan. 1951, 1/9, MSBC; Diaries 1950, 1953–1954, 2c/8, MSBC; Barber Diary 1952, 5/2, MSBC.

8. Marjorie Barber, "Late Rose," 5/6, MSBC; "that tiny ghost": Dorothy Rowe, "Epitaph on a Cat," 8/4, MSBC; MSB to Alzina Dale, 9 Nov. 1977, 4, MSBC; "Meekly we washed": Dorothy L. Sayers, "For Timothy, in the Coinherence," 4, MSBC; "Why are the trees": Dorothy L. Sayers, "Pussydise Lost," 40, MEWC; "pray for the rudimentary": Notice, 423a, MEWC; Barbara Newman, "Charles Williams and the Companions of the Co-inherence," *Spiritus: A Journal of Christian Spirituality* 9, no. 1 (Spring 2009), 6.

9. "It was very kind": DLS to Barber and MSB, 28 Dec. 1951 and 29 Dec. 1950, 4 Jan. 1955, 185a, MEWC; DLS to MSB and Barber, 28 Dec. 1956, 422b, MEWC; "though I go all shy": Barber to DLS, 2 Dec. 1950, 423a, MEWC.

10. "One 'came of age,'" "time and freedom": M. St. Clare Byrne, *No Spring Till Now*, 7c, MSBC; Program, *No Spring Till Now*, 1/7, MSBC.

11. Janet Vaughan to MSB, 29 May 1958, 26 Aug. 1958, 1/3, MSBC; "every doubt expressed": Unsigned to Lady Villiers, n.d., 3/1, MSBC; Adams, *Somerville for Women*, 267; "feminst inferiority complex": DLS to MSB, 9 Nov. 1957, 185a, MEWC; "milder," "quite came up": Barber to DLS, 20 Oct. [1957], 423a, MEWC; "doesn't have to," "we had to": Frankenburg Manchester Studies 1045, Tameside.

12. "But this is just like": DLS to Charles Williams, 28 Dec. 1944, Reynolds, *Letters*, vol. 3; DLS to E. V. Rieu, 12 Mar. 1945, Reynolds, *Letters*, vol. 3; Diary 1945, 2c/8, MSBC; DLS to MSB and Barber, 8 Mar. 1945, 185a, MEWC; "thrilled," "a major literary event": MSB to DLS, n.d., 422b, MEWC; Dorothy L. Sayers, *Further Papers on Dante* (London: Methuen, 1957), 1; Barbara Reynolds, *The Passionate Intellect: Dorothy L. Sayers' Encounter with Dante* (Kent, OH: Kent State University Press, 1989); "to be read": Dorothy L. Sayers, *Introductory Papers on Dante* (London: Methuen, 1954), xii; "enormous new reading": Dorothy L. Sayers, "On Translating the *Divina Commedia*," *Nottingham Mediaeval Studies* 2 (1958), 40.

13. Frankenburg, *Not Old*, 158, 164; "in recognition of her eminent services": *Midwives Chronicle and Nursing Notes*, August 1973, SA/FPA/A14/29 354, Wellcome.

14. Frankenburg, *Not Old*, 165–166; Logan, *Feminism and Criminal Justice*, 29; "to Dorothy Rowe": Charis U. Frankenburg, *Common Sense about Children: A Parents' Guide to Delinquency* (London: Arco Publications, 1970); "half-understood," "theory that thwarting," "violent crime": Charis U. Frankenburg, *I'm All Right; or, Spoilt Baby into Angry Young Man* (London: Macmillan, 1960), 15, 21.

15. "managed to convey": *South Hampstead High School Magazine*, October 1950; "Yours, with more love," "such a civilized," "Household management," "but we at South Hampstead": *South Hampstead High School Magazine* 68 (1954) ("Yours . . . say"); "we, of course, read all": Elvira Niles to author, 25 Apr. 2018; D. A. Burgess to Barbara Reynolds, 22 Mar. 1985, 423b, MEWC; Marjorie B. Barber, ed., *Selections from Chaucer: The Prologue, the Nun's Priest's Tale, the Pardoner's Tale, the Squire's Tale* (London: Macmillan, 1961); Marjorie M. Barber, ed., *A Dorothy Wordsworth Selection* (London: Macmillan, 1965); Austen, *Persuasion*; James Hilton, *Lost Horizon*, ed. Marjorie M. Barber (London: Macmillan, 1967).

16. "rocky pre-eminence": Rowe to DLS, 28 Dec. 1954, 427, MEWC; "when I think," "to come and place": *Old Girls' Chronicle*, Mar. 1958.

17. "is a hobby": Rowe to DLS, 28 Dec. 1954 and [January 1947], 427, MEWC; "In Dorothy Rowe's Golden Days": Program, *Beyond the Pale*, 19–21 Dec. 1962, BLTC; Annual General Meetings, 29 July 1946, 17 June 1947, 10 June 1948, 8 July 1949, 4 July 1962, 1 July 1970, BLTC; Dobson, *Shakespeare*, 191; Rawlings, *Bournemouth Little Theatre Club*, 6, 18; Rawlings, *Just Bournemouth*, 43.

18. "I wish all honours": Frankenburg to MSB, 12 Feb. 1956, 2b/6, MSBC; J. de la Bere to MSB, 5 Oct. 1955, 2b/7, MSBC; "and how on earth," "a glow": Rowe to MSB, 22 Feb. 1956, 2b/7, MSBC.

19. "for my lovely glimpse": Rowe to MSB, 25 June 1948, 1/9, MSBC; Rowe to MSB, 7 Jan. 1951, 8/4, MSBC; Talbot Heath, "Anthea Bell Talks."

20. Programs and notes, 7/6 and 5/1, MSBC; MSB to Ralph Clarke, 5 Mar. 1977, 25.803, DLSA; *The Times*, 13 Jan. 1948; Byrne, introduction, *Shakespearean Production*; Byrne, foreword to *Prefaces to Shakespeare*, vol. 1., *Hamlet*, ed. Harley Granville-Barker (London: B. T. Batsford, 1963), ix, xlii.

21. MSB to Laurence Harbottle, 1 Dec. 1968, 5/5, MSBC.

22. Janet Watts, "How Muriel Byrne Revealed the Private Life of a Tudor VIP," *Observer*, 21 June 1981, PP56/L/1, RHUL; Diary 1977, 2c/8, MSBC.

23. Byrne, *The Lisle Letters*, vol. 1, xxv, 9–10.

24. Byrne, *The Lisle Letters*, vol. 1, 3, 30.

25. "had the benefit," "The piles of books": Janet Watts, "How Muriel Byrne Revealed the Private Life of a Tudor VIP," *Observer*, 21 June 1981, PP56/L/1, RHUL; Byrne, *The Lisle Letters*, vol. 1, xxvi.

CHAPTER 20: LEGACIES

1. "sitting on two," "I should love": DLS to Rowe, [30 Aug. 1957] , 427, MEWC; Death certificate of Dorothy L. Sayers, 6.76, DLSA; Diary 1957, 2c/8, MSBC.

2. Diaries 1957, 1962, 1964–1965, 2c/8, MSBC; "under the lining": MSB to Alzina Dale, 9 Nov. 1977, 4, MSBC; Jennifer (no last name) to MSB, n.d., 1/1, MSBC; Will addition, 21 July 1964, 2a/4, MSBC; "Thank God you've come": Brabazon, *Dorothy L. Sayers*, 271; [Patrick McLaughlin?] to Gordon Clark, 8 Jan. 1958, 612, MEWC; Program, 15 Jan. 1958, 613, MEWC.

3. Frankenburg to Ralph Clarke, 6 Dec. 1972, 25.853, DLSA; "the unpleasant little": MSB to Clarke, 14 Feb. 1975, 25.799, DLSA; Barbara Reynolds to Patrick McLaughlin, 27 Dec. 1957, 612, MEWC; Jean LeRoy to MSB, 5 June 1958, 491a, MEWC; "had a very strong": MSB to H. L. Thompson, 6 June 1968, 491a, MEWC; Diaries 1970, 1973,

2c/8, MSBC; MSB to A. M. Le May, 10 Mar. 1973, 4/3, MSBC; "you cannot discount": Rowe to Hitchman, n.d., 4, MSBC.

4. Ralph Clarke to MSB, 20 July 1976, 25.806 and 2 Sept. 1976, 25.809, DLSA; MSB to Clarke, 4 Sept. 1976, 25.801, DLSA; Clarke to Rowe, 23 Aug. 1976, 25.847, DLSA; MSB to Eileen Bushell, 9 June 1976, 25.804, DLSA; MSB, notes on a biography, 1976, 4/4, MSBC; Clyde Kilby to MSB, 21 Aug. 1976, 4/2, MSBC; Rowe to MSB, 20 June 1979, 4/3, MSBC; Carolyn G. Heilbrun, "Dorothy L. Sayers: Biography Between the Lines," *The American Scholar* 51, no. 4 (Autumn 1982).

5. Wills, 17 Nov. 1958, 21 July 1964, 2a/4, MSBC; Diaries, 1947–1948, 1951–1962, 1968, 2c/8, MSBC; "I don't seem able": [Cullis] to MSB, 12 Dec. 1954, 1/6, MSBC; Kathleen Spears to MSB, 8 Nov. 1968, 1/7, MSBC; Secretary to Cullis, 17 Jan. 1958, 30 Nov. 1966, D352, RHUL; "my great friend": Mary Aeldrin Cullis, last will and testament, 11 June 1964, proved in court 6 May 1971.

6. Diaries 1951, 1953, 1957–1958, 1960, 1962–1963, 1965, 1967–1971, 2c/8, MSBC; Barber Diaries, 1962, 1967, 1970, 5/2, MSBC.

7. Diaries 1972–1973, 2c/8, MSBC; "complete wreck," "our normal Christmas," "highly intelligent": fragment, 5/5, MSBC; MSB to (no first name) Alston, 17 Mar. 1973, 4/3, MSBC.

8. Frankenburg to MSB, 14 Dec. [1974], 5/5, MSBC; MSB to Laurence Harbottle, 13 Apr. 1974, 5/7, MSBC; Ruth Garstang to MSB, 15 June 1974, 5/7, MSBC; Diary 1976, 2c/8, MSBC; "and you may be sure": Rowe to MSB, 29 Mar. 1976, 4, MSBC.

9. *The Times*, 11 Sept. 1976; Diary 1976, 2c/8, MSBC; "I have not had": MSB to Clyde Kilby, 17 Sept. 1976, 4/2, MSBC; "tidy up": Laurence Harbottle to MSB, 12 Mar. 1979, 1/7, MSBC; Muriel St. Clare Byrne, last will and testament, 6 July 1981, proved in court 3 Apr. 1984.

10. "'Frankie', tall, dark": *Guardian*, 5 Jan. 1967, PC/08/F-01, WL; "I do look upon death," "Anyway, I have": *Sunday Citizen*, 2 Apr. 1967, PC/08/F-01, WL.

11. "I felt just": Rowe to MSB, 20 June 1979, 4/3, MSBC; "What we octogenarians": Rowe to MSB, 29 Mar. 1976 and 2 Feb. 1978, 4/3, MSBC; Diaries, 1974, 1977–1978, 2c/8, MSBC; Frankenburg interview, 8SUF/B/144, WL; "much more toffee": Frankenburg, *Not Old*, 182.

12. Diaries 1979–1981, 2c/8, MSBC; "As I write this": Rowe to MSB, 20 June 1979, 4/3, MSBC.

13. "very bright," "worked at desk": Notebooks, 5/3, MSBC; Daphne Park to K. Tillotson, 17 Jan. 1984, PP56/A/6/6 RHUL.

14. Ancestry.co.uk, "England and Wales, Death Index"; Charis Ursula Frankenburg, final will and testament, 17 Sept. 1981, proved in court 10 Sept. 1985.

15. Ancestry.co.uk, "England and Wales, Death Index"; "think I shall": Rowe to Geoffrey Lee, 17 Nov. 1985, 25.859, DLSA; "first and supreme," "that the money": Dorothea Ellen Hanbury Rowe, last will and testament, 30 Mar. 1984 and codicil 27 Mar. 1987, proved 20 June 1988.

16. Notes for funeral service, 9 Dec. 1983, PP56/L/1, RHUL; Dorothy L. Sayers, *The Just Vengeance: The Lichfield Festival Play for 1946* (London: Gollancz, 1946).

CONCLUSION

1. Sayers, *Busman's Honeymoon: A Love Story*, 5.

BIBLIOGRAPHY

ARCHIVAL SOURCES

Balliol College Archives and Manuscripts, Oxford University
  o Papers of Arthur Hugh Sidgwick (1882–1917; Balliol 1901)
Bodleian Library, Oxford University
  o Correspondence of Charis Frankenburg, 1927–1945, MS Eng. c. 7043–7048
Bournemouth Library
  o Bournemouth Little Theatre Collection
British Library, London
  o "Birth Control in the 20s," recording of *Yesterday's Witness* (BBC2 1982), NP6084W British Library Sound Archive
Cadbury Research Library, University of Birmingham
  o Letters Additional Collection
The Syndics of Cambridge University Library
  o 3rd Baron Gorell Correspondence, MS Add. 9439/1
  o T. B. Rowe Papers, MS Add. 8252
John Collett Personal Collection of Muriel Jaeger Papers
Friends Historical Library of Swarthmore College, PA
  o Aydelotte Papers
Harvard Law School Library, Harvard University, Cambridge, MA
  o Felix Frankfurter, letters to his sister Estelle, 1933–1964, Box 2, Folder 2
Houghton Library, Harvard University, Cambridge, MA
  o John Cournos, letters from various correspondents (1916–1936), B MS Eng 998.998.3
  o John Cournos, "Of My Time: An Autobiography," manuscript [ca. 1935], GEN MS Am 1580
  o "The Dates in the Red-Headed League: Typescript, 1932–34", MS Eng 1333
  o Aleksei Remizov, letters to John Cournos, GEN MS Russ 65
  o Dorothy L. Sayers letters to John Cournos, 1924–1925, f MS Eng 1074

Manchester Central Library Archives and Local Studies
  ○ Annual Reports of the Manchester, Salford, and District Mothers' Clinic
National Archives, London
  ○ Board of Education: ED 109/1812-1815; ED 27/7361-7362; ED 35/4370
  ○ Divorce Court: J 77/2083/5253; J 77/1964/1486; J 77/1465/5172
  ○ PRO 30/75/1, Jenkinson Papers
  ○ War Office: WO374/25510; WO339/52964; WO339/1408; WO339/24511;
    WO339/26110
Royal Holloway University Library Archives, London
  ○ BC RF/146/9/3
  ○ D352, Mary Aeldrin Cullis
  ○ D402, Muriel St Clare Byrne
  ○ PP56/A/6/6, Continued links with Somerville College
  ○ PP56/L/1, Advice re civil list pensions and memorials
Salford Local History Library
  ○ U383, Greengate Hospital and Open-Air School Collection
Dorothy L. Sayers Society Archives, Witham, Essex
Smith College Mortimer Rare Books Room, Northampton, MA
  ○ Dorothy L. Sayers Letters and Poems, 1913–1952, MS 308
Somerville College Archives and Special Collections, Oxford University
  ○ ASM Papers and Correspondence on Constitutional Points c. 1934–1937
  ○ Minutes of College Meetings
  ○ Muriel St. Clare Byrne Collection
  ○ SC/AO/RG/RC, Barnett (Mrs. Frankenburg)
  ○ Somerville College Reports
  ○ Student Reports
Tameside Local Studies Library, Aston-under-Lyne
  ○ Charis Frankenburg Manchester Studies, CD 1045
Marion E. Wade Center, Wheaton College, IL
  ○ Dorothy L. Sayers Papers
Wellcome Collection Library, London
  ○ Miscellaneous Photographs, SA/FPA/C/G/9/1/17, Part 1
  ○ PPPBM/A/12/19, Sir Peter Medawar
  ○ SA/FPA/A14/29: Box 354, Mrs. Charis Frankenburg
Women's Library, London School of Economics
  ○ 8SUF/B/144, Charis Frankenburg interviewed by Brian Harrison, April 12,
    1977
  ○ PC/08/F-01, Press Cuttings

PUBLISHED WORKS BY THE MUTUAL ADMIRATION SOCIETY AND ASSOCIATES

An Account of Lord Mortimer Wimsey, the Hermit of the Wash, Related in a Letter to Sir
    H- G- Bart, by a Clergyman of the Church of England. Bristol, 1816.
Austen, Jane. Persuasion. Edited by Marjorie M. Barber. London: Macmillan, 1963.
Barber, Marjorie M. Classified Questions in English Literature. London: Sidgwick & Jack-
    son, Ltd., 1928.

Barber, Marjorie M., ed. *A Dorothy Wordsworth Selection*. London: Macmillan, 1965.

Barber, Marjorie M. Introduction and notes to *Lost Horizon*, by James Hilton. London: Macmillan, 1967.

Barber, Marjorie M., ed. *Selections from Chaucer: The Prologue, the Nun's Priest's Tale, the Pardoner's Tale, the Squire's Tale*. London: Macmillan, 1961.

Berkeley, Anthony, Milward Kennedy, Gladys Mitchell, John Rhode, Dorothy L. Sayers, and Helen Simpson. *Ask a Policeman*. London: Arthur Barker Ltd., n.d.

Byrne, M. St. Clare. *Aldebaran*. Oxford: Blackwell, 1917.

Byrne, M. St. Clare. *Common or Garden Child: A Not-Unfaithful Record*. London: Faber & Faber Ltd., 1942.

Byrne, M. St. Clare, ed. *The Elizabethan Home: Discovered in Two Dialogues by Claudius Hollyband and Peter Erondell*. 2nd ed. London: Cobden-Sanderson, 1930.

Byrne, M. St. Clare. *Elizabethan Life in Town and Country*. London: Methuen & Co. Ltd., 1925.

Byrne, M. St. Clare, ed. *The Elizabethan Zoo: A Book of Beasts Both Fabulous and Authentic*. London: Frederick Etchells & Hugh Macdonald, 1926.

Byrne, M. St. Clare. Foreword, notes, and illustrations in *Prefaces to Shakespeare*. Vol. 1, *Hamlet*, by Harley Granville-Barker. London: B. T. Batsford, 1963.

Byrne, M. St. Clare. *Havelok the Dane, Childe Horne, William and the Werewolf Told from the Originals*. London: Jonathan Cape, 1929.

Byrne, M. St. Clare. Introduction to *A History of Shakespearean Production*. London: Arts Council of Great Britain and the Society of Cultural Relations with the Soviet Union, 1948–1949.

Byrne, M. St. Clare, ed. *The Letters of King Henry VIII: A Selection, with a Few Other Documents*. London: Cassell & Co. Ltd., 1936.

Byrne, M. St. Clare, ed. *The Lisle Letters*. Vol. 1. Chicago: University of Chicago Press, 1981.

Byrne, M. St. Clare, and Catherine Hope Mansfield. *Somerville College 1879–1921*. Oxford: Oxford University Press, n.d.

Byrne, M. St. Clare, and Gladys Scott Thomson. *My Lord's Books*. London: Sidgwick & Jackston Ltd., [1932?].

[Fleming, Atherton]. *Gourmet's Book of Food and Drink*. London: Bodley Head, 1933.

Fleming, Atherton. *How to See the Battlefields*. London: Cassell & Co. Ltd., 1919.

Frankenburg, Charis U. *Common Sense about Children: A Parents' Guide to Delinquency*. London: Arco Publications, 1970.

Frankenburg, Charis U. *Common Sense in the Nursery*. Revised ed. Harmondsworth, UK: Penguin, 1946.

Frankenburg, Charis U. "If You Were a Fairy," music and lyrics. 1927.

Frankenburg, Charis U. *I'm All Right; or, Spoilt Baby into Angry Young Man*. London: Macmillan, 1960.

Frankenburg, Charis U. *Latin with Laughter*. Illustrations by Dorothy H. Rowe. London: William Heinemann Ltd., 1934.

Frankenburg, Charis U. *More Latin with Laughter*. Illustrations by Dorothy H. Rowe. London: William Heinemann Ltd., 1934.

Frankenburg, Charis U. *Not Old, Madam, Vintage: An Autobiography* (Lavenham, UK: Galaxy Press, [1975?].

Frankenburg, Mrs. Sydney. *See* Frankenburg, Charis U. *Common Sense in the Nursery.* London: Christophers, 1922.

Frankenburg, Mrs. Sydney. *Common Sense in the Nursery.* Revised ed. London: Jonathan Cape, 1934.

Frankenburg, Mrs. Sydney. *Common Sense in the Nursery.* Revised ed. Kingswood, UK: World's Work, 1954.

Jaeger, Muriel. *Before Victoria.* London: Chatto & Windus, 1956.

Jaeger, Muriel. *Experimental Lives from Cato to George Sand.* London: G. Bell & Sons, 1932.

Jaeger, Muriel. *Hermes Speaks.* London: Duckworth, 1933.

Jaeger, Muriel. *Liberty versus Equality.* London: Thomas Nelson & Sons Ltd., 1943.

Jaeger, Muriel. *The Man with Six Senses.* Boston: HiLo Books, 2013. First published 1927 by Hogarth Press (London).

Jaeger, Muriel. *The Question Mark.* London: Hogarth Press, 1926.

Jaeger, Muriel. *Retreat from Armageddon.* London: Duckworth, 1936.

Jaeger, Muriel. *The Sanderson Soviet: A Comedy in Three Acts.* London: Samuel French, 1934.

Jaeger, Muriel. *Shepherd's Trade.* Ilfracombe, Devon, UK: Stockwell, [1965?].

Jaeger, Muriel. *Sisyphus: Or, the Limits of Psychology.* London: K. Paul, Trench, Trubner & Co., 1929.

Jaeger, Muriel. *War of Ideas.* London: Watts & Co., 1942.

[Munday, Anthony]. *John a Kent and John a Cumber.* Oxford: Printed for the Malone Society at Oxford University Press, 1923.

Pollard, Alfred W., and Marjorie M. Barber. *Chaucer's Canterbury Tales: The Pardoner's Tale.* London: Macmillan, 1929.

The Recipe-Book of the Mustard Club: A Treasury of Delectable Dishes, Both New and Old, in the Right Tradition of Good English Cookery. Norwich, UK: J. & J. Colman, n.d.

Reynolds, Barbara, ed. *Dorothy L. Sayers: Child and Woman of Her Time.* Swavesey, UK: Dorothy L. Sayers Society, 2002.

Reynolds, Barbara, ed. *The Letters of Dorothy L. Sayers.* Vol. 1, *The Making of a Detective Novelist, 1899–1936.* London: Hodder & Stoughton, 1995.

Reynolds, Barbara, ed. *The Letters of Dorothy L. Sayers.* Vol. 2, *From Novelist to Playwright, 1937–1943.* Swavesey, UK: Dorothy L. Sayers Society, 1997.

Reynolds, Barbara, ed. *The Letters of Dorothy L. Sayers.* Vol. 3, *A Noble Daring, 1944–1950.* Swavesey, UK: Dorothy L. Sayers Society, 1998.

Reynolds, Barbara, ed. *The Letters of Dorothy L. Sayers.* Vol. 4, *In the Midst of Life, 1951–1957.* Swavesey, UK: Dorothy L. Sayers Society, 2000.

Sayers, Dorothy L. "The Beatrician Vision in Dante and Other Poets." *Nottingham Mediaeval Studies* 2 (1958): 3–23.

Sayers, Dorothy L. *Busman's Honeymoon: A Love Story with Detective Interruptions.* London: Gollancz, 1937.

Sayers, Dorothy L. *The Christ of the Creeds and Other Broadcast Messages to the British People during World War II.* Hurstpierpoint, UK: Dorothy L. Sayers Society, 2008.

Sayers, Dorothy L. *Clouds of Witness.* London: Gollancz, 1935.

Sayers, Dorothy L. *The Devil to Pay.* London: Gollancz, 1939.

Sayers, Dorothy L. *Even the Parrot: Exemplary Conversations for Enlightened Children.* 3rd ed. London: Methuen, 1945.

Sayers, Dorothy L. *The Five Red Herrings.* London: Gollancz, 1931.

Sayers, Dorothy L. *Further Papers on Dante.* London: Methuen, 1957.

Sayers, Dorothy L. *Gaudy Night.* London: Gollancz, 1935.

Sayers, Dorothy L., ed. *Great Tales of Detection.* London: Dent, 1984.

Sayers, Dorothy L. *The Greatest Drama Ever Staged.* London: Hodder & Stoughton, 1938.

Sayers, Dorothy L. *Hangman's Holiday.* London: Gollancz, 1933.

Sayers, Dorothy L. *Have His Carcase.* London: Gollancz, 1932.

Sayers, Dorothy L. *He That Should Come: A Nativity Place in One Act.* London: Gollancz, 1939.

Sayers, Dorothy L. *In the Teeth of the Evidence and Other Stories.* London: Gollancz, 1939.

Sayers, Dorothy L. *Introductory Papers on Dante.* London: Methuen, 1954.

Sayers, Dorothy L. *The Just Vengeance: The Lichfield Festival Play for 1946.* London: Gollancz, 1946.

Sayers, Dorothy L. *The Lost Tools of Learning: Paper Read at a Vacation Course in Education, Oxford 1947.* London: Methuen, 1948.

Sayers, Dorothy L. *Love All.* Perth, Scotland: Tippermuir Books, 2015.

Sayers, Dorothy L. *The Man Born to Be King.* London: Gollancz, 1943.

Sayers, Dorothy L. *The Mind of the Maker.* New York: HarperCollins, 1987.

Sayers, Dorothy L. *Murder Must Advertise.* London: Gollancz, 1933.

Sayers, Dorothy L. *The Nine Tailors.* London: Gollancz, 1934.

Sayers, Dorothy L. "On Translating the *Divina Commedia.*" *Nottingham Mediaeval Studies* 2 (1958): 38–66.

Sayers, Dorothy L. *Op. I.* Oxford: Blackwell, 1916.

Sayers, Dorothy L. *The Other Six Deadly Sins: An Address Given to the Public Morality Council at Caxton Hall, Westminster, on October 23, 1941.* London: Methuen, 1943.

Sayers, Dorothy L. *Strong Meat.* London: Hodder & Stoughton, 1939.

Sayers, Dorothy L. *Strong Poison.* London: Gollancz, 1941.

Sayers, Dorothy L., trans. *Tristan in Brittany.* London: Ernest Benn Ltd., 1929.

Sayers, Dorothy L. *Unnatural Death.* London: Gollancz, 1935.

Sayers, Dorothy L. *The Unpleasantness at the Bellona Club.* London: Gollancz, 1935.

Sayers, Dorothy L. *Unpopular Opinions.* London: Gollancz, 1946.

Sayers, Dorothy L. *Whose Body?* London: Gollancz, 1935.

Sayers, Dorothy L. *Why Work?* London: Methuen, 1942.

Sayers, Dorothy L. "The Zeal of Thy House." In *Famous Plays of 1938–1939.* London: Gollancz, 1939.

Sayers, Dorothy L., and M. St. Clare Byrne. *Busman's Honeymoon: A Detective Comedy in Three Acts.* London: Gollancz, 1937.

Sayers, Dorothy L., Freeman Wills Croft, Valentine Williams, F. Tennyson Jesse, Anthony Armstrong, and David Hume. *Double Death: A Murder Story.* Edited by John Chancellor. London: Gollancz, 1939.

Smith, Timothy d'Arch, ed. *The Quorum: A Magazine of Friendship.* New York: Asphodel Editions, 2001.

TWE, DLS, and SS, eds. *Oxford Poetry 1919*. Oxford: Blackwell, 1920.

TWE, EFAG, and DLS, eds. *Oxford Poetry 1918*. Oxford: Blackwell, 1918.

WRC, TWE, and DLS, eds., *Oxford Poetry 1917*. Oxford: Blackwell, 1918.

OTHER SOURCES

Alwyn Ladell, "Miss Dorothy Rowe," Flickr album, www.flickr.com/photos/alwyn
    _ladell/sets/72157653224505489/.

Ancestry.co.uk

Andrew Belsey, correspondence with author

Elvira Niles, correspondence with author

SELECTED SECONDARY SOURCES

Adams, Pauline. *Somerville for Women: An Oxford College 1879–1993*. Oxford: Oxford
    University Press, 1996.

Aiston, Sarah. "A Maternal Identity? The Family Lives of British Women Graduates Pre-
    and Post-1945." *History of Education* 34, no. 4 (2005): 407–426.

Alexander, Sally. "Primary Maternal Preoccupation: D. W. Winnicott and Social De-
    mocracy in Mid-Twentieth-Century Britain." In *History and Psyche: Culture, Psy-
    choanalysis, and the Past*, edited by Sally Alexander and Barbara Taylor, 149–172.
    New York: Palgrave Macmillan, 2012.

Arondekar, Anjali. "In the Absence of Reliable Ghosts: Sexuality, Historiography, South
    Asia," *differences* 25: 3 (2014): 98–122.

Batson, Judy G. *Her Oxford*. Nashville: Vanderbilt University Press, 2008.

Beaumont, Caitríona. *Housewives and Citizens: Domesticity and the Women's Movement
    in England, 1928–64*. Manchester, UK: Manchester University Press, 2014.

Bell, Anthea. "Dorothy Rowe." *Somerville College Report and Supplement 1988*.

Berthezène, Clarisse. "The Middlebrow and the Making of a 'New Common Sense':
    Women's Voluntarism, Conservative Politics and Representations of Womanhood."
    In *Rethinking Right-Wing Women: Gender and the Conservative Party, 1880s to the
    Present*, edited by Clarisse Berthezène and Julie V. Gottlieb, 104–121. Manchester,
    UK: Manchester University Press, 2018.

Bingham, Adrian. "Cultural Hierarchies and the Interwar British Press." In *Middlebrow
    Literary Cultures: The Battle of the Brows, 1920–1960*, edited by Erica Brown and
    Mary Grover, 55–68. Houndmills, UK: Palgrave Macmillan, 2012.

Bourne, Stephen. *Black Poppies: Britain's Black Community and the Great War*. Stroud,
    UK: History Press, 2014.

Brabazon, James. *Dorothy L. Sayers: The Life of a Courageous Woman*. London: Gollancz,
    1981.

Bressey, Caroline. "Geographies of Belonging: White Women and Black History." *Wom-
    en's History Review* 22, no. 4 (2013).

Bright, Brittain. "The Maturity of Lord Peter Wimsey and Authorial Innovation within
    a Series." In *Serial Crime Fiction: Dying for More*, edited by Jean Anderson, Carolina
    Miranda, and Barbara Pezzotti, 87–98. Houndmills, UK: Palgrave Macmillan, 2015.

Bryder, Linda. "'Wonderlands of Buttercup, Clover and Daisies': Tuberculosis and the
    Open-Air School Movement in Britain, 1907–39." In *In the Name of the Child: Health
    and Welfare, 1880–1940*, edited by Roger Cooter, 72–95. London: Routledge, 1992.

Bush, Julia. *Women against the Vote: Female Anti-Suffragism in Britain*. Oxford: Oxford University Press, 2007.

Carter, Laura. "The Quennells and the 'History of Everyday Life' in England, c. 1918–69." *History Workshop Journal* 81, no. 1 (April 2016): 106–134.

Carter, Laura. "Women Historians in the Twentieth Century." In *Precarious Professionals: Gender, Identity and Social Change in Modern British History*, edited by Heidi Egginton and Zoë Thomas. London: Institute for Historical Research, 2019.

Chapman, Siobhan. "Towards a Neo-Gricean Stylistics: Implicature in Dorothy L. Sayers's *Gaudy Night*." *Journal of Literary Semantics* 41, no. 2 (2012): 1939–1953.

Charnock, Hannah. "'A Million Little Bonds': Infidelity, Divorce and the Emotional Worlds of Marriage in British Women's Magazines of the 1930s." *Cultural and Social History* 14, no. 3 (2017): 363–379.

Chettiar, Teri. "Treating Marriage as 'The Sick Entity': Gender, Emotional Life, and the Psychology of Marriage Improvement in Postwar Britain." *History of Psychology* 18, no. 3 (2015): 270–282.

Clark, Anna. *Alternative Histories of the Self: A Cultural History of Sexuality and Secrets, 1780–1917*. London: Bloomsbury, 2017.

Clay, Catherine. *British Women Writers 1914–1945: Professional Work and Friendship*. Aldershot, UK: Ashgate, 2006

Cochrane, Claire. *Twentieth-Century British Theatre: Industry, Art and Empire*. Cambridge: Cambridge University Press, 2011.

Cockin, Katharine. *Edith Craig and the Theatres of Art*. London: Bloomsbury, 2017.

Cohen, Deborah. *Family Secrets: The Things We Tried to Hide*. London: Penguin, 2014.

Collins, Marcus. *Modern Love: An Intimate History of Men and Women in Twentieth-Century Britain*. London: Atlantic Books, 2003.

Cook, Hera. *The Long Sexual Revolution: English Women, Sex, and Contraception, 1800–1975*. Oxford: Oxford University Press, 2004.

Cook, Matt. *Queer Domesticities: Homosexuality and Home Life in Twentieth-Century London*. Houndmills, UK: Palgrave Macmillan, 2014.

Cooter, Roger. *Surgery and Society in Peace and War: Orthopaedics and the Organization of Modern Medicine, 1880–1948*. Houndmills, UK: Palgrave Macmillan, 1993.

Cross, Gwenith Siobhan. "'A Midwife at Every Confinement': Midwifery and Medicalized Childbirth in Ontario and Britain, 1920–1950." *Canadian Bulletin of Medical History* 31, no. 1 (2014): 139–159.

"D. H. R. Member of Staff 1916–1935 B.H.S. 1935–1957 T.H." Bournemouth, UK: Victory Press, [1958?].

Davis, Angela. *Pre-school Childcare in England, 1939–2010: Theory, Practice and Experience*. Manchester, UK: Manchester University Press, 2015.

Debenham, Clare. *Birth Control and the Rights of Women: Post-Suffrage Feminism in the Early Twentieth Century*. London: I. B. Tauris, 2014.

Delap, Lucy. "Conservative Values, Anglicans and the Gender Order in Inter-War Britain." In *Brave New World: Imperial and Democratic Nation-Building in Britain between the Wars*, edited by Laura Beers and Geraint Thomas, 149–168. London: Institute of Historical Research, 2011.

Derry, Caroline. "Lesbianism and Feminist Legislation in 1921: The Age of Consent and 'Gross Indecency between Women.'" *History Workshop Journal* (2018).

Deslandes, Paul. *Oxbridge Men: British Masculinity and the Undergraduate Experience, 1850–1920*. Bloomington: Indiana University Press, 2005.

Dinsman, Melissa. *Modernism at the Microphone: Radio, Propaganda and Literary Aesthetics during World War II*. London: Bloomsbury, 2015.

Doan, Laura. *Disturbing Practices: History, Sexuality, and Women's Experiences of Modern War*. Chicago: University of Chicago Press, 2013.

Doan, Laura, and Jane Garrity, eds. *Sapphic Modernities: Sexuality, Women and National Culture*. New York: Palgrave Macmillan, 2006.

Dobson, Michael. *Shakespeare and Amateur Performance: A Cultural History*. Cambridge: Cambridge University Press, 2011.

Durbach, Nadja. "Private Lives, Public Records: Illegitimacy and the Birth Certificate in Twentieth-Century Britain." *Twentieth Century British History* 25, no. 2 (2014): 305–326.

Dyhouse, Carol. *No Distinction of Sex? Women in British Universities, 1870–1939*. London: University College Press, 1995.

Edwards, Martin. *The Golden Age of Murder*. New York: HarperCollins, 2015.

Ehland, Christoph, and Cornelia Wächter, eds. *Middlebrow and Gender, 1890–1945*. (Leiden, Netherlands: Brill Rodopi, 2016.

Ewins, Kristin. "A History of the *Fritillary*: A Magazine of Oxford Women's Colleges, 1894–1931." *Notes and Queries* 55, no. 1 (2008): 60–64.

Feldman, David. "Conceiving Difference: Religion, Race and the Jews in Britain, c. 1750–1900." *History Workshop Journal* 76, no. 1 (October 2013): 160–186.

Fisher, Kate. *Birth Control, Sex, and Marriage in Britain, 1918–1960*. Oxford: Oxford University Press, 2006.

Freedman, Ariela. "Dorothy Sayers and the Case of the Shell-Shocked Detective." *Partial Answers: Journal of Literature and the History of Ideas* 8, no. 2 (June 2010): 365–387.

Goody, Alex. "Dorothy L. Sayers's *The Man Born to Be King*. The 'Impersonation' of Divinity: Language, Authenticity and Embodiment." In *Broadcasting in the Modernist Era*, edited by Matthew Feldman, Erik Tonning, and Henry Mead, 79–96. London: Bloomsbury, 2014.

Gottlieb, Julie V. "Modes and Models of Conservative Women's Leadership in the 1930s." In *Rethinking Right-Wing Women: Gender and the Conservative Party, 1880s to the Present*, edited by Clarisse Berthezène and Julie V. Gottlieb, 89–103. Manchester, UK: Manchester University Press, 2018.

Hall, Lesley. "'Sentimental Follies' or 'Instruments of Tremendous Uplift'? Reconsidering Women's Same-Sex Relationships in Interwar Britain." *Women's History Review* 25, no. 1 (2016): 124–142.

Hamlett, Jane. "'Nicely Feminine, Yet Learned': Student Rooms at Royal Holloway and the Oxford and Cambridge Colleges in Late Nineteenth-Century Britain." *Women's History Review* 15, no. 1 (2006): 137–161.

Heilbrun, Carolyn G. "Dorothy L. Sayers: Biography Between the Lines." *American Scholar* 51, no. 4 (Autumn 1982): 552–553.

Herbert, Amanda E. *Female Alliances: Gender, Identity, and Friendship in Early Modern Britain*. New Haven, CT: Yale University Press, 2014.

Hitchman, Janet. *Such a Strange Lady: A Biography of Dorothy L. Sayers*. London: New English Library, 1975.

Hollenberg, Donna Krolik. "Art and Ardor in World War One: Selected Letters from H. D. to John Cournos." *Iowa Review* 16, no. 3 (Fall 1986): 125–155.

Hone, Ralph E. *Dorothy L. Sayers: A Literary Biography.* Kent, OH: Kent State University Press, 1979.

Houlbrook, Matt. *Prince of Tricksters: The Incredible True Story of Netley Lucas, Gentleman Crook.* Chicago: University of Chicago Press, 2016.

Hunter, Billie. "Midwifery, 1920–2000: The Reshaping of a Profession." In *Nursing and Midwifery in Britain since 1700*, edited by Annie Borsay and Billie Hunter, 151–176. Houndmills, UK: Palgrave Macmillan, 2012.

Hurst, Isobel. "'Maenads Dancing before the Martyrs' Memorial': Oxford Women Writers and the Classical Tradition." *International Journal of the Classical Tradition* 12, no. 2 (Fall 2005): 163–182.

Jones, Claire L. "Under the Covers? Commerce, Contraceptives and Consumers in England and Wales, 1880–1960." *Social History of Medicine* 29, no. 4 (2015): 734–756.

Jones, Timothy Willem. "Love, Honour and Obey? Romance, Subordination and Marital Subjectivity in Interwar Britain." In *Love and Romance in Britain, 1918–1970*, edited by Alana Harris and Timothy Willem Jones, 124–143. Houndmills, UK: Palgrave Macmillan, 2015.

Kenney, Catherine. "Sayers [married name Fleming], Dorothy Leigh." *Oxford Dictionary of National Biography*, September 23, 2004.

Koven, Seth. *The Match Girl and the Heiress.* Princeton, NJ: Princeton University Press, 2014.

Langhamer, Claire. *The English in Love: The Intimate Story of an Emotional Revolution.* Oxford: Oxford University Press, 2013.

LeMahieu, D. L. *A Culture for Democracy: Mass Communication and the Cultivated Mind in Britain Between the Wars.* Oxford: Clarendon Press, 1988.

Leonardi, Susan J. *Dangerous by Degrees: Women at Oxford and the Somerville College Novelists.* New Brunswick, NJ: Rutgers University Press, 1989.

Light, Alison. *Forever England: Femininity, Literature and Conservatism between the Wars.* London: Routledge, 1991.

Light, Alison. *Mrs. Woolf and the Servants: An Intimate History of Domestic Life in Bloomsbury.* New York: Bloomsbury Press, 2008.

Logan, Anne. *Feminism and Criminal Justice: A Historical Perspective.* Houndmills, UK: Palgrave Macmillan, 2008.

Loss, Daniel S. "The Institutional Afterlife of Christian England." *Journal of Modern History* 89 (June 2017): 282–313.

Lott, Monica. "Dorothy L. Sayers, the Great War, and Shell Shock." *Interdisciplinary Literary Studies* 15, no. 1 (2013): 103–126.

Macdonald, Kate, and Christoph Singer, eds. *Transitions in Middlebrow Writing, 1880–1930.* Houndmills, UK: Palgrave Macmillan, 2015.

Mackinnon, Alison. *Love and Freedom: Professional Women and the Reshaping of Personal Life.* Cambridge: Cambridge University Press, 1997.

Mandler, Peter. *History and National Life.* London: Profile Books, 2002.

Marcus, Sharon. *Between Women: Friendship, Desire, and Marriage in Victorian England.* Princeton, NJ: Princeton University Press, 2007.

Mass, Sarah. "Sunday Rites or Sunday Rights? Anglo-Jewish Traders and the Negotiability of the Mid-Century Sabbath." *History of Retailing and Consumption* 2, no. 1
(2016): 68–83.

McClellan, Ann K. *How British Women Writers Transformed the Campus Novel: Virginia
Woolf, Dorothy L. Sayers, Margaret Drabble, Anita Brookner, Jeanette Winterson.*
Lewiston, NY: Edwin Mellen Press, 2012.

McIntosh, Tania. *A Social History of Maternity and Childbirth: Key Themes in Maternity
Care.* London: Routledge, 2012.

McKibbin, Ross. *The Ideologies of Class: Social Relations in Britain, 1880–1950.* Oxford:
Clarendon Press, 1990.

Medd, Jodie. *Lesbian Scandal and the Culture of Modernism.* Cambridge: Cambridge
University Press, 2012.

Melman, Billie. *The Culture of History: English Uses of the Past 1800–1953.* Oxford: Oxford University Press, 2006.

Moore, Francesca. "Governmentality and the Maternal Body: Infant Mortality in Early
Twentieth-Century Lancashire." *Journal of Historical Geography* 39 (2013): 54–68.

Morse, Elizabeth J. "Jaeger, Muriel." *Oxford Dictionary of National Biography*, September 23, 2004.

Moulton, Mo. "*Bricks and Flowers*: Representations of Gender and Queer Life in Interwar Britain." In *British Queer History: New Approaches and Perspectives*, edited by
Brian Lewis, 68–86. Manchester, UK: Manchester University Press, 2013.

"Muriel St. Clare Byrne 1894–1983." *Somerville College Report and Supplement 1982.*

Myers, Christine D. *University Coeducation in the Victorian Era: Inclusion in the United
States and the United Kingdom.* New York: Palgrave Macmillan, 2010.

Nuttall, Alison. "Midwifery, 1800–1920: The Journey to Registration." In *Nursing and
Midwifery in Britain Since 1700*, edited by Annie Borsay and Billie Hunter, 128–150.
Houndmills, UK: Palgrave Macmillan, 2012.

von Oertzen, Christine. *Science, Gender, and Internationalism: Women's Academic
Networks, 1917–1955.* Translated by Kate Sturge. New York: Palgrave Macmillan,
2014.

Oram, Alison. *Her Husband Was a Woman! Women's Gender-Crossing in Modern British
Popular Culture.* London: Routledge, 2007.

Perry, Kennetta Hammond. *London Is the Place for Me: Black Britons, Citizenship, and the
Politics of Race.* Oxford: Oxford University Press, 2015.

Rawlings, Keith. *Just Bournemouth.* Stanbridge, UK: Dovecote Press, 2005.

Reid, Alice. "Infant Feeding and Child Health and Survival in Derbyshire in the Early
Twentieth Century." *Women's Studies International Forum* 60 (2017): 111–119.

Reynolds, Barbara. "'Dear Jim . . . ' The Reconstruction of a Friendship." *Seven: An
Anglo-American Literary Review* 17 (2000): 47–59.

Reynolds, Barbara. *Dorothy L. Sayers: Her Life and Soul.* London: Hodder & Stoughton,
1993.

Reynolds, Barbara. *The Passionate Intellect: Dorothy L. Sayers' Encounter with Dante.*
Kent, OH: Kent State University Press, 1989.

Robinson, Lillian S. "The Mysterious Politics of Dorothy Sayers." In *At Home and
Abroad in the Empire: British Women Write the 1930s*, edited by Robin Hackett,

Freda Hauser, and Gay Wachman, 222–234. Newark, DE: University of Delaware Press, 2009.

Ross, Ellen. *Love and Toil: Motherhood in Outcast London, 1870–1918*. Oxford: Oxford University Press, 1993.

Rutherford, Emily. "Arthur Sidgwick's *Greek Prose Composition*: Gender, Affect, and Sociability in the Late-Victorian University." *Journal of British Studies* 56 (January 2017): 91–116.

Saler, Michael. *The Avant-Garde in Interwar England: Medieval Modernism and the London Underground*. Oxford: Oxford University Press, 1999.

Satterthwaite, Alfred. "John Cournos and 'H.D.'" *Twentieth Century Literature* 22, no. 4 (December 1976): 394–410.

Schaub, Melissa. *Middlebrow Feminism in Classic British Detective Fiction: The Female Gentleman*. Houndmills, UK: Palgrave Macmillan, 2013.

Schwartz, Laura. *A Serious Endeavour: Gender, Education and Community at St. Hugh's, 1886–2011*. London: Profile Books, 2011.

Schwarzkopf, Stefan. "Consumer Communication as Commodity: British Advertising Agencies and the Global Market for Advertising, 1780–1980." In *Consuming Behaviours: Identity, Politics and Pleasure in Twentieth-Century Britain*, edited by Erika Rappaport, Sandra Trudgen Dawson, and Mark J. Crowley. London: Bloomsbury, 2015.

Shapira, Michal. *The War Inside: Psychoanalysis, Total War, and the Making of the Democratic Self in Postwar Britain*. Cambridge: Cambridge University Press, 2013.

Shepherd, June. *Doreen Wallace (1897–1989), Writer and Social Campaigner*. Lewiston, NY: Edwin Mellen Press, 2000.

Smith, Angela K. "How to Remember: War, Armistice and Memory in Post-1918 British Fiction." *Journal of European Studies* 45, no. 4 (2015): 301–315.

Snell, K. D. M. "A Drop of Water from a Stagnant Pool? Inter-war Detective Fiction and the Rural Community." *Social History* 35, no. 1 (2010): 21–50.

Stableford, Brian. *Scientific Romance in Britain, 1890–1950*. London: Fourth Estate, 1985.

Stewart, Victoria. *Crime Writing in Interwar Britain: Fact and Fiction in the Golden Age*. Cambridge: Cambridge University Press, 2017.

Szreter, Simon, and Kate Fisher. *Sex Before the Sexual Revolution: Intimate Life in England 1918–1963*. Cambridge: Cambridge University Press, 2010.

Tate, Trudi. "King Baby: Infant Care into the Peace." In *The Silent Morning: Culture and Memory after the Armistice*, edited by Trudi Tate and Kate Kennedy, 104–130. Manchester, UK: Manchester University Press, 2013.

Thackeray, David. "At the Heart of the Party? The Women's Conservative Organisation in the Age of Partial Suffrage, 1914–28." In *Rethinking Right-Wing Women: Gender and the Conservative Party, 1880s to the Present*, edited by Clarisse Berthezène and Julie V. Gottlieb, 46–65. Manchester, UK: Manchester University Press, 2018.

Thackeray, David. *Conservatism for the Democratic Age: Conservative Cultures and the Challenge of Mass Politics in Early Twentieth Century England*. Manchester, UK: Manchester University Press, 2013.

Thane, Pat, and Tanya Evans. *Sinners? Scroungers? Saints? Unmarried Motherhood in Twentieth-Century England*. Oxford: Oxford University Press, 2012.

Tisdall, Laura. "Education, Parenting and Concepts of Childhood in England, c. 1945 to c. 1979." *Contemporary British History* 31, no. 1 (2017): 24–46.

Unwin, Cathy, and Elaine Sharland. "From Bodies to Minds in Childcare Literature: Advice to Parents in Inter-war Britain." In *In the Name of the Child: Health and Welfare, 1880–1940*, edited by Roger Cooter. London: Routledge, 1992.

Vicinus, Martha. *Intimate Friends: Women Who Loved Women, 1778–1928*. Chicago: University of Chicago Press, 2004.

Vickery, Margaret Birney. *Buildings for Bluestockings: The Architecture and Social History of Women's Colleges in Late Victorian England*. Newark, DE: University of Delaware Press, 1999.

Walkowitz, Judith R. *Nights Out: Life in Cosmopolitan London*. New Haven, CT: Yale University Press, 2012.

Webster, Peter. "Archbishop Temple's Offer of a Lambeth Degree to Dorothy L. Sayers." In *From the Reformation to the Permissive Society: A Miscellany in Celebration of the 400th Anniversary of Lambeth Palace Library*, edited by Melanie Barber and Stephen Taylor with Gabriel Sewell, 565–582. Woodbridge, UK: Boydell Press, 2010.

Wiggins, Sarah. "Gendered Spaces and Political Identity: Debating Societies in English Women's Colleges, 1890–1914." *Women's History Review* 18, no. 5 (2009): 737–752.

Witchard, Anne. "Sink Street: The Sapphic World of Pre-Chinatown Soho." In *Sex, Time and Place: Queer Histories of London, c. 1850 to the Present*, edited by Simon Avery and Katherine M. Graham, 221–237. London: Bloomsbury, 2016.

INDEX

Page numbers in *italics* indicate illustrations.

Mo Moulton is currently a lecturer in the history department of the University of Birmingham. They earned their PhD in history from Brown University in 2010 and taught in the History & Literature program at Harvard University for six years. Their previous book, *Ireland and the Irish in Interwar England*, was named a 2014 "Book of the Year" by *History Today* and was the runner-up for the Royal History Society's 2015 Whitfield Prize for first book in British or Irish history. Moulton has also written for outlets such as the *Atlantic*, *Catapult*, *Public Books*, *Disclaimer Magazine*, and the *Toast*.